"Meg Moseley fo ... n south where her colorful characters will make you feel southern even if you aren't. When Tish, on a whim, lands in an old family home, she realizes there are secrets to be discovered in small-town Alabama. With a spark of romance, a friend who seems to always land in trouble, and a few healed scars, this inspirational tale is destined to be another winner."

—JULIE CANTRELL, *New York Times* and *USA Today*
best-selling author of *Into the Free*

"What happens when a Yankee ventures south, expecting warm southern hospitality but getting a shoulder as cold as the Michigan winters she left behind? Filled with quirky, endearing characters and a heartwarming story about taking risks and finding reward, *Gone South* will delight you."

—MARYBETH WHALEN, author of *The Wishing Tree*
and director of SheReads.org

"*Gone South* is a prodigal story about second chances, the importance of family, and the complexities of the human spirit. In this compelling novel, Meg Moseley reminds us all that we are more than our reputations and that God truly does make everything beautiful in its own time."

—KATIE GANSHERT, author of *Wildflowers from Winter*
and *Wishing on Willows*

"In *Gone South,* Meg Moseley has created a cast of characters that captured my imagination and drew me into their world. As their stories unfolded, I found myself caring deeply for Tish and George and especially young Mel, whose foibles and shortcomings made her all the more endearing. I have a feeling the folks of Noble will stay with me a good long while!"

—ANN TATLOCK, award-winning author of *Sweet Mercy*

"Some people write books; some tell stories. Meg Moseley does both, drawing the reader into the lives of strangers who, by the end of the novel, have become friends. She captures a southern town that can be as ornery as it is beautiful, and through it shows that 'we all do terrible things.' Things that only a loving God could grant us forgiveness and grace. *Gone South* is not to be missed."

—CHRISTA ALLAN, author of *Walking on Broken Glass*
and *The Edge of Grace*

"Meg Moseley's sophomore novel is the perfect blend of southern charm, fast cars, and endearing characters. With a new twist on the prodigal child, *Gone South* is a literary delight from start to finish!"

—CARLA STEWART, award-winning author of *Chasing Lilacs*
and *Stardust*

"On the spur of the moment, in a bit of northern naiveté, a young Yankee woman moves south to the town where her ancestors lived during the Reconstruction period and opens up a whole can of worms. Get ready for a fun and thought-provoking ride, as powerful as the story's Corvette. In *Gone South*, Moseley spins a lovely tale of prodigals and prejudices and of a courageous young woman who refuses to take the easy way out."

—ELIZABETH MUSSER, author of *The Swan House*
and *The Sweetest Thing*

Gone South

BOOKS BY MEG MOSELEY

When Sparrows Fall

MEG MOSELEY

Gone South

A NOVEL

MULTNOMAH
BOOKS

GONE SOUTH
PUBLISHED BY MULTNOMAH BOOKS
12265 Oracle Boulevard, Suite 200
Colorado Springs, Colorado 80921

Trade Paperback ISBN: 978-0-307-73080-0
eBook ISBN: 978-0-307-73081-7

Cover design by Kelly Howard; cover photo by Ian Cook

Published in the United States by WaterBrook Multnomah, an imprint of the Crown Publishing Group, a division of Random House Inc., New York.

Multnomah and its mountain colophon are registered trademarks of Random House Inc.

Library of Congress Cataloging-in-Publication Data
Moseley, Meg.
    Gone south : a novel / Meg Moseley—First Edition.
        pages cm
    ISBN 978-0-307-73080-0—ISBN 978-0-307-73081-7 (electronic)
    I. Title.
    PS3613.O77876G66 2013
    813'.6—dc23

                                                        2013003030

Printed in the United States of America
2013—First Edition

10 9 8 7 6 5 4 3 2 1

This book is dedicated to the memory of Joseph Moseley, recently departed for a far better world; and to Lizzie, Karis, and the other grandchildren who will join our family someday. I will always love you and believe in you, no matter what.

One

*N*o doubt it was the last time they would ever meet at the hole-in-a-wall Greek place for gyros, but brooding wouldn't help. She had arrived first, as usual, so she placed their regular orders at the counter and settled into a bright orange booth by a window. Wrapped in the cocoon of clatter from the kitchen and an ancient Motown song on the stereo, Tish McComb rested her chin in her hands and watched headlights zip past on the big hill that descended into the south end of town.

Snow flurries twinkled down from the sky, a reminder that the first serious snow would arrive soon. As much as Tish loved the way a winter storm could swaddle an ordinary little Michigan town in a sparkling blanket of white, she wasn't fond of driving in it.

A gust of wind blew a flock of faded autumn leaves past the window. Her mother followed at a trot with a gigantic handbag on her arm and a red scarf hugging her neck. No gloves, probably because she loved to show off her new wedding ring. She pushed the heavy glass door open and stepped inside, smoothing her rumpled gray curls with her left hand.

Spotting Tish, she smiled. "You're always too punctual. Did you order for me?"

"Yes, I did."

"Thanks. Did you remember my avgolemono? And extra tzatziki sauce?"

"Of course," Tish said with a trace of envy. She'd blow up like a blimp if she ate like that. She didn't have her mother's petite figure.

Her cheeks flushed, Barb Miller plopped down on the other side of the booth and unwound her scarf. She looked both wired and tired.

"Pretty scarf," Tish said.

"I knew you would like it. And I see you've been thrifting again. Cute jacket."

"I found it online. It's from the forties, but it still has all its original hardware, see?" Tish patted the brass buttons that marched down the jacket's smooth, bright blue wool. "It has some tiny stains that won't come out, but I couldn't pass it up."

"We vintage items always have our flaws. They're part of our charm."

Tish smiled at her mother, a woman whose gentle wrinkles were like those of a well-ripened persimmon. "Part of your charm is the way you describe how charming you are," she teased.

Mom ignored the quip. "That's a nice blue on you. It goes with your eyes." Peering at Tish's hair, she said, "I wish you wouldn't keep your hair skinned back tight like that. You know it's gorgeous, so turn it loose. Let it frame your pretty face."

Tish refrained from rolling her eyes at her mother's predictable comments. "You know I have to look businesslike for my job, Mom. How's the packing coming along?"

"Slowly. Charles hasn't moved a lot, so he hasn't weeded out a thousand times like we did. It'll be a miracle if we finish before moving day."

"I'll come over a few more times to help," Tish offered. "And I've put in for that week off so I can make the trip with you."

Her mother frowned. "I wish you wouldn't waste your vacation days to help a couple of old fogies move their junk. You should round up some of those nice girls from your church and go someplace special. Someplace warm. Puerto Vallarta, maybe. Isn't Fran a traveler? I bet she'd love to go on a trip."

"Yes, she would." Tish loved Fran, but when they'd roomed together at the over-thirty singles' retreat, she'd snored like an overweight trucker. "But I want to see your new place and help you unpack. It'll be fun—and warm."

"Not as much fun as Puerto Vallarta, but…oh, all right. Thanks, honey." An impish smile overcame the frown. "You know I'm pretty well organized, but I'm still cleaning out your father's storage unit. Yesterday I found a blender in a box he'd labeled 'garden stuff.'"

Tish laughed. "Typical."

"This morning I hauled out a box labeled 'miscellaneous,' and you'll never guess what he'd tucked away with his electric car research." Her mom reached for her bag.

"You're right. I'll never guess."

"A treasure, just for you." She pulled out a large manila envelope and offered it to Tish. "Ta-da!"

Tish sucked in her breath, recognizing that loose, loopy penmanship. "The McComb Letters," her father had written, and he'd underlined it twice.

She took the envelope. "Oh my goodness. Finally, I have my chance to read the letters. He always kept them out of sight, like he thought they'd be stolen or something."

"I still haven't run across the other papers—the genealogy and whatnot—but I'll find them eventually. Will you want them too?"

"Sure. Thanks, Mom." Tish unfastened the metal clasp and reached into the envelope. She smiled at how meticulously he had wrapped the letters in acid-free paper.

Tish slid the packet back into the envelope. "I won't look until I get them home. I'd hate to get grease on them. Or lemon soup."

"Heaven forbid. Your father would roll over in his grave."

"They're for me to keep?"

"Of course. You're the one with McComb blood, not me, and you're at least a little bit interested in family history."

"I haven't given it much thought since Dad passed away, though." Tish closed the envelope again and tucked it carefully between her purse and the wall.

"Remember the time he drove you down to Alabama to see the McComb house? He was such a sweetie, trying to distract you. He never could stand to see you hurt, so he did the best thing he knew—took you on a trip."

Tish nodded. On that slapdash father-daughter adventure, her father had been her rock. Bob McComb might have been a dreamer, chasing the latest get-rich-quick scheme or business opportunity, but he'd made himself completely available when she'd needed him most.

The waitress set the bowl of avgolemono on the table. As her mother sipped the lemony broth, Tish listened to her talk, enjoying the excitement in her eyes.

"Just think, Tish. By the time winter really hits, Charles and I will be in Florida." Her mom sat up straight. "Are you sure you don't want to move south too? You've got enough money to buy a condo or even a house by now. Don't you want to settle down somewhere? All those years in apartments…and it would be a new adventure."

Tish laughed. "You sound like Dad with all his pep talks about greener pastures."

"Talk about greener pastures, honey—we'll have palm trees and orchids. An orange tree in the front yard and mangoes and avocados out back. You could too."

"Trying to bribe me with guacamole and fruit salad? Nice try, but if there's one thing I learned from all our moves, it's that the grass isn't greener on the other side of the fence. It's just another pasture. With its own cow pies."

"At least my pasture's full of tropical flowers instead of ice and snow."

Catching a whiff of lemon, Tish could almost imagine being there. "Oh, Mom, Florida just doesn't appeal to me. Sorry. I like a place that has four seasons."

"Well, ice and snow don't appeal to me. Not anymore. I'm ready to get out of here." Pushing her empty bowl to the side, her mom said, "I'm just glad we don't live in covered-wagon days. We can hop a plane and be anywhere in a few hours. That reminds me. I'll have to buy you a plane ticket so you can fly home from Tampa."

A new idea fluttered into Tish's mind, triggered by the road-trip memories she'd made with her dad. Sunrise over a new town. The crazy place names on road signs and water towers. Different accents in different states. Seeing the landscape change, mile by mile, and coming to a new understanding of what a huge country she lived in.

"You know what I should do, Mom? I should drive myself down. Caravan with you and Charles. Then I can take my time on the way back and see some sights."

"Oh, Tish. Don't try to make that long drive all by yourself. In that old car."

"Mother, I'm thirty-five years old. I can handle it. And the car's in great shape."

The waitress set their plates of gyros and curly fries on the table. As their drinks were being refilled, Tish shrugged her way out of her vintage jacket and placed it on the seat beside her, safe from the drippy, spicy lamb and tangy sauce.

After they'd eaten and settled their bill, they headed outside and stood under the awning. The snow flurries had given way to a fine mist sifting down from the dark sky. Tish tucked the McComb letters under her arm while she buttoned her jacket.

Her mom zipped her parka, wound her red scarf around her neck, and reached into her purse for a matching pair of knit gloves. She pulled them on and clapped her hands, the sound muffled by the fabric. "You can adopt my winter gear, Tish. I won't need parkas and scarves and gloves in Tampa."

Tish smiled, remembering a series of stretchy red gloves tucked into long-ago Christmas stockings. "Thanks. That would be nice. Thank you for giving me Letitia's letters too. I'm glad you found them."

"It's right for you to have them, especially since you're named after her."

"I'll read them with her and her husband staring down at me from their wedding portrait."

"Ugh! That old thing always makes me think of haunted houses and bad smells. He's ghoulish and she looks anemic."

Tish was quick to defend her namesake. "No, she was just fair skinned. And he had a long, thin face."

Her mother laughed. "He sure did. I think he's related to Lurch from *The Addams Family*." She reached out for a hug, and Tish welcomed it. "Well, good night, sweetheart. Let me know if you find anything interesting."

"'Night, Mom. Drive carefully." Tish watched her mom hurry down the wet sidewalk toward her car, a little kick in her step. Her mom really knew how to roll with life, a trait that had served her well through Dad's numerous ventures and so many moves.

While her Volvo warmed up, Tish rubbed her cold hands together and thought about the manila envelope on the passenger seat. Her dad had told her about the letters. About his great-great-grandmother moving from Ohio to Alabama sometime after the Civil War. She'd written home to her mother in Ohio, and her mother had saved the letters. They'd been passed down from one generation to another, treasured but seldom read.

Tish had always wanted to read them, especially since her dad always put Nathan and Letitia McComb on a pedestal. But Dad had been wise to keep them out of the hands of a curious little girl who could damage the fragile old papers. Sometimes, like the lonely child she'd once been, Tish still yearned to disappear into the past. She wasn't quite sure why.

Home again in her second-floor apartment, Tish set her purse on the piano bench and the manila envelope on the coffee table, then kicked off her shoes and walked to the window. Nightfall had completely swallowed the courtyard of the complex.

She touched the cold glass with her fingertips.

Sometimes Florida didn't sound bad…except for the hurricanes and the alligators. And millions of senior citizens clogging the roads. But it wouldn't be hard to find another job in the insurance field if she ever took a notion to move closer to her mother and Charles.

Beyond the courtyard, the parking lot filled as residents came home for the night. Each set of headlights and brake lights briefly illuminated the rows of parked vehicles and then went dark, making the streetlights seem brighter again.

Ever since college, she'd lived in an apartment. She could have bought a house somewhere by now. She could have been building equity. That was what stable, responsible people did. But when a single woman bought a house, it was like admitting that she was alone. Like a widow.

Tish turned toward the antique wedding photograph on the living room wall and pondered her mother's description of Nathan and Letitia McComb. No, they weren't ghoulish and anemic. Their solemn expressions were due to the fact that no one smiled for the camera back then. No doubt they'd been ordered to sit perfectly still.

Posing in a photographer's studio sometime around 1870, young Letitia sat in an ornately carved chair while her much older husband stood behind it, one hand resting on her shoulder. Her slender hands lay demurely in her lap, flaunting a ring set with a dark gem of a respectable size. Matching gems dangled from her ears, and a larger stone hung from a delicate chain at her throat. Her gown was simple; its neckline cut straight across, baring her pale shoulders.

Nathan wore a multitude of layers: a floppy bow tie over a white shirt under a dark vest under a darker jacket. His black hair fell straight and smooth in a cut that ended at his earlobes, while Letitia's lighter hair was severely parted down the middle and pulled back tight.

Tish had always wondered what colors had met the eye of the unknown photographer when he'd settled his subjects for their portrait. Brides hadn't worn white in those days, and for some reason Tish had always imagined the gown as a soft shade of green. The jewelry might have been green too, even if the stones weren't emeralds.

She had no idea what had become of the jewelry. Her dad had known some interesting family stories, but they'd had a lot of gaps. The letters might fill in some of the gaps.

Settling cross-legged in front of the coffee table, she extracted the packet of letters from the envelope and removed the protective paper. Gently, she spread out a couple of the letters. The paper was fragile, the corners crumbling. Some of the folds had become splits. The ink was faded.

Most of them were written by Letitia to her mother in that gloriously graceful style…what was it called? Spencerian. That was it. A useless tidbit of information that Tish had absorbed from her dad's interest in genealogy and historical documents.

At the top left corner of each letter, Letitia had included her address: 525 South Jackson Street, Noble, Alabama.

On a warm spring day over five years ago, Tish and her dad had tracked down that very house. He'd knocked on the door, hoping the current residents would offer a tour if he introduced himself as the great-great-grandson of the man who'd built the place. Tish, mortified, had been relieved when no one came to the door. It was bad enough that they'd stood there on the porch while a little white dog yapped at them from a window.

They hadn't stayed long. They'd prowled around Noble for a few hours, exploring a used-book store and a cemetery. After supper at a local diner, they'd headed back to I-65 and the return trip north.

She picked up a letter that was obviously written by someone other than Letitia. Although the penmanship was large and bold, its flourishes made it difficult to decipher.

My darling Miss Lattimore, as the blessed day of our nuptials approaches, my happiness knows no bounds. I want only to share my joy with you forever, my dear.

That one must have been a special treasure to Letitia. Years after Nathan wrote it, she'd probably added it to the letters her mother had saved.

Setting it aside, Tish chose one that Letitia had written. *Dearest Mother, Nathan and I are wonderfully happy here....*The tiny writing strained Tish's eyes, so she decided to put off further reading until she'd used her scanner to make e-files of the letters. Then she could enlarge them on her computer screen. She'd also e-mail the files to herself for safekeeping.

Unable to resist, she skimmed a few more letters but found nothing especially interesting. She carefully returned all of them to their protective wrapping and slid the packet back into the envelope. Funny how Nathan and Letitia's correspondence was so ordinary. Maybe it meant that they had enjoyed a happy, if uneventful, life.

She picked up her smartphone, opened her browser, and typed the address of the house into the search bar. The first result was an online advertisement.

For sale by owner. Historic home restored and waiting for you. PRICE
IS FIRM!!! THIS IS ALREADY A BARGAIN!!! DO NOT TRY AND DICKER AND
DO NOT TEXT. PHONE CALLS OR E-MAILS ONLY!!!

She smiled at the screaming caps and the abundance of exclamation
marks, then clicked on the photographs. There were only two. Blurred and
dark, they both showed the exterior of the house. It was a shame that the seller
hadn't provided pictures of the interior too. She especially wanted a glimpse of
the parlor where Letitia might have sat, keeping up on her correspondence.

And that was a good reason to drive down to Tampa. On her return trip,
she could take a detour to Noble. The town wasn't too far off the interstate. She
could even call the seller and arrange a time to walk through the house.

It was a crazy idea, like something her fun-loving dad would have come up
with. He'd never thought twice about packing up and hitting the road, whether
for an impromptu vacation or a move halfway across Michigan.

With a fond smile for him, she settled in her favorite chair and studied the
portrait on the wall. The simple dignity of Letitia's expression was what Tish
had sought to imitate every time she was the new kid in school again, facing
bullies on the playground. Holding her head high, she'd managed to keep her
fists to herself by imagining that she was the original Letitia, regal and
composed.

I am Letitia McComb. You can't change who I am.

The more she thought about taking a side trip to Noble, the more she liked
the idea.

Two

George Zorbas ran up the familiar steps and scooped up the runaway. Her little heart raced as she huddled apologetically against his chest.

"If you're not careful, you'll go to doggie heaven a little early," he told the tiny white Maltese.

The dog regarded him with tragic eyes and thumped her tail against his arm.

His late mother's last surviving dog, Daisy could live another ten or fifteen years, barring accidents. But after two years, she still ran back to her former home on a regular basis. The way she darted into traffic, she might not make it to a ripe old age.

"It's a bad habit," he said. "You don't want to die that way."

Daisy whimpered as if to say she understood. Not that she ever honored his wishes about anything.

From his vantage point on the porch, George frowned at the condition of the yard. He had always helped his mother keep the place in tiptop shape, either by the sweat of his brow or by hiring the sweat of someone else's brow, but Si Nelson and his wife had let everything go after they'd learned they had to sell.

When Si bought the place, he'd been gung-ho about the yard. Especially those old camellias. Lately, though, he probably hadn't had the heart to do the yard work himself or the discretionary income to hire someone. But he could have kept up on the pruning and raking, at least.

The front door creaked open on its elderly hinges. George closed his eyes briefly, wishing he hadn't dawdled. Now he had to face Si.

At the moment, with his white hair standing up like the bristles of a scrub brush, the man didn't look like a pillar of the community. "It's about time you picked up your dog, Zorbas. She's been here for an hour."

"Sorry. It took me awhile to notice she was gone." George nodded toward the For Sale sign that had stood on the front lawn for weeks. "Getting any calls lately?"

"Some, but everybody tries to get me down."

"That's the way it's done."

"Not at this price. It's already a bargain, and that's that."

George couldn't argue. The buyers would get a steal of a deal—which would only make him feel guiltier about the hefty profit he'd made when he sold to Si. But business was business.

Stepping onto the porch, Si scowled at the unkempt yard. "I won't miss that steep slope. Or the stairs. Or how big the place is. It's too much to keep up."

George was happy to go along with the excuses that might soothe Si's injured pride. "Yes sir, those creaky old stairs are a pain. You'll be happier in a smaller house with a smaller yard."

"We don't want a house. We'll move to an apartment over in Muldro. We aren't inclined to keep gardening anyway." But Si moved his glum gaze to the camellias he'd loved to pamper.

George racked his brain for an encouraging word. "A lot of apartments have nice big balconies. Y'all can still raise a few flowers and tomatoes and—and things."

"Sure we can." Si stared toward the vacant lot next door where the

Morrisey house had burned down a few years ago. Last summer, he and Shirley had raised a truckload of vegetables there.

"Maybe you'll have some nice neighbors in Muldro," George offered.

"Sure we will." A faint buzzing came from Si's direction. He dug a phone out of his pocket and squinted at it. "Another text. What's wrong with people? Can't they read? When my son put the ad together, he put right in there, 'Do not text,' but these idiots text me anyway." He shoved the phone into his pocket.

A faint sense of alarm began brewing in George. He didn't like texts either, because his big fingers didn't get along with that miniature keyboard. If he wasn't careful, he'd turn into a cranky old geezer too, before his time.

"I'd better get back to minding the store," he said. "Remember, now, if you need to sweeten the deal for somebody, I'll donate a dog. You can say she comes with the house, no extra charge."

Si snorted. "Who'd want her?" He reached into his pocket and slipped Daisy a doggie treat before George could stop him.

"Don't feed her," George protested as she chomped it down. "No wonder she won't leave you alone. Please don't give her any more treats."

Si stumped inside without answering and banged the door shut the way George had banged it shut so many times as a boy.

"Aw, what's the use?" he muttered. He'd never figured out if Si was hard of hearing or if he only faked it when it was convenient.

Daisy whined, struggling to leap from his arms to her usual begging post by the door. George took a firmer grip.

"You don't live here anymore, dog. Get over it."

He wondered if Si would ever get over it, or if he'd spend the rest of his days hating the new owners, whoever they proved to be.

"Not my problem," George said, and carried the resentful dog to his van.

᷒᷒᷒

Tish couldn't get used to it. Orchids just outside the window and Elvis crooning "White Christmas" on the stereo. It was unnatural.

Finished organizing the highest shelf in the last of the tall kitchen cabinets, she lowered herself to sit on her mother's granite countertop and pitched another empty box to the center of the room. In only a few days, her mother and Charles were nearly settled. The gray-haired newlyweds worked hard but stopped often to flirt and smooch. It was cute, but only up to a point. Tish could hardly wait to hit the road, even though she'd be driving into winter weather.

Here in Tampa, it didn't even feel like December. It was an unreal season in an unreal world. Instead of growing poinsettias in foil-covered pots and planning to toss them when they turned spindly after Christmas, Floridians planted them in the ground. Instead of hanging damp gloves to dry near a wood-burning stove, they hung swimsuits and towels to dry on the backs of their patio chairs—and they didn't care if their sixty-something bods weren't quite swimsuit-worthy. Tish grinned, remembering her mom's quip about vintage items. Their flaws, their charm.

The glass sliding door to the patio stood open, admitting the gurgle of the pool pump and the fragrance of tropical flowers. Long-legged Charles stood on a stepstool on the far side of the patio, hanging colored lights on a small palm tree against a brilliant orange sunset. He was whistling along with Elvis.

They would celebrate an early Christmas together before Tish headed north, but it wouldn't be anything like those long-ago visits to Grandma and Grandpa McComb's house just outside Detroit when she was little. Her dad would detour through downtown so she could see the Christmas lights. Sometimes it was snowy, sometimes it wasn't, but steam always rose from the street grates in great white clouds, and her grandparents' house always smelled of roast turkey, sage-and-onion dressing, and the fresh cranberries that popped in a pan on the stove. Every year, Tish had run to the spare room to check the items on the dresser—an antique hairbrush, an ornate music box, a framed photo of relatives she didn't know—and sure enough, nothing had changed. Even the smell of the room stayed the same, as sweet and stale as Grandma's face powder.

Now, high-rise apartments covered the block where that house had stood. Tenants moved in and moved out. Nothing stayed the same, and nothing looked the same. Tish could never point to a particular spot and say it was where she'd once helped her grandma trim the tree and bake gingerbread men.

Her mom bustled into the kitchen. "I just found more boxes that we moved straight from the storage shed into the moving van without opening them. There's no telling what we'll find, but they can wait." She started breaking down one of the empties that Tish had tossed to the floor. "Wow, you work fast."

"You bet. I can't stay all week, you know."

"I still wish you weren't driving back when I could have sent you home on a plane."

"No, this is perfect," Tish said. It was time to share her goofy plan. "I'm going to stop in Alabama and see the McComb house."

Her mother flattened another box and gave her a puzzled look. "Again? Why? You've already seen it."

"The address was on Letitia's letters, so I looked for it online and a for-sale ad popped up. I've swapped a couple of e-mails with the seller—"

"What? When there are so many nice, new homes available? Why would you buy some dilapidated old house, and in Alabama of all places?"

"Who said anything about buying? I only want to see it."

"Oh," her mom said. "That makes a little more sense."

"It's my chance to see the interior while the owner's trying to lure prospective buyers inside. When I went there with Dad, we could only admire it from the sidewalk." Tish made a face. "But I feel bad for the seller. He'll think I want to buy the place."

Her mom chuckled. "Give your conscience a rest. He's selling his house, so he has to expect a few looky-loos."

"True. And I won't take much of his time. I won't haggle over the price. I wouldn't dare. It says right in the ad, 'do not dicker.'"

"Ha! Then you should dicker your little heart out. Get him softened up so he'll be willing to bargain with the next person. You're doing both of them a favor."

Tish smiled. "I like the way you think."

"Did you give him your name?"

"My first name, but he got it wrong. He thought I said 'Trish,' and I just let it go. Why?"

"Just wonder what he'd think of a McComb strolling through the Mc-Comb house."

"Now that you mention it, if he finds out I'm a McComb, he'll think I have my heart set on buying the place, and he'll be even more stubborn about the price."

Her mom laughed and started in on a story about some long-ago real estate deal, but Tish tuned her out.

Why shouldn't she buy the house? For years, she'd been careful with her money. She had enough for a decent down payment. She had excellent credit, and her experience at the insurance company could translate into a managerial position in some other field if need be.

If she bought a house, she could take up piano again. Her neighbors at the apartment complex had complained about the noise, so she'd hardly touched it. In a house of her own, though—

"Earth to Tish."

"Yes?"

"You've got that dreamy look in your eyes. The one your father used to get when he was cooking up some new scheme."

Tish blinked. Of course she wouldn't move to Alabama. It was a crazy idea, like something her father might have done. She was more like her mother. Organized and practical. Not an explorer or a dreamer.

"I only want photos, Mom. Photos of the rooms. That's all."

"Uh-huh."

Tish pushed herself off the counter and onto the floor, the ceramic tiles chilly beneath her bare feet. "What's left on your to-do list? Let's get busy."

Three

After leaving Tampa, Tish had made several touristy stops in Florida, then cut across a corner of Georgia and headed for Montgomery. She'd spent the night there. This morning she'd visited a historical museum before returning to the interstate, where heavy rains and other people's accidents had created the mother of all traffic jams. A four-hour drive turned into six, but the sun had come out, traffic had cleared, and she was almost there.

She took the exit for Muldro, a good-sized town that boasted an outlet mall, a multiplex theater, and more chain restaurants and car dealerships than a girl could ever want. Somewhere in that cluster of commerce was the motel where she'd made reservations for the night.

The mall was a zoo. Everyone for miles around must have decided this was the weekend to finish the Christmas shopping. Except for the lack of snow and the stores that sold Auburn and 'Bama merchandise for sports fans, the mall bore a strong resemblance to the outlet malls she shopped in Michigan. Sometimes she wondered if national chains would blur the country's regional differences someday, making a homogenized blend.

Safely past the mall traffic, Tish yawned and flexed her shoulders. Noble would be another twenty minutes down the state highway, but she would still be early for her appointment with the seller. She wished she had more daylight left for exploring the town, though.

A few miles east of Muldro, the landscape became more rural. Lackadaisical fences separated big country lots. Some people kept chickens or goats; other yards held swing sets or above-ground pools. It wasn't dark yet, but Christmas lights sparkled on trees and fences and houses.

She was on the outskirts of Noble now, a small town nestled among green hills. Everything looked much the same as she remembered it from her trip with her father. The state highway became Main Street, and a sign announced the city limits. She had to stay on the main drag and look for South Jackson on the right, past the downtown area.

Old homes lined Main, many of them converted to commercial use, with a few modern buildings sprinkled into the mix. She passed hole-in-the-wall eateries and local shops, a small park with a gazebo decked out in Christmas garlands, and more businesses. Every light pole held a red bow and greenery. It would be even prettier after dark, with all the lights on.

Retail gave way to residential, and the homes—most of them—were old but lovely. She could get used to the climate too. Instead of winter but never Christmas, like Narnia, or Christmas without winter, like Florida, this was Christmas with a combination of sunshine and a nip in the air.

Most of the town didn't look especially familiar, maybe because she'd seen it in the springtime before, or maybe because she'd seen it through a veil of grief. That trip with her dad hadn't been long after Stephen's death.

Spotting South Jackson, Tish put on her blinker and slowed for the turn. The street curved slightly to the right and rose in a gentle slope, just as she remembered it.

She counted down five houses on the left. There it was, a rectangular, two-story house that was longer than it was wide. Only a small portion of it was visible from the street, and a huge magnolia tree had taken root in the front yard. White pillars held up the roof of the porch. A For Sale by Owner sign stood on a sloping lawn that rippled with clumps of weeds. Overgrown shrubs crowded the first-floor windows. The house could have used some fresh paint and the services of a window washer.

Tish pulled the car to the curb but didn't get out. Mr. Nelson had said he would be home in time for their appointment, but the place looked deserted. No vehicles in the driveway. No lights in the windows. No Christmas lights either.

The house hadn't changed much in five years, except now the lot next door sported a neglected and forgotten garden instead of an old home. She spied the remnants of a pole-bean teepee among the rows of dormant or dying plants. Off to the side stood part of a blackened brick chimney. A house fire? She was glad it hadn't spread to the McComb house.

A small white dog sat by the front door, so still that Tish took it for a statue until the breeze ruffled its fur. Maybe it was the same dog she and Dad had spotted in the window, bouncing up and down on spindly legs and yapping. In dog language, it had said: *Go away. Mind your own business.*

But the house *was* Tish's business. Its history had her name written all over it.

Grabbing her digital camera, she climbed out and stretched. Then she took a few pictures of the front yard, its lawn dissected by a flagstone path. Yellow pansies bloomed around the base of the magnolia, a patch of domestication in the jungle.

Pansies in December? Tish shook her head, smiling. She couldn't get over it.

She turned slowly, sizing up the neighborhood. Directly across the street, a matching circle of yellow pansies ringed a smaller magnolia. The neighbors might have shared a flat of pansies. Maybe they were the kind of neighbors who shared the overabundance of their vegetable gardens with each other too, and weren't afraid to ask to borrow a cup of sugar.

A white cargo van pulled up on the opposite side of the street. The van's door was emblazoned with the words *Antiques on Main*.

A man climbed out. About her age, with thick black hair that needed a trim, he wore a black overcoat that could have fit in nicely on Wall Street. He might have been a laid-back stockbroker, if such a creature existed.

He was halfway across the street already. "Good afternoon," he said.

"Good afternoon," she echoed uncertainly. Could this be Silas Nelson, who'd sounded like such a cantankerous old coot on the phone? About to ask, she decided to wait and see.

The man marched past her and onto the walkway that led to 525 South Jackson. He proceeded up the stairs to the porch, scooped up the dog, and turned around with the tiny animal snuggled against his chest. He kept his head down until he was almost beside Tish, then gave her a brief smile as he passed. He didn't say another word. He just crossed the street, climbed into his van, and drove away with the dog.

Moments later, a silver pickup truck pulled into the driveway. An older gentleman climbed out and gave her a hopeful smile that pricked her conscience.

"You must be Trish," he said in a potent drawl. "I'm Si Nelson."

"I'm glad to meet you, Mr. Nelson. Thanks for being willing to show me around."

"It's a wonderful house," he said. "As I'm sure you can tell."

She nodded, trying not to act too enthusiastic, and he launched into a sales spiel that made her cringe inside. The poor guy seemed to think she was in love with the house and ready to make a full-price offer on the spot. He even mentioned having a purchase agreement ready to go. They only needed to fill in the blanks and add their signatures, and of course he would collect her earnest money.

Only in his dreams.

Although his clothes were perfectly respectable, his hair was as overgrown as his lawn. His dishevelment was the old-man version, not the slightly shaggy and attractive look of the olive-skinned guy in the overcoat.

Nelson seemed to think she'd be fascinated with the good condition of the furnace and the electrical system, important considerations if she'd been serious about buying the place. She tried not to feel guilty about leading him on.

He caught her attention when he said he and the previous owner had been careful to preserve what he called "the originals" of the house. "It's worth the trouble," he said. "A grand old place like this will last forever."

Tish thought of the house fire next door and wanted to argue that no house could stand forever, but she only nodded respectfully. "I can't wait to see the interior."

"It'll be dark soon," he said. "Let's start with the yard and the garage while it's light out."

"Sure. Do you mind if I take pictures?"

"Not at all," he said with a smile. "You'll want to show your friends."

"Well…maybe. Is there any wiggle room on the price?"

His thin lips snapped into a straight, unsmiling line. "No, there isn't. Do you still want to see the place or not?"

"Yes. Yes, of course I do." She straightened, then reminded herself that she was doing him a favor. After a tour with her, he would understand that his house was overpriced and, from the looks of the outside, in great need of some TLC.

He set off around the side of the house and she followed, her black Crocs buried in the tall grass. She snapped pictures of the house, the overgrown backyard, and a pair of sandy tracks worn into the ground by many tires over many years. The tracks led toward a row of tall shrubs and, behind them, a "garage."

They made their way to the far corner of the backyard and rounded the tall hedges. Perhaps a hundred yards in front of them stood a building that,

Mr. Nelson explained, had started life as a carriage house. As big as a barn, it still evoked an atmosphere of horses and carriages. Its twin square doors with weatherworn cross-braces might have been barn doors, and a smaller door on the second floor testified to its history as a hayloft. Tish could easily imagine Nathan hitching a horse to a buggy and taking his young bride for a ride, but she couldn't see a modern homeowner getting much use out of the building.

"It's awfully inconvenient," she said, "being so far from the house."

Mr. Nelson laughed as if she'd said something especially stupid. "Nobody with any sense would build a carriage house or a stable anywhere near their dining room windows."

"Oh, of course. Those horsy smells. Was there a stable too?"

"Yes, but it's long gone." Mr. Nelson went to the door on the right, dealt with a padlock, and shoved the heavy door open. He turned on the lights. The building had a cement floor, two small, high windows on each side, and a few sections of pegboard on the wall for tools. Still, she could imagine it filled with the smells of hay and leather harnesses.

"It was renovated in 1930 or so and again in the sixties," Mr. Nelson said. "As you can see, it has electricity and good lighting." He pointed overhead. "There's plenty of extra storage up there."

Remembering her resolution to keep him from getting his hopes up, she frowned. "It's not practical, though, being so far from the house."

He scowled at her. "Some folks don't mind walking a few steps."

"It's more than a few steps, but never mind. I'd like to see the house."

"Sure thing."

They stepped outside, and he locked up. In silence, they walked through the twilight with the house looming before them. Its rear was a bit shabbier than the pretty face it presented to the street.

"Seems to need some repairs and some paint on this side of the house. Are you sure you can't come down on the price?" she asked.

He offered a sharp sigh and a stony smile. "No ma'am. As I said in my ad, the price is firm."

Apparently he believed the front door would give her a better first impression, because he bypassed the back door and led her around the side of the house and into the front yard. Following him across the lawn, she eyed the white pillars holding up the porch roof.

She smiled, recalling her dad's joke when they'd first found the place, and decided to quote him. "It wants to be Tara when it grows up."

"Wrong state," Nelson said, not cracking a smile this time. "That would be Georgia." A call came in on his cell phone. "Excuse me," he said, heading toward the sidewalk. "Back with you in a minute."

A little miffed that he would let a phone call derail the tour, she proceeded to the steps. She wore jeans and a sweatshirt, but she indulged in a moment of little-girl pretense, imagining herself as the first Letitia, gracefully lifting long skirts and sweeping up the steps with her head held high.

I am Letitia McComb, coming home in the evening...

She crossed the long, narrow porch and peered through every window. But it was too dark inside to see anything.

Beyond the railing at the far end of the porch stood a tall bush with glossy dark leaves like the shrubs near the garage, but this one was studded with bright red flowers. Camellias? Yes. Moving closer, she cupped one of the blossoms in her hand, marveling that its delicate petals and fragile yellow stamens could survive outside in December. It seemed even more miraculous than the pansies.

It would be lovely to cut a single camellia to grace her breakfast table on a winter morning. It would be even lovelier to pick gigantic bouquets for a larger table crowded with people—except she didn't know a soul in Noble unless she counted Mr. Nelson. He had finished his phone call and was walking up the steps. "Sorry about that." He unlocked the door and reached inside to hit a light switch. "Come on in."

She stopped in the doorway, taking it in. Straight ahead, a hardwood floor and an elegant staircase, its dark banister wrapped with Christmas greens. To the left, the corner of a graceful sideboard and dining room table. To the right, a room with high ceilings and tall, narrow windows. A rich red Oriental carpet lay before a fireplace with a mahogany mantel and a marble hearth. Why, it was the parlor where her great-great-great-grandparents might have hung their wedding portrait. If the walls of the room could speak, their stories would weave connections between two Letitias, born generations apart.

Tish mashed her lips together to keep them from trembling.

"Oh, Mr. Nelson," she whispered. "Can't you come down just a little? Please?"

Long before dawn, Tish lay wide awake in a dark motel room in Muldro, listening to traffic roaring past on the interstate. Heading north. The direction she had to go. People were counting on her to be at work on Monday.

But last night, driving out of Noble, she'd nearly cried. This wasn't supposed to happen. She'd only wanted to see the house and the town. She hadn't planned to fall in love with them. The last time she'd visited, she'd still been in love with Stephen. Her aching heart hadn't been capable of forming new attachments, human or otherwise.

After flinging off the covers, she reached for the bedside lamp, then shut off the alarm on her phone before it could go off. The phone had come in handy as a web browser and calculator. She'd stayed up late, looking up interest rates and crunching the numbers. If she could persuade Mr. Nelson to lower his price a little, her payment would be about the same as the rent on her apartment, and she'd be building equity.

While Tish dressed and packed, she watched one of the weather channels, muted. The abbreviated weather forecasts for major cities scrolled across the bottom of the screen. She watched them all the way through, twice. Half the cities in the Midwest and Northeast expected freezing rain, but Florida would have sun, afternoon thunderstorms, and more sun. Her mom and Charles would hit the pool again today, or maybe they'd play tennis with their new friends. Meanwhile, Tish would drive north, into the freezing rain. If the road conditions didn't get too bad, she'd be home by bedtime.

She stepped outside with her bags. The nip in the air was downright pleasant compared to what she'd find in Ames, Michigan.

She drove to the office and turned in her key to a sleepy-eyed desk clerk who pointed her toward the free coffee beside an artificial tree twinkling with ornaments and white lights. In her car again, coffee in hand, she pulled to the side of the parking lot to let the car warm up. A tractor-trailer glowing with lights moved slowly onto the road toward the northbound on-ramp.

If she followed the truck onto the interstate, she might never return to Noble. She might forget how beautiful the house was and how it tugged at her heart. She'd probably end up living in Michigan for the rest of her life.

Dad would buy the McComb house. If he were alive, and if he were able to afford it, he would buy it and not think twice about moving across the country. Despite the fact that Alabama, even at its northern border, was the Deep South. Where a Michigander wouldn't fit in. She'd be the new kid in town all over again.

She was a McComb, though. That should count for something. Moving to Noble would let her reconnect with her roots, and she could forge new bonds too. She closed her eyes, imagining her dining room table in that house, filled with friends, and her vintage percolator bubbling on the sideboard.

She'd never been good at distinguishing between God's guidance, her own wishes, and the way life dictated certain choices sometimes. Her pastor said he and his wife always prayed about big decisions until they both had peace, but sometimes inner peace was only a fleeting emotion. Not something to stake your future on.

Tish didn't have a husband to pray with, and the Lord wasn't talking.

She opened her eyes. The Volvo's sensible engine was still putt-putting away. So quiet and dependable.

"Lord, I'm tired of being quiet and dependable," she whispered. "But if I'm headed in the wrong direction, please stop me."

She punched Silas Nelson's number on her phone before she lost her nerve. It took him five rings.

"Who is this?" he shouted.

"It's T—oh no!" She stared at the clock on her dash.

"Is this the woman from Michigan?"

"Yes. I'm so sorry. I wasn't thinking of the time."

"It's not even six o'clock!"

But it was nearly seven...eastern. Alabama was central.

Her face heated with mortification. "I'm sorry. I forgot what time zone I was in."

"Never mind time zones. It's still dark out!"

"Um, yes. I'm sorry. I wasn't thinking."

He subsided into offended grumbling as another tractor-trailer groaned by, the noise of its engine drowning him out. After it had passed, he was still talking.

"I'm sorry, could you repeat that?" she asked.

"I said you'd better have a good reason for waking me up. Why'd you call?" A thin thread of hope stretched taut in his voice.

"I..." Something close to despair wobbled in hers. "I wanted to talk about the price."

"There's not much to talk about."

"But I really can't go quite that high."

"That's a shame, but there'll be other folks waiting in line."

Other folks hanging their pictures on *her family's* parlor wall?

But he probably didn't have other people waiting in line. He just wanted her to think he did—like she wanted him to think she would walk away if he didn't lower his price.

"There are other houses out there," she said. "Lots of other houses."

"Yes ma'am, and there are other buyers. It's already a rock-bottom price."

"But you've had it on the market for months, and you still haven't found a buyer. If you'll come down just ten percent, I'll sign the papers this morning."

She held her breath, refusing to be the one who broke first.

After a long, tense silence, he let out a weary sigh. "All right, all right."

"You'll come down ten percent?"

"Yes," he snapped. "But you're a thief."

Suddenly weak, she leaned her forehead against the steering wheel. "Thank you, Mr. Nelson."

He sighed again. "Thank you, Trish."

"Actually, it's Tish."

"What's that?"

"My name isn't Trish. It's Tish. Short for Letitia. Letitia McComb."

Silence again. He must have been hunting for pen and paper to write it down. But she didn't have all day.

"I know it's very early, and I'm so sorry, but I'd like to sign that purchase agreement as soon as possible and get on the road."

He sounded utterly dumbfounded by her request. "You mean right this minute, Miss...McComb?"

"I wouldn't be in such a rush except I have eleven or twelve hours of driving ahead of me. More than that if I don't beat the storm that's coming. I'm in Muldro, so it'll take me twenty minutes to get to the house."

"I'll be here. I might even be out of bed." He ended the call.

Tish put her phone away. She put the car in gear and pulled onto the road, heading back toward Noble. Back to the McComb house. *Her* house.

She'd have to give notice to her employer and her landlord, apply for a mortgage, pack up her life in Michigan, say good-bye to Stephen one last time...

"Dear Lord," she whispered, "what have I done?"

Four

With Daisy in the crook of his arm, George paused at the top of the stairs that led from the apartment down to the shop, took a deep breath of morning air, and nearly burst out singing. After wrangling over the price for weeks, he'd finally bought a project car. He'd take possession in about a month, after the O'Neill brothers switched out the engine. Restoring the rest of the vehicle would keep him busy for months more—once he'd found a secure garage for the project. And then...

He imagined himself at the wheel, cruising Main while the monster engine made that long black hood vibrate with pent-up power. Or he'd take the car cross country for the pleasure of turning it loose on a deserted stretch of highway out west. Or he'd take it to classic car rallies closer to home and have the chicks falling all over him.

Because a man who took his mother's ridiculous dog everywhere he went was an irresistible chick magnet.

With a rueful grin, he carried Daisy down the stairs. While she did her business on his scrap of lawn, he studied the parking area and brooded over his situation.

His van stood there, an ugly but reliable workhorse. A ding in the side panel wrinkled the *M* in *Antiques on Main* so it looked more like *Nain*. That didn't bother him, though. Nor did the trees that rained their junk down on the van. But when it came to his project car… That baby deserved a proper sanctuary. But he couldn't even start the project until he had garage space.

He shouldn't have been in such a hurry to sell his mother's house, but it was too late now. Two years and two owners too late. And the new owner, rumor had it, was something to be reckoned with.

The jingling of Daisy's tags jolted him out of his thoughts. Trotting toward the street, she was nearly gone already, her nose in the air. Sniffing freedom.

He chased her, catching up as she rounded the corner onto the sidewalk. He snagged her with both hands and picked her up. She tried to flatten herself against him, her heart beating at an insane pace—which was only appropriate.

"You thought you were on your way again, didn't you? I can't have you off your leash for one minute, can I?"

He carried the neurotic little dog to the front door. His uncle Calv had already turned on the lights and put the Open sign in the window. George pushed the door open with his shoulder, activating the bell above him.

"It's me," he said, the familiar smells of furniture polish and dust tickling his nose. "Don't get up."

"Wouldn't dream of it," Calv answered from the rear of the store.

George ambled down the narrow aisle, pausing to adjust the hanging price tag on an antebellum kerosene lamp, and entered the back room. He set Daisy on the floor and nudged her in the general direction of her crate. She moved just out of reach and looked over her shoulder, radiating self-pity.

Stooped, lanky Calv sat at the worktable, his dirt-gray hair hanging in front of his suntanned face as he oiled a mysterious mechanical gadget he'd picked up at a yard sale. "I keep telling you, the dog's depressed. She still misses your mother."

"No, she doesn't. The little schemer wants us to feel sorry for her."

Calv shook his head. "My neighbor's dog, he got depressed when she kicked her husband out. He moped around for weeks. The dog, I mean, not the husband. He wouldn't play with the kids. Wouldn't even eat."

"Daisy eats. Believe me, she eats. Grain-free, gluten-free, all natural…" George sighed. He'd promised his mother. Now Daisy ate better than he did.

He sat behind his desk in the corner, somewhat cramped but safely removed from his uncle's messy, greasy project. "I guess you've heard the news? Si sold the house to a McComb."

"Yep. I heard it straight from him, ten times over. I've never in all my born days seen him so riled up." Calv flicked his hair out of his eyes and gave George a solemn stare. "I asked him where she's from that she don't know the score, and he said Detroit or thereabouts. Said she had Michigan plates on her car. And an attitude. He said she called him early-early so he'd be half-asleep. She caught him off guard, and then she nagged and nagged until he caved in."

"Si's got his knickers in a knot about needing to sell. He's not trying to put her in the best light."

George frowned, recalling the woman he'd seen leaning against a white Volvo while she took pictures of the house. He hadn't noticed Michigan tags, but he hadn't been looking for them.

"She has exactly the same name," Calv said. "You think it's a coincidence?"

"Buying that particular house? It can't be a coincidence."

"Especially because she lied about it."

George gave his uncle a sharp look. "You sure about that?"

"That's how Si tells it, anyway. She gave him the wrong name from the get-go—Patricia instead of Letitia—and she wouldn't say her last name until she'd worn him down on the price."

"That was pretty shrewd," George said. "Si wouldn't have budged if he'd known who she was."

"It was a steal. I know, I know, that doesn't make her a literal thief, but Si's got his gussy up. He's even mad at her for wanting an inspection."

"An inspection is just standard procedure. Si has really let the place go, too. If I were her, I'd be concerned about some basic maintenance issues."

"I know, but he says she's a penny-pinchin' trash-talker."

"Even if he's right, we will be nice to her."

"Sure we will. She'll need a good dose of nice. She's gonna have a tough row to hoe in this narrow-minded town. Besides the obvious, I mean. Si and Shirley's friends won't take kindly to her either."

"I hate to see them lose the place." George's guilty conscience circled, flapping its ugly wings, and came in for a heavy landing. "I never should have sold it to them. I should have listened to my gut."

"It's not your fault that they came upon hard times. Nobody saw it coming. Poor Si, though. He loved that big ol' garage. So did I, until your mama put an end to that business."

"We both loved it." George shook his head, remembering the day his mother had decided Calv, her youngest brother, wasn't fit company for her fatherless and impressionable son. So Calv had packed up his tools—

A glorious idea lit George's brain like fireworks. If the McComb woman was a penny pincher, she might want to get some rent money out of the garage. He could ask her, anyway, if she proved to be decent. It stood too far from the house to do her much good, but the noise and the fumes wouldn't bother anybody out there. It was huge too. More than enough room.

Everybody would win. It would solve his problem, but it might help the new owner even more, as a sort of goodwill gesture. It would say George Zorbas wasn't afraid to do business with a McComb. Best of all, it would bring

healing balm to an old man's heart—if it panned out. He wouldn't say anything to Calv just yet.

The doohickey slipped from Calv's hand and crashed onto the floor. Daisy
leaped into her crate, her nails clicking, and cowered in the corner.

"Aw, it's okay, Daisy." Calv leaned over to pick up the gadget. "Toss her a
treat, George. Make her feel better."

George reached into his top drawer, pulled out one of those outrageously
expensive treats, and pitched it into the crate. Daisy blinked several times and
finally worked up her courage to inch over to it. She took it delicately in her
mouth and crunched, not so delicately.

Life would get interesting once the house changed hands. Every time the
dog ran away, he would have to fetch her from the porch of Miss Letitia
McComb.

After stopping at the grocery store on her way home from work, Tish
grabbed a shopping cart and pushed it inside at a fast clip. Lately, she
was always running. Literally and mentally. Always running behind, like
some scatterbrained ditz.

Her workday life had always been a whirlwind of paperwork, but now her
at-home life had become that too. The mortgage was in process. She'd given
notice to her employer and her landlord, and she'd started her online search for
jobs around Noble. Her apartment was a mess of moving boxes and piles of
giveaways.

She steered the cart toward the produce department in hopes of finding
the produce manager. He always had boxes to give away, but she liked to ask
him first. She didn't want anyone to think she was taking them without
permission.

Passing a display of Valentine's Day merchandise—a premature display, in her opinion, as it was still early January—she nearly ran into one of the Henderson brothers coming the other way with one of his little boys. Father and son matched from head to toe: John Deere caps, barn jackets, jeans, and brown boots.

There used to be six stairstep Henderson brothers. Out of habit, not because she needed it anymore, she ran down the mental list that had helped her keep the brothers straight at first. This was Matt, who wasn't quite as blond as his brothers. Hank was the one with the boyish, contagious laugh. Paul had curly hair. Ryan had the only big nose of the family. Rob was the short, studious one. And finally there was Stephen, the youngest. The one she'd loved.

Matt's son tugged on his arm and whined for a bag of Valentine's candy.

"No, buddy," Matt said. "Your mom already bought plenty."

"Daddy, please?"

"No, Alex. Sorry."

Tish felt herself softening, feeling sorry for the little tyke. At four or five, Stephen must have looked very much like Alex.

Tears heated her eyes. If that stupid deer hadn't run into the road and ruined everything, Alex would have been her nephew by marriage. She would have sent him a Valentine every year. *With much love from Uncle Stephen and Aunt Tish...*

Laughing at something his son had said, Matt looked up and noticed her. "Tish, how are ya? My mom told me you're moving to Alabama."

"Hi, you two." Tish mustered up the biggest smile she could. "Yep. That's why I'm here. Picking up moving boxes."

"It sounds like a real adventure. Why Alabama?"

"A family connection."

Matt frowned. Maybe he thought she'd gone crazy.

"My mother remarried and moved to Florida," she said. "Now I'll be within a long day's drive of her new place."

Matt nodded. "That gets important as parents get older. It's good to stay plugged in tight with your family."

Easy for him to say. He had family coming out his ears. But Tish only smiled and nodded.

"I hope you'll love it down there," he said. "Best of luck to you."

"Thanks, Matt. Well, give the rest of the family my love. Bye, Alex."

The little boy gave her a shy smile, but he didn't know who she was. He'd never known his Uncle Stephen, either.

Tish continued toward the back of the store, finding it difficult to think about moving boxes.

Stephen had moved on, leaving her behind. He was eternally young and carefree in her memory while she marched on toward middle age in her comfy Naturalizers. Wearing small, sensible earrings, with her hair pulled back tight. Driving a Volvo. She was even buying a house. An old house, frozen in time.

Maybe she should have taken her mother's suggestion and bought a brand-new condo in Tampa. Surrounded by senior citizens, she might have felt like a spring chicken in comparison. Or she might have sped up the process of turning into an old hen.

Five

December and much of January had blurred into a flurry of paperwork, e-mails, phone calls, and money transactions. The closing was just two days away in Muldro. Tomorrow morning, she'd begin her drive south, but she had one thing left to do before she could leave her life in Michigan behind.

Aware that she reeked of cleaning supplies, Tish leaned against her grocery cart like an old lady with a walker. She'd promised her aching muscles a long bubble bath, but this was her last chance to buy flowers. She was cutting it close too. The gates would be locked at dark.

Picking up her pace, she made her way to the floral department. She passed by the sedate arrangements in the cooler and stopped beside the random, cellophane-wrapped bunches of flowers in big plastic tubs. Twelve stems per bunch. She just couldn't decide which mixture she liked best. Each one included something she loved. A bright yellow spider mum, the softness of green eucalyptus, the vivid blue of a bachelor's-button… How could she decide?

Buy 'em all. You know you want to.

Such extravagance! Exactly what Stephen would have wanted.

Tish counted. Six bunches in one tub. Six in the other. At nearly ten dollars each? When she needed to be smart with her money?

But she had a wad of cash in her purse for the trip. More than she needed.

She wouldn't be able to put more than a few of them in water, though, and what could she do with the rest? They'd wilt in no time without water.

They would wilt anyway.

She loaded the contents of both plastic tubs into her cart, balanced the flowers upright, then headed for the shortest checkout line. Through the window, she could see the sun breaching the horizon. Once the sun went down, it would be too late.

The man ahead of her didn't seem to understand how to swipe a debit card. *Hurry up,* she mouthed soundlessly.

Stephen had often picked up flowers at this very store. She would forever wonder what kind he'd chosen, that last time.

Finally, the slowpoke finished his business and moved on. She handed one cellophane sleeve of flowers to the teenager at the register. "I have twelve of these," she told him.

"Got it."

Fast, efficient, and impersonal, he scanned the UPC code times twelve, handed the single bunch of flowers back, and gave her the total—all without really looking at her. She handed over the cash and took her change and receipt, all without really looking at him.

"That's a lot of flowers," he said, as if he'd finally noticed. "Big party?"

Wanting to cry, she met his eyes. He wasn't as young as she'd first assumed. He was in his midtwenties, probably—about the age Stephen was when they'd met.

Her phone rang. Glad for the diversion, she pulled it out of her purse, mouthed a *thank-you* to the checker, and answered the call as she walked out of the store. It was someone from the mortgage company in Muldro, calling to confirm that she'd be there for the closing at five on Monday afternoon.

Tish decided not to mention the storms predicted for her first day of travel. She would get through it, one way or another.

"You bet," she said. "I'm leaving early tomorrow morning. I'll spend the night in Kentucky and pull into town late in the afternoon."

"Perfect! Safe travels."

"Thanks. See you then."

Tish loaded the flowers gently into the backseat of her car. Climbing behind the wheel, she breathed in the scent of the flowers, then drove out of the parking lot and headed south on M-24. She tucked her phone in the console and ran down a mental checklist of everything she still had to accomplish before she left town.

Lost in her thoughts, she'd missed the turn. She hadn't been there in a while. Wasting precious moments of daylight, she drove to the next light, made a U-turn, and went back to the side road she'd meant to turn on.

A quarter mile down, the metal gates still stood open. She pulled onto the narrow gravel road and followed it around three gentle bends, finally recognizing a cypress tree she used to use as a landmark. A few feet taller than she remembered it, the cypress swayed like a skinny dancer against the fading sunset.

She climbed out of her car and looked out at the flat farmland. An earlier generation of Hendersons had settled in the county long ago, and most of their descendants still farmed. The joke was that you couldn't walk through town without bumping into someone with Henderson blood, and you couldn't drive through the countryside without passing Henderson land.

She opened the rear door. Using the tiny knife on her key chain, she freed the flower stems from rubber bands and cellophane. Piled up in lovely abandon in the soft glow of the dome light, they did indeed look fit for a big party.

She filled her arms with flowers and carried them to Stephen's grave. Working quickly, she began to spread them out from the head to the foot. It took her three trips in the fading light before she finally held the last few stems. It was so dark now she could hardly make out their colors.

A yellow lily. A stem of pale alstroemeria blossoms. A red rosebud.

She brought the rose to her lips. She'd be two hours down the road by the time the sun shed its first light on her farewell offering—if the sun came out at all.

A bird trilled in a nearby tree, and traffic kept up a steady hum on M-24. Life went on, as it had for over five years, without Stephen.

"I'll never forget you," she whispered against the soft petals of the rose.

She placed the last few stems close to the headstone, its lettering illegible in the twilight. She knew every inch of it, though. The dates bookmarked the life of Stephen David Henderson, who'd meant to marry her.

"Good-bye, Stephen," she said, her voice loud in the silence. She groped for something more to say, but there was nothing. Her heart felt empty. Swept clean, like her apartment.

Straightening, she saw a trio of deer grazing in the distance. They looked peaceful. Graceful. Harmless.

She returned to her car. It still smelled like flowers. She started the engine and backed up, shining the headlights on the small mountain of blooms. Then she drove slowly toward the exit, knowing she would never visit the place again. She was bound for Alabama in the morning.

Mel wished she had one of those fancy backpacks so she could strap everything on it. She'd left Orlando in a hurry, though. No time to get organized. With her bedroll strapped to her back, she had to shift her duffel bag from one hand to the other. The jacket made the bag heavy. She'd known since last winter that she didn't really need it in Florida. Still, she couldn't just get rid of it. It was borrowed.

Her legs were so tired. One foot in front of another, she'd made her way south, changing her name along the way. Melissa. Melinda. No. Too close to her real name. Belinda? Yeah, she'd be Belinda for a while. She felt safer that way, like she was protecting her identity somehow.

She knew that didn't make sense, though. Hitching a ride was dangerous, especially for a girl as scrawny as she was. If somebody killed her, her parents would never know. For them, it wouldn't be any different from the last two years. Dead or alive, she was already gone.

Stopping for a minute, she pulled the jacket out of the bag and tied the sleeves around her waist. The bag was lighter as she walked on.

Her eyes on the ground, she knew there was a red light up ahead because traffic slowed. She turned and walked backward with her thumb jutting out, trying to look sweet and tough at the same time. Decent people wouldn't pick up a girl who didn't look sweet, but she had to let people know not to mess with her.

She tried to meet the eyes of the drivers, but nobody paid any attention except a guy in a little Honda. He honked and gave a friendly wave but kept going. Like that could help.

When the vehicles were at a dead stop, the drivers all ignoring her, she turned around and reached the corner just when the light turned green. She stepped into the crosswalk, and somebody gave her a wolf whistle.

Her stomach growled. She hadn't eaten a real meal since that last night at Fishy's just before she got fired. She was trying to save her cash. If she could find a campground that didn't charge, she could roast some convenience-store hot dogs over a fire. That would be sort of cool, like the good ol' days when she'd gone camping with Grandpa John.

She looked up at the cloudy sky. "Don't be mad at me."

Hitchhiking was one of the things he'd lectured her about. Hitchhiking, drugs, alcohol, sleeping around, smoking, and tattoos. She had done pretty well, considering.

About to cross the gravelly driveway of a cheapo used-car dealership, she heard a vehicle slowing behind her. She stopped, waiting for it to pass in front of her. It was a white pickup, really old and really small—and it slowed right beside her.

The driver leaned over and opened the passenger door. He had country music on his stereo. "Need a lift?"

She checked him out without moving closer. He was about thirty, maybe. Blue eyes. A nice smile. He wore a clean white T-shirt and jeans. He was a working man, because there were tools all over the floor of the truck.

"Where are you headed?" she asked.

"South a ways. Miami, eventually. How far do you want to go?"

She wanted him to think someone was expecting her to show up somewhere.

"Fort Lauderdale," she said, hoping it made sense. She'd never been good with maps and directions.

"Cool. Throw your stuff in the back."

She hesitated. Her cash was in the bag. Well, nobody was going to steal it when they were flying down the road, so she dropped the bag in the bed of the truck. She had to be more careful with her bedroll, though. She pulled it off her back and climbed in.

She shut the door, memorizing where the handle was in case she had to lunge for it in a hurry, later. "Thanks for the lift."

"Sure." He held out his hand for her to shake. "I'm Mitch."

"Hi. I'm Belinda." She settled the bedroll carefully in her lap.

So far, she wasn't picking up bad vibes. He used his turn signal and checked his mirrors before he pulled onto the road. The tools on the floor reminded her of the hardworking mechanics at her dad's dealership, but he wouldn't put up with a mechanic who left his tools all over the place. Her dad never put up with much of anything.

The muscles in her legs started to relax, finally. It felt so good to sit down.

It didn't seem fair that she was out of work yet she still had to be on her feet all day.

She closed her eyes, remembering some of the jobs she'd had since she moved to Florida. They'd all kept her on her feet for hours. Picking strawberries. Working at a car wash. Cleaning cheap motel rooms. Bussing tables.

Her stomach growled. Embarrassed, she opened her eyes.

The guy laughed. "Hungry?"

"Yeah. Haven't had breakfast."

Maybe he'd buy her fast food somewhere. He didn't offer, though, and she didn't ask. She was afraid he would want something in return.

Neither of them talked for a while. Traffic was slow. They crawled past a Burger King. Even with the windows closed, the smell drove her crazy.

The black SUV ahead of them had decals all over the rear window, bragging about what a big happy family they were. Soccer, softball. A fish that said they listened to a nice, safe radio station. She wished she'd hitched a ride with them instead, but nice, safe families didn't take chances on scruffy hitchhikers, so scruffy hitchhikers had to take their chances with anybody who looked decent.

Traffic started moving, and they flew through three or four green lights in the time it would have taken her to walk to just one of them. She looked out at the palm trees and the white birds that hung out in the roadside canals. Big clouds were building up for another afternoon thunderstorm, but she'd stay nice and dry in the truck.

Her stomach rumbled again. To cover the noise, she started talking.

"I wish people would take down their Christmas lights after New Year's. It all looks so tacky after a while."

"Yeah, it does. Did you have a nice Christmas with your folks?"

Her radar started buzzing. He wanted to know if she had folks. He wanted to know if anybody would miss her if she disappeared.

"Yeah," she lied. "You?"

"We had fun. Good food, better booze. You like booze?"

"In the morning? No, thanks." All of a sudden, her hands were sweaty. She wasn't sure she'd be able to grip the door handle, but the truck was moving too fast now anyway.

"Gonna be a nice day today." He moved his hand to her thigh, bumping her bedroll. She wanted to shove his hand away, but she didn't want to make him mad.

"I guess." She squirmed a little closer to the door. His hand moved with her, making her skin feel dirty through her thin leggings.

"Come on, sweetheart. Get back here."

She held still. Didn't move toward him, didn't move away from him.

Way down the road, she saw another traffic light. It was green. She kept her eyes on it, willing it to turn yellow.

He was saying something. She tuned out the words but didn't miss his tone.

The light changed. A few vehicles sped through the yellow, but the black SUV slowed for the red. The creep hit his brakes too. She braced herself, hugging her bedroll as they moved closer and closer to the SUV. She wanted to slap his hand off her leg, but she could stand it for about one more minute.

No. She couldn't.

The truck was still moving when she opened the door and dived out with her bedroll. She landed with a hard thud, then slid down the slippery green grass on the bank, landing feet-first in a ditch full of trash and muddy water. She fought to keep the bedroll high and dry. Above her, a horn honked. Then the creep yelled something. A door slammed. Maybe he was coming after her.

She turned and splashed along in the ditch for a few feet, then slogged her way up the bank to the shoulder and ran, so close to the oncoming traffic that she was afraid she'd crash into somebody's side mirror.

When she dared to look back, the light had changed. He'd kept going— with her duffel bag. She had her bedroll, though.

Breathing hard, Mel looked down at her water-splashed jacket and muddy leggings and sopping-wet shoes. Now she didn't have anything dry to change into. And no cash except the ten bucks she'd tucked into her bra. All those hours she'd worked. For nothing.

At least now she knew which direction not to go. The white truck was going south, so she'd go north. Maybe she'd even head for home.

Instead of putting her bedroll on her back again, she hugged it to her front and kept walking. First chance she had, she'd stop somewhere and move her treasures into her shirt pocket. That would be safer than the bedroll.

She kept trudging down the road, passing a church and a school and a preschool. None of those places would want her.

Once in a while, somebody honked. Most people ignored her, and she didn't blame them. She looked like a bum.

Sometimes nice-looking people were creeps, and sometimes people who looked like bums were just doing the best they could.

After two days of rest stops, fuel stops, and fast food, Tish's head-lights shone on the sign that marked Noble's city limits. She'd gained an hour driving into central time, but a rainstorm had blurred the day into an early dark by the time she'd arrived at the closing. The rain had let up now, though, and stoplights and neon signs lent dashes of color to the gray.

Slowing for a red light, Tish rolled her stiff shoulders. After seven hundred miles, some of it through hair-raising weather, she had only a few easy blocks to go. Within minutes, she'd unlock her very own front door with her very own keys. Poor Mr. Nelson. At the closing, he'd given her such a resentful look that she'd nearly apologized for buying his house.

A slender young woman in a baggy black jacket and pale orange leggings walked briskly down the sidewalk, a yellow bedroll on her back. Approaching a tiny barbecue joint, she turned toward its window but kept moving. A stoop-shouldered, white-haired woman approached from the opposite direction, but they ignored each other.

The eatery was called the Bag-a-'Cue, and cartoonish pigs in chefs' hats adorned its doors. Lowering her window, Tish inhaled a sweet, smoky aroma that overpowered the smell of wet pavement. She picked up her phone, and saved their phone number under the *B*'s. She wouldn't be cooking for at least a day or two.

The red light winked out. The green winked on, a cheerful beacon of welcome in the gray. Tish hit the gas, the tires slipping a little on the wet road. She tightened her grip on the wheel.

The town's pocket-size park came into view, its gazebo stripped of Christmas lights and greenery. Then she was in the residential part of town, and her heart beat faster. South Jackson was the next right.

Turning the corner, she smiled as she caught sight of the house, as quaint and quirky as ever. She parked in the driveway, killed the engine, and enjoyed the silence. No more engine, no more wipers, no more road noise. Nothing but a wet windshield stood between her and her piece of Alabama. This time, the seller wasn't breathing down her neck. She could walk through the house alone, slowly, savoring a dream come true. Thirty-five years old, she'd finally bought her first home.

"This is for you too, Dad," she whispered.

Crossing the yard, she relished her solitude. The pansies were still blooming, but the camellias were finished—at least in the front yard. She'd read up on camellias and learned that different varieties bloomed at different times. It was possible that she'd have fresh flowers for months at a time.

She climbed the broad steps to the porch and looked over her shoulder. The grass still hadn't been cut. Apparently Mr. Nelson couldn't be bothered to mow the lawn again once he'd collected her earnest money.

In the small green house across the street, a curtain fluttered in a window. Maybe the pansy-planting neighbors would come out to say hello.

She put the key in the lock and gave the door a gentle push, allowing it to swing open. The hinges screeched like a door on a haunted house. She stepped across the threshold, running her hand over the wall for a light switch. There it was.

Bright lights flooded the empty rooms. If the house were an old woman, she would have begged for the softer, kinder glow of kerosene lamps that would have masked some of her flaws.

But when the house made its debut back in 1870 or so, the rooms must have gleamed with newness. Now age dulled the hardwood floors. Discolorations marred the pitted plaster walls and the tall ceilings. A thin crack ran through a corner of the marble hearth. The inspector had mentioned those issues and more in his report, but he'd said the house was basically sound from its foundation to its roof, and the water damage wasn't recent. The house was in a condition appropriate to its age. It just needed sprucing up—a fact that was more obvious now that it was vacant, stripped of its furniture and the Christmas greenery that had dolled up the old stairway.

She walked farther in, the floor creaking under her feet, and entered the kitchen. The gas stove, dating from around 1970, still scared her a little, although it was allegedly in good working order. The tiny fridge at least hailed from the current century.

A sickly green shade of glossy paint coated the wooden countertops. She could hardly wait to change the color or replace them altogether. A Coke can lay on its side with a dried brown spot next to it. A defiant little gesture from the seller, perhaps. He wouldn't cut the grass, and he wouldn't clean up a spill.

She moved on, soaking up the details she'd missed earlier. The sink was too modern to be original to the house, but older than she remembered. She tried the tap. The water was on, as promised.

Without the muffling effect of furnishings and wall-to-wall carpets, every sound was magnified and sharpened. The sheer emptiness of the house made the cold bite deeper too. Feeling all alone, Tish pulled her phone from her pocket and called her mother.

She answered on the first ring. "Tish! Are you there yet?"

"Just got here. I'm standing in the kitchen."

"Still feel good about it?"

"I love it." Her eyes watered.

"I wish I could be there to help you unload, you crazy girl."

"Don't worry about it. That's why I hired movers. And the moving van's right on schedule. They're supposed to arrive tomorrow afternoon."

"Good. How's the weather?"

"It's colder than I'd expected, but the rain stopped."

"Do you have utilities?"

"Water and power. I won't have heat until I go to the gas company and leave a deposit, but I'll be fine. I brought a space heater and blankets."

"Be glad you're out of Michigan. I saw on the news they're having a terrible ice storm."

"I know. Here, it's wet but only in the fifties. Practically balmy," Tish joked. "Well, I'd better get off the phone and get busy. Come see the ancestral home sometime, okay?"

"Sure, but it's not *my* ancestral home, honey. Let me know when the hard work is done, and I'll be right there."

Tish laughed. "Okay, Mom. Talk to you later."

She decided to walk through the whole house again before unloading her car. Her footsteps echoed on the bare wooden floor of the narrow hall. The sellers had left small reminders of their presence in nearly every room: a paper clip on the bathroom windowsill, a pen on the floor of the linen closet, faded blue valances over the tall windows in the downstairs bedroom.

She turned in a circle, considering the bedroom. It was the biggest one, but she'd rather make it the guest room. She'd take one of the upstairs bedrooms where the sunrise would spill in from the east, and the third bedroom would become a combination office and sewing room. She could whip up some new curtains and valances in no time, if she could find a fabric shop.

Her hand glided smoothly over the banister as she ran up the stairs. After turning to the right, she went straight to the bedroom window that overlooked the big backyard with its wilderness of shrubbery. The last vestiges of the storm still dripped from the eaves, and the wet glass blurred her view. Somewhere beyond the tangle of bushes stood the garage.

After a quick peek into the antiquated bathroom, she loped downstairs and back outside to the car in the twilight. She had to bring her special treasure inside first.

She eased the portrait out of the backseat. Padded with multiple layers of towels and cardboard, it was hard to get a grip on. She lugged her unwieldy heirloom across the yard, up the steps, and inside. With care, she pulled off the wrappings and leaned the ornate gilt frame against the wall. Her great-great-great-grandparents looked solemnly back at her.

Maybe Letitia looked a bit anemic after all, but *ghoulish* wasn't the right word for Nathan. His hollow cheeks and deep-set eyes reminded her of Abraham Lincoln.

"Welcome home," Tish said quietly. "You're back where you belong."

She wanted to hang the portrait, but it wasn't a one-person job.

Her stomach growled, bringing her back to the present. Once she'd unloaded the car, she would call in an order to Bag-a-'Cue. That was a privilege Nathan and Letitia had never known.

She'd made it home, and except for her feet, Mel had stayed mostly dry. Wet feet were the worst, though. They made her cold all over. If she hadn't lost her duffel bag, she wouldn't have lost her cash either. She might have had enough to buy shoes and socks and jeans. Of course, if she still had her bag, she wouldn't need replacements.

Lowering the hood of her jacket, she lifted her face to the dark sky. It was a good thing the storm was over. Her folks weren't home, and her house key didn't work anymore.

She was trying not to read too much into it. People changed locks all the time. For lots of reasons. Maybe it didn't have anything to do with the big blowup. After all this time, they should've gotten over it, shouldn't they?

She tucked her keys carefully into the waterproof side pocket of her bedroll with the last of her cigarettes. She couldn't lose those keys. Even if the house key didn't work anymore, the car key was important.

She eyed the tall wooden fence separating her from the backyard. Maybe they'd forgotten to lock the sliding glass door of the sunroom.

It was worth a try, anyway. She crossed the wet lawn to the side yard where the old oak arched its branches over the fence. She edged her bedroll over the top, and it landed with a plop. She shimmied up the trunk, crawled along the thickest branch, and dropped over. Easy-peasy, like high school except this time her bedroom window wouldn't have been left conveniently cracked open. And she didn't dare do anything that would set off the burglar alarm. She didn't know the code to disarm it anymore, and she didn't want the cops all over her. She'd be so embarrassed if Darren was one of them. He would've graduated from the academy by now and maybe he'd stayed in town.

She picked up her bedroll, noticing the new muddy smudge. No big deal, though. She walked over to the sunroom door and tugged on the handle.

Locked. They'd wedged a security bar in the track too.

Peeking through the blinds, Mel scanned the dark room. Even in the dim light, she could tell the rattan furniture had new cushions in a tropical print. Magazines covered the low table, same as always, and houseplants stood against the low walls below the windows.

She loved that room, especially when all the windows were open. It had been the only room in the house where she could breathe. Where she didn't feel suffocated.

After checking the windows and confirming she couldn't sneak in without breaking something, she dragged one of the plastic deck chairs under the wide overhang of the roof in case another storm blew in. She wiped the seat dry with her hand, then unzipped her sleeping bag and spread it over the chair. She patted her shirt pocket to make sure her treasure was safe, then sat, pulling the sleeping bag around her and drawing the jacket's hood over her head.

Her folks wouldn't see her when they pulled in, but she would hear them. Hiding in the backyard was better than waiting on the front porch where the neighbors would see her and start gossiping again.

Now that she'd stopped moving, she ached all over. And her feet and ankles were like ice. She'd give anything for jeans that covered her ankles. Dry socks. Shoes that weren't smashed and filthy.

A freezing wind blew through the yard, reminding her how cold Noble could get. She pulled the sleeping bag tighter, but it didn't help.

Closing her eyes, she tried to pretend she was back in her own room. The room Grandpa John had helped her paint in a soft blue when she was fourteen.

"Same color as my car, almost," he'd said.

"No, it's my car," she'd said, poking his shoulder to make him laugh.

"Yes, sweetie, it'll be your car someday," he'd said.

Grandpa John was the only person she'd never doubted. Because he'd never doubted her. He'd always believed the best about a person.

When she was a little girl, they'd passed a homeless man on the sidewalk. Grandpa John had said he would drop her off at the house and go back to buy the man a hamburger or something. "There but by the grace of God," he'd said.

She'd thought it was a funny thing to say. Grace meant prettiness in your movements. Being surefooted. Not tripping over your own feet and making a fool of yourself. So it didn't make sense. God wasn't a real person with feet.

"Good night, Grandpa John, wherever you are," she whispered.

Then she tried very hard to believe he winked at her from heaven and whispered back, *"Good night, Melanie John."*

It was dark when Tish pulled her car into one of the few empty spots in front of Bag-a-'Cue and ran inside. For a Monday night in a small town, it was a busy joint that attracted a healthy mix of young and old, black and white. Noisy, friendly customers crowded a dozen picnic tables. Everyone seemed to know everyone else. A little boy ran around in red footie pajamas, his chin smeared with barbecue sauce.

She approached the counter and met the heavily lined eyes of the teenage girl working the register.

"Yes ma'am, how can I help you?"

"I called in a to-go order a few minutes ago for—"

"That's the other end of the counter." She pointed. "Where it says Pick Up Orders Here."

"Oh. Sorry. I'm new here." Giving the girl an apologetic smile, Tish proceeded to the proper spot.

A grown woman presided over the pick-up station. Excessive eyeliner seemed to be a locally popular style for all ages. "Hey," she said with a smile.

"Hi. I called in an order to go…"

"Name?"

"Letitia."

The woman blinked. "Okay." She collected Tish's money and counted out her change. "It'll be up in a minute."

"Thanks."

Stepping aside to wait, Tish looked back at the tables full of customers and wondered if any of them were her new neighbors or people she would run into at the grocery store or the post office. Of course, she'd do her shopping and banking over in Muldro, a much larger town with more options and better prices. She'd go there in the morning to get the gas turned on and open a checking account.

But these people probably lived in Noble. Some of them could be her neighbors. Maybe they'd become her friends someday.

A young couple stopped at the condiment station. Loading red trays with plastic forks, paper napkins, and ketchup packets, they bantered back and forth with their friends who were already seated. The little guy in pajamas swiped a fry from his father's plate and giggled.

"Letitia," a man yelled. "Pick-up for Letitia."

She turned toward the counter. "That's mine," she said, speaking into a sudden lull in the conversations behind her.

A burly old employee held a brown paper bag in huge hands. "Letitia," he repeated loudly and unnecessarily. "That you?"

"Yes." Her voice rang in the strange new silence.

The man slapped the bag onto the counter. "Here's your order, Letitia."

The way he said it took her back to whispered mockery of her old-fashioned name in a Michigan schoolyard. Saginaw? Yes. Fourth grade. *Letitia, Letitia, Tish Tish Tish…*

"Thank you," she said. Even the rustling of the bag in her hand sounded too loud. Too conspicuous.

Someone snickered and whispered something she couldn't catch.

She turned around. The people closest to the counter were staring at her. No one was smiling now except the tyke in red pajamas.

Whatever was going on, getting mad wouldn't help. She drew a deep breath and managed a smile.

"I'm new here," she blurted. "My apologies."

No one spoke.

Bag in hand, she fled to her car. Was Noble one of those towns where everybody was related somehow, and they refused to accept outsiders? Or—she looked down at her University of Michigan sweatshirt. Did they hate Yankees? Could they be that provincial?

No. She was exhausted from the move, and she'd let her old paranoia kick in.

"I am Letitia McComb," she said under her breath. "You can't change who I am."

She started her car and pulled out of the lot. In January, without Christmas lights, Main Street had lost some of its friendly charm.

Seven

Mel jerked awake and squinted up at a bright moon glittering above the trees. She'd never been one of those Girl Scout types who could figure out what time it was, or where north was, from studying the sky. She only knew it was full dark, she was freezing, and either her folks hadn't come home or she'd slept through the sound of the garage door going up and down.

She left her sleeping bag on the chair and peered through the blinds again. No lights were burning except the dim ones they always left on, day and night. The kitchen clock didn't show from the sunroom windows, and she didn't have a phone or a watch that worked.

Putting her ear to the cold glass, she listened. No voices. No TV. If it was three in the morning and they were sound asleep, it wouldn't be cool to pound on the door. Last time she made that mistake, her dad almost wouldn't let her in. He'd grounded her instead. Tried to, anyway.

She figured they'd still treat her like a little kid this time too. They would feed her, though, and they'd let her sleep in her own bed where she'd be warm and dry and safe.

Golden light pooled suddenly across the kitchen floor. Someone had turned on a lamp in the living room.

Moving fast, she rolled up her sleeping bag, trying to hide its muddiest parts. She finger-combed her hair, straightened the collar of her jacket—her dad's—and practiced a smile. Smiling was the hard part.

Bedroll in hand, she knocked on the glass sliding door. "Mom? Dad? It's me."

No one came. She tried again, knocking harder and speaking louder.

"Mom! Mom, it's Mel. Let me in, please!"

A shadow darkened the pool of light. Slowly, someone came into view. Someone short. Mom, the soft touch.

Letting out a sigh of relief, Mel made a rat-a-tat-tat on the glass with her fingernails. "Mom, it's me!"

It took her mom forever to unlock the door and shove the security bar out of the way. Then the door slid smoothly across the track, and Mel stepped into delicious warmth.

She met her mother's eyes for the first time since the big blowup. "Hey, Mom."

"Mel," she whispered. Her face looked pale and old without her usual mask of makeup. "You look tired."

So do you, Mel wanted to say. "Well, yeah. I'm tired."

"And thin." Her mom offered an awkward shoulder pat and lowered her hand to her side. "Where have you been?"

Not the best welcome, but she'd take it. "All over. But I'm home, and that's what matters. Right?"

Her mom didn't answer. Only stared, as if Mel were a spectacle at a carnival.

Dread settled in her stomach. They were going to kick her out again. But before they did, she'd make the best of it.

She edged past her mom, across the sunroom, and into the kitchen. She flipped the light switch. The crystal fruit bowl sat in the center of the table, holding apples, oranges, and ripe bananas. She lowered her bedroll to the floor beside the table. Trying to move slowly, as if she didn't really care, she pulled a banana off the bunch, peeled it halfway down, and took a small, ladylike bite. It was heaven. She'd never appreciated bananas before.

"Where's Dad?" she asked.

"In the shower."

"What time is it, anyway?"

"About ten."

"That's all? I thought it was about midnight." Mel couldn't stop herself. She wolfed the rest of the banana like a half-starved bum.

She crossed to the fridge and stared at the new school photos held up by the same old magnets. Her nephews still had their sweet smiles and big, dark eyes, but she couldn't believe how much they'd changed.

She loved her brother's boys so much. Especially Nicky. She shouldn't have a favorite, of course, so she tried hard not to let it show. She knew how it felt to be the un-favorite one.

"Nicky and Jamie look so grown up," she said. "How are they? And Stu and Janice?"

"Fine," her mom said. "They'll be staying with us for a week or two while they have their kitchen remodeled. It's a huge, messy project."

"Is Stu still working at the dealership?"

"He's practically running it himself, these days."

Mel nodded. When her dad retired, Stu would be in charge of all those shiny new vehicles. All those salesmen in their matching polo shirts. All that money.

She opened the fridge. Milk, juice, cans of soda. Half a ruby-red grapefruit covered with plastic wrap. An unopened package of all-beef hot dogs. A clear plastic container of...chili?

Her mouth watered at the idea of chomping into a chili dog. She didn't want to tick anybody off, though, so she'd keep it simple. She found the grape jelly on the door and set the jar on the counter. "You don't mind if I make myself a PBJ, do you?"

"Of course not." Her mom didn't come any closer, though. It was like she was afraid she might catch something.

Everything was exactly where it had always been—honey-wheat bread in a basket on the counter, the peanut butter in the cupboard by the fridge, and the paper plates in the next cupboard. Mel pulled a knife from the drawer and started slapping the sandwich together. A hot meal would have been great, but she was too hungry to care.

She should have washed her hands and scrubbed her chipped and dirty fingernails. Too late now. She probably smelled like a homeless person too. If they'd let her, she'd take a shower and wash her hair. And she'd raid her closet for all those great clothes she'd left behind.

Not bothering to cut the sandwich in half, she bit into it, rolling her eyes at the sweet, soft goodness. She started to put the lid back on the peanut butter jar, one-handed, then reconsidered. She took two more slices of bread from the bag and made a second sandwich.

"My, you're hungry," her mom said.

"Yeah." Mel put away the peanut butter and the jelly. She pulled out the milk. Tempted to drink straight from the plastic jug, she slowed down long enough to find a glass and fill it. She drained half of it and wiped her mouth. "Oh, wow. Everything tastes so good."

"I take it you haven't been eating well."

"Not lately."

Mel took the glass and the paper plate to the table and sat in the chair closest to her bedroll. If she had to, she could stuff her pockets with fruit and be out the door in seconds. But maybe she wouldn't have to.

Finished with the first sandwich, she started the second. "You think Dad will let me stay?"

"Ask him." Her mom nodded toward the family room.

Afraid to breathe, Mel turned her head slowly. Her father stood six feet away, arms folded across his chest. He'd gone gray, making him look like a grandpa. Well, he was a grandpa, but not the huggy kind. In sweatpants, a T-shirt, and white socks so new they were still fuzzy, he was in jock mode. He just might tell her to hit the floor and do push-ups.

"Hey, Dad." Her voice shook. "It's your lucky day. I'm back."

He sighed and shook his head. "And you're broke as a stick, aren't you? You think we'll let you mooch off of us?"

Mel straightened her spine. "If Stu can move back for a while, why can't I?"

Her dad narrowed his eyes. "Your brother would never steal from us."

Mel squinted back at him. "I've never stolen from y'all."

"No? Where's my gold watch?"

Oh boy. Things were going downhill fast. She gobbled more of the sandwich, then grabbed two oranges and put one in each pocket. She'd be pressing her luck if she took a banana too. Better not. Anyway, bananas squished.

She finished the sandwich, thinking carefully about her answer. "I don't have any watch of yours. I never did."

"If you'd tell the truth, it would go better for you."

"I'm telling the truth. I never took your watch."

"Like you never took your grandpa's car? I think you're what they call a pathological liar. As well as a thief." He unfolded his arms and jutted his thumb toward the front door. "Get out. And don't come back—unless you come back with the watch and put it in my hands. With an apology."

"I only took what was mine."

He let out a short laugh. "I guess you think our food is yours too. You about done there? Ready to go quietly, or do I need to call the police?"

Her heart jumped like a scared jack rabbit. "For what?"

"Where do I start? Petty larceny, grand larceny. Breaking and entering."

"I let her in, Duncan," her mom said in a tired, quiet voice. "She didn't break in."

"Not this time."

"I don't think they call it breaking and entering when it's your own house." Mel's voice broke. Furious with herself for caving, she gulped the last of the milk, slammed the empty glass onto the table, and stood.

"It's my house, sweetheart," he said, making the word sound mean. "Not yours."

"Then I'm not yours. Not your daughter. Not anymore."

"That's still my jacket." He held out his hand.

"Sorry if it's dirty. It's been through a lot." She shrugged her arms out of the sleeves and tossed it at him. An orange fell out of a pocket and rolled across the floor, hitting his foot in one of those brand-spanking-new white socks.

Mel nearly cried. She'd forgotten about the oranges. She wanted them. She needed them.

"Stealing our oranges too," he said. "Once a thief, always a thief."

She grabbed her bedroll and charged past him, catching a whiff of fresh-smelling soap that made her feel filthy. Running now, she crossed the family room. The front door was straight ahead. It was all she could see. She was in a narrow tunnel edged with black. She had to get through it, get outside, escape into the fresh night air where she could breathe.

A vehicle passed in the street, the sound jolting Tish out of hazy daydreams of where she might put the furniture when the moving van arrived. Sitting in her old green camp chair by the empty fireplace, too tired to move, she'd lost track of the time. It was nearly midnight.

Tish yawned. The drive had been tiring in itself, and then she'd made so many trips out to the car and up and down the porch steps. Up and down the stairs. Her feet ached.

Closing her eyes, she could still see the rain on the windshield. The green mile markers measuring her progress on the interstate. And, like an echo in her ears, she could still hear the racket her rolling suitcase had made as she pulled it across the hardwood floor to the foot of the stairs.

She'd brought in her box of essentials—TP, light bulbs, cleaning supplies—and her sleeping bag, floor mat, blankets, and pillow. The camp chair. The vacuum. The cooler with the remains of her road-trip food and drinks. The space heater.

After she'd emptied the car, she cleaned, and while she still had a scrap of energy, she put up the brand-new shower-curtain liners she'd bought for the claw-foot tubs in both bathrooms. But the real work wouldn't start until the moving van showed up.

Yawning again, she stood. She made sure the doors were locked and then trudged upstairs. She'd already made her "bed" for the night, and the space heater had raised the bedroom's temperature to an acceptable level. In her warmest, dorkiest pajamas and thick socks, she'd be fine.

After brushing her teeth, she studied her wavy reflection in the old mirror on the 1950s-style medicine cabinet. For days now, she'd been playing with the idea of dropping her nickname and going by Letitia, but she didn't look like a Letitia. She didn't feel like a Letitia. Going by her great-great-great-grandmother's name would be like wearing clothes that were too big and completely out of style. She might get used to it, though, and it would begin to feel right.

She walked into the dark bedroom. Away from city lights, the moon was so big and clear and bright that it seemed to jump halfway through the uncovered window. She couldn't remember the last time she'd seen the man in the moon so distinctly.

Oddly spooked, she climbed into her sleeping bag and straightened the blankets on top of it. She'd lived alone for years, but this house was different. It was totally empty. It was nearly a hundred and fifty years old. And the past seemed to lurk in every corner, whispering to her.

Nobody wants you here.

Again, she flashed back to the bullies in grade school. They'd lurked around corners or behind bushes, mocking the new girl's old-fashioned name. They'd hissed it, over and over, making a singsong chant of it.

Letitia, Letitia, Tish Tish Tish Tish Tish. Nobody wants you here.

Like the people at the barbecue place.

Oh, that was ridiculous. She held her pillow tightly against her ears, as if that could shut out an imaginary voice.

"Letitia, you need a good night's sleep," she told herself. "And a job. That's all."

She settled back on the pallet and looked out the window. There he was, the man in the moon. The only man in her life.

The flowers from Kroger must have been pelted by sleet the day after she'd left them there. Then they would have frozen. By now the sun would have melted the ice, thawing them to mush. They'd been beautiful for a few hours, though, lying there in the dark with no one to see them.

Tish shivered. The house felt so cold. So empty. It didn't have to stay that way, though. Even if she never had a family of her own, she could make new friends or take in strangers. One way or another, she would fill her empty house with love and laughter. With good food. With fresh flowers from her own yard. She would make the place her home.

But that day seemed very far away as she lay awake, watching the man in the moon watching her.

eorge had stayed up half the night to do his online wheeling and dealing, and he felt no more than half-awake as he wandered down the book aisle at his shop. It would be a good day to weed out the slow movers and put them in a clearance bin on the sidewalk.

He smiled, picking up a couple of books by Harriet Beecher Stowe. A woman who'd had a lot on her mind. She'd never been a bestseller in Noble, Alabama, though.

Calv approached with the Bissell sweeper and a dust cloth. "You payin' yourself to stand there and read?"

Before George could defend himself, the bell at the door tinkled and the first customer of the day walked in. Tiny, gray-haired Mrs. Rose swapped greetings with him and Calv, then took herself off to visit the Victorian umbrella stand that she'd been coveting for weeks. The wife of a prosperous businessman in Muldro, she was a regular customer who never failed to get on George's nerves.

"Now there's a woman with a lot on her mind," he said quietly as he and Calv retreated toward the back of the store. "How to fill her house with the most antiques for the least money, for instance."

"Someday her kids will sell 'em for pennies on the dollar. You can buy 'em back and start over with somebody else."

George grinned. "I like the idea, but hush. She's about to commence haggling."

Sure enough, Mrs. Rose strolled slowly toward them, pausing to feign interest in everything from fishing creels to spatterware crocks. At last she drew up in front of the ornate old cash register and fixed her pleading eyes on George.

"It's a shame about the scratches on the umbrella stand," she said.

"Yes ma'am, it's showing its age. That's part of its charm, though."

"Seems like you'd come down a little on the price."

"I might, at that. I'd take, say…two hundred."

"Dollars?" she asked in an incredulous tone.

Did she think he meant pennies? "Yes ma'am."

"Oh, I don't know. That's still awfully high."

"It's an awfully nice piece."

Mrs. Rose shook her head slowly, as if overwhelmed with grief. "It's not *that* nice." She turned and walked away without saying good-bye.

George took a deep, relaxing breath when the bell tinkled again to mark her exit. "Frankly, my dear, you're not that nice either."

Calv chuckled. "But she thinks she is."

"How did I wind up in this business?"

Calv gave him one of those Yoda looks. "Had something to do with wanting to sell used merchandise instead of sweatshop merchandise, didn't it?"

"It was a rhetorical question, Calv."

"No it wasn't. And don't be embarrassed. I was young and idealistic once too." Calv started whistling, then broke off. "Hey, I was gonna ask you. Have you heard anything about Miss Mel coming home?"

"Mel Hamilton?" George looked at his uncle. "No. Did you?"

"I thought I saw her last night, hustlin' down the sidewalk, but I couldn't be sure."

"If you'd stopped to say hey, you could've been sure."

"But if it was Mel, she might've picked my pockets." Calv said, with a hint of humor in his voice.

"You wouldn't have let her get away with it."

"That's probably what her dad thought too, the day she got away with his gold watch in her pocket."

George scratched his chin. "I heard she hid it in her hair because she knew they'd check her pockets."

Calv narrowed his eyes while he thought about it. Finally he shook his head. "Somebody must've made that up. She'd be the only one who would know, and she sure wouldn't tell. She hasn't even been around to tell."

"Good point."

"Have you noticed her mess-ups always have something to do with abusing other folks' property? Taking things and breaking things. She swiped the watch and her granddaddy's car. Put a dent in her daddy's truck. Dropped her mama's library books right into a mud puddle. And who knows what else."

"Books shouldn't be treated that way." George shut his eyes.

"They were just paperbacks, but you're missing my point. Think about it."

There was something to it, George had to admit. Yet Mel had never been careless with her grandfather's car. She'd loved it a little too much.

He opened his eyes. "You're saying it's all deliberate? Even the so-called accidents?"

"Seems like it to me. Maybe her folks hurt her somehow, so she tries to hurt them back."

George thought back to his younger days, when he and Mel's brother had been good friends. "Could be," he admitted. "She used to be a sweetie, though. At least until she was three or four." He chuckled, remembering the holy terror on a Big Wheel.

"One thing's for sure. If she's home, Dunc and Suzette won't kill the fatted calf."

George sank onto the tall stool behind the register. "I don't think she'd have the guts to go home. If I were her, I sure wouldn't."

"I'm just glad I'm not the one who had to raise her." Calv laughed softly. "Remember the time she rode her Shetland pony up the back steps and into her mama's living room?"

George smiled. "In the middle of the tea party. I think the whole town remembers."

But when Calv walked away, George stopped smiling. Young Mel, if she was in town, wouldn't find much of a welcome anywhere. She'd be about as popular as a McComb. If anybody needed a goodwill gesture, it was Mel.

And if anybody didn't deserve one, that would be Mel too.

The heavy glass door closed behind Tish, and she took stock of her surroundings. Muldro National Bank looked remarkably like her bank in Michigan. Two tellers stood at their stations, chatting with customers, while a third dealt with a drive-through window. On the right, the door to the vault stood trustingly open. Behind her, more employees worked in small, glass-walled offices.

A tall woman with steel-gray hair and eyes to match emerged from one of the glassed-in cubbyholes. "May I help you?"

"Yes, please. I'd like to open a checking account."

"That's what I'm here for," she said with a smile. "If you'd like to have a seat, I'll be back directly." File folder in hand, she motioned toward her office.

Tish took one of the two cushy red chairs posed at an inviting angle on the customer side of the desk. Family photos and a small bowl of lollipops sat atop the gleaming surface and gave the room a faint air of coziness. A shiny nameplate on the desk indicated that this domain belonged to Marian Clark-Graham. The name sounded too snooty for semirural Alabama.

The woman returned, offering her hand. "I'm Marian. Welcome to Muldro National Bank. Are you new in town?"

"Yes, I just moved to Noble."

"I live there too." Marian settled into the chair behind the desk. "Actually, I live between Noble and Muldro, but I have a Noble mailing address."

Tish smiled at the way the town's name worked as an adjective. "It's a cute little town. Not many job openings, though."

"Frankly, no. Muldro is healthier in that respect. Now, you say you'd like to open a checking account?"

"Yes, please. I don't have my new driver's license yet, but I have proof of residence." Tish burrowed in her purse for the papers she'd brought. "Here's my name on my utility hookup bills. I hope that's enough for opening an account. And I have a check to deposit, of course."

"As long as you bring some kind of money, we'll work with you, darlin'." Marian gave a short laugh. "Let's see what you've got." She reached into a file drawer behind her and pulled out some forms.

Tish spread her papers on the desk with her Michigan driver's license on top. "I'll be glad for another chance at a driver's license photo. This one's awful."

"Aren't they always? My last one makes me look like a serial killer." Marian slid the forms and a pen across the desk. "Here, you can start on the paperwork."

Tish picked up the pen, a snazzy little blue number printed with Muldro National Bank—Hometown Loyalty with National Connections. Whatever that meant. It had been a tossup between this bank and the one kitty-corner to it. She'd picked this one because it had prettier landscaping.

"And will your name be the only one on the account, Letitia?" the woman snapped.

Startled more by the icy tone than by the unexpected use of her name, Tish lifted her head.

Marian, holding the driver's license, regarded her with unfriendly eyes. Ah. She must have realized she was dealing with a Michigander. A Yankee.

Determined to be a very polite Yankee, Tish smiled. "Yes ma'am. I'm single."

The woman turned to her computer keyboard. For a few moments, there was no sound but the clicking of keys, the hum of the printer, and the scratching of the pen.

Recording 525 South Jackson Street as her home address brought Tish a surge of joy and gratitude. She'd gone from peeking wistfully at online photos to actually buying the place. Now she couldn't imagine living anywhere else.

A McComb had bought the McComb house. The symmetry of it gave her a beautiful sense of having come full circle. As if God had ordained it. No doubt about it, God had been good to her. He had blessed her crazy decision to move.

"I'll need your signature in a number of places." A reasonable request, but it was, again, delivered in a snippy tone.

"Certainly." Tish took the papers and signed her name in her best penmanship. Letitia had always been fun to write, full of pretty swoops and loops. Fun to say too. Yes, she could get used to being called Letitia.

"I'll be right back." Her jaw set, Marian rose and walked out.

Hometown loyalty, indeed. Tish let out a small sigh. It wasn't surprising that the locals would turn a cold shoulder to newcomers. It wouldn't last forever, though.

A friendly person wouldn't have much trouble making friends. Her father gave her that pep talk every time they moved. She'd never told him exactly how hard it was to be the new kid on the block, over and over. Anyway, she'd survived.

Finished signing the papers, Tish checked the time. She still had to get the gas turned on and then be home by noon to meet the movers. She turned in her chair to see what was taking Marian so long. In the doorway to the vault, she and a white-haired man stood with their heads together, speaking in undertones. He bore a striking resemblance to Ted Turner in his prime. The guy wasn't young, but he was a head-turner in his sharp gray suit, shiny black shoes, and tasteful tie. Every inch of him said "quality."

Marian shot a frown at Tish. Were they talking about her? Tish tried to muster a smile anyway.

The man laughed softly, patted Marian's shoulder, and strode toward Tish. "Welcome to Noble," he said with a twinkle in his eye. "I'm Ed Farris. My official title here is head honcho."

Laughing at that, she rose and offered her hand. "Hello, Mr. Farris. I'm Letitia McComb."

"So I've heard." His hand engulfed hers in a quick, firm shake. "I hope you'll feel right at home in no time."

She warmed to his genial attitude, so different from his employee's chilly demeanor. "I'm starting to. I'll feel even more at home once I find a job."

"What's your background and training?"

"Most recently, I've had a managerial position with a large insurance company in Michigan. I'm a good manager of people, computers, numbers, and money, and I have excellent references." She stopped. "Sorry. I don't mean to sound like a walking résumé."

Deeper amusement kindled in his eyes. "It sounds like a good one, though. You deal with other people's money, eh? Your employer must trust you a great deal."

"Of course. I was at the same firm for thirteen years. Is there any chance you're hiring?"

His expression sobered. "Before I answer that, let me tell you I require my employees to be of impeccable character. A bank's most important commodity isn't money. It's trust. And the most valuable asset an employee brings to the table is personal integrity."

"I agree. Absolutely. And I assure you, I'm squeaky clean. I've never even had a parking ticket." She liked him more every minute. He was proof that some locals were as friendly as could be.

His smile returned, broader than ever. "We might have a position opening up soon, but it's not official yet. Check back in a few weeks. And send me your résumé."

"I'll do that, Mr. Farris. Thank you. And thanks for making me feel so welcome."

"I'm glad you're banking with us, Miss McComb. I'm very interested in seeing what the future holds for you here."

"I am too," she said.

He chuckled. "I bet you are. You have a great day, now." Moving with the natural grace of a born athlete, he turned and walked away, disappearing into an office with real walls, not glass ones.

Marian marched across the room, her eyes cold. "Let's finish up this paperwork."

"Yes, let's. I need to get home and meet my moving van." Tish's lips didn't want to cooperate, but she managed a smile.

Marian didn't return the smile, and the muscles around her left eye seemed to have developed a nervous twitch. It wasn't too much of a stretch to see her as a serial killer. A serial killer who hated Yankees.

Black dribbles of sticky goo had run down the sides of the nasty-smelling Dumpster behind the gas station, and every few minutes Mel heard faint rustling and squeaking inside it.

All that good food going to waste at her folks' house, and she was waiting for pizza that should have gone to rats.

She peered around the Dumpster. The beat-up back door of the convenience store was still closed.

"Hurry up, Hayley," she whispered, hugging her stomach.

With a sigh, she went back to her uncomfortable spot on the curb. She didn't have much padding on her rear anymore.

Closing her eyes, she tried to focus on the afternoon sunshine baking her face. She wished she could absorb the heat and save it for later. When the sun went down, she'd be freezing again. Especially without a jacket this time.

And she'd thought she was miserable in that crowded little apartment in Orlando. Her roommates hadn't been the best, but she'd stayed warm, and there'd always been plenty to eat at work.

Hearing footsteps, she opened her eyes and braced herself to run if it was Hayley's boss.

The Dumpster lid rose. She caught a glimpse of a black trash bag sailing in. It landed with a thud, followed by a clank as the lid fell closed.

Hayley scurried around the corner, curly wisps of hair framing her face where they'd escaped her ponytail. She unzipped her gray hoodie, reached in, and pulled out a plastic bag. "Here. It's too old to sell, but it's not too old to eat."

Mel seized the bag and opened it, her mouth watering. It held two burnt-looking slices of pepperoni pizza. "Thanks, Hay. Wow, you even thought of napkins." But no drink.

"Sorry, I know you hate pepperoni."

"No, it's awesome. I'll eat every crumb."

"I can't believe your dad is so mean. Well, yeah. I can."

"I should start calling him my ex-dad." Mel nodded toward the building. "You think they're hiring?"

Hayley's dark eyes darted over her. "I don't think so."

"Or at least they're not hiring people who look like they've been sleeping in the gutter."

"Well, yeah," Hayley said, sounding apologetic. She looked over her shoulder. "Don't eat here. Go somewhere else. I don't want to get fired."

Mel shivered, remembering the big scene at Fishy's. "No, getting fired is no fun." She stood, reaching for her bedroll. "I'll move on. It doesn't smell great here, anyway."

"Wow, you're so thin. And you look cold." Hayley unzipped her hoodie the rest of the way and pulled it off. "Here. Take it."

"You don't have to—"

"It's okay. I have more at home." Hayley stepped closer and draped the hoodie around Mel's shoulders. "Just go before somebody sees you hanging around. Shoo."

Mel tried to smile. "Thanks for making me feel like a stray cat."

"I'm trying to keep my job. Gotta go."

"Wait—Hayley!"

Hayley turned around. "What?"

"Quick, tell me the news. Like who's still in town and who's not. I don't have a phone so I can't text or call or whatever."

Hayley shrugged. "What do you think? The smart ones went off to college. The rest of us are still here."

"So, what about Darren?"

"He's around, but don't tell me you still have the hots for him." Hayley's voice softened. "I know why you've got a thing for cops, but guys like him are out of our league, doll."

"He made it through the academy?"

"Top of the class. What did you expect?" With a quick wave of her hand, Hayley was gone.

Mel sighed. It was all true, including the part about Darren being way too good for her.

At least she wouldn't starve tonight. She pressed the plastic bag's fading warmth against her cheek. She'd better hurry up and eat. Not behind a Dumpster, though. Someplace that smelled nice. Someplace with flowers, maybe. She'd pretend she was having a picnic like she and Hayley used to do when they were about eight.

Walking across the parking lot with the hoodie draped around her shoulders the way old ladies did with their sweaters, Mel headed south on Main, toward the park. Even rich people ate in parks sometimes. Too bad she looked like a bag lady.

Waiting for the light to change at the corner of Third and Main, she heard air brakes and a deep rumble. She turned to see the cab of a big truck, trembling with power, edge up next to her. A moving van. She thought about faraway places, about making a fresh start somewhere tropical or exotic. But she'd tried that once already. Now she was back, and her folks wouldn't even let her take a shower in their house.

They'd let Stu and his family stay, though, while their kitchen was torn up. The boys would have fun camping out in the basement for a couple of weeks. It was practically an apartment down there, with its own mini kitchen, and they'd have plenty of room to hang out.

Mel swallowed hard. She wasn't about to start crying, right on Main where everybody could see her.

Of course her folks would let Stu stay. He'd always been the perfect son. He hadn't stolen anything from them like Mel had. Or so they thought. But she hadn't taken anything that didn't belong to her, and what she borrowed, she brought back. Even the black jacket, once her dad reminded her.

He didn't want to be her dad anymore, though.

"Fine," she whispered. She didn't want a thief for a dad.

Nine

*I*t wasn't quite ten in the morning, but Tish already wanted to take a break. She'd stayed up past midnight, unpacking and organizing after the movers left, and she'd returned to it at seven. Already, the house was beginning to feel like home. Instead of being too empty, now the living room was crowded with furniture and boxes.

The portrait still leaned against the wall. She wished she'd asked one of those burly movers to hang it for her. At some point, maybe she'd meet her next-door neighbors and see if they could help. Judging by the bumper stickers on the vehicles in their driveway, they were into hunting, fishing, quilting, 'Bama football, and their grandchildren, but she hadn't laid eyes on their faces yet.

She took a swig of her ice water. Once again she located the utility knife she kept losing. She cut the strapping tape on half a dozen boxes of books. Trying to remember how she'd had the books organized in her apartment, she loaded them onto shelves. She placed her special favorites at eye level: *The History of Clothing. Fashion Through the Ages. Why Flappers Bobbed Their Hair.*

With the boxes emptied, she flattened them and carried them onto the front porch. A brisk wind threatened to blow them out of her arms, but she wedged them between her wicker furniture and the wall.

Energized by the gusts of air, she walked into the yard and looked up and down the street. All in all, it was a great neighborhood. Old but nice, and within walking distance of Noble's quaint little downtown area. Only twenty minutes from more practical shopping in Muldro too. The house suited her more and more, and as long as the roof didn't leak and the furnace held out, she'd be able to make some repairs and decorate a little.

She smiled, thinking of Mr. Farris at the bank. If she landed a job within a few weeks, she'd be on her way to finding new friends and settling into the social life of Muldro and Noble—if they had any.

Catching a movement from the corner of her eye, she faced the house directly across the street. The house with the pansies that matched hers. A woman was cracking the screen door open to let a black cat in.

Tish waved. "Good morning," she called, good and loud.

The screen door banged shut, followed by the solid sound of the wooden door closing.

With her optimism dissolving, Tish put her hands on her hips. "Well, be that way then," she said quietly.

It was time to admit the truth. The unfriendliness wasn't her imagination. She was sure she'd find plenty of friendly people too, like Farris, but a good number of the citizens of Noble and Muldro were hostile toward newcomers.

That woman at the bank, Marian Clark-Whoever, had an attitude. So did the mail carrier. Even the guy at the gas company had acted like he wished she'd go back where she came from. Now, the neighbor.

"I'm staying," Tish said under her breath.

She turned to run up the steps and stopped short. A tiny white dog sat expectantly by the front door.

"Who are you? You don't live here."

Looking more like a toy than a real animal, the dog blinked its black eyes and wagged an unrepentant tail.

"Oh, I remember you. You and the guy in the van. Do you belong to him?"

She'd noticed the shop, Antiques on Main, a few blocks away. She'd driven past at dusk when the ground-floor windows were softly lit. Upstairs, the wrought-iron railing of a balcony stood out against the bright lights shining from behind drawn shades.

Tish knelt and held out her hand. Quivering all over, the dog licked her fingers with a moist pink tongue. The quivering became a whole-body wiggle with most of the movement coming from the hindquarters.

"Aren't you cute. Here, let me see your tag." Tish took hold of a pale pink harness and worked the dog's tags out from a tangle of clean white fur. "Okay, your name is Daisy. You must be a girl."

Most men didn't like frilly little dogs, so she probably belonged to a woman. The guy in the van had a wife or a girlfriend then.

Tish pulled her phone from her pocket. Phone in one hand, dog tag in the other, she called the number on the tag.

"Antiques on Main. This is George. If this sounds like a recording, it must be a recording." His slow drawl heightened the dry humor of his words. "Our hours are nine to five every day but Sunday. If you'd like to leave a message, you know the routine. No texts, please. I don't do texts."

Instead of waiting for the beep, Tish closed her phone. "Come on, Daisy." She picked up the featherweight dog. "You're the perfect excuse for taking a break, and I love antiques."

The dog wriggled with joy but didn't make a sound.

"Well, at least there's one friendly soul in Noble." But when Tish started down the steps, the dog whimpered and strained her whole body in the direction of the house.

"Tough luck, puppy," Tish said. "I'm taking you back to your owner."

She decided to introduce herself as Letitia McComb, partly to get in the habit and partly to see if this George would recognize the name. It would be an interesting experiment.

Halfway down the block, she realized she'd forgotten to lock up. She slowed for a moment and then picked up her pace again. This wasn't Detroit. It was a small and peaceful town where most people probably left their doors unlocked. Besides, if anybody had the patience to sort through her ragtag possessions for something worth stealing, they were welcome to it—as long as they didn't mess with her vintage costume jewelry.

Enjoying the morning sunshine, George sat on the balcony with his coffee and the online version of the Mobile news. Now and then he cast an idle glance down to the street as the town woke up. In thirty minutes he'd have to leave for his appointment with a seller in Huntsville, but Calv had already taken charge of the shop and, thankfully, that blasted dog.

If Calv ever found a real job again, George was up a creek.

Hearing the distinctive sound of an old Corvette, he leaned forward in anticipation of the pretty sight. The mint-condition '56 tooled around the corner with its V-eight rumbling and its original arctic blue paint gleaming like ice.

Duncan Hamilton was driving, of course. He took the 'Vette out on a regular basis for the mechanical benefits, but he didn't appreciate the car as his late father-in-law had. Miss Mel had always loved it too. From the time she was a chunky little kid, she'd helped her grandpa when he washed and waxed it. She'd even earned a whipping once for taking it on a joyride.

She'd pitch one of her famous tantrums if she found out Dunc was selling it. She'd find out soon, too, if she was really in town.

Turning a corner, the car disappeared from view. George sighed. He would have endured a whipping too, for one hour at the wheel of the Corvette. His project car was going to be a sorry substitute.

Below him, a shiny red Jeep pulled up and over the curb, one tire gaining the sidewalk. The driver pulled it back down with a thump. Mrs. Rose climbed out. Cheeks flushed, she checked to see if anybody was watching, then hurried into the shop.

Maybe she'd soothe her embarrassment by finally buying the umbrella stand. But if she didn't, somebody else would. Sooner or later.

About to click on the sports section, his hand stilled. A woman was marching down the far side of the street with a small white dog in her arms. Couldn't be Daisy, though. The mutt was in Calv's custody—wasn't she?

Directly opposite the shop now, the woman checked for traffic and jay-walked, unaware of her audience on the balcony. In jeans and a red T-shirt, she had her reddish hair pulled back in a no-nonsense ponytail.

Daisy lifted her head, locked eyes with George, and let out an apologetic whimper. It was her, all right. Therefore the woman was the new resident of 525 South Jackson. Daisy wouldn't have gone to any other house.

Yep, it was the woman he'd seen taking pictures of the house, weeks ago. Letitia McComb, the contemporary version. But she had to be a decent person if she took the time to return a stray dog to its owner. He ought to speak up and welcome her to Noble—right in front of Mrs. Rose, whose grandmother had allegedly scared the original Letitia McComb right out of town with a fierce, old-fashioned tongue-lashing.

The woman passed out of sight beneath the balcony. Remembering his crazy idea of renting some garage space, George decided it wouldn't hurt to try. He'd start with a low offer. Real low.

He gathered his things and went inside, then downstairs and into the shop through the back door. Leaning around the corner into the showroom, he had a good view of Calv and the newcomer in profile. Still holding the dog, she faced him over the counter—and there was Mrs. Rose, peering through the filigree case of the Luminaire funeral fan and eavesdropping for all she was worth—as if its cast-iron pole could hide her from the neck down.

"Good mornin'," Calv said. "I see you found the runaway."

"Yes. Are you George?"

"No ma'am. I'm his uncle, Calvary Williams." He stuck out his hand.

She shook hands, keeping Daisy cradled against her shoulder. "I'm Letitia McComb," she said with no hint of apology.

Mrs. Rose's mouth dropped open, but she didn't let out a peep.

"That's a nice, old-fashioned name," Calv said.

"Thank you. And Calvary is an unusual name. A meaningful one."

"Yes ma'am. My daddy was a traveling evangelist," he said as if that explained everything. "He named my brothers Gethsemane and Zion, or Geth and Zi for short. He named my sister Jerusalem, but she much preferred to be called Rue."

"Interesting," Miss McComb said with a smile.

"Yes ma'am, but whatever name your mama and daddy slap on you, it won't make you a good person or a bad person."

Afraid Calv would say too much, too soon, George walked into the showroom. "Hello," he said. "I'm George Zorbas."

She shook hands with him while Daisy made guilty eyes at him. "Tish McComb. Or—well, I answer to either one. Tish or Letitia." She thrust the dog into his hands. "Does she belong to you?"

"I'm afraid she does," he said as Daisy wilted against him. "Thanks for bringing her back. Every chance she gets, she hightails it to her old house, and I have to fetch her back. I swear, my mother named her Daisy just so I'd always be driving Miss Daisy."

That line usually drew a laugh, but Letitia only frowned. "Shirley Nelson is your mother?"

"No. I'm sorry, let me back up. My mother—who was Calv's sister, Rue—owned the house until a couple of years ago when she passed away and I sold it to the Nelsons. Daisy thinks she still lives there."

"That's an awfully long time for a dog to stay attached to her old home."

"Si gave her doggie treats. Against my wishes."

"Oh. I won't do that, so maybe she'll stop coming." She reached over to scratch Daisy's head. "I'm glad it's not a terribly busy road, but I hope you'll keep a better eye on her."

"Yes ma'am." George hesitated. He couldn't assess her character from one casual conversation, but she seemed all right so he plunged in. "I'm looking for some work space to rent for a while. Would you consider renting your garage to me?" He glanced at Calv, whose eyes had gone round.

"My garage?" she asked.

"Yes ma'am. I need a place where I can work on a project car for six months or so. I could pay you…say…a hundred…and fifty?"

"A month?"

He nodded, ready to raise his offer if necessary. "I wouldn't need more than half of the garage, and I wouldn't need the upper level at all."

"I understand the upper level was a hayloft when the building was a carriage house. I can just imagine horses out there…"

"Yes, well, my project car has quite a few horses under its hood, and they would love to stay in the old carriage house for a while."

She let out a burst of laughter, blue eyes sparkling. "Let me think about it. I'll never park my car back there because it's so far from the house, but I might need the storage space."

George lifted one of his cards from the holder on the counter. "Sure. Think it over and let me know. Here's my number."

She reached for the card, her fingernails tipped with pale pink polish, thoroughly chipped. "Okay. The sooner I finish unpacking, the sooner I'll know if I'll need the space for anything. I'll be in touch. Bye."

"Thanks again for bringing the dog back."

"No problem." She walked toward the entrance and stopped short near the door. Eyeing the vintage mannequin wearing the black velveteen ball gown from the Helm estate, she reached out to touch the cap sleeve. He'd set the dress in the place of honor, but she'd missed it on the way in.

"Oh my goodness," she said softly. "That's gorgeous."

"It's nice, isn't it? Circa 1955 or so. It's not from a big-name designer, so it's more reasonable than some."

She checked the price tag that hung from one sleeve and laughed out loud. "For me, until I find a job, it's not the least bit reasonable." She gave the dress a farewell pat and breezed past Mrs. Rose, who turned slowly to watch her exit, then followed her right outside as if she were attached by a tow rope.

George blew out a long breath. "There she goes. The modern-day Letitia McComb." And she would have looked mighty fine in that dress.

"I'm more interested in the modern-day Letitia's garage," Calv said. "Sure would be nice to work there again."

"We'll see what happens," George said. They couldn't go back to the good old days—and for Calv, they hadn't been good anyway—but it would be something.

"She has that forward Yankee way about her, but she's tolerable. And she brought the dog back." Calv frowned. "I don't think anybody's told her anything yet."

"Nope. Nobody likes to be the bearer of bad news."

"If you're gonna move your project car into her garage, maybe you're elected."

"Maybe."

"Now you'd better get off to your appointment. And take that crazy dog. I can't watch Daisy and the shop both."

"You had her shut up in the back room, didn't you?"

"I thought I did. I'm telling you, the dog's middle name is Houdini."

"What am I supposed to do with the dog when I'm busy wheeling and dealing?"

"That's not my problem." Calv grinned. "Maybe you can arrange a trade."

"I wish."

George took his mother's dog into the back room to gather the leash and other canine accoutrements. It was past time to leave on the ninety-minute drive to Huntsville.

Ten

Mel's fingers made a soft rippling sound against the school's chain-link fence. As the sunset glowed orange behind the school building, she thought of nasty-nice Amanda, one of the bosses of the playground. She was probably the boss of her whole college by now.

Inside, the lights were still on, so the custodians hadn't left yet. They'd be mopping hallways or cleaning bathrooms or straightening rows of tiny desks.

The playground hadn't been much fun since first grade. Mel's dad was on the school board then, and they'd voted to take out the jungle gym and that scary-fast, old-fashioned merry-go-round before somebody got hurt and the parents sued. Now there were only swings, not-too-tall slides, and a climbing wall so low it wouldn't be a challenge even for an itty-bitty kid.

She tried to remember being a happy, noisy kid playing on the jungle gym. She couldn't. It was like trying to remember being a Martian. She sort of remembered the school lunches, though. Syrupy canned peaches. Meatloaf Mondays and Taco Tuesdays.

Earlier, in half-day kindergarten, they'd only had morning snack. She'd loved kindergarten. It was all crayons and games and funny stories, and then a nap on a striped mat. Even the talent show was fun until she had stage fright. She'd practiced her song at home for days, but then nothing would come out of her mouth. Her brother had acted as if she were the star of the show, though.

Stu had whooped and whistled and clapped, hollering "Melly, Melly, Melly!" like she'd done something special just by showing up.

He'd even taken the morning off work so he could be there, but her dad— her ex-dad—hadn't bothered. She didn't remember her mom's reaction. She'd probably been embarrassed.

She stepped over weeds growing in a crack in the sidewalk. Step on a crack, break your mother's back.

She'd never wanted to hurt her mom, and her mom probably hadn't meant to hurt her. Doormats didn't hurt people. They only lay there. They could keep a clean house and cook great meals and raise beautiful tomatoes, but in the end they were something for somebody to walk on.

Carefully stepping over another crack, Mel daydreamed about sneaking into a classroom and making it a free motel room for the night. The kindergarten classroom might have nap-time mats to soften the floor under her sleeping bag. First, though, she'd stop in the school kitchen and raid the humongous refrigerators. Her dad would call it stealing, but she wouldn't feel guilty. After all the hours he'd put into school-board business, she'd just be collecting a little bit of what they owed him.

She'd wash her hair in one of the gigantic stainless-steel sinks. She'd have to use dish soap for shampoo. Maybe she'd find some kitchen towels to dry her hair with, or she could use one of the hot-air hand-dryers in a bathroom. Then she'd find a cozy spot to spread out her sleeping bag.

Except none of it would happen. She didn't dare trespass on school property. That was a federal offense, she was pretty sure.

Not letting herself think about all the food in those giant fridges, she tried to read the street signs as she approached the corner. She couldn't stay on any one street too long. People didn't want scruffy people with bedrolls hanging out in their precious neighborhoods.

Third and...Mimosa? Good. She hadn't walked down Mimosa yet.

She picked up her pace, partly so she'd look like she knew where she was going and partly to warm up. The hoodie was paper-thin compared to her dad's big black jacket.

"He's not my dad," she said under her breath. "Not anymore."

Tempted to stop and dig out a cigarette, she slapped her right hand with her left. She didn't have a light anyway, and she didn't want to draw attention by asking somebody for one. If she bothered people, they'd call the cops. Then the cops would have to crack down on her. Besides, she had to make her cigs last. Once she ran out, she would quit for good.

Mel kicked a stone off the sidewalk. If she could find a way to get into her folks' house, she'd take some things from her room. Some to keep, like clothes and shoes, and some to pawn or sell so she'd have cash for food. Everything in her room was hers too. It wouldn't be stealing.

But Noble didn't have a pawnshop. She'd have to hitch a ride to Muldro, and hitchhiking scared her every time.

At Mimosa and Fourth, she got the idea of walking to Fifth and all the way to the dead end where Hayley's family lived. The Mitchells used to be so nice to her. They wouldn't kick her out, would they?

Probably. Mel made a face, remembering the last time she saw Hayley's folks. Senior year. She and Hayley had been out all night, which the Mitchells didn't appreciate. They'd called her incorrigible, over and over, like it was one of Mr. Stinchfeld's weekly vocabulary words and they'd get extra credit every time they used it. Before that, they'd worried that Mel wasn't a good influence on Hayley—Mel's bad grades probably had something to do with that—but her dad's status around town kept them from banning the friendship.

When she stopped at the corner of Mimosa and Fifth, the sun had nearly faded behind the trees. Once it was really dark out, she might find an unlocked vehicle to hole up in. But she couldn't try it until most people were sound asleep, and by then she'd be so frozen she wouldn't warm up all night.

Mel turned toward Main. If she hung out where there'd be more people, she might run into somebody she knew. Somebody who didn't hate her. At least she wasn't on drugs or sick or pregnant. She was just hungry and broke and cold.

The cold went all the way to her core when she remembered that morning in the park, just after she'd lost her job at Fishy's and had to move out of the apartment. The palm trees and flowers made her feel like she was on vacation, soaking up the same sun that the rich folks soaked up on the balconies of their million-dollar condos. She'd just unzipped her sleeping bag and spread it out on the grass to air out when an old man walked by and gave her a sad smile that reminded her of Grandpa John. Standing there in the sun, she'd shivered. She'd become one of those homeless people he'd always felt sorry for.

There but by the grace of God…

But there she was. She kept going, trying not to step on the cracks.

Climbing into her car with a double order from Bag-a-'Cue, Tish still couldn't figure out what was going on. The teenagers behind the counter were friendly enough this time, but several of the customers gave her the evil eye.

How could they tell she wasn't one of them? She'd purposefully worn a plain black sweatshirt instead of anything from U of M or her old Red Wings shirt, and surely nobody could tell her origins by her speech. She'd hardly said anything.

With growing frustration, she searched for the ignition key among the many other keys on the ring. Why couldn't the front door, the back door, and the cellar door all be keyed alike? Then there were the padlocks for the garage.

After finding the right key, she started her car and pulled onto Main. The streetlights had come on, stretching out before her in an orderly line of white. After a long day of unpacking, she could hardly wait to eat one of the barbecue sandwiches. She would heat up the second one for lunch tomorrow. The stuff was addictive.

Yawning, she slowed for a traffic light, and her brain switched gears with a jolt. On her way to pick up her order, she'd seen that skinny young woman again, this time near the park. Still carrying a dirty bedroll, she'd looked lost. And she must have been freezing.

The light changed. Tish pulled through the intersection. Keeping her speed at a crawl, she scanned the shops and sidewalks on the block before the park. A man and a woman jogged east. Another man strolled west with a large brown dog on a leash.

There was George's shop. She hoped Daisy was safe at home.

She'd better make up her mind about the garage. She didn't need the extra storage space, but she wasn't sure she wanted to have some guy out there all the time, working on an old car. Maybe it would end up on blocks in the yard. But George was no redneck. He was a reputable businessman and a longtime citizen of Noble—and she couldn't help but notice his good looks too. His dark, almost black eyes with long eyelashes. The olive skin that gave him a perpetual tan. That thick, black hair curling over his collar.

Tish smiled at the direction her thoughts had taken. Maybe she *did* want him to hang out in her backyard.

If she agreed to rent out the garage, his old car would have a better sanctuary than the girl with the bedroll—assuming she was homeless. Tish knew some young people who chose to backpack across the country, like a rite of passage or something. Maybe this girl had a home to go back to.

Tish could practically hear the lecture her mom would deliver: *If she needs help, some kind policeman can handle it. Or maybe a church. They're better equipped. A lot of homeless people are addicts or worse.*

But anyone could lose a home. A lot of people were one paycheck away from eviction. If Tish didn't find a job before her savings ran out, she could be in a tight spot too. The bank job would materialize, though, and Farris would be a good employer, although that persnickety Marian would be a pain to work with.

Nearly to the park now, Tish took her foot off the gas and searched the benches, the dark shrubbery, the gazebo—and there was the girl with the bed-roll strapped to her back. She was moving slowly up the steps to the gazebo, her shoulders slumped. At the top, she stopped as if she didn't have the strength to move farther. Her ankles were exposed, and her skinny thighs in those pale orange leggings reminded Tish of the yellow-orange, spindly legs of a sea gull. But a sea gull would have made a racket, crying for someone to feed it. The young woman stood motionless. Silent.

Tish remembered the promise she'd made to herself and the man in the moon. She would fill that big, empty house with people, one way or another.

Her mom wouldn't approve. She would say it wasn't safe, and she might be right about that.

The temperature would only keep dropping. The night would only get darker.

Sure, a church could handle it, but it wasn't a church that happened to be driving by at the moment. It was Tish.

Well aware that she was heading toward a potentially disastrous situation, she parked at the curb and climbed out. The girl didn't react to the sound of the door shutting. Lost in her own world, deaf to outside sounds, she looked utterly defeated.

With no idea of what to say, Tish walked across the grass to the gazebo. She planted one hand on the railing and one foot on the first step. "Hello up there."

The girl spun around, fists raised and eyes wide. "Oh! You scared me."

"I'm sorry. I didn't mean to."

The girl lowered her hands but kept them clenched by her sides. Thin and short, she had dark brown eyes in a heart-shaped face that made Tish think of a painting by some Renaissance artist. An angel, maybe. Or a teenage Mary Magdalene.

"And?" the girl asked.

"Well, I think I've seen you hanging around for a couple of days. I was wondering if you're okay. If you have a place to go."

Tish heard a vehicle approach nearby and slow to a crawl. She turned to look. A police cruiser pulled just past her car and stopped. The window rolled down, and a young officer with a chiseled jaw and a crew cut studied them.

"Everything all right here?" he called out.

"Just fine," Tish said.

"Fine," the girl echoed, giving him a big smile. "It's cool that you found a job back here, Darren."

"Mel?" He let out a startled laugh. "Is that you?"

"Sure is."

"Welcome home, then, and behave yourself." He smiled, tipped an imaginary hat and drove away slowly.

"You know him, huh?"

The girl nodded. "I went to school with his little brother." She shrugged her backpack off her shoulders and lowered it to the gazebo's floor. "He'll probably come back later and warn me that camping in the park isn't allowed. I'll pretend to leave, and he'll pretend to believe I'm gone."

She was a vagrant, then, but the young officer must have decided she was harmless or he would have dealt with her.

Tish moved up another step. "Don't you have anywhere to go?"

"Well, there's my parents' house, but they don't claim me anymore." The girl flashed a quick smile. "If they lock me out, how can I show them what a good girl I am? It's sort of a...what do you call it? A Catch-22?"

"Why did they lock you out? Not that it's any of my business..."

"I've messed up a few times. Nothing superbad, but my dad wants perfection or nothing." She rolled her eyes, a typical teenage show of bravado, but the trembling of her lower lip gave her away.

"You want to make things right with them, though?"

"Sure I do." The girl shivered.

"Have you had anything to eat lately?"

"It's hard to find much to eat when you're broke." The girl closed her eyes. "My mom always makes these awesome dinners, like something out of those magazines she's always buying. But will she feed me? No way, José." She opened her eyes. "Well, maybe she'd let me sneak a PBJ."

Tish couldn't imagine parents who would treat their own child that way, nor could she imagine enjoying her order from Bag-a-'Cue while this girl, Mel, hid out in the park, cold and hungry and alone.

"I just picked up a big order at Bag-a-'Cue," Tish said. "Tonight you can have a hot meal and a warm bed. If you're interested, that is."

"Mmm." The girl smiled. "You bet I'm interested. I haven't had Bag-a-'Cue in ages."

"What's your name?"

She picked up her backpack. "Melanie Hamilton."

Tish frowned. "Like Melanie in *Gone with the Wind*?"

"You got it. My folks already had the last name, and my mom was a *Gone with the Wind* freak, so she thought she might as well give me the first name too. Ridiculous, huh?"

"Just don't marry anybody named Wilkes."

Melanie smirked. "I get that a lot."

"Sorry. I'm Tish."

"Hey, Tish. Glad to meet ya."

Already feeling at home with her, Tish led the way to her car. The dome light showed the grime of a hundred highways on the yellow backpack. In close quarters, Melanie smelled strongly of cigarettes. Offering help was the right thing to do, though.

Tish started the car and pulled away from the curb. "I live really close. It's a mess because I just moved in, but it'll be warm."

"I don't mind a mess." Melanie sounded like a sleepy child.

She didn't say another word until Tish was pulling into the driveway, and then she sat up straight. "Oh, wow! This is where you live? The McComb house?"

Tish grinned. "It's fun that you know it by name. My great-great-great grandparents built the place. That's why I wanted to buy it."

"Seriously? You're related to the McCombs?"

"Yes, I'm Letitia McComb. I'm named after the Letitia who lived here shortly after the Civil War."

Melanie opened her door. The dome light came on, illuminating her dumbfounded expression. "And you think that's something to be proud of?"

Tish stared at her. "Excuse me?"

The girl shook her head slowly. "I guess you don't know much about the McCombs, do you?"

"What do you mean? What's wrong with them?"

"I'm not sure, really. I'm not into stuff like that. You need to talk to somebody who knows some local history. Like…like, um…I don't know."

Tish recalled the Civil War memorabilia she'd spotted in the antiques shop when she took the dog back to its owner. "What about the guy who runs Antiques on Main? Do you know who I mean?"

"George? Sure, I know him. He and my brother were friends in high school or something. Back in the Dark Ages." Melanie yawned. "You should call him, but can we dig into that 'cue first?"

Tish grabbed her purse and the food. "Come on in. You can start eating while I find his number."

Eleven

As the van's headlights flashed across the driveway, Daisy thumped her tail on the seat and broke wind. George didn't rebuke her. He had weightier matters on his mind.

He parked in the lot behind the shop, beside his uncle's truck. Calv had come over to help unload the van, but George would almost have preferred to take care of it himself this time. He wasn't in the mood for company.

"Come on, Daisy." He hooked up her leash and set her down on the lawn.

He could hardly stand the thought of supervising the dog's potty breaks for another ten years. It would be an eternity. A dog should be useful. A watchdog. A coonhound. A dog to go on hikes with, not to carry around like a furry baby.

There must be somebody who'd want her.

Letitia McComb, maybe. She already lived in the right house, and she would need some companionship. Money couldn't buy friends. Not real ones, anyway.

With a deep sigh, George turned his face to the night sky. He didn't want to get involved, but this Yankee woman needed not just a dog, but a friend. He was afraid he was elected.

He shook his head, wanting to disappear for a while. Women never failed to complicate everything, but a McComb woman would be in a class by herself.

Finished cleaning up after Daisy, he carried her up the stairs and walked in. The place smelled like red beans and rice. His uncle lay on the couch with his Alabama hat over his face.

"I'm back," George said, setting the mutt on the floor.

Calv stirred. "Good for you. Find much?"

"Nothing spectacular, but it's stuff we can sell. The man had a hodge-podge. Victorian tchotchkes. Sheet music. A few art-deco smalls and some nice items for the Windies."

"Any big pieces?"

"Not this time."

Calv opened one eye. "Let's eat before we unload."

George nodded. "And remember, I'll need a ride to Muldro, early, to pick up the car."

"You and that car. When you don't even know a wrench from a jackdaw." Calv hauled himself into a sitting position. "And you don't have a place to park the thing either—or do you? Did Miss McComb call you?"

George hated to see Calv so excited about the garage when it might not pan out. "No, I haven't heard from her."

"Why don't you call her? While you're at it, why don't you tell her—"

"Because, like you, I avoid unpleasant subjects."

"Yeah." Calv stared into the distance. "You know, if she hadn't practically stolen the place from Si, I'd see a little less resemblance to her ancestors."

George's defenses rose a bit. "There's nothing wrong with finding a bargain. It's business. It's capitalism. You know that."

"But it seems worse when it's somebody's home instead of a car or an antique, you know?"

"It's the same principle, though. A desperate seller makes the buyer happy."

The reverse was also true. A desperate buyer made the seller happy. George had taken full advantage of the Nelsons' eagerness to own the place, and because his mother hadn't owed anything on it, he'd made out like a bandit. He still felt like one too.

Wondering if even his own uncle realized how much money he'd made on that deal, George walked into the kitchen and lifted the lid of the dutch oven. Red beans and scraps of ham simmered gently in a garlic-rich broth.

His phone rang. He pulled it out of his pocket, checked the display, and winced. "Oh boy. It's her. Letitia."

"Be brave," Calv said from the living room.

George took a deep breath. "Hello, Letitia. I hope you're calling about the garage."

"We'll get around to that eventually," she said. "First, someone told me you're fairly well informed about local history."

"Well, yes. I'm afraid I am."

"Good. I'd like to get your opinion about my ancestors. Nathan and Letitia McComb."

Unaccustomed to such directness, he floundered for an answer. "Oh. Right. I—I've been wanting to…to talk to you. Why don't you come over? I have a book you should read."

"There's a *book* about them?"

"It's not all about them," he said hastily. "But they're in it. The shop's closed for the night, but you can come around to the back and up the stairs."

He held his breath, listening to a short silence backed by muffled whispers. She must have covered the phone with her hand while she conferred with somebody. Maybe she wasn't quite sure she wanted to visit his apartment.

It didn't take her long to decide. "I'll be there in three minutes," she said in a grim tone, and ended the call before he could answer.

He returned to the living room. "She seemed pretty sweet when she brought Daisy back. Now she sounds like a Yankee and a McComb."

"That's exactly what she is."

"How did I get in the middle of this mess?"

"Blame it on the dog," Calv said. "If Daisy hadn't introduced you, so to speak, you wouldn't have asked about the garage, and you wouldn't feel obligated to be nice."

George glared at the dog. She whined and hid her nose under her paws.

He sighed. "Common human decency obligates me to be nice," he said.

"Get off your soapbox, Zorbas. You know what I mean."

"Yeah. We both want that garage, and we want it bad."

Calv stood, putting his cap on his head. "I'll start unloading." He walked out.

"Coward," George muttered.

He started to straighten the apartment, then realized he didn't have time to make a dent in it. Living above the shop meant he was always bringing his work home with him.

He pulled the book off the shelf and flipped to the fourth chapter where he'd already left a bookmark. He was as ready as he'd ever be.

Tish parked the Volvo in a small, unpaved parking area behind the shop, where security lights shed their stark glare over the Antiques on Main cargo van and a blue pickup truck. George's uncle looked up from the rear doors of the van, most of his face hidden by a red-and-white ball cap with an oversized bill.

Upset as she was, she managed a smile as she climbed out of her car. "Hi."

"Hey, Miss McComb," he said. "George is upstairs." He pulled a large cardboard carton out of the van and hurried toward the back door of the building.

The door at the top of the stairs swung open, and George stood there. "I'd planned to talk to you sometime soon," he said. "Come on up."

She climbed the stairs quickly. He stepped aside, and she entered his homey but cluttered living room. The little white dog crouched on the floor, and she twitched at the shutting of the door. No friendly wiggles. No happy tail-wagging.

"Is that the same dog that turned up on my doorstep?"

"Yes," George said. "That's Daisy."

"She doesn't look like the same cheerful little dog."

"No. She has issues."

Savory smells drifted in from the kitchen. Tish hadn't eaten since noon, but she wasn't hungry anymore.

"Why don't you sit down." George indicated the couch. "Can I get you anything to drink?"

She waved away the offer but sat on the couch beside the January issue of *Hemmings Motor News*. That had been one of her dad's favorite publications, although he'd never owned an expensive car. "I'm fine, thanks."

Piles of old magazines covered a coffee table six inches from her knees. The cover photos dated them from the late sixties or early seventies. Vietnam, Ed Sullivan, Woodstock. An era she was glad to have missed. The fashions were horrendous, maybe a reflection of the age.

George sat in a chair across the room and placed his hands on his knees. "All right, then. Let's get to it."

"Yes, let's. Tell me everything you know about the McCombs."

"Everything?"

"Please."

"They—" He blew out a breath. "They weren't well thought of by...by most folks. Around here."

It was true, then, what Melanie had said. Tish fought the impulse to stand up and walk out, to pretend there was no truth to it.

"Why?" she asked.

"After the War, they came down here from somewhere up north. Ohio, Pennsylvania, something like that."

"Ohio," Tish said.

"Ohio? Right. And...they were carpetbaggers."

Tish's mind recaptured a page from some middle-school history textbook: an old-fashioned caricature of a man whose carpetbag overflowed with loot as he traipsed happily through a war-ruined town.

Carpetbaggers. It was a comical word. A caricature, like the picture.

"Opportunists show up after every war," she said.

"That's a mighty kind way to describe Nathan McComb. He built his fortune on the misfortunes of others. The book brings up some stories of his lying, cheating, and stealing. According to some accounts, his wife was worse than he was."

Tish stiffened, hit with a pain that was nearly physical. "You must be exaggerating. My grandfather on the McComb side knew some wonderful stories about them, and he was proud to hang their wedding portrait on his wall. I am too."

"You and your grandfather didn't grow up in Noble. Here, most folks have a story or two about their great-greats and how Nathan or Letitia did 'em wrong."

"Excuse me? People hold grudges over things that happened generations ago?"

"You hold on to your grandfather's stories, don't you? We still have our stories too. It's just that in ours, Nathan and Letitia are the villains."

Tish swallowed hard, wanting to argue but unable to forget Melanie's reaction when she realized the people in the portrait leaned against the wall were the McCombs. She'd actually shuddered.

"I had no idea," she said. "I thought my roots here would help me fit in.

I thought the McComb name was something to be proud of." A sigh escaped her. "You'd think the seller would have spoken up as soon as he learned who I was."

"The way ol' Si tells it, you're the one who did the blindsiding. If you thought the name was so special, why didn't you mention it right away?"

She studied the carpet, trying to remember how that had happened. "I wanted to stay anonymous because it would've been hard to explain my connection to the house. I only wanted to see it, not to buy it. Once I decided to make an offer, everything happened so fast. I didn't take time to explain."

"And you gave him the wrong first name because…?"

She looked up. "That wasn't intentional. He thought I said Trish, not Tish, and I just let it go. It didn't seem important."

"I can understand that."

"Okay, so I'm Letitia McComb. Does the whole town hate me? The whole county?"

"No, not at all. Folks from outside Noble aren't likely to be aware of the town's history. Even here, young people don't know or don't care. It's mostly the older folks who do."

"If most people don't care, why does everybody glare at me when I pick up an order at Bag-a-'Cue? Why does the neighbor across the street slam her door shut when I say hello? Why did the woman at the bank in Muldro act as if she'd rather slit my throat than let me open an account?"

"Muldro National? A tall woman with gray hair?"

"Yes. Marian Clark-Something."

"Clark-Graham. She's a descendant of the Carlyles, the folks who…well, the details are in the book."

"Whatever happened, it was bad enough to go into a book? But nobody had the guts to tell me until tonight?"

He frowned. "How did you learn the basics? Who told you?"

"A girl named Melanie."

He gave her a blank look. "Melanie?"

"Hamilton."

His dark eyes widened. "Mel? She's in town then?"

Tish tried to smile. "Melanie Hamilton. A character from *Gone with the Wind*."

"Sorry, but this Melanie is a character from the police blotter. No, that's too harsh. As far as I know, she has never been in jail. Yet."

Tish shook her head, remembering the friendly exchange between Melanie and the young policeman. Being on a first-name basis with local law enforcement wasn't necessarily a good sign. "She's sweet, though. And she was half starved. I left her back at the house, tucking into an order from Bag-a-'Cue."

His eyebrows shot up. "You left Mel alone in your house?"

"She needed a place to stay. I met her in the park, and I liked her."

George ran a hand over his face. "I like her too, against my better judgment. She's staying with you? Why isn't she staying with her parents? They wouldn't let her in?"

"That sounds about right."

"Yes, it does. You'd better run home and lock up your valuables."

"But she seems so nice. Down on her luck, that's all. She even offered to help with the unpacking and organizing tomorrow."

"I bet she did. Mel has some bad habits—or at least she used to. Stealing, for one. A couple of years ago, she slipped out of town with her grandpa's gold watch. Used it to finance a trip to Vegas, apparently."

"When I was a teenager, I did a few things I'm not proud of now."

"I'm not talking about typical adolescent mistakes, Letitia—or would you rather be known as Tish now?"

She raised her head a little higher. "Letitia's fine."

"Even knowing how some folks around here remember the original?"

"Yes. It's like Melanie told me tonight. Sometimes people misjudge other people."

"That sounds like something she'd say. She's slick." He shook his head. "If she's staying with you, I'm not sure I want to keep my car in your garage."

Tish stared, unable to speak for a moment. If half the town hated McCombs, she'd be hard-pressed to find a job. Farris would never hire her at the bank. She needed George's rent money—and more besides. She fought the urge to panic.

"Oh, come on," she said. "Do you really think she'd steal your car?"

"I wouldn't put it past her. She took a vintage Corvette for a joyride when she was only fifteen."

"That's hard to believe. How do you know so much about this girl?"

"She has an older brother, Stuart. Stu and I were good friends in high school."

"I see." Tish pulled her keys from her purse and started hunting through them. "The garage doors are padlocked. How could she get in?"

"The kid's smart."

"Smarter than the two of us put together?"

"Let's hope not."

"All right, then." She found the twin keys to the padlock and pulled one of them off the ring. "You need a garage. I need some income—especially now, because I might have a hard time finding work around here." She held up the key. "Let's talk about the garage."

"Yes." He stared at the key the way a starving man might stare at a steak dinner, opened his mouth and shut it again, then nodded. "A hundred and fifty a month ought to be about right."

"Three hundred," she shot back.

He didn't even blink. "Deal. Can I deliver the car tomorrow morning?"

"Any time." She should have asked four hundred.

He reached into his hip pocket for his wallet and pulled out three hundred-dollar bills—and his wallet was still fat. Now she wished she'd asked five.

"Do you need a receipt?" she asked.

"At some point, sure. I'm easy."

They made the trade, the key for the cash. She stashed the money in the inside zipper pocket of her purse. He slid the key into his front pocket and returned his wallet to his hip pocket.

"All right," he said. "And I invite you to check on my project anytime, so you can rest assured I'm not running a meth lab or any such thing."

"I'm not worried about that."

"I'm worried about a few things. Don't let Mel get anywhere near your copy of the key."

"That's ridiculous. She's sweet."

"I never said she wasn't sweet. Seriously, though, get home and make sure she isn't helping herself to anything she could pawn."

She thought of the vintage jewelry she'd acquired piece by precious piece at yard sales and flea markets. It had little monetary value, but a thief wouldn't know that. She could imagine worse scenarios than theft too. Drugs, violence, even murder. Her spine tingled with cold.

"She wouldn't…do anything violent, would she?"

"No. She wouldn't hurt a fly." He smiled. "But if flies had pockets, she might pick 'em."

Tish stood up. "I'll get on home. I guess we're done here anyway."

"Not quite." George took a slender green book from a bookcase behind him and handed it to her. "Read this. It was written when the memories were fresh. Some of the stories were likely embellished through the years, but the basics are accurate."

"Thanks, I guess."

Small, elegant lettering marched across the worn cover. *The Proud History of Noble, Alabama, as told by its citizens and recorded by Miss Eliza Clark.*

"One of Marian Clark-Whoever's ancestors?" she asked.

"Yes ma'am. I'm afraid so. There's a bookmark where the info about the McCombs starts."

"You were ready for me, huh?"

"I'd like the book back when you're finished, please, so don't let Mel steal it."

Tish opened her mouth to say the girl with the warm brown eyes and cheerful smile surely wouldn't steal a musty old book, but George's stony expression made her shut her mouth and walk to the door without further comment.

Twelve

George still couldn't quite grasp it. Mel was really back in town and staying with Letitia McComb. He turned to walk downstairs.

Dunc and his wife should have taken their daughter in. She'd burned that bridge behind her, though, and they'd taken a match to it on the other side.

Mel must have found Miss McComb's offer downright irresistible—the way George had found the lure of the garage irresistible.

He found Calv in the back room, solemnly spreading the new batch of 1920s-era sheet music over the battered Formica surface of the worktable. He was sorting the pages into his usual categories: extra fine, fine, and trash.

He looked up with curious eyes. "Did you tell her?"

George nodded.

"She take it all right?"

"Pretty much." George slipped his hands into his pockets. His right hand found the key to the padlock.

Calv returned to his sorting. "Did you talk to her about the garage?"

"Yes sir. We're in."

The delight on Calv's face made it worth every penny. "The Lord's gonna restore the years the locusts have eaten." He hooted and slapped his thigh. "The blessing of the Lord is gonna make us rich, and He'll add no sorrow with it."

"Well...there may be one small sorrow this time. A skinny little sorrow, about five feet tall."

"Huh?"

"Mel's staying with her."

Calv's smile faded. "You mean Mel Hamilton?"

"Do we know another Mel? Of course I mean Mel Hamilton."

"That was really her, then. The girl I saw on the sidewalk."

"Yes sir, apparently it was."

"She's staying with this Letitia?"

"Yes." George squeezed his eyes shut against his own insanity. "But I'm still putting my car in Letitia's garage tomorrow morning."

"Say what? Say *what*?"

George wheeled around and walked out. He didn't want to discuss Mel's hankering for fast cars.

~~~~⦿~~~~

The living room reeked of cigarette smoke when Tish walked in. "Oh no you don't," she said. "Not in my house."

A matchbook lay on the coffee table. She recognized it as the kind she'd stashed in a kitchen drawer. If Melanie had rummaged through drawers, she might have helped herself to more than matches.

In the kitchen, Tish opened the drawer where she'd placed her Victorian napkin rings. There they were, the silver plate gleaming. She pulled them out and dropped them into her purse for temporary safekeeping.

She saw no sign of the food she'd picked up at Bag-a-'Cue. Not on the table, not in the fridge. Tish checked the trash and found the bag, crumpled and empty. Melanie had devoured two huge barbecue sandwiches and all the fries.

Tish returned to the living room. "Melanie? Where are you?"

No one answered, but light spilled from the doorway of the guest room.

Melanie lay curled up on the bed, sound asleep, her hands under her cheek. On the floor were her filthy, worn-out sneakers and filthier socks.

Tish spread a blanket over the girl. Turning out the light but leaving the door ajar, she then took her purse up to her bedroom, still cluttered with unopened moving boxes.

She pulled the four napkin rings out of her purse. She'd always loved their unusual design of cherries and leaves. Somehow, they'd ended up at a yard sale in rural Michigan where the items on the next table included tractor parts and goat collars. Seeing them again made her homesick for the farmlands and orchards of her home state. More than that, she was homesick for a place where she'd had friends. Acceptance. Community. Here? She might be an outsider forever.

She found the box labeled *jewelry,* still taped shut, and scratched out the word with a fat black marker. She wrote a new label—*old magazines*—and hid the box under an empty duffel bag in the back of her closet. She tucked her purse out of sight there too, and hid the napkin rings in the pocket of an ugly windbreaker at the back of the closet. Later, she would buy a safe or a locking cabinet. If she could afford one.

After gathering some clean clothes for her guest, she headed downstairs again. She left the clothes on the chair in the guest room and retired to the couch with George's book. She opened it where he'd left the bookmark.

While Mary Ellen Carlyle lay dying of consumption in a convalescent home, knowing her adored husband and all four of their sons had sacrificed their lives on the altar of the Cause, foul carpetbaggers and Yankees invaded the family home. Perhaps it was by God's mercy that the grieving widow and mother perished far from home, never knowing that Nathan McComb, that liar and blaggard from the North, had stripped her beloved abode of its remaining treasures.

Fancying the mahogany mantelpiece and marble hearth that
Hudson Carlyle had bought at a great price, McComb hired a
crew of darkies to disassemble it in the Carlyle manse and then
assemble it again in the home he was building on South Jackson
Street.

Tish looked up at the fireplace. A mahogany mantelpiece, a marble hearth.
She went back to reading.

The entire edifice is polluted with the fruits of his thievery, from
delicate drawer-pulls to elegant doorknobs and sturdy door-hinges.
     The house still stands at this writing, a vile monument to Mc-
Comb's rapaciousness and greed. Although the home was long ago
sold into the hands of innocents who knew not its history, our town's
long-established families still remember the evil that swooped down upon
us from the North.
     Long may the people of Noble hold the Carlyle name in honor
and remembrance, while giving the name of McComb the con-
tempt it deserves. Nor let us forget the wife, Letitia McComb, that
most unchaste and unkind of women. Undeserving of the name of
"lady," she will forever share the infamy and dishonor of her spouse.

Unchaste? Tish closed the book, her cheeks burning. It was a pack of lies,
though, put together by people who'd lost almost everything in the War—
everything but their pride and their hatred for Yankees. And at least some of
the locals believed every word of the book was true.

No wonder the woman at the bank had changed her friendly tune when she
saw the name on the driver's license. No wonder the burly guy at Bag-a-'Cue had
relished repeating her distinctive, old-fashioned, infamous name to announce

her presence. She was lucky the kitchen crew hadn't slipped something nasty into the barbecue sauce.

Or maybe they had. She shuddered.

Mel was the one who'd eaten it, though. Every bite.

Tish opened the book and read that scathing account again. Surely there was another side to the story. Those old letters might shed some light on it. Once she'd set up her computer, she'd find them and scan them.

Thirteen

Idling at a red light, the 454 engine made the long hood tremble. Tuxedo black, the original color.

George wished he was seventeen, cruising Main on a Friday night with one of those cute cheerleaders who'd always ignored him. But he was a couple of years from forty. It was a Thursday morning, a workday. And his passenger was a prissy little fluff ball with no brain to speak of. He groaned at the memory of his mother dressing her little dogs in sweaters this time of year.

The light changed. Letting out the clutch, he unleashed the beast. The bass vibrato bounced off the brick buildings, waking a laugh from deep inside him.

Then unhappy thoughts intruded. Mel might have swiped some valuables already, or she might have thrown one of her legendary tantrums. Worse, the kid might have used her angelic smile to win Letitia's trust and pave the way for some con game.

He slowed for the turn onto South Jackson. Daisy put her paws on the window and peered out, shivering with so much excitement that her leash shivered with her.

"Calm down, dummy. You don't live on this street anymore, okay?"

She let out a faint yip.

Maybe he should count his blessings. Daisy was the quietest dog his mother had ever adopted. If he had to be stuck with the surviving dog, at least she wasn't one of the loudmouth yappers.

He downshifted, turning into the familiar driveway, and the growl of the engine made him grin. He finally owned a muscle car—a '70 Chevelle SS 454, no less—and he'd wangled his way back into the garage that Calv had been so rudely evicted from. They had plenty to work on too, from brakes to wiring problems to upholstery.

George's smile fell away. Mel sat on the porch steps, knees together, feet splayed out, a cigarette in one hand and a Coke can in the other. She turned her head, giving the car a faint smile—of mockery or approval? He couldn't tell. She gave no sign that she recognized him.

He cranked the window down. "Hey, Mel."

She squinted at him through a blue haze of smoke. "George? What are you doing here?"

"That's what I'd like to ask you. Letitia let you spend the night?"

"Tish, you mean? She sure did. She's nice." She glowered at him. "I can't believe nobody wanted to be honest with her about the McCombs."

He tried to bury the defensiveness welling up inside him. "We hashed it out, last night. Part of it, anyway."

"So, why are you here?"

"Dropping off my project car. I don't have a garage so she's letting me rent hers."

Leaving her Coke on the steps, Mel stood and sauntered across the shaggy lawn. She was wearing baggy jeans and a Detroit Pistons sweatshirt, very different from the semi-Goth styles she'd favored for a while. He hoped they were borrowed, not swiped, from Letitia's closet.

"Doesn't look like a project car," Mel said.

"Nice paint job, isn't it? I bought it that way, but there's still plenty of mechanical work to keep me busy."

"You? Doing mechanical work?"

"I'll rely on Calv's expertise."

"Poor Calv. I bet he doesn't know what he's in for." Trailing her cigarette-bearing hand across the trembling hood, she crossed in front of the car and went to the passenger door.

"Lucky for you, I didn't see any ashes falling on that pretty paint job," he said when she started to climb in. He'd smiled when he said it, but she scowled at him anyway. "No smoking in my car, please. Or around it."

"You grumpy old grump." After one more pull from her cigarette, she dropped the butt and ground it out with the heel of her shoe.

"Don't litter, please."

"I'll pick it up later." After nudging Daisy to the floor, she climbed in. "Cute dog."

"You want her?"

"I can't afford dog food. I can't even afford Mel food."

"You haven't had steady work lately?"

"Jobs are scarce. Especially after, you know, the big stink about the missing cash."

He frowned, trying to remember the particulars. She'd worked at a produce stand and later at the Howards' chintzy little gift shop downtown, but both places let her go because the money kept coming up short. She'd blamed it on her lack of experience. Nobody bought it.

He let the car crawl forward on the rutted lane that curved around the side of the house. The kitchen window shook with the car's passage, making sunlight shimmy on the glass.

He tried for a relaxed and patient tone, like an uncle dishing out advice. "Well, I hope you'll find a good job and prove that you've turned into a reliable and law-abiding adult who respects other people's property."

She bristled. "I haven't taken anything that isn't mine."

There she went again, proclaiming her innocence and irritating the patience right out of him. "Just keep your mitts off Letitia's things, all right?"

"Why do you call her that? She calls herself Tish."

George frowned. The nickname seemed too familiar, but he preferred it to Letitia, which always made him think of carpetbaggers.

"And why do you think I'd steal her things?" Mel started playing with the knobs of the radio, trying in vain to make it come on. "Everybody always thinks the worst about me. Everybody but Grandpa John. He loved me when nobody else did."

"Your parents loved you. They still do."

"You wanna bet? They don't want me. They never did. They were your age when I was born. Forty."

"I am not forty."

"You're close, anyway. Would you want a baby that messed up your life like that? I was born when Stuart was already in high school."

"Have you forgotten how they showered you with everything your little heart desired? The playhouse? The pony? The electric car?"

"Ooh, I loved the car. I remember racing the mail truck down the street."

He tried not to smile. "I heard about that."

"All that expensive stuff, though, you know what that was all about? They felt guilty for not wanting me, so they tried extra hard to act like they wanted me. But then, every time they spent too much money on me, guess who they blamed?" She splayed her hand over her chest. "Me. The oops baby."

"Mel, you have a wild imagination."

She didn't answer. He could only hope she would think about what he'd said.

He pulled the car around the line of camellias. The garage came into view, flooding him with memories. When he was a kid, his uncle had practically lived there, tinkering on cars and sharing his expertise. But when Rue Zorbas caught her brother drinking around her young son, she'd banned Calv from the premises. She'd meant it too. She didn't relent until shortly before her death—years and years after he and George had started spending time together again. Once her son was an adult, she hadn't had much say in the matter.

Stopping the car in front of the right-hand door, George savored the engine's throaty roar one moment more before shutting it off. It ticked placidly in the silence like a black dragon settling its shiny limbs for a power nap.

Mel didn't move. She only sat there frowning. Scheming, probably.

"How are you and Letitia getting along?" he asked.

"Too soon to tell. I conked out last night before she got back from your place, and when I got up this morning, she was asleep on the couch with a book on her stomach."

George had a good idea which book that was.

"So, was it fun to explain about the McCombs?" Mel asked.

"What do you think?"

"There you go again. Grumpy old—"

He got out, slamming his door on the rest of her commentary. Proceeding to the garage, he then unlocked the sliding door and shoved it to the side. "We're in, Calv," he said under his breath.

Mel climbed out, bringing the dog, and followed him around to the trunk of the car, the way she used to follow him and Stuart long ago. Daisy lolled happily in her arms, wagging her tail. If she'd been a cat, she would have been purring.

That gave him pause. Daisy was a wreck at the shop and upstairs, but perfectly happy at the house. Maybe it was the location, or maybe she trusted women but didn't trust men. With rescue dogs, you never could tell.

After opening the trunk, George pulled out a socket set and a small toolbox filled with screwdrivers and pliers. He placed them against the interior wall and went back for more, the small tools neatly stored in toolboxes and the larger ones loose. The pry bars clinked and clanked against the cement. Finally he added the electric drill he'd bought himself for Christmas, still in its orange plastic case.

"That's a lot of tools," Mel said.

"This is only the first load. Calv's bringing—" George shut himself up when he imagined her strolling into a pawnshop with one of the expensive power tools that the old man had scrimped and saved for.

When he had finished emptying the trunk, George slammed it shut. "Now I'd better put this baby to bed and lock her up tight."

"A car like that isn't cheap. Did your mom leave you a ton of money?"

"It's no Maserati. It's only a Chevelle, and it still needs work."

"You didn't answer my question, George."

"And I don't intend to."

Letitia's voice floated across the yard. "Melanie? Where are you?"

"I'm out here harassing George," Mel called. "He deserves it."

Letitia stumbled around the camellias, looking like she'd slept in her clothes. Yep. She had. She was still wearing the black shirt she'd worn when she stormed up his stairs with war in her eyes.

She stopped short and stared at the car. "That explains it. I thought we were having an earthquake or something."

He squelched a proud smile. "Sorry. I didn't mean to wake you."

"I didn't mean to sleep in." Running a hand through her messy hair, she looked back and forth between them like someone who'd been asked to keep an eye on a rat and a snake simultaneously. She settled on Mel. "Did you sleep all right?"

"Yes, thanks." Mel smiled, all innocence and charm. "Sorry about eating all the 'cue last night. I couldn't stop."

"It's okay. By the time I got back from George's place, I didn't feel like eating."

Mel's smile changed to a sympathetic pout. "Of course you didn't. It's terrible the way you had to drag the truth out of him."

"That's enough, Melanie." He turned to Letitia. "Did you read the pertinent parts of the book?"

"I certainly did. Several times." She put her hands on her hips. "I can't believe it. It's like the whole town has conspired to keep me in the dark."

"How long have you been in town?" he asked. "And you've hatched a conspiracy theory already? You persecute easy."

"I *what*?"

"Stop fussin', y'all," Mel said. "George, can I take the car for a spin? Please?"

"No. You may not drive it. You may not touch it. Understand?"

"Just one little touch." She reached out and caressed the fender, watching from half-veiled eyes for his reaction.

He folded his arms across his chest and kept his mouth shut.

Something was brewing in Letitia, though. She glared at him and opened her mouth as if she were about to commence arguing with him. Then she pushed her hair out of her eyes and faced Mel instead, leaving him feeling slighted.

"Tell me the truth," Letitia said. "Did you really steal a Corvette?"

"No!" Mel jutted her chin. "No way. It was my grandpa's. He'd just died, and taking the car out made me feel like—like he was still around. I brought it back without a scratch, but my dad whipped me anyway. That made me so mad. I was too old for whippings."

George raised his eyebrows. "A whipping is better than being charged with grand theft auto when you weren't even legal to drive."

"It's not theft when you take what's yours. Grandpa John always said he'd leave me the car when he died."

"He was only teasing," George said gently.

Mel swung her head stubbornly from side to side. "No, he meant what he said, but my stupid, selfish father wanted the car, so he took it. *He's* the thief. Oh, I forgot. Duncan Hamilton isn't my father anymore. He's my ex-father. Ask him if you don't believe me." She deposited Daisy in George's hands, turned around, and stalked toward the house.

He sighed. "She accuses Dunc of taking whatever he wants, but she does the same thing. Was anything missing this morning?"

"I hope not, but I don't intend to take inventory every day," Letitia said. "I can't live that way."

"No, you can't. She needs to stay somewhere else."

"Such as?"

"I don't know, but you don't want her under your roof. Not with her history of stealing."

"But where's your proof? Your suspicions aren't necessarily based on facts. What if you're wrong? And as for your smart remark about how I persecute easy—"

"I apologize for that," he said hastily.

"Thank you, and I apologize if I've overreacted to that nonsense about the McCombs, but there must be another side to that story. I'll let you know when I find it." She turned around and rushed off, disappearing behind the camellias before he could corral his scattered thoughts.

It was possible that those old McComb stories were highly exaggerated, but the Mel stories were recent, and he'd heard them from reputable citizens soon after they'd happened. She had a lot of pluck, coming back to town. And now, if she thought she had nothing left to lose, there was no telling what she might do. Especially if she heard about Dunc's plans for the Corvette.

George climbed into the car again, putting the dog on the passenger seat. The Chevelle made a glorious racket when he drove it into its new, temporary home. With the dog straining against her leash, he padlocked the door behind him. He sure hoped Letitia kept her keys where Mel couldn't find them.

⤳⟡⤺

Standing at the parlor window with that awful book in her hand, Tish watched George walk down the sidewalk toward Main with the dog padding reluctantly behind him. Daisy looked mournfully over her shoulder, then sat. The leash went taut.

George stopped short, picked up the dog, and started walking again. He kicked a rock, sending it into the street, and picked up his pace.

Tish explored her hair with her hand, and it was as tangled as she'd feared. She hadn't brushed her hair or her teeth. She'd just run outside looking like a nightmare, and there was George. With his thick, wavy, dark hair and his crazy-fast car.

Her dad had grown up in the Motor City, and he'd given her a pretty good education about Detroit's finest products. She knew what a Chevelle Super Sport could do.

Zero to sixty in about six seconds, probably. The thought gave her a peculiar feeling in the pit of her stomach. She didn't like fast cars.

The floor squeaked behind her. She caught a whiff of cigarette smoke mixed with shampoo—*her* shampoo. Tomorrow, maybe, they could hit Target and buy Mel some necessities.

"You're too nice to be a McComb," Melanie said. "Thanks for letting me borrow the clothes."

Turning, Tish studied Melanie—or Mel, as she preferred. "You're welcome. We can round up some more clothes later. Some things that fit you a bit better," she said, eyeing how baggy the clothes were on Mel.

Mel moved closer to the portrait. They seemed to be sizing each other up—Nathan and Letitia with their deep-set eyes staring out of the past, and the skinny, big-eyed waif regarding them solemnly from the present. Crooks, all three?

But it was far easier to picture Mel as a demure young miss in a gown from the Civil War era, her brown hair bound back in a snood. Her face was as lovely and delicate as Olivia de Havilland's when she'd played the fictional Melanie on the silver screen.

"Maybe they did some bad things," Mel said, "but people can change. People can be sorry for what they've done, you know?"

"I do. But being sorry doesn't always repair the damage."

Tish sat on the couch and looked around her half-unpacked living room. She'd hoped to spend the day working on the house and enjoying it—but now she shared it with a stranger she couldn't trust. She couldn't enjoy it anyway, though. Even the doorknobs reminded her of Miss Eliza Clark's tall tales.

Tish held up the book for Mel to see. "Have you ever read this?"

"No, I'm not much of a reader."

"In this case, I'm glad."

"Pretty bad, huh?"

"Very. If it's true."

"But maybe they weren't as horrible as everybody says." A small smile warmed Mel's face. "Maybe I'm not horrible either."

"But George tried to talk me out of letting you stay, and he must have his reasons. He's known you all your life, hasn't he?"

Mel's eyes brimmed with tears. "Yes, but he doesn't know the new me. Please let me stay. Please. I'll pull my weight. I'll scrub toilets. I'll wash windows. I'll do anything, but I don't want to be on the street again."

The tears were very nearly contagious. Putting the book down, Tish regained her composure. "Maybe I can help you out for a little while, if you'll meet my conditions."

"What are they?" the girl whispered.

"Without getting into fussy details, pretend I'm a strait-laced, old-maid schoolteacher. No, a Sunday school teacher. Anything that would offend an uptight, old-maid Sunday school teacher is something you can't do. No alcohol, no drugs, no men in your room." Tish inhaled a whiff of tobacco that reminded her of a crucial rule. "And no smoking in the house."

"Oh. Sorry. Okay."

"And you'll look for a job, and you'll help with the groceries when you can."

"Yeah, sure."

"And you'll help around the house and the yard."

Mel nodded with enthusiasm. "I love to work outside."

"But this is the most important thing. You'll try to make things right with your parents."

Mel's tears spilled over. "You think I haven't tried already?"

"Of course, but you need to try again. And again and again. Will you do that?"

Mel didn't answer right away, but maybe that was a good sign. She was giving the question serious thought. She frowned, she worried her lower lip with her teeth, and finally she nodded.

"With my mom, it might work," she said. "My dad, though, he'd rather not see me again. Ever."

"Will you at least try, though? You don't know how long he'll be around. Don't miss your chance."

Mel gave a slow, reluctant nod.

"All right, then. You can stay. But be on your best behavior. And please, always be honest with me? Please?"

"I will. Thank you." Mel grabbed her in a fierce hug. "I'll make you proud."

"That's what I want to hear." Tish gave Mel's shoulders an encouraging squeeze but stepped away again quickly. At such close range, the smell of smoke nearly made her ill. "I'm going to sit on the front steps and enjoy the sunshine for a few minutes before I get to work. You can join me if you'd like."

"Sounds like fun. I love fresh air. I love having room to breathe, you know? Do you mind if I smoke?" Mel grabbed the matches from the coffee table. Pulling a smashed pack of cigarettes from her back pocket, she headed for the front door. The hinges creaked when she opened it.

The fruits of his thievery...elegant doorknobs and sturdy door-hinges.

But that was then. This was now. Tish wasn't responsible for Nathan Mc-Comb's wrongdoing—if it was even true. His reputation had put a damper on her excitement about living in the house he'd built, though. She might as well pin a scarlet *C* for carpetbagger on her shirt. That was how people saw her—especially if they thought she'd taken unfair advantage of Silas Nelson when he was desperate to sell. She was a villain who'd swooped in from the North and cashed in on his troubles.

Joining Mel on the porch, Tish pondered her policy on cigarettes. Never having lived with a smoker, she'd never had to consider a no-smoking rule. For that matter, she'd never had to hide her valuables either.

Hiding important papers and her jewelry was only sensible, but hiding the napkin rings seemed miserly and mean. They were symbols of hospitality and festivity. She'd always used them when she invited friends over and wanted to set a pretty table. But they would never grace her table again if someone stole them and pawned them.

Who was she kidding? An anonymous someone didn't worry her. Mel did.

Tish sat on the top step and far to the left, hoping to escape the smoke, but a faint breeze wafted it right into her nostrils. Blowing it out again, she gazed down at the neat part in Mel's clean, shiny hair. A new wreath of smoke drifted up and hovered over the girl's head like a halo.

This was not the way Tish had pictured her new life in Noble.

Fourteen

*A*t the Super Target in Muldro, Mel leaned into a rack of raspberry-colored sweaters and inhaled. She'd already changed into the jeans and one of the tops from the thrift store, and she was grateful for them, but there was nothing like the smell and feel of new clothes.

Someday, she'd have spending money again. Someday, she could drive past the dealership without feeling a thing too. She wished it wasn't so close to Target.

"Here, see if these fit." Tish handed her a couple of T-shirts on hangers and a pair of folded jeans.

Mel shook her head. "We already found jeans at the thrift—"

"A girl can never have too many jeans, and they're on clearance. And you need to pick out pajamas and socks and underwear."

"Um, when you say underwear, do you mean a bra too?"

"I mean bras, plural. Get a couple."

"But you already spent thirty bucks on me at the thrift store. It's too much."

"No," Tish said gently. "No, it's not."

To hide her tears, Mel pretended to examine the tags on the T-shirts. From the corner of her eye, she saw Tish checking the tiny notebook that held her shopping list.

Tish pointed her cart toward the grocery section. "Grab a cart and pick up whatever toiletries you need too," she called, walking away. "We can meet somewhere around the checkouts."

"Okay," Mel managed.

She felt like such a jerk. She'd thought Tish asked her to come along because she didn't trust her alone in the house, but it was really all about the shopping. With Tish's money. She was like a fairy godmother.

Mel latched the dressing-room door behind her and pulled off her thrift-store shoes. The floor was cold and gritty beneath her bare feet.

She could hardly wait to break into a bag of new white socks. And to have good jeans again. Jeans that fit. The thrift jeans fit okay, but they weren't exactly in style, and the ones she'd borrowed from Tish were way too big.

But when she zipped up the brand-new jeans, they were baggy too. They gapped at the waist. Instead of hugging her thighs and hips, they fit like mom jeans.

She pulled them off, found the size label and turned it this way and that. Was it a 5? No, it was a 3. She was skinnier than she'd thought.

When she tried on the Ts, she forced herself to take a hard look in the mirror. Her ribs showed, like the ribs on the stray cat she'd tried to feed in Florida when she'd still had some money. Bra shopping wouldn't be any fun at all. She'd probably only fill out an A-cup. Making a face, she changed back to her own clothes and left the dressing room.

It was a cinch to find pajamas, panties, and socks, but it took half an hour to find a bra that fit right and wasn't too expensive. Then she pushed her cart through the health-and-beauty section, making herself stick to the basics. Shampoo, deo, toothpaste, a toothbrush, and a box of what her mom always called "feminine products" in the special, soft voice she saved for talking about subjects like that.

Mel stopped by the men's toiletries and allowed herself a tiny sniff of Old Spice. She closed her eyes and pretended Grandpa John was right there beside her, about to crack a joke or pull a quarter from her ear.

"Stop it," she whispered. She returned the container to the shelf and sneaked her hand up to wipe her eyes so quickly that nobody would notice. Then she maneuvered her cart through a traffic jam in the main aisle and hurried toward the checkouts.

Tish was browsing through a display of half-off calendars, her fully loaded cart beside her. The cold foods were piled on top—yogurts, ice cream, freezer waffles. Chocolate milk too. Mel's mouth watered.

Tish looked up with a smile. "There you are. Find everything okay?"

"Mostly, but the jeans were baggy."

Tish's smile faded. "Size 3 is baggy?"

Mel tried not to roll her eyes. "I'm not anorexic. I just haven't been eating right."

"I don't think you've been eating at all." Tish glanced down at the food piled high in her cart. "We'll put an end to that. Come on, let's find a short line."

Tagging along with her own cart, Mel decided she'd better not ask Tish to buy cigarettes. She seemed like the clean-living type who wouldn't want to. Besides, she'd already been way too generous.

As Mel helped pile the groceries on the conveyer, she gave herself a lecture. She would not sneak the trail mix in the middle of the night. She would not drink all the chocolate milk. She would not hoard the fresh fruit in her room— not much of it, anyway.

Tish pushed her empty cart out of the way and pulled Mel's forward.

"It's too much," Mel said. "I'll put some things back."

"Don't be silly. You've only picked up a few basics. Are you sure you have everything you need?"

Mel nodded. She wanted to say a big, loud "Thank you," but she knew she'd start crying. So she only nodded and emptied her cart.

Needing a distraction from the bank of cigarette cartons behind the register, Mel checked out the magazines. Her mom thought she was too high class to read the gossip rags, so she only bought the women's magazines that were full of recipes and health stuff and decorating ideas. The same old same old, every time. Mel picked up *People* instead. She hadn't seen one in so long that she didn't recognize half the celebrities in the photos.

"That'll be two-ten thirty-six," the checker said in a sweet, high-pitched voice. Like baby talk.

Mel froze—partly because she couldn't believe the total came to over two hundred bucks, and partly because she'd known that cutesy-baby voice since first grade.

Turning slowly, she held the magazine in front of her face and took a peek. Yep. The checker was Amanda La-Di-Da Proudfit. Maybe she'd flunked out of that fancy college, or maybe her folks ran out of money, but she was back. Even in a Target shirt, she looked like a model. Shiny hair, clear skin, perfect makeup. She wore gold hoop earrings and a sweet little gold heart on a gold chain.

Mel had never felt so ugly, wearing thrift clothes and very uncool shoes and no jewelry. Her lips were chapped. Her hair was full of split ends, and it probably smelled like the cigarette she'd smoked on the porch in the middle of the night. Well, she'd only be uglier if she acted like Amanda.

Returning the magazine to the rack, Mel worked up a friendly smile. "Hey, Amanda."

Amanda glanced her way. "Hey," she said in her baby voice.

Mel had never known anybody who could make one little word sound so snotty. It still hurt too, like it always had. Like she meant *I don't care how much money your dad has, you're still a loser.*

Mel wanted to smack her. Or at least cuss her out. Gripping the handle of her cart, she strung a few nasty words together in her mind.

Tish looked over her shoulder, frowning at her. A silent signal: *You okay?*

Mel let her breath out. Nodded.

Holding Tish's credit card in perfectly manicured fingers, Amanda stared at it. She looked up at Tish, then down again, moving her lips as if she were sounding out the name. Mel groaned a little on the inside. Amanda knew the old McComb stories too.

Tish smiled. "Is there a problem with the card? Is it expired or something?"

"No…"

"Oh, good. I'd hate to hold up the people behind us."

Amanda swiped the card and handed it back, giving Tish another long stare. It didn't wilt Tish's friendly expression as she waited for her receipt.

Amanda handed it to her. "Have a nice day."

"You too," Tish said, pushing her cart toward the exit.

Amanda had already turned toward her next customer. Tired of feeling invisible, Mel made sure Tish was out of earshot, then got right in Amanda's face.

"Okay, Sweetsie-Pie Proudfit. You don't like Tish because she's a Mc-Comb, and you don't like me because I'm me, and you don't have to, but don't ignore me. Got it?"

Amanda's eyes nearly bugged out. "Got it."

"Good." Mel smiled politely, like Tish. "Bye, then. It was nice to see you." She walked through the automatic doors, holding her head high. Like Tish.

Maybe George was right, Tish thought. She was hypersensitive. Imagining things. The name on the credit card hadn't really flummoxed the checker at Target.

Tish rolled her shoulders to rid them of tension. The ride back to Noble would be relaxing if she would take time to enjoy the rolling landscape and the piney woods. Northern Alabama in winter was almost as green as Michigan in the spring. The morning chill still hadn't burned off, though.

She glanced over at Mel, dressed more appropriately for the weather now. Before they'd pulled out of the Target lot, she'd put on a pair of her new socks. She'd practically cooed over them.

Now she'd opened the bag of trail mix. One handful after another, she sorted it out in her palm, eating it in the same order every time. Nuts first, then raisins, then sunflower seeds, and finally the M&M's, saving the red ones for last. It would have been funny except she was so reverent, as if she were performing a religious ritual.

At the checkout, Mel had been like a little girl at Christmas, her eyes shining but timid. Afraid to believe all those special presents were really hers. But really, it was nothing special. Just toothpaste and socks and cheap clothes. The look she'd given the employee at the register, though…that was decidedly not like a sweet little girl.

"The checker at Target was somebody you went to school with?" Tish asked.

"Yeah. Nobody important."

"Everybody's important to somebody."

"Especially if you're Amanda La-Di-Da Proudfit," Mel said in a perfect imitation of the girl's prissy, infantile voice. "She's so special. She's a cheerleader and an honor student and a teacher's pet."

"Sounds like you two have some history, and it's not especially pleasant."

"It's nothing personal." Mel sounded like herself again. "She was one of the people who decided who got to be popular and who didn't, starting in first grade. And I didn't."

"I didn't either."

"You know what I'm talking about, then." Mel reached for the bag of trail mix again.

"Take it easy, there. Don't make yourself sick."

"Sorry." Mel closed the bag in a hurry.

"No, I didn't tell you to stop. Just slow down a little."

Mel shook her head and dropped the package into the shopping bag where she'd found it. "I'd better save some for you."

"I don't really like trail mix myself, but I thought you could use the extra calories."

"You bought it for me? To fatten me up? Wow, thanks. Thanks for everything. The clothes, the shampoo and stuff. You're too nice."

"I can't spend this much money every week, but I think we both needed a jump-start on groceries and essentials."

Tish frowned, hoping she had a job waiting. She'd check in with Farris soon, to make sure he'd received her letter and résumé. He didn't seem like the type to believe wild stories about a woman's ancestors. Or even if he believed them, surely he wouldn't hold them against her.

Mel straightened and pointed ahead. "Hey, see that street sign up there? Rock Glen Drive? Can you turn off there?"

Tish took her foot off the gas. "What for?"

"That's where my folks live. I just…I just want to drive by."

"Sure, we can do that." Tish signaled for the turn. "Is this the house where you grew up?"

"Yeah. My brother grew up in a little house closer to town, but they built this one later when they had more money."

"That's amazing. A family that lived in only two different houses, all those years. When I was a kid, we moved so many times I can't keep it all straight in my head."

"How come?"

"Nothing too terrible. It's just that my dad was always chasing the American dream. He never quite caught it."

Mel let out a quiet snort. "My dad thinks he caught it, but I think it caught him."

She'd forgotten to say ex-dad, for once.

Making the turn, Tish was already impressed. The homes were spaced far apart and set a substantial distance from the road. Long driveways curved between pines, hardwoods, and carefully planned landscaping. Some of the driveways were gated, but the gates stood open as if to say the residents were prepared to be friendly or defensive, as necessary. These weren't cookie-cutter homes. They displayed individuality, good taste, and prosperity. Maybe the homeowners made a living in the hustle and bustle of Muldro but preferred to *do* their living in the more rural atmosphere on the outskirts of Noble.

It didn't seem like Mel's kind of neighborhood. Pondering that, Tish cast a sidelong glance at her passenger.

"It'll be awesome to drive by in a car they won't recognize," Mel said with a grin. "Totally awesome."

That was it. Twenty years old, she had the vocabulary of a twelve-year-old. She didn't sound well-read. That was true of a lot of young adults, though, and she'd already admitted she wasn't much of a reader.

Tish slowed for a speed bump. "I hate speed bumps."

"Me too, but my dad hates 'em worse. Ex-dad, I mean. He got into a big argument with one of the neighbors. He's this old banker dude who runs every morning when it's still dark out. I guess he nearly got run over a couple of times, so he started a petition to add the speed bumps."

Tish's mind spun in circles. A banker with an athletic build... "Do you know the banker's name?"

"Yeah. Farris. He's nice, but he and my ex-dad can't stand each other."

"Please stop calling him your ex-dad. It's disrespectful."

"Yeah, because I don't respect him."

Tish shook her head, wondering what kind of man he was. If a personable businessman like Farris didn't like him, maybe the man simply wasn't likable.

Mel pointed again. "It's up there on the right. The last house before the side street. Slow down a little so we can get a better look."

"What are we looking for, exactly?"

"I wonder what they're up to. That's all."

Tish checked her mirror. Nobody was behind her, so she slowed to a crawl.

It was a sprawling, one-story brick home with a large porch. Four white rocking chairs sat there, two on each side of the door. A wooden privacy fence enclosed the backyard. The house had a two-car attached garage and a separate two-car garage off to the side.

"Nice setup," Tish said. "A man can never have too much garage space."

"He added the second garage when I was about ten. To make room for his toys. His boat, his Jet Skis, stuff like that."

"Beautiful landscaping," Tish said, turning onto the side street. "I wish I could see the backyard too, but that's a pretty effective privacy fence."

"Yeah, they're really good at keeping people out. See the tree that hangs over the fence? That's how I always used to sneak in if I was locked out."

"Were they in the habit of locking you out?"

"It got to be that way." Mel leaned toward her window. "I didn't learn much in high school, but there's one poem I remember. Our teacher read part of it out loud, and we were supposed to read the rest ourselves, but I never did. I guess it's about an old hired hand who comes back—"

"Robert Frost?"

"Yeah, that's him. The dude who wrote it, I mean. There's this line that goes, 'Home is the place where, when you have to go there, they have to take you in,' but for me it's more like 'Home is the place where, if they won't take you in, you know it's not home anymore.'"

"Aw, Mel, I wish I could help you get past feeling that way. I'd love to see you reconnect with your folks. I think it'll work out if you'll just give it another chance."

"I'm not the one who won't give it another chance," Mel said.

Tish wanted to pin her down, but it didn't seem like the right time.

"When I was a little, I had a Shetland pony in the field behind the house," Mel said, pointing. "His name was Buddy."

Tish smiled at the evidence that Mel's parents had given her something that most little girls could only dream of. "That must have been fun." She proceeded to a home farther down the road and made a careful T-turn at the driveway. "You said your dad sells cars for a living?"

"Yeah, he owns a dealership in Muldro. Makes big bucks." Mel made a face.

As Tish drove down Rock Glen toward the main road, a big silver SUV came from the other direction. Mel whipped around to follow it out of sight.

"Aw, geez, that was my brother. He's pulling into the driveway. They kicked me out, but they're letting him stay while he's getting his house remodeled. That's so unfair."

"Patience," Tish said. "Things might still turn around."

Mel only shook her head. She was silent all the way home. She helped unload the car, but then she shut herself in the guest room.

Tish left her alone and unpacked groceries, praying for Mel the whole time.

Fifteen

At her bedroom window, Tish stood entranced by a cloud of golden diamonds glittering at the back of the lot. They winked and trembled in constant motion. They were only the garage lights, seen through wind-blown trees and shrubbery, but it was a magical sight from a distance.

She kept catching snatches of laughter and music. It was like eavesdropping on a party. She was invited, though. George had said she was welcome anytime. After all, it was her garage.

He and his uncle had arrived, driving separately, when she and Mel were finishing their supper. Mel wolfed down her last few bites and searched for her hoodie, but Tish stayed at the table, saying two men intent on fixing a car wouldn't want female interference. That was probably true, but the deeper truth was that she needed some time to herself. Mel had all the emotional maturity of a thirteen-year-old, and her presence was draining.

Speaking of maturity… Tish wrinkled up her nose and faced the real problem: although she and George had apologized to each other, they still had their differences. She didn't look forward to their next conversation, but if half the town despised her for being a McComb, she'd better take good care of the few semifriendly relationships that she had.

Tish pulled on a sweater, sailed down the wooden stairway she loved more and more each day, and went out through the back door. By moonlight, she navigated through the dense plantings without running into anything. A bluesy guitar solo grew louder as she approached the last barrier, a thick hedge of camellias so tall they were practically trees.

She rounded the hedge and stopped. The cloud of diamonds had vanished. Ordinary light spilled from the opened door on the right of the garage, and music poured out of an ancient boom box on the floor.

George stood in the wide doorway, wearing a bulky jacket and taking pictures of his big black car with a tiny camera. Mel and Calv stood farther inside, poring over a magazine. Daisy's leash dangled from Mel's other hand, and the dog snoozed at her feet.

"Hello," Tish said.

George turned toward her with a cautious smile. "Hey there. How's everything going?"

She smiled too, equally cautious. "Pretty well. No new conspiracy theories."

He laughed softly. "That's good news."

Once she'd stepped out of the nippy wind, the temp in the garage wasn't bad. "How's it going for you?"

"We're not trying to accomplish anything tonight," he said. "Just having fun. Celebrating."

"That explains why it sounds like a party from the house."

Calv chuckled and turned a page of the magazine. "It's a party, all right."

George snapped a picture of Calv and Mel. "Tell you what," George said. "When I finish the work on the car, I'll throw a real party."

Calv lowered his half of the magazine—no, it was an automotive parts catalog. "Listen carefully, Zorbas. You ain't never gonna finish. If you want a finished car, go see Miss Mel's daddy and buy a brand-new one right off his showroom floor."

So, Mel really was who she claimed to be.

Mel let go of the catalog. Its pages fluttered as Calv grabbed her half of it. "No, you'd better not do that. Never trust a car salesman, especially if he's named Dunc Hamilton. And by the way, he's not my daddy anymore."

"Sure he is," George said in a mild tone.

She jammed her hands into the pockets of her hoodie. "He's not. Ask him sometime."

"Is Stu still your brother?"

"I doubt it. He's his daddy's boy." Mel handed the leash to Calv. "And don't anybody argue with me. I know what I'm talking about. He told me not to go to his house, ever—" She brushed past Tish, broke into a run, and disappeared in the darkness.

George tucked the camera into a little black case and shook his head. "That's one crazy, mixed-up kid."

"Yep." Calv transferred the leash to George without waking the dog. "Looks like the party's breaking up. I'll mosey on home and look up the particulars on the wiring harness and all. See ya later, George. Good night, Miss McComb."

"Please, call me Tish. Or Letitia. I don't care anymore. Good night."

"All right, then. Good night, Tish." Calv walked away, catalog in hand. The lights reflected off the slick paper, then the darkness swallowed him too.

"See?" she said. "A McComb shows up, and the place empties."

George flashed her a quick smile. "There's that conspiracy theory again," he said. "No, Calv was itching for an excuse to leave. He's addicted to reality TV, and his favorite show comes on at eight."

"I hope that's all it was." Tish turned toward the car, admiring its sleek lines and glossy black paint. A Chevelle Super Sport in decent shape could be pricey, but George lived in a dinky bachelor pad above his shop. Maybe a nice house wasn't important to him.

Remembering the Hamiltons' neighborhood, she frowned. "How well do you know Mel's parents?"

"I used to know them pretty well, from a kid's perspective anyway. Her dad was my coach in Little League. Dunc's a jock. He sells cars for a living, but his world revolves around sports. Suzette—his wife—is a small-town Martha Stewart."

"And what's the brother like?"

"Stu? A nice guy, last time I checked, but I haven't seen much of him the last few years. When Mel was little, she practically worshiped him."

"Not anymore, huh?"

"Doesn't sound like it. I'm assuming she hasn't contacted him since she's been back. Is she behaving herself?"

Tish nodded. Nothing had gone missing. She'd even dropped a crumpled five-dollar bill in the corner of the kitchen by the trash as a test. Mel had found it and brought it to her immediately. Of course, she might have known it was a test.

"She's ridiculously grateful for little things," Tish said. "And she works hard. This afternoon she washed windows for hours and never complained."

"Hard work might keep her out of trouble anyway." George stepped away from the car. He crossed his arms and stared. "She's so pretty."

It took her a second to realize he didn't mean Mel. "Very pretty, but she'll cost you a fortune in gas."

"It'll be worth every penny. Calv says it's my midlife crisis project, a little early." George checked his watch. "He expects me to bring some eats over to his place, so I'd better get going. Mind holding the dog for a second?"

"Not at all. Come on, Daisy." Tish picked up the dog, who blinked once and snuggled against her. The warm little butterball certainly wasn't starving.

George turned off the music and the lights, shoved the heavy wooden door shut, and locked up. He pulled a stocking cap over his head, and they began walking slowly toward the house. She glanced over her shoulder, recalling the image of Nathan and Letitia setting out on a buggy ride from their carriage house. That notion was tarnished now with harsh realities.

Her shoes crunched on dry leaves in the dark, and then there was the softness of grass again as they made their way around the side of the house. George kept pace with her as if he were shepherding her safely home. A gust of wind blew through from the street, whipping her hair into her eyes.

"Cold?" he asked.

The question made her want to giggle and snatch that silly cap off his head. When she was a kid, she'd run around outside barefoot in colder weather than this.

"It's a little chilly," she said.

"Careful, there's a big exposed root coming up," he said. "Right about... there."

Now she saw it, like a pale snake lying across her path. She stepped over it. "Do you know every inch of the yard?"

"Just about. Remember, I grew up here."

"I keep forgetting that."

George stopped at the corner of the porch. Amber light from the living room filtered through the blinds. As he reached out to take Daisy, he asked, "Apart from its history, is the house what you'd hoped it would be?"

Was that a hint of sentimentality in his voice? "It has its eccentricities, but I love it."

"It's solidly built."

"So that's one positive about Nathan McComb. He built a solid house as well as a terrible reputation. I wonder which will last longer."

"It'll all work out as long as your descendants hear nice stories about you...a few generations from now."

Tish laughed. "When I'm moldering underground. That's a cheerful thought." She tipped her face toward the magnolia tree whose leathery leaves were rattling in the wind. "That reminds me. If all the Carlyle sons died in the Civil War, how can Marian at the bank be a direct descendant? Did they leave children behind, or were there daughters too?"

"The sons died young, without heirs, but there were two daughters. Marian's descended from one of them. Have you tangled with her again?"

"No, but you should have seen the looks I got from the checker at Target. I don't know if that was about being a McComb, though. Maybe she hated me for being with Mel. It was obvious that they didn't like each other."

"That's no surprise. Mel was never very diplomatic."

"But she can be sweet too. She tries so hard to please. And she's so...needy. She didn't even own a decent pair of socks. She told me she lost a bag full of clothes in Florida. That's why she wasn't dressed for the weather."

"Florida? I thought she went to Vegas."

"Maybe she went there too. I'm trying not to be too nosy."

"Be nosy enough for your own good, though." He started toward his van and then turned around. "The rent money I paid you. The cash. Did you stick it in the bank?"

"No."

"Keep a close eye on it, then. And on your keys."

"I'm not stupid about things like that."

"Of course not." Shaking his head, he proceeded to his van.

Tish climbed the steps to the porch, wondering once again if she'd hidden her valuables well enough.

George was exiting the Shell station with a pizza box warming his hands when a monster-sized SUV pulled into the parking space directly in front of him. Stu Hamilton climbed out, looking half-asleep as usual, and his two boys scrambled out of the back. George could never keep their names straight, but he'd sized up their dispositions. They weren't bad kids, just typical daredevil sons of the South whose tolerant parents used the old "boys will be boys" excuse to cover a multitude of mischief.

It was hard to believe that Stu had kids approximately the same age he and George were when they tackled their first business. A lemonade stand. Stu had made the signs, George had handled the money, and they'd conned his mother into providing the lemonade at almost no charge. It was his introduction to the buzz of making a huge profit and had probably set him on the road to majoring in business.

"Evening, Stu," George said. "How's everything going?"

"If I said everything was fantastic, I'd be lying." Stu offered a weary smile. "We're staying at my folks' house while our kitchen's torn up for remodeling. I thought it was fine the way it was, but I'm not the cook so my opinion doesn't count."

"Learn to cook, then. Problem solved."

"Too late now. Stop that," Stu told the younger boy, who was kicking white pebbles out of the landscaping strip and into the darkness on the side of the building.

"Yes sir." The kid hopped backward and collided with the older boy, who shoved him off in a fairly civilized manner.

George glanced at the van, parked a few spaces down from where he stood. Daisy paddled her front paws against the passenger window while she whimpered and carried on. Two more minutes of abandonment, and she'd be in hysterics.

"So Mel's back in town," George said. "You must have been glad to see her."

"Actually, I haven't—"

The older boy went airborne. "Dad!" he shouted. "You didn't tell me! Aunt Mel's so much fun. You gotta call her. I know her number." He rattled off a phone number.

"Impressive memory," George said with a smile.

"But the number's no good," Stu said. "Sorry, Nick."

The kid frowned up at him. "Why is it no good?"

"Your grandpa stopped paying her bills when she moved out."

"Maybe she has a new number. We need to find her."

"No we don't," Stu said. "She's a bad influence."

"Huh? No, she's not. She's great, Dad. I like her."

"That's the problem," Stu said in a dry tone. "If she wants to mess up her life, that's her decision, but I don't intend to let her affect yours. Jamie, stop that." He grabbed the younger boy's shoulders and propelled him away from the landscaping pebbles again.

"No fair," the older boy said. "So she messed up. Everybody does sometimes."

"And it's my responsibility to protect you from messed-up people." Stu pointed to the entrance. "Get moving, boys. We'll talk about it at home. Nice seeing you, George."

"You too. See you around." George continued down the sidewalk and climbed into the van. Daisy flung herself at him, doing the dog version of heartbroken sobs, and nearly knocked the pizza box out of his hands.

"Stop that and sit down," he said, suddenly reminded of Stu trying to keep his boys in line.

She wept, she whined, she pawed his arm.

He pointed at the floor. "Sit!"

She dived for the floor and sat, trembling.

"Aw, Daisy. It's okay. Good girl."

He placed the pizza on the passenger seat. By the time he'd dug his keys out of his pocket, Daisy had jumped up beside the pizza. At least she was sitting next to it, not on it.

All the way to Calv's place, he tried to process the inner workings of the Hamilton clan. Nick must have been about eight when Dunc kicked Mel out of the family on the heels of those accusations of theft. Now it seemed she was unwelcome at Stu's place too. No doubt about it, he was right to protect his sons from the influence of their bad-news aunt, but it wouldn't kill him to reach out to her. Stu was in no danger of being corrupted by his kid sister.

George sighed. Other folks' problems weren't his to solve. Still, he hated to see Mel's family treat her like a pariah.

At the house Calv was renting, George parked at the street and climbed out with the pizza in one hand and the leash in the other.

"You have four good legs," he told Daisy. "Come on."

She cast him a resentful look and refused to budge.

There were a few advantages to having a cat-sized dog. He reached down and picked her up, one-handed, shut the door with his hip, and walked across the lawn to the front door, where he engaged in a great deal of juggling pizza and dog in order to manage the doorknob.

He walked in. "Pizza's here."

"About time." Calv messed with the remote, no doubt trying to find his Friday night favorite.

"You keeping track of the hours you're working on the car?"

Calv turned toward him. "You bet I am, and it's gonna cost you."

"If you weren't the best shade-tree mechanic in three counties—"

"Four. And as I am also your esteemed uncle, you'd better treat me right."

"Yes sir." George smiled, seeing his mother in her brother's eyes. It was good to see him still sober and happy after all these years, proving that her pessimism had been misguided. "Sure is nice to work in that garage again," he added.

"Work? I didn't notice you working, Zorbas. I noticed you taking pictures and flirting with Miss McComb."

"I was not flirting."

"Could've fooled me," Calv said, grinning.

George decided to ignore him.

After turning the dog loose, he set the pizza box on a newspaper Calv had placed in the center of the coffee table alongside chilled Coke cans, paper plates, and napkins. His idea of fine dining was to keep the grease off the furniture.

"I saw Stu and his boys at the Shell station," George said, popping the top of a Coke.

"Yeah?" Calv found his station, but it was a commercial so he muted the TV. He opened the pizza box, put a gigantic slice on each plate, and handed one to George.

The folks at the gas station advertised it as Greek pizza because they topped it with feta, purple onions, and ordinary black olives. They'd probably never heard of Kalamata olives. George took a bite. As usual, it wasn't bad. But it wasn't Greek. He was beginning to educate himself about such things.

"Stu knows Mel's in town," he said.

Calv scratched his chin. "And?"

"That's all. His son was more interested in Mel than he was."

"Somebody needs to get his attention, then."

Whenever Calv said *somebody* in that particular tone, he meant the person he was addressing.

George brooded over the problem for a while, and then tried to put it out of his mind. It would come back to haunt him, probably in the middle of the night.

Daisy sighed deeply. Showing no interest in the pizza, she curled herself in a ball at his feet.

"If she's not begging, something's bad wrong," Calv said.

George nodded. Calv's comment wasn't proper English, but it was accurate. "She must have helped herself to somebody's trash tonight when Mel was supposed to be watching her. Hey, I wonder if the new and improved version of a McComb would like to adopt Daisy."

Calv frowned. "You'd give your dog away?"

"Daisy isn't my dog."

"After two years?" Calv shook his head slowly, putting a world of condemnation into it. "She's your dog. Stop fighting it."

"No. If a man's going to have a dog, it should be useful somehow. What's Daisy good for besides fattening the vet's wallet? Every time I take her in, it's another hundred bucks."

"You got a cash register where most folks have a heart."

"And it serves me well."

"Okay, Moneybags." Calv handed over the parts catalog with a pizza coupon serving as a bookmark. "Call the 800 number and order the parts I circled. They'll get here pretty fast. Meanwhile, there's plenty to work on. Plenty." He shook his head. "But I hope Mel won't hang around every night. She makes me nervous."

"Relax. A girl wouldn't steal car parts."

"But Mel's not like most girls," Calv said. "She's more like, you know, what's-'er-name. The NASCAR girl."

"Danica Patrick?"

"Yeah. But Danica wouldn't steal. She don't need to." Calv frowned. "You think Mel meant what she said about her dad?"

"That he's not her dad anymore? Sure, she meant it. One thing about Mel, she's honest."

The absurdity of the statement hit him and he started laughing. Calv joined in, hooting so loudly that Daisy woke with a jerk and hid behind the couch.

When the creepy guy slowed for a red light, Mel opened her door and jumped out with her bedroll. The truck roared after her, its horn blaring, and chased her into a ditch full of alligators—

Gulping for air, she sat up. Just a nightmare. A nightmare. She couldn't place where she was, though. Couldn't remember—

An angel-shaped night-light shone by the door. Now she remembered.

She was staying with Tish. In the McComb house.

There hadn't been any alligators. Just muddy water and trash. And the guy hadn't chased her. He'd yelled and hit the horn, but she was already running away in the opposite direction. She never saw him again.

She never saw her duffel bag again either, but her real treasures were safe.

Her heart wouldn't stop pounding. Still, a nightmare was better than the panic attacks when she lay there and felt all alone in a universe she'd never asked to be born into. The ceiling would get closer and closer, like it might fall and smash her. After a couple of minutes of that, her chest always felt crushed and she had to run outside where she could breathe.

She was glad to be on the ground floor. Whenever she needed to slip outside in the middle of the night, she didn't wake Tish.

Mel pulled socks on, opened her door, and walked into the kitchen. The clock on the microwave said it was…nearly five. It didn't feel like morning, though.

After finding the gray hoodie where she'd hung it on the back of the couch, she put it on and unlocked the front door. "Brrr," she whispered.

She'd be warm enough, though, in her new flannel pajamas. Grammy jammies. A couple of years ago, she would have thought they looked stupid. Now she loved them just because they were pajamas. She would never sleep in her clothes again, as long as she lived. Clothes weren't for sleeping in.

She moved quietly across the porch and settled into one of the wicker chairs. It held a nighttime chill that spread all through her, making her wish she'd brought a blanket. And her cigarettes. She had to hoard them, though. Once she finished the pack, she would quit for good. She wanted her hair to smell nice, not nasty, next time she ran into Darren. If she ever had any money, she'd put it toward clothes, not smokes.

The sky was clear, sparkling with stars. Stormy weather was more fun, though. More interesting. She'd always loved to sit in the sunroom with the windows open when a big storm was rolling in. The wind would rush through the pecan tree in the backyard first, then flatten the grass and whip toward the house. She'd breathe deeply, so deeply that she felt like she was eating and drinking the air instead of inhaling it.

"You're not safe there in a thunderstorm, not really," her mom always said. "Not with the windows open." She would stand there and frown at the windows, but she never closed them. Maybe she'd been hungry for the excitement of the storms too, but she could never admit it.

Poor old Mom, trapped in a boring life. She kept her days cluttered up with busywork. She was always redecorating a room or sewing new curtains or trying another fancy recipe, but nobody appreciated any of it. Well, maybe Nicky and Jamie appreciated the homemade cookies anyway, if they weren't too fancy.

The sky was a little less black now, the stars fading. A few birds chirped in the trees. Mel stood, rubbing her cold arms with her hands. If she didn't get back to bed now, before hundreds of birds woke up and started their racket, she'd never go back to sleep.

Her gaze drifted to the driveway and the little old Volvo that showed up as a blob of white in the dark. When they got back from Target, Tish had locked it as carefully as if it were some expensive car.

Grandpa John's Corvette wasn't just locked. It was locked up tight. A prisoner. As trapped as Mom. Mel would rather fight off a thousand creeps than be trapped like that.

She went inside, careful not to make noise so Tish wouldn't know she'd been sitting on the porch in her pajamas in the middle of the night. Tish was funny about things like that. She was the proper type.

Sixteen

The open window helped, but the nasty fumes still made Mel cough and gag. She scooted backward into the hall, but the air there wasn't much better.

"Mel," Tish called from somewhere, "are you still scrubbing the grout?"

She stifled a cough. "Yes."

"Stop it right now." Tish came around the corner with a dustpan in her hand. "I appreciate all your hard work, but give yourself a break. It can't be good for your lungs."

Mel sat back on her haunches. "No, it's okay. I mean, this was the deal, right? I can't stay if I don't work."

"But you don't have to work all afternoon. It's a beautiful day. A Saturday." She laughed. "I guess that doesn't matter to two people who don't have jobs. Anyway, go take a walk or something. You're the girl who loves to be outside, right? The fresh-air kid."

"Right."

Tish smiled at her. "Shoo, then." She walked away, humming.

With a sigh, Mel pulled off her yellow rubber gloves and dropped them on the counter. She'd get back to the job in a few minutes. She didn't want to leave it half-done.

She washed her hands and checked her reflection in the mirror. She looked awful. Bags under her watery eyes. No makeup. Her long brown hair with its scraggly ends. Thrift-store clothes. She stuck out her tongue at herself and walked out to the porch, where she took a big breath to clear her lungs.

It was weird to be sent outside like a little kid. Shoo, go outside…and do what? Play hopscotch? It was like being grounded, in reverse. At least she had a house to go back to, which beat walking around for hours and waiting for night to fall just so she could find an unlocked car to sleep in.

She headed down the sidewalk, farther into the neighborhood instead of toward Main, where she might run into somebody she knew. A few houses down the block, she heard a vehicle coming up behind her. Slowing down.

She looked over her shoulder. A white car with a bar of lights on the roof. A cop.

She hoped it wasn't Darren, when she looked and smelled gross, but then she hoped it was him. Everything about cops made her feel mixed up. She hated them and loved them. They could throw a girl in jail, but they could help her find her way home too.

Right now, her feet seemed to be glued to the sidewalk. She couldn't move, just stood there staring as the driver's window slid down. It *was* Darren. His eyes were that gorgeous baby blue, and his mouth had a delicious curve to it.

"Hey, Mel."

"Hey, Darren." She gave him a quick glance, then pretended there was something interesting down the street a ways.

"You get around, don't you?" His voice was so soft and sexy that she had to look again.

"What do you mean?" she asked.

"Sometimes you hang out at the park. Sometimes you walk around residential neighborhoods."

Her insides went chilly. He'd been watching her, but not like a guy watching a girl he liked. He'd been watching her like a cop because she was a suspicious person.

"I live on this street now." She pointed behind her. "See the big house with the white car in the driveway? That's where I live. My friend owns it."

"I see," he said slowly.

"I'm not shacking up with some guy. My friend's name is Letitia. The one who was, um, at the gazebo with me. She's cool."

Darren nodded. "What else have you been up to? Going to college?"

"I was working in Florida for a while," she said with a shrug. "I've been around a little." Then, realizing what she'd said, she quickly added, "Not in a bad way."

"I know." He smiled, giving her hope, but then his radio crackled. "Gotta go," he said.

It was her last chance to flirt with him. "Yeah, you have places to go. People to bust." Then she groaned inside. She couldn't have picked anything stupider to say.

"Don't be one of 'em," he said. "See you around, kid."

Kid? She wanted to argue that she was a grown woman, but he was already pulling away so she gave him a quick wave and started walking. Her face burned.

If he was watching in his rearview mirror, he didn't see Melanie Hamilton who loved him. He saw Mel the little kid. Or Mel the delinquent. Definitely Mel the freak who smelled like bathroom cleaner. And Mel the idiot who didn't know how to talk to a guy.

She should have asked him how he'd liked the police academy, or where he was living now, or how his brother was doing. She should have said anything but what she'd said.

Okay, so she had to learn how to talk to guys. She had to buy clothes and makeup and get her hair done. But that meant she had to get a job, and nobody would hire her when she looked like a homeless person and everybody thought she was a thief.

༺ৎৎৎ༻

Tish ate alone at the kitchen table, eyeing some of the cleaning projects she hadn't tackled yet: dusty light fixtures, scuffed woodwork, the stove's greasy knobs. In Nathan and Letitia's day, most people had housekeepers to do the dirty work, but Tish only had Mel. Now it seemed she'd gone on a hunger strike.

Finished eating, Tish stopped in the hallway near the guest room and listened. Again, she thought she heard sniffles.

She knocked gently. "Mel? You okay?"

"I'm fine," said a muffled and miserable voice from behind the door.

"There's food still on the table for you. Do you want to eat?"

"No. Thank you."

"Okay. I'll put it in the fridge. If you get hungry, let me know. Or help yourself to the leftovers."

Mel didn't answer.

About to walk away, Tish smelled cigarette smoke. She sniffed to make sure. It was faint but unmistakable. "Mel? Are you smoking in there?"

"What?"

"Are you smoking?"

There was a short silence. "Sorry."

"No smoking in the house, ever. Put it out."

"Yes ma'am."

"I didn't buy this house just so you can set it on fire." Tish couldn't believe her ears. When had she started to sound like a mother?

"Why are you so in love with this stupid old house? Don't you care about me? And my lungs? No, you only want me to stop smoking so I won't set your stupid house on fire!"

Well, maybe *that* was why Tish had fallen into the maternal role. Mel sounded like a spoiled teenager who claimed to be mistreated by her parents. Tish put her hands on her hips so she wouldn't be tempted to yank the door open and say what she was really thinking. "You know the vacant lot next door? The house that used to be there burned down. I don't want my house to burn down, especially with somebody in it. You or me or anybody else."

Mel snorted and said something Tish didn't catch. Maybe that was a blessing.

"This old house could go up in flames in no time, Melanie. There is to be absolutely no smoking in the house." Again, the mother. "Do you understand?"

"Yes!" the girl screamed. "I'm so sorry I'm not perfect like you!"

Clenching her hands into fists, Tish shut her eyes and took a deep breath. She probably shouldn't have taken in the girl in the first place, but now she couldn't see kicking her out.

"Melanie," Tish said, making her voice even, "don't speak to me that way again."

Tempted to say much more, she walked away and grabbed a sweater. She had to get out of the house before she strangled somebody.

She ran out the back door and through the backyard. When she neared the garage, the soft music calmed her a bit. She stepped out of the twilight and into the brightness where the boom box rested on the cement floor. Calv sat on a tall stool holding a screwdriver in one grimy hand and a small metallic item in the other. He looked up, tossing his hair out of his eyes, and smiled.

"Hey there, Miss Tish."

She smiled back, feeling as if she'd swum out of a stormy ocean and into a deep pond of peace where she could float for a while. "Hi, Calv. Where's George?"

"He ran over to the auto-parts store in Muldro." Calv lost his grip on the tiny metal part, and it bounced off his bony knee and onto the cement. "Oh, foot. Where'd that thing go?" He climbed off the stool. After a leisurely hunt, he retrieved the part and climbed onto the stool again. "Would've roont my whole night if I'd lost that little doohickey."

Roont. It took Tish a second to translate. Ruined.

"Where's the dog?" she asked. "With George?"

"Yes ma'am. She ain't my problem—she's his." Calv laughed. "Poor George. His mama adopted one itty-bitty dog after another. Sometimes two or three at the same time. Maltese, all of 'em. One would die, and she'd bring another one home. Daisy was the only one left when Rue passed away, but she was barely out of the puppy stage. The week after the funeral, I caught him online looking up the life expectancy for a Maltese."

Tish stifled a laugh. "He wants Daisy to die?"

Calv shrugged. "He treats her right. He just don't love her."

"I'll bet she knows it too. Poor baby."

"You're too soft-hearted to be a McComb."

"I'm a few generations removed from Nathan and Letitia, you know."

"Good thing too. I had a great-aunt who was a little girl when the stories were fresh."

Tish propped one elbow on a massive red toolbox very similar to the one her dad had hauled all over Michigan. "Well…are you going to share them with me?"

"Sure, but they're not pretty." Calv bent over his project and lowered his voice. "My great-aunt used to say Letitia kicked kittens and slapped other folks' children and wasn't too particular about the bonds of holy matrimony."

Tish sighed. "Right. Unchaste and unkind. Forever sharing the infamy and dishonor, et cetera."

"Say what?"

"That was in an old book George let me borrow. It also said the house is a vile monument to Nathan's greed."

"I guess it is, but no monument can stand forever."

"Especially if somebody burns it down," Tish said.

"Excuse me?"

"I just caught Mel smoking in her room."

"Ah."

"I have a smoke detector right in the hallway. I don't know why it didn't go off."

"There are ways, and I know 'em all. I know all about bad habits too. Mine almost earned me an early grave. Miss Mel's a smart girl, though. She might turn around before she goes too far down that road."

"I hope you're right. Do you think George might hire her at the shop? Just to give her a chance?"

Calv shook his head. "He's got about enough business to keep one person busy, most of the time. I help out sometimes, but he don't need me. Not really."

"Okay. Just thought I'd ask." Tish frowned. "This is nosy, but how can George afford a project car like this if he doesn't have more business than that?"

"He's a smart boy, ol' George. He makes his real money online, buying and selling. He started that years ago, before most people figured out how."

"I see." Why had she asked that? It was none of her business.

"And if I could just teach him how to text, he'd make more money still," Calv added with a grin.

Tish had no idea what he meant. "Well, I'd better make sure Mel isn't setting the monument on fire."

"Yeah, and if you've got any silver spoons, you might want to count 'em." Calv gave her a sad smile, softened with a wink.

He was a nice old guy. Kindhearted. Like George, he seemed to like Mel but didn't trust her any more than Tish did.

Walking back through the chilly night, she wondered if there was even one person in Noble who trusted Mel.

George exited the parts store approximately fifty dollars poorer than when he'd walked in, but he wasn't complaining. At least they'd had the necessary tools and cleaning agents in stock.

About to run for the van to rescue Daisy from the terror of five minutes of solitude, he stopped to wait for a disreputable-looking pickup truck to pass. Si Nelson was in the driver's seat, his scrub-brush hair wilder than ever. He must have sold his nice silver truck. This one was a downgrade in size and age, and he wasn't keeping it clean. It worried George a little. Not just that Si's prosperity had vanished, but that his spunk was gone too.

The truck slowed to a crawl, its ticking engine a clue to its ill health. Si lowered his window. "George," he said with a deep sigh.

It was appropriate, George decided, for a man who sighed so often and so theatrically to call himself Si.

"Hey," George said. "How goes it?"

"Not good. I'm here to buy a fuel pump for the wife's car."

"Ouch."

"Yeah." Si studied the bag in George's hand. "I guess you're buying parts for your fun car. Must be nice to have money to spend on frivolity like that."

George wanted to argue that he'd earned every penny he spent, and the Chevelle could be seen as an investment anyway, but arguing Si out of his opinions was like trying to talk a tiger out of his stripes.

"It's not a rich man's car," George said. "It's a 'Velle, not a 'Vette."

"You're a durned sight richer than I am now. So's that McComb woman. That crook."

"Come on, now. She didn't hold a gun to your head to make you accept the offer."

"She might as well have. I was barely awake. She's a thief."

"Jesus welcomed at least one thief into paradise, you know."

Si pointed his forefinger toward George. "Only because that one repented." He hit the gas. The truck lurched forward.

"You have a nice evening too," George told the truck's taillights.

Approaching the van, he frowned. Daisy wasn't hurling herself against the windows or making her ungodly and undogly howls and moans. Hope stirred in his heart. Maybe some idiot had swiped her.

No. There she was, delicately sneaking cold fries from the container he'd left on the console.

He yanked the door open. She dived for the floor, her tail between her legs, and peered up at him with guilt-stricken eyes.

"Bad dog," he scolded, climbing in.

She whimpered and flattened herself on the floor.

George let out a sigh as dramatic as one of Si's and patted the seat. "Come. Sit."

She obeyed, all happiness and gratitude, and kissed his hand.

Wiping his hand on his jeans, George decided that if dogs went to heaven—which was doubtful—Daisy would fit right in.

Seventeen

*A*s far as Tish could tell, Mel hadn't ventured out of her bedroom all evening. The good news, though, was that when Tish came in after her visit with Calv, she didn't smell fresh cigarette smoke.

After tidying up the kitchen and locking the front door, she was about to head for bed when her phone rang. It was her mother. "I found your dad's box of family papers," she said. "I'm looking through it right now. You wouldn't believe what a mess it is."

"Oh yes I would."

"Genealogy charts, copies of deeds, and marriage licenses. A few old photos. Oh, here's a copy of somebody's will. Somebody named…I can't make it out. Anyway, it's from both sides of your dad's family. You do want it all, don't you?"

"Yes, but there's no rush. Can you bring it when you come for a visit?" As soon as she'd said it, she remembered the guest room was occupied.

"Sure," Mom said against a backdrop of rustling noises. "Let me just dig to the bottom of the box and see if there's anything besides genealogy junk in here. Oh, here's a book. Hmm, looks like it's about the town's history."

Tish froze. "Which town?"

Her mom chuckled. "Oh, what a title. It's called *The Proud History of Noble, Alabama, as told by—*"

"Dad had his own copy and never told me? He knew about the McCombs?"

"Knew what?"

"Turn to the fourth chapter, Mom. Take it with a grain of salt, but read the first page or so." Silence ensued while Tish paced the living room with the phone to her ear and Calv's remarks about his great-aunt's stories playing through her mind like a recording.

"Letitia kicked kittens…" Tish managed to shut it off before it reached the worst part.

"Oh my," her mother said at last. "Nathan McComb was a liar and a blaggard?"

"You don't have to read it to me," Tish said. "I've practically memorized it."

"Why? How?"

"It's pretty wild. There's a guy here, George, an antiques dealer, who let me borrow his copy of the same book. Dad must have bought one when we made that trip down here."

"I see…I guess."

Reality was sinking in fast, and Tish didn't like it. "Mom, this is strange. It means Dad knew the dirt on the McCombs but kept it to himself."

"Well, no wonder! Listen. *Letitia McComb, that most unchaste and unkind—*"

"Please stop. But now I know why Dad wrapped up our visit to Noble in such a hurry. It was after we'd hit the used-book store. He must have read that section, and that's why he switched his focus to his mother's side of the family."

"Honey, my head is spinning. You mean you've known about it for a while?"

"No, I haven't known long at all. I can't believe *he* knew. Dad used to laugh at people who scrubbed their family histories to make them look respectable, remember? But that's what *he* did!"

Her mother clicked her tongue. "Your Grandpa McComb's family stories weren't exactly accurate, then. Or the book isn't."

"That's what I'd like to think. It isn't an academic work. It's just a collection of local stories without any references to back them up. I know what I need to do, Mom. I need to unpack the McComb letters and see if they show another side to the story."

"No, sweetheart. You need to forget ancient family history and make some new friends."

"It's not that ancient, and I *am* making some new friends. I just want to settle this once and for all. I know where the letters are too." Tish hurried into the dining room where several moving boxes still sat, unopened. "There. I found them already. Gotta go, Mom. Thanks for calling."

Hardly hearing her mother's good-bye, Tish found a pair of scissors and used them to cut the strapping tape on the box labeled *Letters, perc, gloves.* It was one of the hodgepodge boxes that she'd packed when she was running out of boxes and time. She was only being practical, tucking items in wherever they fit, but anyone who'd seen the box would have thought she was as disorganized as her father. He wouldn't have seen anything wrong with packing gloves, old letters, and a vintage electric percolator in the same box.

She lifted the box's flaps. The manila envelope lay on top, supported by a layer of thick cardboard, with her mother's red scarf and gloves snuggled into a corner beside it. They might come in handy during northern Alabama's brief, mild winter. Even if Tish never used them, they were a reminder of the gloves she'd always found in her Christmas stocking. Those childhood gloves were never high quality. They weren't even especially warm, but they'd added color to gray days, like colorizing a black-and-white photo.

Tish decided to pull out the percolator too, so she'd have one more box emptied. She reached into the nest of papers and unwrapped the percolator, enjoying its shiny belly and the exuberant scrolls and folderols of its curvy handle. Its chrome finish had stayed as clean and beautiful as it had been when it was brand new in 1940 or so, only seventy-five years after the Civil War had ended. The percolator still worked perfectly too, but it wasn't practical for fewer than a dozen people.

Tish sighed. She wasn't sure she could round up even a dozen friends in Noble.

She placed the percolator on the sideboard she'd bought at a yard sale years ago. Then she stashed the scarf and gloves in her rattan étagère before reaching for the manila envelope. She held it flat in her palms like a little boy carrying a ring-bearer's pillow and made her way up the stairs to her office, where her scanner waited. She would stay up for hours if she had to, scanning the letters and searching them for clues to the past.

It had been at least half an hour since Mel had heard water running in the upstairs bathroom, and she hadn't heard the computer chair rolling around after that. Tish was probably in bed by now, so it was safe to come out. About time too. Mel was so hungry she hardly cared if Tish popped out of hiding and wanted to know what was going on.

Not that Mel had done anything wrong. She hadn't. But if she had to explain, she would cry.

She tiptoed to the door and turned the knob slowly, slowly, trying to take the noise out of the clicking of the latch. Not too bad. But then the hinges creaked like crazy.

She held her breath for a long time and then started breathing again. She opened the door the rest of the way and tiptoed into the hall. All the lights were out so she walked into the living room.

Out of nowhere, it hit her again. Darren had looked at her like she was a criminal, not a woman to fall in love with. He'd called her "kid" like he was the grown-up and she wasn't. He thought she was too young and stupid and criminal for him.

She had to stop thinking about it. Maybe after she'd had something to eat.

She walked quietly into the kitchen. The fridge was a paradise of food, but she had to find something she didn't have to nuke. The *ding-ding-ding* of the microwave might wake Tish.

Settling on yogurt, a banana, an orange, a PBJ sandwich, chocolate milk, and cookies, Mel carried everything back to the bedroom. It took two trips, scurrying around in the night like a sneaky little mouse. Sitting cross-legged on the bed, she ate every bite.

"Thanks, Tish," Mel whispered, raising the last of the milk in a toast. "You're awesome. And I'm really sorry about smoking in my room. And screaming at you and everything."

Someday, she would get better about apologizing out loud.

She stuffed the fruit peelings into the yogurt cup, tiptoed back to the kitchen, and put everything in the trash. After rinsing her glass and leaving it in the sink, she walked into the bathroom.

It was the coolest bathroom ever, with a claw-foot tub and a medicine cabinet that looked about a hundred years old. It was also cool because all the toiletries from Target reminded her again how awesome Tish was. She'd bought them without squawking about the cost.

Mel pressed her lips together, hard, so she wouldn't cry. Nobody had ever been that sweet to her before. Nobody but Grandpa John.

He might not approve of her crazy plan.

He would like Darren, though. Darren was what Grandpa John would call a stand-up guy. But a stand-up guy wouldn't fall in love with the girl who'd been walking down the sidewalk in thrift-store clothes, who'd been camping out at the park. He'd been sweet to her, but his eyes had been missing the spark that said he was interested even if she wasn't exactly a model citizen.

Next time she ran into him, she had to look good. She'd been working on her plan to get some of her own clothes back. Except for some details, she nearly had it worked out.

"Mirror, mirror, on the wall," she whispered, "help me do this."

Closing her eyes, she tried to get into her mom's skin. Into her mom's head. Her way of thinking, her way of moving. Even her way of breathing fast and shallow because she was on edge, all the time.

Mel opened her eyes and threw herself into the role. The way Mom always tilted her head when she wanted to ask a favor. The way she smiled, her eyes so big and innocent that you could almost forget the way she treated you sometimes.

"Hey, baby, it's me," she said softly. "Be a sweetheart and do me a favor."

Mel shook her head. That was all wrong. It was too whispery.

She cleared her throat and tried again, putting some volume into it. "Hey, baby."

Now she was too loud. She couldn't risk waking Tish.

But she'd never get it right if she couldn't say it out loud. She'd have to wait until she was home alone, or she'd have to go somewhere private to practice, but then she'd need an excuse for being gone.

She wished Tish would find a job in a hurry so she wouldn't always be hanging around the house.

No, that was wrong. Mel made a face at her reflection in the wavy old mirror. She was the one who needed a job, ASAP. She couldn't keep mooching.

But she didn't even have transportation. She'd be limited to jobs within walking distance—in Noble, where everybody knew her and nobody trusted her.

"Help me figure it out, Grandpa John," she whispered.

This time, she couldn't imagine his answer floating down from heaven. He was too far away. She was on her own.

Eighteen

$\mathcal{S}$eated cross-legged on the garage floor and petting Daisy, Mel looked up at Calv, who was leaning over the Chevelle's engine. "Where's George?"

"At church."

"Why aren't you at church?"

He looked over his shoulder at her. "Why aren't you?"

She shrugged. "I'm not a churchy kind of person."

She'd started the morning with a fierce headache from her crying jag, but it might turn out to be a pretty good day if she could find a private place to nail down the details of her plan. The house was no good because Tish was there, doing something on her computer upstairs, and the garage was no good because Calv was there. He was fun to hang out with, though. Mel wasn't exactly trying to avoid Tish, but things had been a little weird ever since that screaming match.

"Now we're gettin' somewhere," Calv muttered at something under the hood.

"Why did George buy this car? It's an old-person kind of vehicle."

Calv let out a hoot that made Daisy twitch her ears. "Don't tell him that. He's already mighty sensitive about his greatly advanced age."

"Yeah, I know he's really old, but why does he like this kind of car?"

"It's probably about the money. He buys things he knows he can sell at a good profit."

"I don't think so. I mean, I know that's what he usually does, but I think he's like in love with this car even if it's all out of date and stupid looking."

"Out of date? Stupid looking?" Calv faked a stern look, but she could tell he was about to bust out laughing. "This car's a classic, and it ain't stupid."

Yes it was, compared to the Corvette's pale blue paint and shiny chrome, not to mention the way it could move. She shut her eyes and tried to bring back one of those Sunday drives. Her hands on the wheel, her foot on the gas. Her grandpa in the passenger seat, laughing his head off and calling her Melanie Andretti. Once he'd explained who the Andrettis were, she'd thought it was a pretty cool compliment.

"Remember," Calv said, "don't say nothin' bad about the car when ol' George is around. You don't like it, you don't have to talk about it."

She nodded. She didn't want to hurt George's feelings. "The car's okay, really. I bet it's fast."

"You have no idea, young lady." Calv frowned at her. "But you'd better not get any notions about taking an unauthorized test drive."

"Don't worry. I don't have any designs on it." Somebody might, though, and it would be safer in a garage with no windows, like her dad's. "Matter of fact, I have an idea for keeping it safe."

"What's that?"

"Cover the windows," she said. "The garage windows, I mean. Tape newspaper over them or something."

Calv looked back and forth from the windows on one wall to the windows on the other. "Why? I like the light."

"But car thieves could look in and see the car and want it. That's what I think."

"You think funny, sometimes. Nobody's gonna poke around back here. It's too far from the street, and there are all those trees and bushes between. I bet half the folks in town don't know this garage is even here."

"That's good." Daisy was tangled up in her leash, so Mel untangled her and gave her a hug. "It's awful to lose something that means a lot to you."

"Careful with Houdini there," Calv said. "She'll run off if you give her half a chance."

"No, she only runs away from other places. Once she's here, at this house, it's where she wants to stay." Mel pulled Daisy into her lap. "Do you think it's because she lived here when she was a puppy?"

"Maybe, but I'm no expert on dogs. I don't even like dogs, especially when they have issues."

Mel leaned over Daisy, cuddling her. "I know," she whispered in the dog's ear. "Nobody likes me either. Because I have issues."

Daisy let out a happy whimper and relaxed, like she'd decided to stay in Mel's lap forever. Ruffling the curly white fur with her fingers, Mel looked around the garage. It was way bigger than most garages, but really old. More like a barn than a garage, it didn't have a security system.

A barn! Mel held her breath, happy with her new idea. The barn she and Hayley had explored years ago when they were looking for a new hangout. It was out past the old vacant bank, on the outskirts of town.

She stood up, holding Daisy. "Can I take her for a walk? If she runs away, she'll head straight back here, so I can't lose her."

Calv laughed. "Sure, take her for a walk. I don't think George would mind. Keep a good grip on the leash, though."

"Okay. I'll take her down Main Street a ways. See you in a while."

Mel carried the dog all the way to the sidewalk and set her down. "Heel," she said, moving forward, but the leash went tight because Daisy wasn't moving.

"Come on, Daisy, let's go." She tugged at the leash. "Heel."

Daisy turned toward the house and gave a sad little moan, but she started walking in the right direction, her head low.

"Good dog! Good girl, Daisy. I'll carry you if you get tired."

Walking down the sidewalk, smelling spring in the air, Mel could almost pretend everything was going to be fine. She'd find a job somewhere, and she'd find a permanent place to live. Someday, she would have her own dog. It wasn't the kind of goal the school counselors had always harped on, but it seemed reasonable.

Reaching Main, Mel turned to the right. Away from downtown and toward that old barn. If it was still abandoned and if it wasn't falling down, it would be perfect.

Having showered and dressed, Tish checked the time and let out a sigh of relief. Too late to go to church. It was one thing to get the cold shoulder at the bank or the store, but she couldn't handle the idea of being excluded at church too, especially now that she'd seen some of Nathan and Letitia's good qualities revealed in the letters.

She sat at her computer desk to return the letters to the safety of their acid-free paper wrap. She was still groggy from her late night. It wasn't just physical tiredness; it was emotional exhaustion too. She'd scanned every letter into her computer and enlarged each one for easier reading, but there was something endearingly human about the originals, passed down to a generation that rarely corresponded with pen and ink. Tish couldn't recall the last time she'd written an actual letter, by hand. It was becoming a lost art.

Most of the letters had been written by Letitia to her mother, Ann Lattimore. A few were addressed to Letitia, from people Tish had never heard of, and then there was the love letter from Nathan to Letitia before their marriage.

He'd had a warm and tender way with words. The lines she'd written about him, decades later, had shown her affection for him too.

In spite of an age difference of nearly twenty years, Nathan and Letitia had remained devoted to each other—at least on paper—until the end of his life. They'd loved their children too. It was hard to reconcile that devotion with the account in the book, but Tish had to admit that it was possible for a man to be a cheat and a liar who happened to love his wife and children.

Gently, she picked up a fragile sheet of paper, a letter that Letitia had written shortly before she'd moved back to Ohio. *Dearest Mother, may God grant us grace to endure. I have grievous news again for...* The next word was smudged and paled by an irregular patch that looked suspiciously like a splash of water. A teardrop, maybe, spilled from Letitia's eyes as she wrote the words—or from her mother's eyes when she opened the letter in Ohio.

Tish placed a fingertip on the tiny water stain, wondering who had dried Letitia's tears once Nathan was gone. Her news had been grievous indeed. The rest of the letter gave the details. Only weeks after losing her husband, Letitia had lost her daughter too. Malaria.

If only the letters had also included some evidence to contradict what that old book presented as fact. But there were only twenty-three letters that spanned more than two decades, and none of them referred to the construction of the house. Or where and how Nathan had obtained the beautiful mantel and hearth.

Resigned to the fact that the story would always have large gaps, Tish placed all the letters in the manila envelope and slid it into her desk drawer.

After scanning the letters, she'd saved the files to her computer and e-mailed them to herself for safekeeping. Even if the house went up in smoke someday, she could retrieve the files from her e-mail account or from her online backup service. She could share them with other people too—not that she knew anyone who would be particularly interested.

She sat up straight, enlivened by a new idea. She could take copies of the letters to Marian at the bank so she could see Nathan and Letitia's devotion to each other and to their children. Whatever they'd done, the McCombs hadn't been monsters. The "unchaste" bit in Miss Eliza Clark's book might have been a big fat lie—and where there was one lie, there were usually others.

Sitting on the front steps, nearly finished with a cigarette, Mel wished she had a paying job. Smoking was an expensive habit, but it calmed her down. And she needed that right now since she was about to put her plan into action.

The abandoned barn had been perfect for her rehearsal. She'd loved the birds swooping in and out, and the soft smell of dried grass and the coziness of a secret hiding place. Daisy had been the perfect listener, perking her ears and making a hundred different expressions, which had to be hard to do with a fur-covered face.

But now it was time for Mel's real audience. She'd never prayed so much in her life. She wasn't exactly comfortable talking to God, but she sure couldn't share her plans with anybody else, and she figured He already knew anyway, so it wouldn't do any good to try to fake Him out.

He'd answered the first part of her prayer. Maybe He liked her plan. She had some time alone because George had gone somewhere after church, taking Daisy with him, and then Tish had gone off to run errands.

Mel had to act now, while Stu and Janice and the boys were still staying at the house. It would only work when Nicky was there.

Mel stood up. If she had some money, she'd buy a disposable cell phone. But she'd have to borrow one for a minute or two. Less, if the wrong person answered. If it wasn't Nicky, she would hang up.

She'd practiced until she'd nailed it, but even if he thought she was the real deal, what if he didn't know the code?

"Please, God, make it work," she whispered. "All I need now is a phone."

Everything else was perfect. Her ex-dad and Stu spent Sunday afternoons at the dealership doing paperwork, and her ex-mom always did her Sunday shopping thing at the mall. Maybe Janice went with her, dragging the boys along, or maybe they'd stayed home. Janice wouldn't pick up the phone, but if Nicky still pounced on it every time it rang…

But what if they didn't have the land line anymore?

Time to find out. Mel took one last drag on her cigarette and tossed the butt on the lawn. She smashed it with her shoe and kicked it under a bush.

She tilted her face toward the sky. "God, here goes. Make Calv help me. Please. Without knowing he's helping me. I mean, without knowing why. You know what I'm trying to say, God?"

She walked around the house and headed toward the garage, ever so slowly so she wouldn't look like she was up to something. Calv had pulled the Chevelle into the sunshine, and he was tinkering on the engine.

She strolled up to him, casual as could be. "Hey again, Calv."

"Hey again, Miss Mel."

"Still workin' on that thing? I thought it had a new engine."

"That don't necessarily mean it's fit to drive. George is bound and determined to take it to a car show in a few weeks. Halfway across Alabama." He leaned farther over the engine and tugged on a fat black hose.

"You're not going with him? To keep it running?"

"Nope. A good friend of mine is getting married in Pensacola that weekend, so that's where I'll be."

Mel wrinkled her nose at the idea of someone as old as Calv getting married. "Why do you have so much spare time? I mean, why don't you have a real job?"

"I'm what they call a shade-tree mechanic. I'm my own boss."

"Oh. That must be nice."

"It's not. I've had a hard time finding what you call 'a real job' because I used to abuse certain substances. I recommend that you avoid that path, Miss Mel. It's not a good one."

She frowned, trying to put it together. She knew he'd had a drinking problem when she was a little kid, but it didn't seem fair that he still couldn't get a real job when he'd been sober for so long.

"Yes sir," she said. "I'll remember that."

"See that you do. It wasn't just jobs that I lost," he said. "I lost my marriage, and I nearly lost my sister and my nephew. I loved them, but I loved my booze more until the good Lord got ahold of me."

Mel nodded and asked the good Lord to make Calv stop preaching. Just like that, he shut up. She smiled. She was halfway starting to believe that God heard her prayers.

She watched Calv work a little longer, then decided to go for it. "May I borrow your phone, please?"

He straightened up to squint at her. "Why?"

"Tish isn't home so I can't borrow hers. Come on, Calv. I only want to call my mom and dad's house." She didn't dare say "ex" to Calv.

"Well, all right then." He dug his phone out of his pocket and handed it to her.

"Thank you. Do you mind if I walk across the yard so I'll have a little privacy? Because I've hardly talked to her in a couple of years."

"Go ahead, but don't hog my phone too long. And don't go calling all your friends too."

"I'm only calling my folks' house. That's all. I promise." It was the absolute truth.

"All right, but can I tell you something first?"

"Sure." Her face felt hot. Afraid he was onto her, she stared at the grass and twisted one foot around and around in it.

"I don't like that you're tryin' to be sneaky," he said. "Sneaky sins are the worst."

Was that all? He must have smelled the smoke on her.

She met his eyes. "I'm not sneaking. Tish knows I smoke. She just won't let me smoke in the house, that's all."

Calv crinkled up his eyes like he was about to start laughing. "Well, if you gotta sin, sin boldly, but don't try to pull the wool over anybody's eyes. You understand?"

"I think so. God knows everything anyway, right? So we can't fool Him."

"Something like that, but I suspect we could both use a little more training in theological matters." He scratched his head. "When *did* you start smoking?"

She tried to remember. "I'm not sure. Sometime after Grandpa John died."

"Well, at least you spared him that." Calv went back to working on the car. "Get on with your call, now, and be sweet to your mama. I'd give you some better advice if I had any, but I don't."

"Yes sir. Thank you."

She walked all the way to the back steps, where she sat down and tried to think. She'd have to keep it short so she wouldn't have time to blow it. This wasn't another rehearsal. This was the real thing.

She played with the phone for a minute, remembering what it was like to be able to call or text any time. Someday, she'd have a phone again.

Then she said another prayer and made the call with shaky fingers. If they didn't have the land line anymore, all her practice was for nothing.

But the phone didn't make that annoying "this number is out of service" noise. It rang. And it rang again. And someone answered.

"Hello?"

It wasn't—yes it was. It was Nicky, but he sounded older now. She'd missed two years of his life.

Now she had stage fright again, like in kindergarten. She almost forgot her lines, but they came back to her just in time.

"Nicky? Do me a favor, baby." She breathed fast and shallow, keeping her voice soft. "Remind me of the security code."

He laughed the raspy little laugh that always made him sound like an evil genius. "Come on, Grandma. Are you serious? Why don't you ask Grandpa? Wait! If you're out there trying to get in, why don't you get out of your car and ring the doorbell?"

She was so stupid. Now he would look out the window, but his grandma's car wouldn't be in the driveway. And that was only one of the big holes in her plan.

She smiled, hoping a phony smile would help her stay in character. "It's easier to call you, sweetheart."

He let out a big, dramatic sigh. "Oh, all right. It's 3808."

"Oh, sure. Why can't I remember that?" Her brain was spinning with lame explanations. Now he would expect the garage door to go up. He would expect his grandma's car to pull in. She hadn't thought it through.

"Thanks, Nicky," she said. "You're a wonderful grandson."

"Yeah, I know I am." He snickered. "I'm a wonderful nephew too. Nice try, Aunt Mel, but I know it's you."

The gasp was halfway out her mouth before she could stop it. She held her breath and waited.

"As soon as you called me 'Nicky,' I knew," he said. "Grandma never calls me that anymore. She calls me Nick. Everybody does."

Mel let out her breath. "You brat. You were just playing me."

"You were playing *me*. What do you want?"

She could feel her heart beating fast. "Who's there? Is anybody listening?"

"No. Grandma's at the mall. Mom's online, looking at kitchen stuff. It's all she ever does. Dad and Grandpa are at work, and Jamie's doing tomorrow's homework."

"No way. Jamie's not old enough for homework."

"Yes he is. But what do you want?"

"Nicky—I mean Nick—I'm really sorry. I only wanted to trick you. I didn't want to drag you into it. But I'm not doing anything wrong, really. I just need to get my own stuff out of my own room."

"What kind of stuff?"

"Jeans and shirts. Shoes. That's all I want. Please don't tell them you gave me the code. They'll say I'm corrupting you. I don't want to corrupt you. I only want what's mine."

"You'd better not take much, then, or they'll notice."

"You're too smart for your own good."

That was what they'd always said about her, even when she was stupid in other ways, like tests and grades. But Nicky was nothing but smart.

"When are you gonna try it?" he asked.

"I can't tell you."

He giggled, sounding like the little kid she remembered. "I'll figure it out."

"Don't even try to. Please. I don't want you to be my—my accomplice. If I get in trouble, I deserve it. But you don't."

"I won't tell anybody." Now he sounded solemn. Older than ten. "I promise. Because I don't think they're treating you right."

"They're not." A lump rose in her throat. "If they won't help me, I'll have to help myself."

"Yeah. Good luck, Aunt Mel. I miss you."

"I miss you too. I love you, Nicky."

"Nick," he corrected. "Love you too. Mom's coming. Bye." He hung up.

Now that the code was stuck in her head, she wasn't sure she wanted to use it. If she never did, nobody would ever find out what she'd wanted to try, and Nicky wouldn't be her partner in crime.

But she only wanted her best jeans. Her favorite shirts. Was that too much to ask?

A metallic clanging came from the direction of the garage, reminding her that Calv would want his phone.

Walking slowly toward the garage, she decided to scrap her crazy plan. She just had to find a job and buy some new clothes. They'd have to be cheap, but at least they'd be new. Maybe they'd help Darren look at her the way he'd looked at her before she'd messed up her life.

Nineteen

Standing in Mel's doorway on Monday morning, Tish wondered how much to say about appropriate attire for job hunting. The girl didn't own anything but jeans.

"Want to borrow some clothes, Mel? They'd be a little big on you, though."

Mel smiled. "They'd be a lot big. No, I think this is fine. If I get all dressed up, I'll be even more nervous. It's better just to be myself."

"There's something to that. But if you don't land a job today, maybe we should try to find some clothes that are a little dressier but still comfortable."

"Yeah, maybe. I remember the counselors in high school were always harping about that."

"Did they give you any career guidance? Aptitude tests or anything?"

Mel nodded. "My top picks were like forest ranger and pet groomer. I forget the other ones. I don't want to go to college for anything anyway. I barely made it through high school."

"What made it so hard? Did you not apply yourself?"

"I sort of gave up when I figured out I couldn't compete with my brother. And I was never good at school anyway."

"How was there any competition? He's so much older, he's almost like a different generation."

"Yeah, but some of my teachers had been there forever and they remembered him. I'd walk into class on the first day of school and the teacher would say, 'Oh, you're Stuart's little sister so I'll expect big things from you.' A week later, she's saying, 'Are you sure you're Stu's sister? Did somebody swap babies at the hospital?' because I had so much trouble with the work. And no matter how hard I tried, I couldn't measure up."

"Sounds like those teachers needed some sensitivity training." Tish offered a smile that she hoped would soften things for Mel.

Mel let out a hard-edged laugh. "So did some of the kids. They were a bunch of bullies."

Tish was beginning to understand the chip Mel had on her shoulder. "It's no fun to be bullied. I remember. I was always the new kid in town."

"That might be better than being the same old kid. Never having a chance to start over."

"If you can find a job, though, there's your new chance. Do you have your driver's license handy in case somebody offers you a job? They might ask for your ID."

"I don't have one." Mel glanced at the bedroll in the corner. "I lost my wallet in Florida. It was in my duffel bag."

"Did you report it to the DMV?"

Mel shook her head. "Not yet. I've got more important stuff to think about right now." She smoothed a hand down the thigh of her jeans. "I'll start at the Shell station. My friend Hayley works there. Maybe she'll give me a reference. Recommendation. Whatever you call it."

"You might want to ask her before you go in."

"Yeah. But I have to go in anyway. To take her hoodie back. She let me borrow it when—when I didn't have a jacket anymore."

Tish smiled again. "That was kind of her."

"Yeah. She's a good friend. I'd better go. Do I look okay?"

"You look very nice."

"Anything stuck between my teeth?" Mel bared her teeth.

Tish shook her head. "Nothing. No bad breath either. No smell of ciga-rettes. You're all set."

Mel took a deep breath and squared her shoulders. "Then I'd better go."

Tish wanted to offer a ride, but that would set a precedent. And the gas station wasn't far. In Noble, nothing was far.

"Good luck," she said. "I'll be praying for you."

"Thanks," Mel said with a tight smile. "Sometimes God answers prayers. I think."

"He does."

Mel blinked rapidly, stared down at her feet, and looked up again. "Um, I'm really sorry about...you know. Smoking and yelling and stuff. Forgive me?"

"Sure, Mel. I kind of lost my temper too. Forgive me?"

"Yeah. We're good." Mel walked out of the room and out of the house, shutting the door gently.

Tish followed to the porch and watched Mel plod down the sidewalk. Now her shoulders sagged. Her head drooped. She seemed to have lost two inches of her already small stature, as if she'd shrunken down to her twelve-year-old self. Who on earth would hire her?

Tish whispered the promised prayer for Mel's success and then for her own plans. She intended to visit Muldro National Bank with a copy of the Mc-Comb letters for Marian Clark-Whoever.

On her way to change into nice clothes, Tish stopped at the piano and banged out "When the Saints Go Marching In," a song that always made her think of football games and victories.

⌒◯⌒

Somewhat hesitantly, Tish approached Marian's cubicle. It wouldn't be professional to interrupt her work, but dropping off the copies wouldn't take more than a minute of her time.

Marian sat at her desk, her fingers flying across a keyboard. "May I help you?" she murmured without quite looking up.

"Good morning," Tish said.

Marian lifted her head. "Oh, hello." Tiny lines of irritation made tight little parentheses around her lips, but her eye hadn't started twitching yet.

"I brought you something." Tish held out the envelope, nearly a twin to the one that held the originals in her desk drawer. "These are copies of letters, most of them written by Letitia McComb. I hope you'll read them and start to see her and Nathan…well, in a kinder light."

"I see." Marian took the envelope and set it on the corner of her desk. "Thank you, but please don't expect to change my opinion. I have proof that Nathan McComb was a thief and a liar."

Tish kept her tone calm. No need to make a scene. "Proof? Really?"

"Proof. From the county historical society. Copies of old deeds and so on. It's very clear that he never owned the Carlyle house. Everything was chaotic after the War, and he used it to his advantage. He stripped the house of a number of beautiful items that he wanted for himself while Mary Ellen Carlyle lay dying over in the next town—"

"Of consumption. Yes, unfortunately I've memorized those lines, but are you sure?"

"Quite sure, yes."

"I…I'm sorry to hear it." Tish hesitated, wanting a truce but not wanting to back down completely. "Before I read the book by Miss Eliza Clark, I had no idea there were any hard feelings between Clarks and McCombs."

"Now you know."

"I'm very sorry if my ancestors allegedly wronged your ancestors. I apologize on their behalf."

Marian gave her a prim smile. "I accept your apology, although I don't believe the words 'if' and 'allegedly' have a place in any apology."

Like a stab given with a honey-coated knife, it still hurt. Mel's apology was far more sincere.

Tish managed to refrain from speaking her mind. "Please read the letters, though, if only to understand some of the tragedies of Letitia's life."

Marian's attention seemed to stray toward her keyboard. "I hope you'll visit the historical society's museum sometime, so you'll understand some of the tragedies of the War and its aftermath."

As if Tish didn't understand! She was tempted to offer a condescending jab of her own, or a pointed remark about the tragedies created by people like the Carlyles, who'd treated "darkies" as if they weren't quite human. She needed a job, though, and women who threw fits in banks weren't likely to land jobs there.

She managed a tight smile. "You have a great day." She turned and hurried toward the exit, afraid she might kick the next living creature that crossed her path. But white-haired Mr. Farris began to stride across the lobby. Right toward her.

"Miss McComb," he said with an amiable grin.

She forced a smile, her heart still pounding with rage. "Hello, Mr. Farris. It's nice to see you again."

"It's nice to see you too." As nattily dressed as before, he motioned her toward his office. "Let's chat."

"Okay." In the back of her mind, she entertained the crazy notion that he was about to offer her a job—working with Marian? Well, a job was a job.

Seated in a cushy chair before his desk, she met his eyes. As angry as she was, she could still enjoy his resemblance to Ted Turner.

He cupped his chin in his hands and regarded her in silence for a long moment, then spoke abruptly. "I'm sorry, Miss McComb. I really did want to hire you, but things have changed."

"Did Marian tell you she has evidence that Nathan McComb was a thief?"

"Yes, but I don't care what your great-greats did. I care about what you do. In the here and now." He smiled faintly. "For that matter, just because you have something to prove, you may be more honest than the average bear. I have no problem believing that you're an upright individual."

"Well, that's good to hear. What's the problem, then?"

He leaned forward. "If I were, say, a farmer, I wouldn't be so concerned about this issue, but I run a bank. Integrity is my business. People put their money in my hands. Their life savings, their dreams. I can't betray their trust by hiring someone whose character may be called into question because of the company she keeps. In your case, it's Melanie Hamilton."

"Excuse me?" she faltered.

"She's staying with you, correct?"

Tish nodded numbly. "Yes."

"She's a hometown girl who went bad, then rubbed her parents' noses in it. To some folks, that makes her worse than outsiders. Worse than Yankees who don't know any better." His eyes twinkled. "I hope you know I don't believe that myself. Some of my best friends are Yankees."

Tish couldn't quite smile at that. "If you're trying to make me feel better, it's not working. But let's go back to what you said about the company I keep. Didn't Jesus sit down with sinners?"

"Absolutely—but my customers aren't Jesus."

"And Melanie Hamilton isn't the world's worst sinner."

"Not even close, but I know the people she stole from at local businesses. They're my friends and neighbors—and they bank here."

Tish let out a long breath. "So, I can either kick Mel out, or I can be her friend and keep looking for a job." She stood. "I'd better get busy."

He rose too, and offered his hand. "Your loyalty is commendable. I only wish you'd picked someone more worthy of your loyalty."

"I hope I'll be able to prove you wrong." She shook his hand. "Good-bye, and thanks for your time."

Refusing to look in Marian's direction, Tish walked out of his office and across the lobby. Imagining every eye in the place watching her, she held her head high and kept herself to a ladylike pace, although she wanted to run. At the exit, an elderly gentleman waited to hold the door open for her although he hardly looked strong enough.

Glad for an excuse to hurry, she ran the last few steps. "Thanks," she told him, wondering if he would have let the door slam shut on her if he'd realized who she was.

Halfway across the parking lot, she realized she shouldn't try to please the locals. They'd already made up their minds. She'd taken Mel in, so her reputation was tarnished already. Next time she ran into Marian or Farris, she might as well speak her mind.

She backed her car out of the parking space and pointed it toward the street. Light traffic streamed by, two lanes in each direction. She wanted desperately to peel out of the parking lot, just to make a statement.

Seeing a break in traffic, she punched the gas. The Volvo's tires produced a screech that wasn't so much a statement as a whimper.

She straightened the steering, picked up speed, and rolled down her window, her hair blowing in the wind. "Who cares?" she shouted.

Nobody could have heard her over the noise of traffic, but she felt better anyway.

∼◎∽

George stood at the counter, taping up a box full of carefully packed Victorian Christmas ornaments for an online customer and brooding over the unfixable wrongs of the world. An internship in college had shown him the ugly truth about big business that relied on sweatshop merchandise, but it had been years before he'd realized that the antiques trade had its dirty little secrets too. Victorians had had their sweatshops. Precious metals and jewels had started untold wars over the centuries. All over the globe, every form of commerce was tainted by someone's misfortune for someone else's profit.

The bell tinkled. He looked up, and Mel's forlorn face nearly broke his heart.

It wasn't right for parents to shut their only daughter out of their home. Never in a million years could it be right.

"Good to see you, Mel," he said. "You want to borrow the dog again? Please?"

"Is she here?"

"Sleeping in the back room."

She came closer, slowly. "Let her sleep." She stopped beside the 1941 Coke machine and inspected it. "This is a gloomy store. All these things used to belong to dead people."

George smiled. "When the merchandise belonged to them, they were still very much alive. You're right, though. I go to a lot of estate sales and buy merchandise that belonged to people who've died."

"See what I mean? It's creepy."

He shook his head. "It's only a business. Like any other business."

She kept her eyes downcast. "Any chance you could give me a job?"

He hesitated, wanting to spare her feelings. "I probably don't need anybody right now."

"Nobody does. Well, that's what they say, anyway. I applied at the Shell station and a few other places, but everybody turned me down. They'd already made up their minds before I walked in." She looked up. "Maybe they really don't need help, but I think they don't trust me."

And you don't either, her eyes said.

"Tell me about your recent employment history," he said.

"What do you mean?"

"Where have you been for the last couple of years? Where have you worked? Actually, start before that. Start with the jobs you had before you left town."

"Well, I worked for the Engelbrights at their produce stand, and then I worked at the Howards' gift shop. And…then I hit the road."

"For Vegas?"

"Vegas? I've never been to Vegas. I went to Florida. I figured if I couldn't find work, I'd at least stay warm. And I'd heard there'd be oranges growing alongside the road so I wouldn't starve." She paused. "That's not exactly true."

"No," George agreed. "Where did you work in Florida?"

She gave him a crooked smile. "I can't stand the smell of fish, so where'd I end up working? At a seafood joint. Blech."

"Where was this?"

"Orlando. A girl I knew from high school was working there, and she helped me get in. I got fired, though. They said I stole some cash, but I promise I didn't. I was framed."

"Sounds like your two jobs in Noble too. That's a little coincidental, Mel."

"I was framed," she said, enunciating the words with precision.

She sounded utterly sincere, of course. Utterly truthful. But she was quite the actress. Or maybe she'd talked herself into believing she'd been framed. Three times.

"Look, Mel," he said as gently as he could. "I don't need an employee right now. If I have to go somewhere, I can lock up and leave. Or sometimes Calv helps me out."

"I know," she said in a quiet, tired voice.

"And if I hired you…" He took a breath and let it out, wishing he didn't have to say it aloud. "Frankly, I'd be afraid to leave you here by yourself."

"I know," she said again. "I just thought I'd ask." She turned away, her shoulders sagging.

He couldn't hire her. If he did, he'd have to watch her all the time. But Tish was giving her a chance. And she was Mel, like a kid sister. Maybe, given a second chance—or was it her seventeenth chance or so?—she'd straighten up simply because somebody finally believed in her.

"Mel, wait," he said.

She shook her head and started walking.

"We could do a trial run. Maybe."

She stopped but wouldn't face him. "What do you mean?"

"I might be able to hire you. Part time, on a trial basis. But you'll have to fill out an application and be very clear about what my conditions are." He waited, studying the back of her head.

She straightened, seeming to grow an inch. "For real?"

"For real, but only two or three days a week. Minimum wage. And you'll have to abide by my rules."

She spun around and came back to the counter, her face alight. "Well, it'd be something anyway."

"But if you steal so much as a paper clip, you're fired. If you're one minute late, you're fired. If you're rude to a customer, you're fired."

"Fired? For being rude?"

"Yes ma'am. You'll have to be courteous to the customers. Every single one, even the ones you don't like. Think of it as a game. Fool them into thinking you like them."

"I know people who try to do that to me. People who pretend to like me and trust me when they don't. But they don't fool me."

George leaned against the counter, bringing himself down to her eye level. "I won't pretend to trust you. I want to, but I'm not there yet. I'm willing to give you a try, though. Don't let me down."

She returned the look, her eyes solemn. "I won't let you down."

"Okay, then. Can you come back tomorrow morning and we can go over the details and conditions?"

She nodded eagerly. "What time?"

"Eight thirty, and don't be late. I'll have some paperwork for you to fill out. Come around to the back door because the front will be locked."

"Oh, wow, I can't wait to tell Tish," she said breathlessly. "Thanks, George. Thank you so much."

"But it's not quite official yet," he said.

Ignoring or not hearing that last warning, she hustled toward the door. The bell tinkled to mark her exit.

What had he done? He was halfway to hiring an employee he didn't need and couldn't trust. Already, he found himself worrying about the small and valuable antiques that might wander into Mel's pockets.

Twenty

After retreating from the bank in defeat, Tish had spent the rest of the morning diligently job-hunting online and tweaking her résumé. She'd hoped to stay so busy that she wouldn't have time to be mad at herself, but it hadn't worked.

She shouldn't have counted on the job at the bank. She shouldn't have invested so much time and emotional energy in reading those stupid old letters. She shouldn't have assumed that she'd be welcome in Noble. She probably shouldn't have moved in the first place.

Now it was late afternoon. The mail truck had gone by already, but Tish decided she wouldn't run outside for her mail until the truck made its return trip on the other side of the street. Pacing the living room, she kept one ear on the street and rehearsed what she wanted to say to her neighbor.

"Look, lady," she said under her breath. "Don't pretend to be nice. You hate me for being the idiot who gave that terrible Mel Hamilton a place to stay when her own parents wouldn't."

Hearing the mail truck, she cracked the door open to watch. The truck pulled up in front of the green house, paused for a few seconds, and moved on to the next house.

"Okay, snotty neighbor," she said. "Stop avoiding me."

Mel had told her the woman's name was Mrs. Nair and she used to be the school nurse. That was all Tish knew, besides the fact that Mrs. Nair seemed to be allergic to contact with her new neighbor. Twice now, Tish had stepped outside to introduce herself, and the woman had nipped back inside as if she'd seen a ghost.

Mrs. Nair's screen door opened, and she stepped onto the porch. Slowly, limping a little, she made her way down the steps and across her yard. When she was busy unlatching the gate of her white picket fence, Tish made her move.

Trying to be quiet about it, she hurried out of the house and across the yard. After a quick check for traffic, she jogged across the street, gaining the curb just as Mrs. Nair reached her mailbox. Perfect timing. The woman couldn't retreat now, with her mail only inches away. Up close, her beaky nose and spiky hair reminded Tish of some exotic bird—in a lavender pantsuit.

"Hi, Mrs. Nair," Tish said with forced cheer. "I've been hoping you'd give me a chance to introduce myself. I'm your new neighbor, Letitia McComb." She stuck out her hand.

Mrs. Nair clasped it. "Annalee Nair, and I'm so glad to finally meet you. A couple of times when I was letting the cat in or out, I was too embarrassed to come out and say hey. Sometimes I'm up all night with my husband—he's in poor health—so my days and nights get turned around, like a baby, and there I am, still in my pajamas in broad daylight." She leaned forward, dropping her voice. "They're scandalous too. About twenty years old and threadbare."

Rapidly reassessing the woman, Tish could only laugh. "I have some awful pajamas too. They're not threadbare, but they're ugly. Pink with yellow duckies."

Mrs. Nair whooped with laughter, a delight to Tish's ears.

"Woo-hoo!" someone shouted. "Yeeeeeee-haw!" Mel charged up the sidewalk like a schoolgirl turned loose for summer vacation.

Tish took a quick breath. "I was just about to tell you I have a houseguest, and here she comes. Mel Hamilton."

Mrs. Nair peered down the street. "Is that Mel? I don't know how many children I knew in my forty-five years as a school nurse, but she's one I'll never forget."

Mel was approaching rapidly, her face aglow and her hair a mess. "I got a job!" she yelled. "I got a job!"

"Congratulations," Tish said. "Where?"

"George! George's shop! He hired me."

Great, Tish thought. She'd lost the bank job because Farris heard she'd taken Mel in. Now Mel had a job—with George, who didn't need an employee.

Mel slowed her pace for the last few feet and drew up beside them. "Hello, Mrs. Nair," she said, panting a little.

"Hello, Melanie. My, you do favor your mama."

Mel rolled her eyes. "Better her than—" She stopped short and flashed a grin. "Tish is awesome, Mrs. Nair. She's really generous and everything." She turned to Tish. "Now I can be generous too. I'll have moneeeeeeeeey!"

"You'll need to be careful with your money before you can be generous," Tish said. "Once you know how much you'll be making, I can help you set up a budget. And I can take you to the bank to open an account."

Mel's smile faded. "A budget?"

Calv's blue pickup slowed in front of the house. He lifted a hand in a lazy wave and pulled onto the track that led back to the garage.

"Oh! I have to tell him about the job," Mel said breathlessly. "Yee-haw, the job!" She raced across the street, her sneakers slapping hard on the pavement, and chased the truck around the house.

"My goodness." The retired nurse reached into her mailbox for her mail. "So much energy. She's a handful, that one, but I always had a soft spot in my heart for her. She wasn't favored in school, you know."

"She mentioned that, but I don't know the details."

Mrs. Nair started sorting her mail and sighed. "Well, I'm glad she found a job when jobs are so scarce. I hope it will work out well for both her and George."

"Me too." Tish said good-bye and walked across the street to her own mailbox. Junk mail, a magazine, and bills. Bills, bills, bills. She didn't want to look at them, much less open them.

A quick glance at her next-door neighbors' house confirmed that they weren't venturing out for their mail. Sooner or later, she would meet them too. She headed inside, grateful for so much but worried at the same time. If she couldn't find a job, she wouldn't be able to pay her bills. She'd get behind on her house payment, and that would add to her reputation as one of those less-than-respectable McCombs. An unemployed McComb. A slouch. And a Yankee to boot.

She walked slowly up the stairs and lay across her bed. Calv's laughter rang out, muffled by distance, and she imagined Mel out there in the garage, regaling him with her tale of landing a job the first day she started looking.

Closing her eyes, Tish revisited the day, starting with Mel trudging away that morning, looking defeated before she'd begun, and ending with the way she'd raced home, screaming that George had hired her. He could have played the just-protecting-my-business card, like Farris, but he hadn't.

Tish smiled. "Bless you, George," she whispered, suddenly smitten with him for taking a chance on Mel.

On the other hand, it was aggravating that Mel found a job when she was the reason the bank job hadn't worked out for Tish.

Tish frowned, remembering her conversation with Farris, and before that, her encounter with Marian. The anger, the frustration, the pitiful attempt at peeling out of a parking lot in a Volvo. Well, none of it mattered now, at least for a little while.

She needed to come up with a celebration dinner for Mel. A cheap one.

⌒◉⌒

Carrying the pizza box toward the garage with Daisy scampering beside him, George felt considerable trepidation about sharing his news. Several times during the afternoon, he'd nearly called Calv but chickened out every time.

He heard music long before he rounded the camellias. When the garage came into view, George had to grin. Calv had hauled so many amenities into the garage that it had started to resemble a clubhouse. His boom box was pumping out some Stevie Ray Vaughan, as usual, and now he'd added a large cooler, four sun-bleached camp chairs, and a giant oscillating fan, although the weather hadn't even warmed up yet.

Calv was occupying one of the camp chairs and reading one of the old newspapers he swore by for their glass-cleaning properties. Looking up, he let out a deep sigh of contentment. "I just love readin' about other folks' troubles. They make mine look a little smaller."

"When did you turn so hardhearted?"

Calv reached into the cooler and pulled out two dripping cans of Coke. "When did you turn so grumpy?"

Ignoring that, George got Daisy situated with her own dinner and water bowl in the corner, then took one of the camp chairs. His hands black with grease, Calv tore off paper towels to use as plates and napkins, then opened the box. The pizza seemed greasier than usual, and that was saying something.

George cast a furtive look into the yard, half expecting Mel to show up before he'd said anything to Calv. Or maybe she'd already told him. "I have a confession to make."

"Sounds serious. You killed somebody? You stole something?"

"No. I've lost something."

Calv regarded him in silence, took another bite, and waited while Stevie Ray's guitar carried on. And on.

"My mind," George said. "I've lost my mind."

"Ah. What did you do this time, Zorbas?"

"At the shop, I…I hired Mel. Well, not officially. I told her we had to talk about my conditions, but she seems to think it's a done deal."

Calv's smile was sly. "She sure does. She came running out here, screaming her fool head off. Said you gave her a job."

"You let me suffer in silence when you already knew?"

"Yes sir, I think it's good for you to stew in your own juices sometimes."

George shook his head. "Speaking of juices, that's disgusting." He studied the paper towel in Calv's hand, smudged with pizza sauce, pizza grease, and automotive grease. "Good thing the ladies aren't around to comment on your table manners."

"Or yours. No, the ladies went out to celebrate Mel's job. Tish gave her a choice. Pizza or Bag-a-'Cue." Calv frowned. "Mel wanted Bag-a-'Cue. She said pizza makes her think of Dumpsters."

"Dumpsters?"

"And stray cats. And after she said that, she started squalling like a baby."

"Crying, you mean?"

"Yeah, except she was laughing at the same time." Calv shook his head. "I hope you didn't hire yourself a crazy girl."

"At any rate, it's too late to change my mind now."

"It was too late the minute you said anything to Mel."

George nodded glumly. "I'm an idiot."

"You won't get no argument from me." Calv laughed. "Actually, I see what you're doing."

"Hanging my head in despair?"

"No, you're trying to impress Miss Tish with how kind and generous you are."

George shook his head emphatically. "She hardly knows Mel, but she gives her a place to stay. I've known Mel all my life. I can at least hire her a few days a week."

"Uh-huh."

"It's only on a trial basis, and I'll give Mel some strict rules. If she can't abide by my rules, she's gone."

"Uh-huh."

Grease oozed from the pizza onto George's paper towel, reminding him of Mel's strange comment about Dumpsters and stray cats. "I wonder how my loyal customers will react when they find out."

"Dunc won't want his wife shopping with us anymore, will he? Just when you bought another big batch of *Gone with the Wind* garbage."

"Collectibles," George corrected. "Moneymakers." He frowned. "You think he's afraid Suzette will do the right thing and be nice to their kid?"

Calv shook his head. "She's been under his thumb so long that she's forgotten how to think for herself. No, I think he'll order her to stay away to spite the both of you. You and Mel. Behind the Mr. Nice Guy act, he's ugly mean. And sometimes I wonder about Stu."

"Nah. Stu's all right. He just needs to grow a backbone, if it's not too late for that."

"It's never too late for a man to change," Calv said. "Or a girl."

George nodded, hoping he was right.

Twenty-One

Sitting cross-legged on a blanket, Mel licked barbecue sauce off her fingers and let out a huge sigh. It was awesome to sit in the park and watch the town begin to close up for the night without feeling homeless.

She loved to be outdoors, and she would be happy to sleep in the park again someday—when she didn't have to. That made all the difference. If she slept under the stars because she wanted to, then it was camping out. If she slept under the stars because she had nowhere else to go, then she was a loser.

She wiped her mouth with a napkin. If Darren came by again, she didn't want to have sauce on her face. Like a messy little kid. Especially because Valentine's Day was coming up and he might be looking for a special date.

Tish peeked into one of the bags. "Have some more, Mel. There's plenty. Come on, eat up."

Tish sure was antsy to finish and get home. Okay, she was probably upset because she wasn't the one who found a job, but still, she needed to chill out.

"I'm stuffed, but—well, I'll have some more fries. Bag-a-'Cue has the best fries." Mel grabbed a handful and dipped one in ketchup. "I loved the way you walked right up to the pick-up counter and said your name, loud and clear. 'Carry-out order for Letitia McComb, please,' and the old guy behind the counter nearly had a heart attack."

Tish laughed. "I ran into him there once before, when I first came to town. Before I knew my name would be a black mark against me."

"It shouldn't be. It's a nice name."

"When I was a kid, I hated it. My first name, I mean. It's so old-fashioned. I was probably your age before I decided it was a name I could be proud of." Her eyes went squinty for a second. "It still is."

Mel thought about that while she ate her fries. Someday, she would be proud of her name too. She would walk into Bag-a-'Cue and say "Carry-out order for Mel Hamilton," or maybe she would say "Melanie" to sound more ladylike.

"Maybe it's time for me to stop being a tomboy," she said.

"There's nothing wrong with being a tomboy," Tish said. "You'll have to dress and speak appropriately for your job, but be yourself. It's healthier than putting on an act."

"Yeah. I never want to be like Amanda."

"Amanda?"

"The nasty-nice checker at Target, remember?" Mel started imitating Amanda's voice. "The one with the sweetsie-peetsie baby-doll voice. I'll never be a prissy-face like her."

Tish laughed around a mouthful of fries. "Thank God."

Mel smiled, glad Tish saw through Amanda's act. Tish was almost like another Hayley. Another friend.

This morning when Mel took the hoodie to the Shell station, Hayley wouldn't let her give it back. Mel had cried, just a little, once she was outside again. When people were supernice like that, she felt soft as a marshmallow inside. Then crying made her like a marshmallow in the rain, turning into a soggy mess.

There was a certain kind of cop that made her feel that way too. Darren for one, and the old cop who'd talked her out of running away when she was little. If he'd been hard nosed about it, she never would have climbed into his car.

"The sunset makes a nice backdrop for our fancy dinner," Tish said with a smile.

Leaning her head back, Mel stared out at the red-orange sky. "Yeah. I love to eat outside. When I was little, I'd go to Hayley's house and her mom would let us have a picnic in the backyard. It felt special, even if it was only PBJ sandwiches."

"Like coffee tastes special when I make it in my vintage percolator and pour it into a beautiful porcelain cup. But we don't all have the same ideas about what's beautiful and what's not."

Mel snickered. "George thinks his Chevelle is beautiful."

"But it is."

"To him, maybe."

"Whatever you think of his taste in cars, he's a nice guy who's giving you a chance to prove yourself. I hope you'll be a good employee, and that starts with 'Do unto others as you'd have them do unto you.'"

Mel nodded. "Yeah, I'll try. I always try."

A woman walked by with a tiny dog on a leash, and it reminded Mel of the last time she walked Daisy. She'd never lied to Calv. She'd said she would take the dog down Main Street, and she did. She just hadn't mentioned she'd go all the way to the edge of town. She'd carried Daisy most of the way, of course. She was too little for a long, long walk.

But it was all for nothing. Even though the code was stuck in her head, she wouldn't use it. She had a real job now. She could buy brand-new clothes, maybe one or two things with every paycheck. Nicky was more important than the clothes she could have grabbed from her closet.

Nick, she reminded herself. He wasn't little-boy Nicky anymore.

A cop car cruised by, and her heart did a somersault. She thought she saw Darren at the wheel. Hoping he was close enough to see her, but not close enough to notice her crappy clothes, she waved.

The driver waved back, but it was a cop she'd never seen before. An older dude. He was blond like Darren but had a hard, square face. Like a robot. She shuddered and zipped up her hoodie.

"It gets cold when the sun goes down," Tish said. She straightened as if she'd been looking for an excuse to leave. "Are you ready to go?"

"Sure." Mel picked up their trash while Tish closed up the carry-out containers. "Thanks, Tish. That was fun. I wish you'd found a job already too."

"I'll find one, sooner or later. It might take awhile."

Walking toward a trash can, Mel watched traffic backing up for a red light half a block away. It was getting too dark to recognize faces inside the vehicles. They were like cocoons made of glass and metal, keeping people boxed up and separated from each other when they were only a few feet apart. Like people could be boxed up in separate rooms in a house, so close to each other but never talking.

She wished she could call her mom and tell her about the job. Maybe she would be just a little bit proud.

On foot in the brisk night air, George turned onto Jackson. Away from the streetlights on Main, he could hardly see the sidewalk curving away in front of him.

He'd chased Daisy down Main for half a block, then slowed to a walk and let her run ahead. He knew where he'd find her. And he didn't blame her. He was drawn to the old house too, and not just because he used to live there.

When he'd nearly reached Tish's place, piano music floated into the night. Someone was playing "When the Saints Go Marching In"—but slowly, like a dirge. The playing broke off in the middle of a line. After a short silence, light spilled onto the porch as Tish opened the front door. She turned on the porch light and stepped outside. About to call out, he decided to approach quietly. He wanted to know if Tish, like Si, secretly encouraged the dog's visits.

Now he was close enough to see Daisy bounding up the steps and into the light. Tish, barefoot and wearing jeans and a sweatshirt, crouched in front of the door, wasting a perfectly beautiful smile on the mutt.

"You little nuisance," she said. "You think it's still your house, don't you?"

George stopped at the beginning of the flagstone walk as the dog rushed Tish in a frenzy of joy. While Daisy feinted attacks and play-growled, Tish played with her and lapsed into baby talk.

"But this is my house, yes it is! Nobody's gonna run me off. Nobody. I'm staying, yes I am! I live here. If people don't like me, who cares?" Her voice wavered on the last two words.

George wanted to blurt that he liked her just fine, but he kept his mouth shut.

After one more play-growl, the dog trotted to the door and lifted her head to stare at the doorknob.

"No." Now Tish's voice was firm. "Sorry, baby. *I* live here. You don't. We'd better call George."

He cleared his throat and entered the yard. "No need. I'm here."

"George?" Her cheeks rosy with the cold or maybe with embarrassment, she picked up the dog. "Were you listening while I blathered on?"

"I caught a little bit of it. I just wanted to see if you'd be like Si and give her doggie treats and then complain that she won't leave you alone."

"Nope. No treats here. I just hope I didn't sound like an idiot. It hasn't been a great day."

"I'm sorry to hear that. Sorry about the little nuisance too. I stayed late in the shop to do paperwork. When it was time to head upstairs, she pulled her disappearing act."

"She's quite the repeat offender. How does she get out so often?"

"She has a crate in the back room, but I can't latch it. If I shut her in or tie her up, she makes an unending, ungodly howl that turns my brain inside out. So I give in. I leave the crate open. Sometimes she makes a run for the door before I can get a leash on her."

"I see," Tish said slowly. "Well, since you're here, can you stay awhile? I'd like to talk about a couple of things."

"Sure."

They sat halfway down the steps, out of the porch light's glare. Daisy curled up in Tish's lap, happy as could be.

"It was kind of you to offer Mel a job," she said. "She's so excited."

"I know. I warned her that it's not official until we've talked about my rules and requirements, but she didn't seem to hear that part."

Tish was silent for a moment, scratching the dog behind her ears. "I'm just glad you're more merciful than Farris."

"Ed Farris at the bank?"

"You know him?"

"Everybody knows him. He's a nice guy. What did he do?"

"He practically offered me a job when I first came to town, but that's all changed. Long story short, I went to the bank to give Marian copies of some letters that Letitia wrote and—"

"You have Letitia's letters?"

"Yes. A couple dozen, and I scanned them. I can e-mail the files to you if you're interested, but I won't let the originals out of my sight."

Her earnestness made him smile. Old letters written by ordinary people weren't worth much money, but that wouldn't affect their nostalgic value. "I'd like that. Thanks. But what happened with Marian?"

Tish let out a sharp sigh. "I thought the letters would soften her attitude, but now she claims to have proof that Nathan was a thief. Not just hearsay but proof from the historical society. To top it all off, Farris changed his mind about me. Now I'm persona non grata."

George frowned. "Because you're a McComb? Or because you got into a row with Marian?"

"Neither. Farris won't hire me because I keep bad company."

It took a moment for that to sink in. "Mel? He won't hire you because you took her in?"

"Precisely. All his employees must be beyond reproach."

"Seems a little over the top."

"You think?" Tish let out a wobbly laugh. "I don't want that job anyway. Marian would be awful to work with."

Afraid she was about to lose it, George reached for her hand, then lost his nerve and petted Daisy's head. "So Marian claims to have evidence from the historical society. That's the key word. Historical. Whether or not the stories are true, they're in the past."

"I know. I should focus on the present." Tish turned toward him, her face framed softly by long locks of red-brown hair. "No matter what happened here in 1870, this is my home now. Nobody's going to scare me away."

"You know the difference between a Yankee and a...well, a Yankee who's bound for eternity in the lake of fire?"

"The ones who visit versus the ones who stay? Yeah, I've heard that old joke, but I'm staying. I don't care what people call me. I don't care what they think of me either."

"No?"

"Okay, sometimes I do. Sometimes I care too much. I want very badly to be accepted, but sometimes I forget to mind my manners and I speak my mind instead. Someday, I'm afraid I'll say things I shouldn't say. Do things I shouldn't do."

She could be direct, all right, and maybe she didn't always think before she acted, but at least she *did* something. "If your heart's right, your actions can't be too far off. Case in point, the way you reached out to Mel."

"You did too," Tish said. "It's very generous to hire her, and I don't mean just about the wages you'll pay. It's…moral generosity."

George squelched a grin. If he'd known hiring Mel would cast him in such a noble light, he might have hired her sooner.

"I see moral generosity on your side too," he said. "Even though you're a Yankee."

She laughed. "Careful there, Mr. Zorbas. You're skating on thin ice."

"I know, but I grew up listening to my grandfather always preaching against the world, the flesh, and the devil. Sometimes he mentioned Yankees in the next breath, so I started to think Yankees and devils were one and the same."

"Gee, thanks."

He leaned closer, enjoying her cynical little smile. "But I'd be first to admit that some of y'all aren't too bad. And some of y'all are mighty pretty."

"And some of you southern gentlemen are mighty forward." She moved Daisy to his knee and got to her feet.

"Forward? I only—"

"My feet are freezing. Good night, George."

He rose too. "Tish, I—"

She'd already escaped inside, shutting the door firmly behind her. He carried the dog home, brooding over his extraordinary talent for ruining good conversations.

Twenty-Two

*I*n the back room of the shop, Daisy moaned and nudged her empty bowl with her little black nose.

"Don't give me that," George said. "I fed you."

She collapsed on the floor as if she'd succumbed to starvation.

"Knock it off. I don't need a diva dog on top of everything else."

He half dreaded Mel's first day on the job and half welcomed it. She would be a challenge, but she'd give him something to think about besides the way Tish had shut him down.

Long before Mel was scheduled to show up, he'd moved the change drawer from the safe to the cash register. He'd found a sales-tax chart too, and placed it beside the receipt book and a pad of paper for Mel's benefit.

He'd left the pricier jewelry in the safe where it always stayed overnight. He wasn't sure how long he would keep it there. If he didn't have it on display, he couldn't sell it. But he couldn't sell it if Mel stole it, either. It was a dilemma.

The back door swung open, and she stuck her head in. "Is it okay if I walk in like this?" she asked in a timid voice.

"Sure. Come on in."

She entered, carrying a lunch bag, and scooped up the dog with her other hand. "Daisy! How are you today?"

Suddenly recovered from her swoon, Daisy sniffed the bag, her tail wagging.

"You might want to stick that in the fridge." George pointed to the tiny refrigerator in the corner. "So the dog can't get to it."

Mel stashed her lunch beside his and then nuzzled the dog. "Poor baby," she murmured. "Doesn't grumpy old George feed you enough?"

"I feed her plenty. She's a glutton. She has a food dish here, and upstairs, and now out in Tish's garage too."

"She's not a glutton. She's a hungry girl." Mel smiled at him over the dog's head. "I'm ready to get to work if you are."

"First things first. We need to have a little talk."

She hid her face in the dog's fur. "Am I in trouble already?"

"No, but I want to remind you that this is your chance to prove to your dad—"

"Ex-dad, you mean."

"Show a little respect. If you refuse to call him your dad, at least call him Dunc or Mr. Hamilton. But back to my point. I'm afraid he's tired of giving you second chances. If you wind up in trouble again, that's it."

"Isn't it 'it' already if I'm not even allowed in the house? How much further can he go, George? Anyway, it's hopeless. I know I'll mess up again someday, somehow, so I might as well mess up ten times. Or a million times."

"I see your point, but don't give up. Just do your best."

"I do," she said fiercely. "I always do."

"And that's all I ask of you as an employee. I'll forgive honest mistakes, but I won't tolerate dishonesty, laziness, or rude conduct. Do you understand?"

"Yes."

"Okay, then. I'd like to have you work three or four days a week, but the particular days might change from week to week. Will that work for you?"

"Yeah, sure."

He placed an application and a pen on the worktable. "Here's your paper-work to fill out."

"Fun, fun, fun." She sat with the dog in her lap and picked up the pen.

Leaving her to it, he walked through the showroom, turning on lights and straightening merchandise. At the front door, he unlocked and flipped the Closed sign over to the Open side. When he returned to the back room, Mel was scrawling her signature at the bottom of the application.

"Here ya go," she said, holding it up.

He took it and looked it over. Her penmanship was wretched, and her spelling was worse.

"You didn't write down your driver's license number."

"I don't have one. I lost it."

"Lost it? As in…the state took it away?"

"You mean like for a DUI? What kind of girl do you think I am? Geez, George. No, I lost it. It was in my wallet, and my wallet was in my duffel bag, and I lost the bag in Florida."

"A duffel bag is a pretty big item to lose track of."

"I was hitchhiking, okay? And the guy turned out to be scary so I jumped out at a red light. I didn't have time to grab the bag, but I saved my bedroll."

"And your life, maybe. Hitching a ride is dangerous."

"Tell me about it."

He squinted at her application, trying to decipher her chicken-scratch printing. He made out her date of birth. She was coming up on her twenty-first birthday, but she'd listed only two previous jobs, both in Noble.

"Didn't you tell me you worked in a restaurant in Orlando? Where's that info?"

"I didn't put it down because I don't remember the phone number. Or the manager's name. I mean, his name was Rocky, but I don't think that was his real name."

George imagined a swarthy, tattooed hoodlum running a biker bar. "No, probably not. Name of the restaurant?"

"Fishy's."

"A high-class joint, obviously."

"It was all right. They had good fries."

"Were you a waitress?"

"No, I bussed tables."

"It's the restaurant where you got framed for stealing cash?"

"Yes." Her cheeks colored.

"Did you have access to the register?"

"No. It was a jar. A glass jar. You know, one of those charity things? For a little girl who'd been burned in a house fire. Somebody was collecting money to help with the hospital bills. Geez, I wouldn't steal from a three-year-old with third-degree burns. The jar just sat there on the bar. Anybody could have taken the money. They said it was me, but I didn't take it. I put money in a few times. Not a lot, but I wanted to help."

"You're sure you were framed?"

"I'm sure. Go ahead and call, if you can find the number. Ask for Rocky or Marlene. They'll tell you I was a hard worker. They didn't want to let me go."

"But they did let you go. Because they thought you stole from a charity."

"That's what they thought, but they were wrong."

She said it so sincerely that he found himself believing her. Wanting to, anyway.

He studied the sloppy application again. "Did you work at Fishy's the whole time you were out of town? Two years?"

"Well, no. There were a few other jobs too, but I didn't want to put them down because"—she squirmed in her chair—"it's embarrassing."

He waited. Remembering stretches of Florida interstate that were crowded with billboards for strip clubs, he felt sick. Not Mel. Not Stu's baby sister.

"Okay, okay!" she said. "I was a housekeeper at a trashy motel just off I-75. It was horrible. And I picked strawberries with a bunch of people who didn't speak English, and I worked for an old guy who sold orchids and oranges by the side of the road." She paused. "Oh yeah, and I worked at a car wash."

"There's nothing dishonorable about manual labor. You don't need to be embarrassed unless you were doing something illegal." Thinking of a blue Corvette and a gold watch, he dropped the application on his desk. "Okay. We're open for business. Customers seldom show up before 9:30, but that gives us time to do a few chores."

She wrinkled her nose. "What kind of chores?"

"Like chores at home. Basic housekeeping."

She heaved a dramatic sigh. "All right."

"Melanie," he said in his sternest voice, "if you don't want to do the work, save both of us some grief by telling me right now."

"No, I'll do it."

"With a good attitude."

"With a good attitude." She mimicked his severe tone perfectly.

"Your attitude is especially important when you're dealing with customers. Pretend you love working here, even if you don't. Even if you can't stand the customers. Even if somebody wastes an hour of your time while she makes up her mind about a cheap teacup, and then asks you to gift-wrap it."

She puckered her lips as if she'd eaten a lemon. "You want me to be a phony?"

"I want you to be courteous." He pointed toward the front of the store. "Let's make sure you remember how to work an antique cash register."

She followed him behind the counter. Hands clasped behind her back, she studied the ornate gilt surfaces of the machine. "Wow, that's a fancy one."

"Of all the registers I've restored, this one's my favorite." Not for sentimental reasons, though, but for its extravagant style. Every curlicue of the design seemed to celebrate the process of collecting money.

"It's even older than the one the Howards use at their gift shop," he added.

She showed no reaction to the name. "Huh. Can't you afford a newer one?"

Enjoying the irony, he refrained from telling her how valuable an antique NCR could be. "I love the old ones. There's never a paper jam or a problem with the power supply. But as you know, a 1910 model can't tell you how much change to give back. You have to use your head."

"Yeah, yeah. I know."

"Show me. Pretend you're ringing up a sale. Let's say it's a twenty-dollar item, plus tax." He handed her the chart for calculating the sales tax.

She flashed him a look of unadulterated irritation but consulted the chart. Twice. Then she rang up the sale, seeming to enjoy the clash and clang of the machine as much as he did.

"There," she said. "Happy now?"

"Yes ma'am. That's the sound of commerce, even if it's only a trial run. Now, here's an important tip. If somebody gives you, say, a twenty, don't put it in the drawer right away. Leave it on the ledge above the drawer until the customer takes the change and seems happy with it."

She frowned. "Why?"

"So somebody can't give you a ten, wait until you've closed the drawer, and then claim they gave you a twenty."

Comprehension dawned in her eyes. "Oh, wow! Sneaky!"

Hoping he hadn't given her a brilliant new idea to try sometime, he led her into the back room and introduced her to his vintage Bissell sweeper. Never having seen one, she was intrigued.

"You mean you don't have to plug it in?"

"No ma'am."

"Does it run on batteries?"

"No. When you push it back and forth, the little brushes pick up almost everything."

"Awesome. It's like those weird lawn mowers that don't have motors."

He fought to keep a straight face. "It's a similar concept. Sweep the floor mat by the front door and the carpet in front of the register, please. When you've finished, you can clean fingerprints from the front door and display cases and so on. But never use any of the cleaning supplies on the merchandise without checking with me first. One squirt of Windex can ruin a valuable antique. Got it?"

"Got it." She hurried away with the Bissell, her ponytail swinging.

George shook his head. If she could learn some new habits, even if it started out as playacting, maybe the habits would do her good. Or maybe she'd only be whitewashing a sepulcher. If she ran into trouble with the law at some point, his new status as her employer put him in danger of being dragged along for the ride. He tried to dismiss the unsettling thought, but it lingered.

It was a quiet day, as Tuesdays often were, but the slow pace was perfect for training her. Early in the afternoon, he decided she'd observed enough transactions. It was time for her to work the register alone.

The customer currently browsing the store was a retired teacher who stopped in perhaps twice a year and never spent more than ten dollars. If Mel somehow offended Miss Meyers and she never came back, it wouldn't be a great loss.

"Here she comes," he said softly as the woman approached the counter. "This one is all yours."

"No," she whispered, in a panic.

"What's wrong? You did fine on your practice run."

"But I know her. She'll hate me."

"Get over it, Mel. Do your job."

It was too late for her to argue. Miss Meyers was nearly upon them, her bad hip making her list to the left like a car with a flat.

Mel looked terrified but attempted a smile. "Hello, Miss Meyers."

"Hello, dear," the woman said. "Do I know you?"

"You were my teacher," Mel said faintly. "Second grade. I'm…I'm Melanie."

Miss Meyers lowered her glasses and smiled at her. "I'm sorry, dear, but I've taught so many children. I can't possibly remember them all." The woman placed three doilies on the counter. "These were in the three-for-four-dollars pile." She reached into a cracked leather handbag and pulled out an equally decrepit change purse.

Mel tucked the doilies into a bag. Then she ran her forefinger down the sales-tax chart. "That'll be, um…um…four twenty-four, please."

From the tiny coin purse, Miss Meyers extracted a ten-dollar bill, folded in fourths. Mel unfolded it and placed it on the ledge above the drawer.

She hesitated, moving her lips, apparently going over the process in her mind. Then she pulled out four ones, two dimes, and four pennies, and placed them in the woman's hand. "That's four twenty-four," she said breathlessly.

Too stunned to speak, George raised his eyes to Miss Meyers' face. She appeared to be oblivious to this highly irregular method of making change.

Mel reached into the cash drawer and pulled out a penny and three quarters. "Four twenty-four," she repeated under her breath. "Twenty-five," she said, her voice gaining strength as she dropped a penny into the woman's outstretched palm. "Fifty, seventy-five, five," she chanted, counting out the quarters. Then she placed a five-dollar bill on the woman's palm. "And five makes ten."

"Thank you, dear." Miss Meyers stuffed the money into her coin purse.

"Thank you." Mel beamed and handed her the bag. "Have a wonderful day."

"You too." Miss Meyers beamed back and leaned closer to George. "Keep a sweet girl like her at the register and you'll do twice as much business."

"Er, yes," he said. "Thank you, ma'am. Come see us again sometime."

Miss Meyers hobbled away, humming.

"Cool," Mel whispered. "She doesn't remember me."

Glowing with pride, she watched her former teacher walk out with the three doilies and not a penny less than she'd arrived with.

George massaged his scalp, hard, with both hands. The good news was that Mel might not have stolen from her previous employers. Not intentionally, anyway.

The bad news? He needed to confront her immediately. If she overreacted and stormed off, then he didn't want her working there anyway.

He cleared his throat. "Mel, we need to have another little talk."

Upstairs at her desk, Tish checked the time. Past five. Mel wasn't back, so George hadn't found cause to fire her yet.

He was a good man. A kind man. Tish had already admitted to herself that she liked him, so she didn't understand why he sometimes spooked her so. When he spoke to her so gently…or teasingly…she froze inside. The night before, on her porch steps, she'd half expected him to lean in for a kiss, but then she'd panicked. He would want to know why, and she wouldn't know what to tell him.

Part of it was that he'd apologized for the "little nuisance," quoting the first words she'd said to the dog at her door. Knowing he'd heard the whole thing, she felt as if she'd opened a window to her heart just when he happened to be passing by.

She didn't want to think about it anymore. She'd had enough of the online job hunt too, so she decided to take another look at the McComb letters. If nothing else, they would remind her to be grateful. Compared to Letitia, she lived a cream-puff life. Being unemployed for a while was nothing. Absolutely nothing.

Tish zoomed in on one of the most poignant letters.

I'll be home soon, dearest Mother. I have lost everything but Nathaniel, who was once the delight of his father and his sister who now repose in the vile earth of Alabama...

When Tish had visited Noble with her dad, he'd driven to the town's oldest cemetery, thinking Nathan might have been buried there. She'd stayed in the car, trying not to cry. She hadn't been ready to visit a cemetery—any cemetery—but she hadn't wanted her dad to know how hard it was. He hadn't found Nathan's grave, but when he'd climbed into the car again, he'd been more angry than disappointed. Pressed for an explanation, he'd said he'd found a separate area where slaves were buried, but their graves weren't marked.

"As if they weren't God's children too," he'd said. "It's evil."

She'd agreed with him, but she'd been more focused on her private grief. Even now, she couldn't comprehend the wickedness of slavery or the way it had bled into succeeding generations, long after the Civil War.

She lifted her gaze from the letter, recognizing that the "darkies" mentioned in that old book were former slaves, as were the people Nathan and Letitia must have hired as household help—for a pittance, probably. Carpetbaggers hadn't been known for their generosity.

The front door slammed. "Tish! Tish! Are you up there?"

"I'm up here, Mel," she hollered back. "I'll be right d—"

Mel's feet pounded up the stairs. "I gotta tell you," she yelled, halfway there already.

Tish shook her head. There went her plan to keep the second floor as her private sanctuary.

Mel burst into the room, her socks sliding on the smooth wooden floor. "George cleared my name! I mean, he practically called me stupid, but I already know I'm stupid. It was, like, really embarrassing, but he taught me the right way to make change. Sheesh, I'm an adult, I'm nearly twenty-one, and I can't do something that simple?"

"What are you talking about?"

"He watched me counting change for a customer, and I did it all wrong. See? It proves I didn't steal from anybody's cash drawer. It was all an accident. A dumb mistake—every time!"

Tish's natural skepticism kicked in, but she decided to ignore it. If George believed this new theory, she would too. "That's great, Mel."

"Isn't it?" Smiling, she looked around the room. Her eyes lingered on the sewing table in the corner. "This reminds me of my mom's sewing room. You really like to sew? That's weird."

"What's weird about it?"

"It's kind of a mom thing to do. Or a grandma thing. Anyway, my mom's sewing room is half filled up with Scarlett O'Hara stuff. She spends a ton of money at George's shop 'cause she's a Windy."

"A what?"

"A Windy. That's what we call people who collect *Gone with the Wind* junk. Except we don't call it junk. We call it memorabilia. Collectibles."

Tish smiled at Mel's wholehearted adoption of George's terminology. "I see. Well, do you think you're a good fit for the job?"

"Yeah. It's fun except for the chores. I get to wait on customers and everything, but he'll only need me part time so it won't be much money."

"Maybe you can find another part-time job too."

"Maybe. Hey, I'm starving." Mel headed toward the doorway. "I'm gonna grab something to eat. You want anything?"

"No, thanks. Save some room for supper. I'm making stir-fry."

"Okay."

Mel was back in two minutes with a yogurt and a spoon in one hand and an apple in the other. She set the apple on the sewing table and started the yogurt. Leaning in, she studied the computer screen. "What's that?"

"A letter that the original Letitia McComb wrote to her mother after her husband died."

"The mother's husband?"

"No. Letitia's husband. She lost her daughter too."

"That's sad."

"Yeah. Maybe the whole town had good reason to hate them, but I feel sorry for them anyway. According to Letitia's letters home, they went through some real tragedies."

"What happened?" Mel pulled the chair away from the sewing table and straddled it while she ate.

"From clues in the letters, I think Letitia couldn't get pregnant for a long time, and then one baby was stillborn and another one died when he was only six months old."

"That's sad," Mel said again, scooping a spoonful of yogurt from its container.

"She finally had two healthy children, a boy and a girl, when she was in her early forties."

"Huh. My mom was almost that old when she had me."

"And Nathan was a lot older than his wife, so he was probably in his mid-seventies when the two children were teenagers."

Mel laughed. "Geez, and I thought my dad was old."

"Nathan made a bundle of money when he and Letitia first came to town, but apparently he lost most of it in the last few years of his life. He died when their son was sixteen."

"What did Nathan die of? Old age?"

"The letters don't say, but a few weeks after he died, their daughter died of malaria. She was only fifteen."

Mel stopped with a spoonful of yogurt halfway to her mouth. "That's awful. That's like…tenth grade. Before she'd had a chance to go to prom or anything."

"Yes, and Letitia was afraid she'd lose her son too. She wanted to move home to Ohio, but she hadn't been aware of Nathan's money problems. He was so far in debt that she wasn't even sure she could afford to leave town."

"What did she do?"

"From what I've read, my best guess is that someone pressured her to sell this house, dirt cheap. Then she and her son headed for Ohio with almost nothing."

"You mean somebody cheated her out of her house? Right after her husband and daughter died?"

"It was probably legal, even if it wasn't kind or honorable."

Mel shrugged. "What goes around, comes around. He wasn't exactly honest himself, was he?"

"Apparently not."

Mel set down the empty yogurt cup, crunched into her apple, and leaned toward the computer again. "So that's Letitia's writing? It's pretty."

"It's called Spencerian penmanship. A whole generation of schoolchildren grew up learning that style." Tish scrolled down the page to show Mel the closing lines. "Can you make it out? The writing is so small in the actual letters that they're easier to read on the screen, zoomed in."

Mel squinted at it and shook her head. "Read it to me."

"Monday next," Tish read, "abandoning our loved ones to their graves in this hostile land, young Nathaniel and I shall leave for Ohio and your faithful affection. My dear Mother, you have never ceased to keep the door open for us. Lord willing, we will see your face soon, and you shall embrace your grandson for the first time amid the gentle landscapes of home."

"It sounds like she was really homesick. I know how that feels." Mel made a face. "At least her mother wanted her back."

"Maybe yours does too."

"Ha!" Mel glared at the sewing machine, picked up her empty yogurt cup, and walked out.

Tish stared out at the trees and wondered about Suzette Hamilton and Mel. Ann Lattimore and Letitia McComb. Barb Miller and Tish McComb. Mothers and daughters, of all people, should try to stay connected.

Twenty-Three

Tish made awesome stir-fry. She left out the yucky vegetables like broccoli but added plenty of pineapple chunks and crunchy water chestnuts. It was so good, Mel didn't mind getting stuck with the supper dishes, even without a dishwasher. Not that she should've minded anyway. She had a roof over her head and a comfy bed and hot showers and even somebody fun to talk to. Sure, sometimes Tish acted like an old-maid Sunday school teacher, but she was nice. Mel wanted to make her proud, and George too.

She hung up the dishtowel and did a happy dance around the kitchen. She had a job, a real job, and her boss was cool even if he was old. He wasn't like Rocky, who'd groped her, or old Mrs. Howard, who'd called her a moron and a liar. George wasn't exactly a friend, but he wasn't an enemy either.

With everything drying on the rack, Mel walked into the living room and looked up the stairs. She wished she could sneak up there sometime and use the computer, but a computer was a personal kind of thing. Besides, she hadn't been online in so long she couldn't remember her user names or passwords for anything. She'd have to start fresh. That wasn't a bad idea anyway.

Tish came up behind her, carrying a laundry basket full of neatly folded towels that smelled like fabric softener trying to smell like flowers. "I went into your room and opened the window this morning," she said. "Just to air things out. And I noticed your sleeping bag smells like smoke."

Mel's chest froze, squeezing her lungs. She couldn't breathe. "You didn't wash it, did you?"

Tish studied her for a long, scary moment. "No. I'm not your mom. You do your own laundry."

"Yeah. Sure. I'm sorry, that's not what I—yes, I'll wash it."

"You can start it right now. This was my last load." Tish headed up the stairs. "After I put the towels away, I'm going to run out to the garage and say hello to George."

"Say 'hey' for me." Mel hurried into her room, shutting the door behind her. Her heart raced as she grabbed her sleeping bag from the floor and unfolded it on the bed.

Of course her treasures were right where she'd left them. She slid them under her socks and underwear in the top drawer of the dresser. They'd be safe there, temporarily, but she'd have to think of a better hiding place, especially because she'd be at work three or four days a week. Tish probably wouldn't snoop, but there was no way to know for sure.

She sniffed the sleeping bag. It did smell like smoke—and made her crave a cigarette, but she didn't want to make Tish mad. Wadding it up into a big, slippery armful, she took it into the laundry room and set the washer for an extra-large load. She poured detergent in. While the water ran, she spread the sleeping bag across the floor and squirted stain remover on the mud stains.

"Poor old sleeping bag," she said, her voice drowned out by the noise of the water flooding into the machine. They'd been through a lot together.

Most of the mud came from that ditch in Florida. She'd been caught in the rain plenty of times too, with vehicles speeding past and splashing her with dirty water. The yellow fabric had been bright and pretty when her folks gave it to her for her sixteenth birthday, but that was almost five years ago. She would buy another one someday.

She crammed the puffy, bulky bedding into the washer and tried to figure out how much money she'd earned so far. Shoot, a day's wages wouldn't buy one little corner of a good sleeping bag. Clothes were more important right now, though—and groceries. She'd promised to help with groceries.

Maybe she could find a baby-sitting job. Nah. Nobody would trust her with their kids.

She heard Tish's feet coming down the stairs. A minute later, the back door slammed. It wasn't an angry slam, just the kind that happened when a door didn't want to latch and needed some encouragement.

Mel wandered back to the kitchen, craving a dessert. A bowl of ice cream would work, with fun stuff sprinkled on top. Banana slices. Chopped peanuts. Chocolate syrup. It could be an upside-down banana split, with the bananas on top. She pulled out a bowl, found the ice-cream scoop, and created her masterpiece.

She'd just sat down to eat when a horrible racket burst from the laundry room, as if the washer wanted to fly through the wall. Mel ran into the dinky room and yanked the lid up. The tub kept spinning, off center, but it slowed and finally stopped.

She didn't know what to do. If she'd broken the washer, she'd have to pay for it. She couldn't afford to, though. Tish would kick her out.

About to panic, she remembered her mom sometimes stopped a load to move things around. She reached in and shifted the heavy, sopping-wet sleeping bag so it filled the tub evenly. With a silent prayer, she banged the lid shut. Then she restarted the washer and held her breath while the spin cycle worked up to speed. This time, it sounded right.

Back in the kitchen, she sat down at the table. The ice cream had started to melt around the edges, and it didn't look yummy anymore.

Her dad always liked chopped peanuts on his sundaes. She did too. It made her miss him, and that was crazy because he was a jerk. He didn't love her. He never would. It was hopeless.

She picked up her spoon and ate a bite of her upside-down banana split. It didn't taste as good as she'd hoped.

Tish peeked around the camellia bushes in the twilight. Daisy was sprawled on the garage floor, lazily gnawing on a roll of duct tape, and George sat at the wheel of his Chevelle with the windows rolled down. He was humming.

Would he remember the way she'd ended their last conversation by dumping the dog and running inside? Of course he would, but awkward or not, she had to talk to him about Mel.

She stepped out of hiding. "Hi, George."

He stopped humming. "Hey, Tish. Want to check out my ride?"

"Sure." First, though, she took the duct tape away from Daisy and put it out of reach on the big red toolbox. "That can't be good for your digestion, baby."

She walked around to the passenger side, and George reached over to help her open the incredibly heavy door. "My dad would have loved this car," she said, climbing in. "He always raved about how solid cars used to be."

"He would have liked your Volvo, then."

"Nope. It's an import, and he was a GM man all the way." She settled back in the cushy bucket seat. "I love the old-style gauges and knobs. Everything's so big and chunky."

"What? No, it's sleek and sporty and classic."

She decided not to argue. "How's the project coming along?"

"Slow as molasses. I'll drive Calv to the brink of insanity before we're done. He gets discouraged when I break things or buy the wrong parts."

"You don't get discouraged?"

"Nah. It's all part of the process." George ran one finger around the steering wheel. "He's making another run to the parts store. Said he'd rather not have me there to complicate things."

"I'm glad you're here. I need to talk to you about a couple of things. Starting with Mel."

"Did she tell you she's learning how to count change, finally?"

"Yes, but I'd like to hear it from you too. I'm not sure I understood what she meant."

He laughed. "It's hard to explain. I wouldn't have believed it if I hadn't seen it. The first time she rang up a customer, instead of counting back from the amount of the sale, she gave back the amount of the sale. Counted the purchase price right into the customer's hand—and then she counted the change from there."

"You mean…in effect, she was giving away the merchandise?"

"Exactly. The customer was a sweet old gal who didn't even notice. Fortunately, it wasn't a big sale." George shook his head. "With Mel's crazy method, the drawer would always come up short. Her employers assumed she was stealing. Actually, the customers were the bad guys if they noticed but didn't speak up."

"Are you sure this theory makes sense?"

"It makes perfect sense. She worked at a produce stand and a gift shop here in town. The woman who ran the produce stand didn't even use a register—just an adding machine and a cash box—and the folks at the gift shop used a vintage register I sold them."

"Do you think the register wasn't accurate?"

"It worked perfectly, but that's irrelevant. The issue is that an antique register can't tell you how much change to give back, and Mel couldn't figure it out."

"Couldn't? Or wouldn't? What if she faked it? Maybe she'd rather be thought stupid than be thought guilty of stealing. She might have deliberately miscounted, right in front of you, to give herself an excuse for any missing money in the past. Or in the future."

"Why are you so suspicious all of a sudden?"

Tish hesitated, remembering the night George had said Mel was a character from the police blotter. "Tonight when she thought I'd thrown her sleeping bag in the wash, her face went absolutely white. Like she had something to hide."

"Hmm. That doesn't sound especially good."

"No. Has she ever used drugs?"

"Not that I know of, but even before she skipped town, some of her friends were on the wild side. And God only knows what kind of friends she made in Florida. She worked at a fine establishment called Fishy's, managed by a gentleman named Rocky."

Tish smiled at George's deadpan wit. "It sounds terrific." Then she sighed. "You think she even has a chance of making it? Not just eventually being able to pay her own way, but reconciling with her family?"

"It won't be easy. Dunc kicked her out the second time someone accused her of stealing. And then she left town with her grandfather's gold watch. Stu told me Dunc won't take her in again until she returns it. She must have sold it already, though, at the first pawnshop she ran across."

"How can he hold that over her? How can he demand something she'll never be able to give him?"

"He's that way. In public, of course, he's Mr. Congeniality."

"I'd better get back inside and make sure Miss Innocence is behaving herself." After finding the door handle, she heaved the door open, shut it, and leaned over to speak through the open window. "Sometimes I worry about my valuables, but I don't want to spend any money right now on a safe or a locking cabinet. If I had extra, I'd buy a lawn mower instead."

"If it would help you sleep at night, you can leave your valuables in my safe at the shop."

"You might laugh at my so-called valuables. I'm talking about vintage costume jewelry from garage sales and flea markets. Anyway, I hope Mel won't swipe anything. I want to believe the best about her. Really, I do."

"I do too. She's like a kid sister to me. A troublesome kid sister."

"But her own brother ignores her?"

"He hasn't always," George said. "The night she went missing, he cried."

Sensing that she was about to hear quite a tale, Tish lowered herself to a crouch. "Mel went missing? When?"

"She was about eight or nine, I guess. Hated school. Decided she was big enough to make it on her own, so she packed some things in a little bag and took off walking. She was missing for hours. Half the town was out searching. An old cop, Rivera, found her and brought her back. It turned out she'd heard me and Stu calling her name but she wouldn't come out. She knew we would take her home and Dunc would give her a whipping."

"She went with the policeman, though?"

"Rivera had grandkids, so he knew how to handle a stubborn little girl." George gave her a mischievous smile. "It probably had something to do with letting her operate his lights and siren. But when he brought her back, she wouldn't go to Dunc. Rivera handed her to Stu instead, and that's when he started crying."

"At least we know he has a heart. Or he used to, anyway."

"I'll work on him," George said. "I'll see what I can do."

"Let me know if you get anywhere. Good night."

"Good night, and brace yourself. I'm about to fire up the monster."

Tish laughed at the excitement shining in his eyes. "Thanks for the warning. Won't it scare Daisy, though?"

"No, she's used to it."

She'd nearly reached the camellias before he started the engine, but the roar of it still made her jump. She turned around. "Now that's a car that makes a statement!" she yelled, knowing he couldn't hear her.

He gunned it, drowning out everything else, but she knew he was laughing.

Maybe, just maybe, she could learn to like fast cars again.

Twenty-Four

George never bought himself a cup of coffee if he was within a few miles of his own coffeemaker, but he'd made an exception this time because Stu had always liked the Starbucks wannabe on Main—especially on Wednesdays when they had their specials.

Sure enough, there he was. Wearing his usual half-asleep expression, Stu huddled at a tiny table in the rear. Coffee in his left hand, he picked at a keyboard with his right. The tables around him were empty, as if the other customers had decided to avoid his gloom. Everybody else stayed at the front of the shop where the sun shone in and the barista kept everybody smiling.

After claiming his own coffee, George approached. "Well, look who's here. Good morning, Stu."

Surrounded by a clutter of papers and sticky notes, Stu looked up, over the frames of reading glasses. "Morning, George. Sit. Sit." He took off his glasses and made motions as if to shut his laptop.

George signaled to him to stop. "I don't want to interrupt what you're doing. Not for long, anyway." He took the other chair. "How's the kitchen remodel coming along?"

"Slowly. I wish I hadn't agreed to camp out at my folks' house."

"A little too crowded?"

"That too, but the real problem is that Janice knows we won't do this twice, so she's slow to decide about her color choices and so on. If we were home, living without a functioning kitchen, she'd make up her mind a little faster."

George nodded, imagining Stu's wife agonizing over the color of her countertops while her twenty-year-old sister-in-law relied on charity from a virtual stranger. But that was a topic to be broached sideways, so to speak, a little later.

"Did you hear the Nelsons sold to a Letitia McComb?"

"That's old news, George. I hear she's a typical loudmouth northerner."

"I'll have to argue with that. I like her."

"You've met her?"

"I have." George finally tried his coffee. It burned his tongue.

"How's business?" Stu asked.

"Not bad. It's a little harder to turn a profit these days when anybody can go online and find out if great-grandma's china is worth five bucks or five hundred. The Internet has come a long way since you and I played on your parents' PC. But I'm doing well with my specialty items."

"Still restoring old cash registers?"

"Yes. I sold a beautiful 1912 NCR last week."

"For how much?"

George smiled. "Plenty. I earned it too. It can take months to track down replacement parts, and months more to put all those fiddly little parts back together so everything works. In some ways, it's more challenging than restoring a car, but don't try to tell Calv that."

Stu's eyes glinted with good humor. "It must be fun to set your own prices. Run your own show, so to speak."

"It is." With a flash of pity for anyone who had to work under Dunc's thumb, George tried his coffee again, more cautiously. "How's everything at the dealership?"

"Good, except I didn't go to college just so I could sell cars for a living." Stu gave a rueful smile to his laptop, maybe wishing he'd pursued graphic arts like he'd talked about in high school. "On the other hand, it's nice to know the dealership will be mine someday."

"You'll cut Mel right out of it, eh?"

Stu's eyes went to the other end of the room. "She's never been part of it."

"She's still part of the family, though, isn't she?"

A long silence ensued. While Stu played with his sticky notes, George worried that he'd crossed the line. They'd been buddies from Little League through their college years, but that didn't give him the right to butt in to the Hamiltons' business.

"Look," Stu burst out. "Have you forgotten that she helps herself to whatever she wants? The gold watch that was supposed to go to me, for instance."

"Even if she took the watch, she's still your sister. It might mean the world to her if you'd stop by and see her."

"I don't know where to find her."

"I do."

Stu picked up a pad of bright blue sticky notes, pulled one off, and folded it in half. "I'm glad somebody knows where she is, at least."

"But you don't care to know?"

He drew the folded rectangle of blue paper between rows of keys on his laptop. "This is a great way to get lint out of keyboards. Sticky side out."

"That's terrific, Stuart. I'm thrilled. Now see if you can dig deep in your heart, if you have one, and scrape up some brotherly love for Mel."

He looked up. "It's not my fault that she blows up her bridges behind her. My folks are fresh out of patience with her. Dad told me she came home, mouthed off, tried to swipe a couple of things—"

"When? What kind of things?"

"He didn't give me the details." Stu ran the sticky note between another two rows. "Look, you know she'd be a bad influence on Nick and Jamie. Isn't that enough reason to draw the line?"

Remembering Tish's suspicion about drugs in the sleeping bag and Nick's obvious loyalty to Mel, George couldn't argue with that part. "Even if you don't want her around the boys, you could go see her. Your schedule's flexible. If you're afraid to cross your dad, you can sneak out to see her sometime when he's at the dealership."

The taunt made a muscle tighten in Stu's jaw. "I'm not afraid of him…but I don't want to get on his bad side either. You have no idea what it's like to deal with a difficult parent. To walk on eggshells all the time."

"Sure, but try to see it from Mel's perspective. She's back in town after a two-year absence, and her big brother hasn't even tried to see her. Don't you want to know where she's working? Where she's staying?"

Keeping his eyes on the laptop, Stu shrugged. "Sure."

George checked his watch. Mel would show up at the shop in about fifteen minutes, so he had to run. He picked up his coffee, stood, and decided there was no reason to keep his voice down. Let the whole town know.

"I hired Mel. She's working in my shop."

Stu's head jerked up. Squinting and blinking, he focused on George's shirt, not his face. "Do tell."

"And she's staying with a very fine person named Letitia McComb."

Stu rubbed his eyes like a man waking from a long nap. "She what?"

"You heard me. Do with it what you will. Have a great day, Stu." George headed toward the door, noticing with great satisfaction that several of the shop's customers were staring at him over their overpriced coffees. Their ears must have been burning hotter than his tongue.

Twenty-Five

*A*nother Wednesday had rolled around, but even if Stu had hit the coffee place again for the specials, George hadn't. He'd missed his chance, and the day was over. Dark had come early with the rain. He'd already sent Mel home, locked up, and closed out the register. He dimmed the main lights, leaving his merchandise in an artificial twilight, and pondered his plans for the evening.

The storm was a mean one, and it had settled in to stay awhile. Fat raindrops spanked the sidewalk so hard that it sounded like hail. He and Calv had decided they wouldn't work on the car tonight. It just seemed like a good night to stay home.

He tucked the dog into his jacket, took her out the back door, and ran up the stairs. He was soaking wet by the time they got inside, but he'd spared Daisy the worst of it. She was indignant anyway, shaking herself violently. After he'd fed her, he stood by the window to the balcony and watched the rain.

Ever since he'd seen Stu, he'd been waiting for Mel to say that her brother had called or stopped by. But a week had passed and she'd said nothing about it.

What did he have to lose? The friendship wasn't exactly flourishing anyway.

George called the number but reached voice mail. "Stu, it's George," he said. "Get off your duff and do something before you lose your sister. She's not working tomorrow so you can't use her work schedule as an excuse. If you don't want her around your boys, then keep her away from them, but you're no longer at a young and impressionable age so I don't think she's a bad influence on you."

He ended the call. It was an abrupt way to end the message, but he didn't care.

With Daisy's crunching noises as the backdrop for his thoughts, he booted up his computer so he could research his hunch about Mel. He didn't have much to go on. Just the atrocious spelling on her job application. The way she'd always loathed school. The problem she'd had in making change for customers.

He typed the words into the search engine: learning disabilities.

Mel's stomach growled. This wasn't the way she'd pictured her day off, but she couldn't think of a polite way to tell Tish it was time for lunch.

For three hours, they'd worked around the house. They'd oiled creaky hinges, unpacked one box of kitchen stuff, and then they'd hung blinds, then curtains, and then pictures, including that ugly old portrait. She didn't know why Tish would even want it anymore.

Tish set her pink plastic toolbox on the coffee table and turned her head slowly as if she were trying to get the panoramic view of the living room. "A woman isn't fully dressed without her accessories, and a house is never fully dressed without her window treatments."

Mel tried to act enthusiastic. "Yeah, they're pretty." But curtains and blinds just felt like walls between her and the outdoors. They made her feel trapped.

At least Tish had opened the slats so they didn't block the view completely. Not that the view was anything special. Just Mrs. Nair's house.

Tish took a pen and scratched out a couple of lines in her tiny notebook. "It feels great to have so many items crossed off my to-do list. Thanks for your help, Mel."

"You're welcome. Now we can eat—" A big silver SUV pulled up in front of the house. Mel squinted to see through the blinds. "Oh boy. That's my brother."

"Wonderful! I'm so glad he's coming to see you."

"But I don't know why he'd want to."

"Because you're his sister. This is good, Mel. It might be the first step toward working things out."

"Fat chance. I wonder how he found out I'm here."

Already moving toward the front door, Tish said, "George knows him, right? Maybe they talked."

She sounded so excited, but Mel worried that if Stu and George had talked, they would've dragged up every bad thing she'd ever done—or every bad thing they thought she'd done. All that old garbage would be fresh in Stu's mind, and he might spout off in front of Tish. Then Tish would kick her out.

Mel decided she'd better meet him at the street. She put herself between Tish and the door.

Walking around his vehicle, Stu ran a comb through his hair. It didn't take long. He didn't have as much hair as he used to. He put the comb in his pocket and made a face at the front yard.

Tish laughed. "Think he'll volunteer to help with the yard work?"

"Not a chance," Mel said with her hand on the doorknob. "Wish me luck."

"You don't want to invite him in?"

"Maybe another time." Like when the devil and all his demons needed ice skates.

That was the way Grandpa John had always said it, and the memory made her want to cry. Now she'd never be able to hold herself together.

Tish came closer. "I'll come out and meet him, then."

"No, don't bother." Mel shut the door behind her and ran down the steps. She kept herself focused on the walkway's big, flat stones and the way their odd shapes fit together like a jigsaw puzzle. Once she reached the sidewalk, she let herself look at Stuart.

He was going bald. Definitely. He'd gained some weight too, so he looked older than George even if they were the same age. Stu used to be a teddy bear, grumpy but sweet. Now she only saw the grumpy part.

"Hey, Stu." She smiled, trying to make it real, but she felt as phony as Amanda.

"Hey." His face belonged on a middle-aged Ken doll. Plastic. Cold. The opposite of a cuddly teddy bear. Then he looked past her, putting on that carsalesman friendliness. "Hello there. You must be the Tish McComb I've heard about."

Tish and Stu shook hands, but then they only made small talk until he said something about wanting to see Mel on his lunch break but he had to make it snappy. Tish stepped back, grinning like she thought everything was just fine. They said good-bye to each other, and that was that. Tish headed back to the house.

Mel took a big breath and looked up at Stu. "So, where are we going?"

"I don't know."

"Well, we can't stay here. You wouldn't be caught dead hanging around the McComb house, would you?"

He frowned like he wasn't sure she was joking. "I've been wondering why you landed here, of all places."

"Rejects like to hang out together."

"You're not a reject. Or at least you wouldn't be if you would straighten up so people could trust you."

"George trusts me. He hired me. And he cleared my name, Stu. He figured out why everybody thought I was stealing. From my old jobs, I mean."

Stu gave her a skeptical squint. "I had coffee with him about a week ago, and he didn't say anything about clearing your name."

George hadn't stuck up for her? That hurt.

"So what?" she said. "Even if he didn't tell you about it, it's still true. But where are we going?"

He opened the passenger door. "We'll think of something."

She climbed in, and he shut the door. She patted the leather seat and inhaled the new-car smell. It smelled like the showroom at the dealership. Like money and power and pride.

He climbed in, buckled up, and eyed her seat belt while he started the engine. She ignored the hint.

"So, you hungry or anything?" he asked.

Not anymore. "No, thanks."

"Just want to ride around and talk?"

"Sure. I've got lots of time. No money, but lots of time."

He backed a little ways into Tish's driveway, nearly tapping bumpers with her Volvo, then pulled out, pointing the SUV toward Main. "So, where have you been? I heard Vegas."

"I don't know how that rumor got started. I was in Florida. Orlando, mostly."

"What did you do there?"

"I worked at a restaurant. A seafood restaurant."

Stu laughed. "That's funny. The kid who hates the smell of fish, working at a seafood restaurant."

She laughed too, glad he'd remembered that about her. "It wasn't too bad." Except she was always low man on the totem pole, and she never moved up from bussing tables because she'd admitted she had a hard time counting change.

"Who did you stay with?"

"I was in an apartment. I had some pretty cool roommates." Some terrible roommates too, but nobody stayed long. "The girl who got me the job lived there, and she gave me a ride if we were working the same shift. I had a bike too, but that wasn't great when it was raining. Then somebody stole it anyway."

"Couldn't afford a car, huh?"

"Nope." She relaxed a little. It was almost like old times, talking things over with her big brother.

He turned right at Main, heading away from town. "You already blew what you got for my watch?"

So much for a happy reunion. "Who says it was yours? You only cared about how much it was worth, and Grandpa John knew it. He said he was giving it to me because I loved it and you didn't."

"Did he put it in writing? That he'd give it to you?"

Mel thought Stu sounded like a spoiled brat. "No. He died without a will, remember?"

"I remember. I sure do. It was a crime, especially after all the times we tried to tell him to get his affairs in order." He stepped on the accelerator.

"You know what's a crime? The way this thing slurps up about five bucks' worth of gas every minute."

"Don't try to change the subject, Melanie. Taking the watch was a crime. Grand larceny. It was worth a lot of money."

"You're driving a huge, expensive gas hog, but you'll fuss at me about an old watch? I don't even have shoes except these because I had to throw my old ones out." She propped her sneakers up on the fancy dashboard. "These are from a thrift store."

"You've made bad decisions, so you have to live with the consequences. You can turn your life around, though. Find a job. A *real* job."

"It's hard when you don't have a college degree."

"What's stopping you? You can work and go to school at the same time. A lot of people do. And there's financial help."

"Like anybody would give me a scholarship."

"Scholarships aren't given. They're earned."

"Then it's hopeless."

"I didn't pick you up just so you could argue with everything I say."

"No, you picked me up so you could lecture me like I'm five."

"Because you still act like a five-year-old."

Out of her window, green trees rushed by in a blur. Sometimes she wished she could be five again. Back before she'd figured out she was an oops baby. No matter how hard she tried, she could never make her folks proud. They'd never wanted her in the first place. They'd only wanted Stuart, their perfect son.

Rage bubbled up inside her. "Most five-year-olds have better manners than you do, Stuart. You're a jerk like your father, who isn't my father anymore, so I guess you're not my brother anymore either."

"That's it. I've had it."

He veered into the turning lane and swung left in front of an oncoming car. Mel slid across the seat, shrieking. A horn blared. She caught a glimpse of a woman at the wheel, her lips moving as she gave them the finger.

Once Mel could breathe again, she realized they were on the long driveway that led to the abandoned barn. "You trying to kill me?" she asked.

"I can't say I've never considered the idea."

He hung a U in the weeds. It was all so familiar to her now—the barn's sagging roof, the rusty hulk of an old pickup with no windows. She wanted to smack him for trespassing on her private property. It was amazing, though, how fast they got there, and how fast they were flying away from it now. On foot, it seemed like a five-mile walk from Tish's house. Driving, it was only a minute or two.

He drove back toward Main with the engine roaring and made a right. "I'd better drop you off and get home."

Their folks' house was home to him, then, at least for a while. Lucky Stu. If he showed up in time for lunch, nobody would tell him to get lost.

Mel swallowed and stared straight ahead. They'd gather around the table,

Stu and Janice and the boys. Nicky and Jamie would grab fruit from the crystal bowl with their grubby hands. Mom would wait on them, hand and foot. Even Janice.

Can I get you some lemonade, Stu? Janice, baby, you want some potato salad?

"Drop me off somewhere, okay?" Her lips were frozen rubber.

"I'll take you back to the house." He smirked. "The McComb house, I mean."

No, she'd scream if she didn't get out now. "Drop me off here."

"If you insist."

He swerved into the parking lot of a vacant bank building and braked so sharply she had to throw her left hand against the dash.

"This okay?"

"Perfect." She climbed out, sucked in a big breath of fresh air, and stood there holding the door open. "You used to be nice, Stuart. What happened? When did you change?"

"What about you? No, I guess you've always been this way."

"What way?" She held her breath, hoping he would explain.

"Never mind. Sorry. I'm under a lot of stress." He let out a long sigh and faced the windshield. "There's something you should know. About the Corvette."

She felt like a thin sheet flapping on a clothesline in a strong wind. "No," she whispered. "No."

"Dad decided to sell it. Before something happens to it and it loses its value."

"It's not his," she said between clenched teeth. "It's not his car."

"Sure, technically it's Mom's." He faced her again, his eyes hard. "What difference does it make?"

What *difference*?

Mel's throat had closed up. She slammed the door and ran.

Twenty-Six

George wasn't in an especially good mood. He'd stayed half an hour past closing time to court a fussy customer who'd finally walked out without buying a thing. Calv had probably been working on the car for an hour already.

George parked at the curb and climbed out, dog in hand. Daisy trembled with excitement. "You don't live here anymore, dummy," he said.

She yipped and went into full wiggle mode.

"But that doesn't mean I'm not tempted to leave you here," he added.

The front door opened, and Tish poked her head out. She'd tied a red bandana around her head, slightly askew and filmed with cobwebs. "Hey, George. How's the project car coming along?"

Like the Tish project, it was too soon to tell. "She's prettier every day," he said. "How's everything going for you? Is Mel behaving herself?"

"I'm delighted to report that her brother picked her up about noon, and I haven't seen her since."

So, Stu got the message. Maybe he hadn't become a complete jerk after all.

"Excellent," George said, "but don't count on Mel patching things up with her family right away. Even if it happens, it might not last."

"I know, but I'm hoping for the best." Tish's face brightened. "Hey, can I get your professional opinion on a little bitty antique? At least I think it's an antique."

"Sure."

"It's upstairs. Come on in. I'll run up and get it."

He secured Daisy's leash to the porch railing and walked in. While Tish went upstairs and Daisy lay down at the door that was once hers, he surveyed the living room. He hadn't been inside since he sold the place to the Nelsons.

Tish owned an old upright piano. A beautiful rosewood Fischer of Victorian vintage, it would be worth a pretty penny if the innards were in good shape too. Her other furnishings, though, were Early Attic at best.

Seeing the place filled with Tish's possessions made it seem less like his mother's domain, but the furnace still grumbled like an angry troll in the cellar, and his mother's last dog sprawled on the porch, perfectly content. He shook his head, wanting to forget the succession of Maltese puppies that had piddled on those beautiful hardwoods.

Turning again, he faced a large portrait of a cadaverous old gent and his colorless bride. One of those studio photographs that had become common shortly after the War, it was set in an ornate gilded frame that outshone the couple. Then it hit him. This was the portrait Tish had mentioned. The notorious Nathan and Letitia McComb looked sickly—but not evil. They didn't look like villains who would steal doorknobs and whatnots from the home of a dying widow.

He hadn't read the scanned letters yet. He almost hated to. Reality was seldom as interesting as tall tales.

"Found it." Tish ran down the stairs, moving so fast he was afraid she would slip and tumble to the bottom.

"Next time, slide down the banister," he said. "It's faster."

"Did you, when you were a kid?"

"Sometimes, if my mother wasn't home. What have you got?"

"It's just a button I picked up at a yard sale. It's so pretty I thought I could make it into a pin."

She opened her hand, revealing a metal button about an inch in diameter. A delicate honeybee resting on a lotus leaf. The nature motif hinted that it was Victorian, but the style leaned toward art nouveau.

He pulled his jeweler's loupe from his pocket. "May I?"

"Sure." She handed it over.

Under magnification, the details popped—the veins in the insect's wings, the dewdrops on the leaf. He turned it over. A shank back. No marks.

He looked up at Tish in her bandana and had to smile. He'd never seen her in anything dressier than jeans, yet she'd fallen in love with this little delicacy.

"How much did you pay?"

"Four dollars for a whole tin of old buttons. This is the only really interesting one, so that was probably a ripoff."

"No, you did well. I'd say it's from sometime around the turn of the century. Victorian verging on art nouveau. It's in good condition. You go making a pin out of it, and it won't be worth as much to a collector."

"What do you think it's worth?"

"Retail, as is, probably between forty and fifty."

Her eyes widened. "Dollars?"

George smiled. "Dollars," he repeated. She sounded like Mrs. Rose, who'd said the word in the same incredulous tone but for a different reason.

"For one little button?"

"Yes ma'am. If you want to sell it, I'll pay—"

She snatched it from his fingers. "I don't want to know. I never said I wanted to sell it."

George stifled a laugh and returned the loupe to his pocket. "Why did you want to know its value, then?"

"Just to know if I found a bargain, I guess, but I'll never sell it. I love tangible connections to the past. Even to parts of the past that have nothing to do with me. Does that sound crazy?"

"Not at all."

"I knew you would understand. You deal in antiques. Connections to the past."

Her earnest expression compelled him to confess. "I hate to break it to you, but my connections to my merchandise are strictly mercenary. I have no sentimental attachments to anything in my shop."

"Really? None?"

"None. You're not too disappointed, are you?"

"Well…yes. Yes, I am." She examined the button again, then looked up. "What about the Chevelle? Is that just a pile of metal and chrome to you?"

"Of course not. It's a big, noisy toy—and an investment as well. And if anything should happen to it, now it's insured to the hilt." He made his way to the door and stepped onto the porch. "I'd better get out to the garage before Calv starts thinking it's his toy, not mine."

Daisy had stretched herself out like the Sphinx, except her posture was more relaxed. She rested her chin on her leash. Too lazy to raise her head, she lifted her gaze, showing the whites of her eyes.

"Come on, Daisy. Let's go work on the car."

She blinked, sighed, thumped her tail once, and closed her eyes.

Tish leaned in the doorway. "You can leave her here if you want. She looks perfectly happy."

"Thanks, but I'd better take her with me. I don't want to encourage her delusion that this is still her porch."

Catching a movement from the corner of his eye, George looked down the block. Mel trudged along the sidewalk, her head hanging and her shoulders slumped.

"Here comes Mel," he said. "And she doesn't look like a girl who spent the afternoon in the bosom of a forgiving family."

Tish moved to stand beside him. "Maybe she's tired."

"But if they parted on good terms, Stu would have dropped her off at your door. Especially if she was tired."

Mel turned into the yard and looked up. "Hey, y'all." Her glum greeting matched her body language.

"Everything okay?" he asked.

She stopped at the bottom of the steps. "Well, yeah. Sure. Except—" She met his eyes. "Except they're selling my car."

She looked so forlorn that he tried to speak as lightly as possible. "It's not your car."

"Yes it is," she said in a quiet but controlled voice. "Did you know? You knew they were selling it and you didn't tell me?"

Obviously, the gentle approach wasn't working. "It was never yours anyway."

She moved up the steps. "It was. Grandpa John told me it was."

"Funny thing is, nobody else ever heard him say that."

"I know, George. I know. Nobody ever believes me." Her words came faster now, spilling over each other in a small, frantic stream. "Even if he didn't officially leave it to me, it should've gone to my mom, not my dad, but he took it because she never learned to drive a stick, and now he thinks it's his to sell, but it's not."

"Melanie—"

"I'll never see it again. He'll sell it to somebody who doesn't even live around here, because nobody around here can afford it. Almost nobody." She edged closer to George. "I know you have tons of money. Please, please, buy it back for me. I'll pay you back someday."

If it had been anyone else making the ludicrous suggestion, he would have laughed out loud. "I'm sorry, Mel, but I don't have that kind of money. Not even close."

Her shoulders drooped. She turned to Tish.

Tish shook her head. "Don't look at me. I don't even have a job."

Mel shifted her gaze to something in the distance. Like a rag doll retrofitted with a spine, she straightened her posture. "I'm not the thief. *He* is."

Tish tried to wave her inside. "Come on in. Did you have supper?"

"No, but I'm not hungry. I'm tired. I'm going to lie down. Thanks, though." With a faraway look in her eyes, Mel stepped past them and into the house.

George braced himself for the slamming of a door. He only heard the faint click of a latch as Mel shut the door to the downstairs bedroom that used to be his mother's.

Tish leaned toward him. "That's not like her," she whispered. "Mel's never not hungry."

"She must have had a hard day. Emotionally draining." But his brain marched double-time toward a different explanation. The brat was plotting something.

"She was talking about the Corvette, right? The one she took for a joyride?"

"Yes, and if she knew how much it's worth, she'd be on a rampage right now."

"How much is it worth?"

"Ballpark figure? Sixty grand, probably."

Tish inhaled sharply. "Sixty *thousand*?"

"Yes ma'am. Sixty thousand dollars. It's nearly mint, it's rare, and it's beautiful. And I can't blame Dunc for selling. Actually, I'm surprised he's kept it this long."

"Sentimental value, maybe?"

"Dunc, sentimental? No, more likely he was waiting for the economy to pick up."

"Didn't her grandpa make a will?"

"He never got around to it, I guess, or maybe he didn't want to write one. He was an eccentric old guy who made a killing in the stock market. I think Suzette was always ashamed of her dad even after he made his money, but he and Mel always got along." George paused, thinking. "Maybe he took a shine to her because her folks named her after him—and that might have been a calculated effort to encourage him to be generous in his will. The will he never wrote."

"Wait. I thought they named her after Melanie in *Gone with the Wind*."

"They did, but her middle name is John, for her Grandpa John Hoff."

"John? As in J-O-H-N? For a girl?"

"Why not? My mother's middle name was James, after her father."

"Must be a southern thing."

He decided to live dangerously. Venture onto thin ice again. "Watch your tone, Yankee woman."

She smiled. "You'd better be joking."

The dark humor in her eyes made him want to stay longer, sparring with her, but Calv let out a yelp followed by a long string of unhappiness, the words muffled by distance.

"I'd better get back there," George said. "It's not fair to make Calv suffer all the skinned knuckles."

"If you guys ever need first aid, come on up to the house," Tish said.

"I'll keep that in mind." Maybe he could arrange a gently smashed thumbnail for himself.

Tish smiled as if she'd read his mind. "You do that." She went inside, shutting the door.

Feeling vaguely guilty about something, he picked up the dog. When he was halfway down the steps, his conscience explained itself to him: he was ashamed of himself for cheerfully flirting with Tish when Mel was miserable.

Carrying the dog down the steps and around the house, he pondered the market for high-end vintage cars in Hunt County. It wasn't a wealthy area, but Dunc was a dealer. He knew how and where to advertise, and he had connections. He'd find a buyer in no time, and Mel's crazy little heart would break all over again.

Twenty-Seven

M el dried a plate and added it to the stack in the cupboard. Her feet hurt from working all day, but her heart hurt worse. She couldn't stop thinking about the 'Vette. She had to see it one more time. She just had to. But if her dad—Dunc—didn't want her in the house, he wouldn't want her in the garage either. He *especially* wouldn't want her in the garage.

Tish breezed through the kitchen, putting on a pair of funky, dangly earrings and then fluffing her hair. "I'm going out back. To get the latest updates on the Chevelle."

"Have fun." Mel could have given her the latest about the wiring harness, whatever that was, but she knew Tish didn't give a flip about the car. She wanted to see George.

It would be fantastic to be able to talk to the guy you loved, any old time.

With a sigh, Mel dried the last plate and put it away in the cupboard. She was so tired of acting happy. At work, George kept watching her. Not like he thought she'd steal something, but like he was afraid she'd fall apart in the middle of polishing a candlestick or whatever. She'd held it together, though. Even when he acted like he thought she was about to throw a fit, which was exactly what made her want to throw a fit, she'd held it together.

Praying helped. She kept asking God to keep the car from selling, and to help buyers find other cars before they saw Dunc's ads. She prayed about a million other things too, like money and clothes and figuring out how to get along without a family and how to go to college when she could hardly read. Last night, instead of crying herself to sleep, she'd prayed the night away.

She hung the towel over the handle on the oven door, then circled around to make sure she hadn't missed anything to wash or put away.

Tish's phone lay on the table.

Thinking hard about how to make the most of her big chance, Mel waited for a minute to make sure Tish wasn't coming back for the phone. Then, keeping an eye out for her, Mel dialed her mom's number.

Please, God, don't let Tish look at her call records—

"Hello?"

"Hey, Mom. It's me. Mel."

A brief pause. "Where are you? It's the wrong area code."

"I borrowed a phone from a friend."

"Are you all right? Are you still in town?"

"Yeah! Yeah, I got a job. I've been working for George."

"That's nice."

Mel had hoped she'd sound more excited. Maybe it wasn't the best time to ask about the car. The clothes shouldn't be a big deal, though.

"I'm not making much money yet," she said. "And I need clothes. Can I stop by sometime for some of my things?"

"I don't think that would be wise."

"It would only take a few minutes. Come on, Mom. You can throw some things in a bag and leave it by the front door if you don't want to see me."

"It's not that. Your father doesn't want you on our property. He says you're a bad influence on Stu's boys. You know they're staying with us for a while."

"Yeah, but how long can it take to remodel a kitchen? Anyway, I don't even have to see the boys. I can come when they're in school. Pick a day and I'll be there. Well, if I'm not working." Mel swung around to look at the calendar on the wall. "Hey, your anniversary is coming up. Are you planning anything?"

"Yes. Nothing fancy, though. Dinner and a movie in Muldro."

Mel waited for her mom to say something about a birthday dinner too, but she didn't. Not one word. And she was the one who always planned things weeks and weeks ahead of time.

"I guess we're not getting together for my birthday, huh?"

"If you weren't a bad influence on Nick and Jamie—"

"Don't give me that." Mel felt hard and mean inside, as sharp as the blade of her mom's food processor. "Even if Nicky and Jamie weren't around, even if they didn't exist, you'd still wish *I* didn't exist. And you say *I'm* a bad influence? What kind of influence do you think you are on me?"

Mel ended the call and put the phone back where she'd found it. She picked it up again, wiped it with her shirt, and put it down carefully. No fingerprints. Then she stared out the window at branches bobbing up and down in the wind.

Her parents weren't going to do a thing for her twenty-first birthday. The big one. She was a stranger to them. A nobody. She was dead to them, but they weren't crying for her. Well, she wouldn't cry for them either.

She might cry for Nicky and Jamie, though. And even for Stu.

She remembered looking over her shoulder after he'd dropped her off at the vacant bank building. A crazy thought had hit her hard: *What if I never see him again?* For one little second, she'd loved him for being the big, grown-up brother who whooped and cheered for her at the kindergarten talent show and cried when the cop brought her home after she'd run away.

But then she saw the dealership license plate on the back of the big silver gas hog, and she remembered he was part of Dunc Hamilton's business. That made Stu the enemy, almost.

She wouldn't cry for him anymore either. She was done.

Walking into the warmth of the kitchen after a chilly half hour in the garage, Tish smiled. She'd been cold, but she'd enjoyed having George all to herself for a while. No Calv. No Mel, although her troubles had come up in the conversation. Just Daisy, who didn't matter…and George, who was beginning to matter a lot.

She had to call Mom soon. She would want to know all about George, like Tish had wanted to know all about Charles. The mother-daughter bond had grown stronger through their losses—first Stephen, then Dad—and sometimes Tish thought they were more like sisters than mom and daughter.

She turned in a circle, inspecting the kitchen. Mel had done a great job of leaving it spick-and-span, as usual. Tish headed toward the guest room to express her appreciation. The poor kid probably didn't get enough pats on the back, especially if George's new theory held any water. An undiagnosed learning disability could explain a lot of Mel's issues.

Reaching the bedroom doorway, Tish stopped, picking up bad vibes from Mel's furtive body language. Unaware of her visitor, Mel tiptoed to the dresser and opened the top drawer, being awfully quiet about it. She pulled a white sock from the back of the drawer and squeezed the toe of it, then glanced over her shoulder. Seeing Tish, she jumped, dropping the sock, and slammed the drawer.

"What are you hiding, Mel?"

"Nothing." But she stood squarely in front of the dresser, her face as white as the day she'd thought her sleeping bag had gone in the wash.

Hugely disappointed, Tish shook her head. "Wasn't honesty one of the things we talked about when I laid down my house rules?"

Mel's eyes narrowed. "I can be honest without telling you absolutely everything."

"What are you hiding?"

"What do you *think* I'm hiding?"

"I don't know. If it's something harmless, you shouldn't be afraid to show me."

"It's none of your business."

"If it's under my roof, it's my business."

Mel's cheeks turned red. "Fine. You want to see my horrible, awful, illegal secret? I'll show you." She yanked the drawer open, picked up the sock, and pulled something out of it. She opened her hand, revealing an old-fashioned gold pocket watch. "It was Grandpa John's. He gave it to me."

Tish drew in her breath. "Well! Farris was right when he decided not to hire me because of you."

"He what?"

"Farris refused to give me a job because he heard I was harboring a criminal. I stuck up for you, Mel, but I shouldn't have. You're a thief, all right, and you cost me that job."

"Grandpa John promised me the watch. Why don't you believe me? Why don't you trust me?"

"You don't seem to be trustworthy. The evidence is piling up, and it's all going against you."

"Like the evidence against the McCombs is piling up?" Mel spat out. "It doesn't feel good to have your reputation in the Dumpster, does it? But you're doing the same thing to me." Mel stalked across the room, almost invading Tish's personal space. "I am not a thief."

Tish glanced down at Mel's hand clenched around the watch. "You stole the watch. You need to give it back."

Mel opened her fist. With her other hand, she ran a fingertip over a monogram engraved on the smooth golden case. "It's mine."

Tish hated to act like Mel's mother again, but somebody had to. "It's not legally yours. I won't have stolen property in my house, Melanie. If you won't give it back to your father, move out of my house. Today."

"Grandpa John told me he was going to give me the watch someday, but for a long time, I didn't know what he meant." Mel's voice shook. "When I figured it out, I said I didn't want it if he had to die to give it to me. He said that was exactly why he wanted me to have it." She let out a little sob and shoved the watch into Tish's hand. "Go ahead, give it back, but I'm never talking to Dunc again."

"Mel—"

But Mel pushed her way past Tish and ran down the hall. The front door slammed.

Weak in the knees, Tish wobbled over to the bed and sat on the edge. Opening her hand, she studied the watch case. The monogram read *JMH,* presumably for John M. Hoff. Mel's initials were *MJH,* the same letters in different order. Remembering her conversation with George, Tish wondered what it would be like to live in a world where letters and numbers shuffled their order when you weren't looking.

She opened the case. The watch ticked quietly in her hand, keeping perfect time. It had survived two years in Mel's possession without a scratch, and she'd never intended to sell it.

Now Dunc's demand wasn't impossible. He might let Mel rejoin the family, especially if he understood why she'd taken the watch. He might even let her keep it.

Twenty-Eight

Bright with banners and balloons, Duncan Hamilton's dealership stood near the interstate on the outskirts of Muldro, not far from the outlet mall. His main building included a two-story tower of steel and glass topped with a gigantic American flag. Dunc's office, according to Mel, was on the second floor, where he enjoyed an unobstructed view of Muldro and the green hills beyond.

Tish parked in the customer parking lot, climbed out, then reached into her purse to make sure the watch was still there. According to George, it was worth much more than she'd guessed. They hadn't told Mel how much, and maybe they never would. She'd returned at midnight, afraid she'd be locked out and find herself on the street again. She'd fallen apart when Tish offered a hug instead of a lecture.

She took a deep breath and started walking across the lot. Returning the watch was the responsible and proper thing to do, so she would do it. Arriving without an appointment with the head honcho on a busy Saturday, she could only hope he was available, but she wanted to take him by surprise.

In the showroom, she encountered a pair of hungry-looking salesmen in matching polo shirts.

"I'm here to see Dunc," she said before they could pounce. "Upstairs, yes?"

The salesmen pointed her toward an elevator, and she took it to the second floor. The view was beautiful if she looked beyond the outlet mall and restaurant row. Turning from the window, she proceeded along a broad hallway lined with offices open to view behind glass. Telephones rang, printers hummed, and employees laughed. It seemed like a pleasant enough place to work.

Farther down the hallway, it was quieter. A door with a brass nameplate caught her eye. She moved close enough to read it. Dunc Hamilton.

Until she'd shared her plan with George and absorbed some of his pessimism, she'd thought it sounded easy enough. Just walk into Dunc Hamilton's office and return the watch. Now she wasn't so sure.

The door was ajar by a couple of inches. Hoping he wouldn't be there, she knocked gently on the door frame. "Mr. Hamilton?"

"Come on in, whoever you are." He sounded genial enough.

Cautiously, she pushed the door open. A muscular figure stood silhouetted against a sunny window. She couldn't make out his features, but his stance was like that of a high school football coach on the sidelines of a game: legs apart, hands on his hips. In polo shirt and khakis, he only needed a coach's whistle around his neck to complete the stereotype. That impression was confirmed by photos of sports teams on display all around the office: Little League, soccer, youth football.

As he stepped away from the window, his features became visible. She saw Mel in his smile and his warm brown eyes.

"Hello," he said. "I'm Dunc Hamilton."

"Hello," she said. "My name is Tish McComb."

The warmth drained from his expression. "I've heard about you."

"I've heard about you too. I'm one of Mel's friends."

"I'm sorry to hear that. She's a troublemaker."

"She's your daughter, Mr. Hamilton. Please don't talk about her that way."

"It's the truth."

"People can change. She's a sweet girl, really. Give her a chance."

Dunc sighed. "I'll be happy to work with you if you ever want to buy a vehicle, but if you show up again to preach at me, I'll have security throw you out. Is that clear?"

Tish's hopes deflated. "It's a little too clear, actually."

"Good day to you, then."

"Wait. I—I wanted to tell you…" She blinked, trying to remember the carefully crafted lines she'd rehearsed on the drive over to Muldro. They'd all fled her mind.

"Yes?" he prompted.

She reached into her purse for the watch but kept it hidden in her hand. "Mel still believes this was meant to be hers, but she's returning it to you. To make things right." Tish opened her hand, displaying the watch on her palm.

He let out a delighted laugh. "I thought she sold that thing." He was an imposing figure as he moved closer.

She hid the watch behind her back. "She could have sold it, but she didn't. She hung on to it even when she was flat broke and homeless, because it was her only memento of her Grandpa John."

"Give it here."

"You don't need it, do you? And it means so much to Mel."

"I guess that's why she stole it." He held out his hand. "Give it to me."

"If I give it back, will you stop shutting her out of the family?"

"*If* you give it to me? It's my property. My wife's, actually, and she'd planned to give it to our son. If Mel ever has the courage to face me in person, maybe we'll talk about letting her back in the family."

Tish laughed in disbelief. "What if your father-in-law really meant to give it to her?"

"Then he should have given it to her before he kicked the bucket, or he should have made a will. The law is the law."

Tish backed toward the door. He followed, his hand still extended.

"Give me the watch before I call security."

"What would you do if you lost her suddenly? Wouldn't you wish you'd treated her better? She's your daughter."

He shook his head slowly. "She says she's not my daughter anymore."

"I'm starting to understand why."

She took another step backward, calculating her chances, but she knew he would sic his security goons on her. She, the woman who'd never had a parking ticket, would be charged with grand larceny. Her name would be mud.

So what? The McComb name was already mud. It was like her dad's joke that he drove a dented old vehicle so he would win parking-space battles. People in nice vehicles could see he had nothing to lose.

She had something to lose, though. Her conscience. Her self-respect.

"Hand it over," Dunc said with a smug smile.

Tish dropped the watch in his outstretched palm and left him to gloat over his victory.

Waiting for the elevator, she stood by a wall of glass and surveyed row after row after row of glittering new vehicles awaiting their new owners. Dunc Hamilton had everything he needed, but Mel, more than ever, had nothing.

Having failed to talk Tish out of her crazy mission, George had spent the day keeping an eye on Mel. She worried him. She managed to act perky for their customers, but every time the shop emptied, she retreated into silence and gloom. He wished Tish would call, at least, but the lack of communication told him it hadn't gone well.

It was nearly closing time when he heard a knock on the back door. He checked to be sure Mel was in the showroom and out of earshot before he opened the door, but when Tish walked in, she didn't need to speak. Her tearful eyes said it all.

"Bad news, huh?"

She nodded. "Where is she?"

"Out front. Sit." George pulled out the chair at the head of the ugly old worktable. "What happened?"

She sank onto the chair and looked up at him. "I thought returning the watch was the key to patching things up with her family. I even thought he would let her keep it. Now she doesn't have the watch or the family." She covered her face with her hands. "I guess I'm the only one who isn't surprised."

"You're the only one who doesn't know Dunc." George reached down to give her shoulder a squeeze. "Are you ready to talk to her?"

She nodded, still hiding her face.

"I'll get her."

It was a matter of three minutes to lock up the shop and return to the back room with Calv and Mel. Silent and expressionless, she faced Tish and waited.

"Mel, I'm sorry," Tish said. "Your dad took the watch, but he didn't...well, getting it back didn't soften his heart any."

"He always takes things." Mel's eyes were dry, and her voice was soft but steady. "Like he took the car. Like he took the black jacket when it was so cold..."

"I'd feel better if you'd scream at me and tell me what a stupid idea it was."

"It's okay, Tish. I just want to be alone for a while." Mel found her hoodie and walked out the back door, shutting it gently.

Silence settled upon them until Calv let out a heavy sigh. "The prodigal went to a far country and lost everything," he said.

Tish's face hardened. "She didn't lose everything. She had the watch—until I made her give it back. I wish I hadn't."

Unperturbed by her tone, Calv kept going. "Dunc ain't in the business of killing fatted calves. He don't fit the father mold. Mel don't fit the repentant prodigal mold either."

"She's hungry, isn't she, just like the prodigal in the Bible," Tish snapped.

"Yes ma'am. I'll give you that one." Calv widened his eyes at George as if to invite him into the discussion.

George shook his head and pursued his thoughts in silence. It was safer that way.

Instead of asking for her inheritance, Mel had swiped her older brother's watch. And instead of asking forgiveness, she'd steadfastly maintained that she'd only taken what was hers. No wonder Dunc hadn't given her a fancy robe or fired up the grill.

Tish glared at Calv. "I wish somebody would do something practical."

He gave her a reproachful look. "Like what, young lady?"

"I guess punching Dunc's lights out wouldn't count."

"We don't want to do that, Miss Tish. Cross that man, and he turns into ten gallons of mean in a five-gallon bucket. It sloshes all over everybody." Calv pulled keys from his pocket. "I gotta get off to my AA meeting before somebody draws me into some kind of altercation. Bye, y'all." He left by the back door, his shoulders stooped.

Tish rose. "I should head back to the house too."

"Hold on a minute," George said. "Was Stu there?"

"I didn't see him. It was only Dunc and me in his office. I felt like a peon, and he was the king who had the power to say 'off with her head.'"

"He has that way about him."

"I seriously considered making a run for it. With the watch." She laughed sadly. "Farris was right. Bad company has corrupted my good morals."

"Don't be too hard on yourself. Most people would never have the courage to confront Dunc in the first place."

"He had every right to be angry with her." She sighed and moved toward the door. "I've been thinking about it all day. The Carlyle family had every right to be angry with Nathan for stealing too, but it's wrong to hang on to the anger forever."

George opened the door for her, his mind teeming with troubled thoughts about Yankees and carpetbaggers, prodigals and parents and siblings. Every story had more than one side to it.

Twenty-Nine

Walking out of the parts store with Calv on Sunday afternoon, George shook his head, recalling a snatch of a dream he'd had when he drifted off to sleep in church. In his dream, Tish had been preaching, and she was mad as heck about something.

Then he'd snapped out of it, waking in a church that didn't allow lady preachers. He'd found himself wishing mightily that it did. Tish would wake up a few people.

Returning to reality, he peered into the brown paper sack and shook his head. "I can't believe one little gizmo cost me forty bucks."

Calv snorted. "Your shorts too tight? You've been grouchy all day. No, all week. Ever since Tish took the watch to Dunc."

Had it been a week? Yes. Eight days, actually. Tish had stormed Dunc's office on a Saturday. A week ago yesterday. Meanwhile, Stu and his family had moved back to their own house. When George told Mel, she'd said she didn't care if they moved to the North Pole. They weren't her family anymore.

She had worked four days over the past week. Her job skills were improving, and she'd started to master the art of making cheerful chitchat with even the most obnoxious customers. But when things got slow, she hardly said a word.

Calv squinted into the sunshine. "Speak of the devil. Two of 'em."

Dunc and Stu ambled across the parking lot, their heads bent together, heading toward a silver SUV parked only a few spaces away from George's van. That was convenient.

"Good afternoon," George said when they were too close to ignore him.

Stu mumbled some kind of greeting—he'd never responded to George's voice mail—and Dunc nodded but didn't speak.

George's temper began to wake up. "May I have a word with you, Dunc?"

"Sure. Fire away."

George stopped a few feet from them and put his hands on his hips, the paper bag probably detracting from what he'd hoped would be a gunslinger stance. "Why do you act like Mel isn't part of the family anymore?"

"If she wants to play by the rules, I'll let her back in the game."

Calv dropped a heavy hand on George's shoulder. "This ain't goin' anywhere good," he said quietly. "Leave it."

Still feeling Calv's crushing grip, George moved closer to Dunc. "I understand you're shutting her out even after she's tried to make amends."

"I told her already that I want an apology, but the little coward couldn't even face me in person. She had to send Letitia McComb, of all people, to apologize for her. To do her dirty work." Dunc shook his finger in George's face. "Keep that woman out of my hair, Zorbas."

George laughed. "I don't try to tell Tish what to do. But what's the big idea? You used to say you wouldn't welcome Mel home until she'd returned the watch. Now she's still not welcome after she's returned it?"

Stu's head jerked up. "She did? She never sold it?"

"She had it all this time," George said. "She gave it back, via Tish."

A storm stirred in Stu's eyes, usually so drowsy. "It was supposed to be my watch. When did this happen, Dad?"

"Over a week ago," George put in quickly.

Stu stared at his father. "Dad? You somehow forgot to tell me?"

"Relax," Dunc said. "I would've given it to you."

"Yeah, sure. Sure you would."

Stu hit a remote to unlock his vehicle, and both Hamiltons climbed in. He reversed the vehicle so quickly that neither of them could have buckled up yet. Exiting the lot, he cornered that big SUV as hard as if it were the Firebird he'd driven in high school.

Calv let out a low whistle. "Somethin' tells me Stu and his old man are having a highly entertaining discussion about the ownership of that watch."

"I hope Stu's giving him an earful."

Calv laughed softly. "Has Stu ever given anybody an earful?"

"There's a first time for everything."

But the real problem was that Stu, like his old man, seemed to value the watch more highly than he valued Mel.

It was a typical bad-news Monday. None of Tish's job leads had panned out lately. Trying to put a positive spin on it, she remembered her dad's favorite quotation from Thomas Edison: "I have not failed, not once. I've discovered ten thousand ways that don't work." But she wasn't sure her dad had the wording exactly right, and Edison had been talking about inventions, anyway. Not job hunting.

"I have not failed, not once," she told Mel, sitting behind her at the kitchen table. "I've just discovered a whole mess o' jobs that won't work for me."

"You're almost starting to sound like a southerner," Mel said. "Pretty soon you'll start saying 'y'all' instead of 'you guys.'"

Tish forced a laugh. "Maybe, but I refuse to say 'all y'all' or 'who-all.'"

Mel didn't answer, fortunately, because Tish couldn't have come up with another quip.

On top of everything else, now she'd burned the grilled cheese. She wanted to cry, but with Mel setting such a fine example of maturity and fortitude in spite of her family's issues, minor issues needed to remain that. Minor.

Tish swallowed hard, manufactured a smile, and turned from the stove with the plates in her hands. "Sorry." She slid Mel's plate across the table with the least burnt sandwich and kept the blacker one for herself. "It won't hurt my feelings if you want to scrape the burnt part into the trash."

"No, it's fine. I like things crispy." Mel gave her a thoughtful look. "You had a bad day, huh?"

A terrible day. "I'm never late for anything, not even a dentist appointment. Never. I always allow myself plenty of time, but everything went wrong. I was five minutes late."

"Five minutes? That's not bad."

"For an interview, it's terrible. Then I was flustered and I botched the interview. The woman pretended to love me, but I could see right through it."

"Yeah. I wish people would be honest. If they love you, they should show it. If they don't love you, they should show that too, instead of faking the love." Mel nibbled at the darkest corner of her sandwich. "Yum. Toasty."

Tish smiled. "I think you're faking your love for that burnt sandwich."

"No, I'm not faking it. I like burnt popcorn too. I'm weird that way."

Tish took a brave bite of her sandwich and wanted to spit it out. It was far beyond toasty, but she made herself eat it.

Out at the garage, Calv revved up the Chevelle's engine. "Sounds like a NASCAR garage out there," she said. "Calv has been working on that thing all day."

"Yeah, George is taking it to some kind of car show over the weekend, and Calv wants to make sure it won't fall apart on him."

"I heard about that," Tish said.

It made no sense, the way her throat closed up as if she were about to start crying. They weren't even talking about her job hunt anyway. They were talking about a stupid car.

"Don't be sad," Mel said gently. "I'm sorry about your interview, but something will come up. Hey, you should do some networking, you know? Join some clubs or something. A singles group or a dance class or whatever. Maybe you'll connect with somebody who's looking to hire somebody, and you'll have some fun too."

Tish breathed deeply and collected herself. "That's not a bad plan, as long as it isn't expensive. There must be a community college around here somewhere. Sometimes they offer interesting classes, cheap."

"There's one in Muldro. I checked it out after high school, but then I went to Florida instead."

"You could still look into it."

"Except I don't have a way to get to Muldro. Not yet, anyway, but at least I have a job. That's a start."

"It's definitely a start."

"There's even bingo," Mel said suddenly. "For networking, I mean. At the VFW hall. My grandpa used to go."

Tish smiled at the idea of networking for jobs among bingo-playing senior citizens. "Your grandpa had enough money to own a classic Corvette, but he'd play bingo at the VFW hall?"

"Yeah, he was funny. He lived in a dumpy little house and drove an ugly little truck and raised half his own food like he was poor, but he took the 'Vette out a couple of times a week and never griped about putting gas in it. We'd sing along with the radio and play the alphabet game. You know the one I mean, with billboards and stuff? You always have to look for a Dairy Queen for the *Q* and I forget what for the *Z*, and it's almost impossible to find an *X*. Especially if you're not a fast reader."

"I remember playing that game with my mom," Tish said. "Your grandpa sounds like he was a lot of fun." He was crazy too, to let his teenage granddaughter drive his hugely expensive car with only a learner's permit.

"He was a ton of fun." Mel blinked and looked at her. "A garden club!"

Startled by the non sequitur, Tish shook her head. "What does that have to do with anything?"

"The networking thing. You want to learn about southern plants anyway, right? Why don't you look for a garden club? There's a little local paper that has a calendar section for things like that. George has a stack on the counter. They're free."

"I could check it out."

"You should. It would be good for you to get out of the house."

"You're right, and that's a good quality in you."

Those big brown eyes got bigger. "What is?"

"You're going through a tough time, but you're still interested in other people. You still care about other people. Some people only care about themselves."

"Oh." Mel wiggled a little in her chair, obviously uncomfortable with the praise. With downcast eyes, she arranged the potato chips on her plate from smallest to largest, then picked up the tiniest one and ate it. "Grandpa John was like that," she said softly. "He cared about people."

"Then he would be proud of you. Love God and love your neighbor. That's the whole thing, right there."

Mel didn't answer, but her lower lip trembled. She picked up another tiny chip and ate it, keeping her eyes on her plate.

Thirty

*A*bout the time George fell in love with the unseasonably warm weather, it broke his heart. A cold snap hit hard on Monday night. Tuesday morning, he wasn't surprised to see half his customers bundled up in multiple layers although the sun was shining.

Tish, though, strolled up to his counter in jeans and a light sweater. No jacket, no hat, no gloves. No jewelry either, but she didn't need accessories when she had that smile.

He smiled too, glad for a chance to chat. "I guess this is balmy weather by Michigan standards," he said.

"You betcha. We'd call it a heat wave and drive around town with our windows down." Tish's eyes searched the counter. "Mel told me you always have a stack of these local papers…"

"Like this?" He took one of the freebies and gave it to her.

"That must be it."

"As a newspaper, it's a very good fish wrapper," he said. "It's mostly ads and coupons. Once in a while, you might find some useful information."

Mel joined them and slouched against the counter. "That's the one I was telling you about, Tish. Look on the back."

Tish flipped it over to the community calendar page and took a moment to read it. "Imagine that. Remember your idea about a garden club? There's one called the Noble-Muldro Garden Club."

"Really?"

"And it meets Friday night."

"Perfect," Mel said. "You should go."

Tish kept reading. "It's a potluck, it starts at six, and it's followed by a discussion of springtime gardening essentials. Whatever that means. There's a phone number for RSVPs."

Mel crowded closer to see. "Call right now, and then you won't back out. George, you still going to the car show?"

"Yes, I am."

"Too bad, or you could go to the garden club too."

"I don't have a garden," he pointed out. "Just a scrap of grass for the dog's business."

Tish looked up from the paper. "I love car shows. My dad used to take Mom and me to the big show at Meadow Brook Hall in Michigan. Classic cars all over the lawn."

"I've heard of that one," George said. "This one won't be in the same class. It'll have muscle cars instead of Rolls Royces, but I'll learn a lot from talking with other folks who've already restored cars like mine."

"Is Daisy going with you?"

"Unfortunately, yes. Unless you'd like to adopt her for the weekend."

"No, thanks," Tish said. "She's cute, but I'm not a dog person."

"I am," Mel said. "Please, Tish? Can I?" She turned to George. "Please, George?"

"It's up to Tish."

"Oh, I don't know," she said. "It would make it that much harder to convince her that she doesn't live with us. Not that we're making much progress with that anyway."

Mel gave a little hop. "So does that mean I can? Please, Tish?"

"All right, as long as you're the one taking care of her. Not me."

"And don't let her piddle on those nice floors like she used to," George said.

"I won't," Mel said solemnly, and he believed her.

Tish smiled, folded the paper, and tucked it under her arm. Steadfastly ignoring the black gown on the mannequin, she browsed the rest of the vintage clothing.

"Is there a particular era you're interested in?" he asked.

"Not really. I just know what I like when I see it." Tish rifled through the clothes on the rack, wasting no time. "Of course, that doesn't mean I can afford it. Mostly, I pick up vintage scarves and costume jewelry. And I've bought some cute old hankies at yard sales."

"Handkerchiefs are a popular collectible," he said politely, although he would never understand the appeal of a used snot rag.

Finished with her perusal of the clothing rack, she turned to the shelves. "Ooh, look what I found." She went straight to the satchel-style bag he'd picked up for a song at an estate sale. "Not bad," she said, checking the price tag. "Practical and pretty, and it's real leather. Made to last."

"With the right care, it'll last a long time yet. Those little wrinkles and imperfections are part of its charm."

"You sound like my mom," Tish said with a laugh.

George frowned. Was it a good thing to sound like a woman's mother? No. Definitely not. He'd have to work on that.

Tish held up the purse for Mel to see. "Beautiful, huh? In a retro way. And it's not very expensive."

"It's awesome," Mel said, coming closer.

"It's much better than the little purse we picked up at the thrift store." Tish started exploring the multitude of zippered pockets inside. "Look at the details. It's great craftsmanship."

"Yeah, but I need to be supercareful with my money."

"Do you really like this one?" he asked. "Or are you only being polite?"

Mel ran a tentative finger over the buttery brown leather. "I really do like it. I'm starting to get hooked on old stuff. Antiques are all different, you know? It's not something you can buy at the mall."

"Only one girl in town will have one like this," he said.

Mel sighed. "But it won't be me. I wish…but it ain't gonna happen."

With a pang for the profit he was losing, he pulled the price tag off, tugged the bag out of Tish's hands, and gave it to Mel. "Happy birthday, a little early."

Mel's mouth dropped open. "George, you can't do that."

"I just did."

"Thank you! I love it." It was the only genuine smile he'd seen on her in days.

"You're going to be twenty-one, right?" Tish asked. "One of those special birthdays. A milestone."

Mel nodded, keeping her gaze on the bag.

It might be her only birthday gift. Her family would ignore the day. And George couldn't help. He'd be at the car show.

But Tish gave him a tight smile that told him she understood the situation. The woman who'd charged into Dunc Hamilton's private lair wouldn't have any problem coming up with some kind of birthday plan.

She picked up one of the black velvet evening bags, stroked it, and returned it to the shelf. "I'd better go before I find your vintage jewelry and get myself in real trouble. I'll come back sometime when I have a job. And money. See you guys later."

But she wouldn't get rid of him that easily. He opened the door and followed her onto the sidewalk. "Thanks for stopping by."

Tish gave him a grave smile. "It was kind of you to give Mel the purse. She needs all the encouragement she can get."

"She seems to be doing well, though, don't you think?"

"She's doing *too* well. Sooner or later, she'll let herself feel the hurt. That's when she'll fall apart." Tish twinkled her fingers at him in a wave and left, empty-handed except for the free paper.

George returned to the warmth of the store and scrutinized Mel, who was still rooting through the handbag's inner pockets. She looked perfectly happy, but he remembered her as a kid, moving easily from a full-blown tantrum to sunshine and giggles—and back again. She'd never been predictable.

She looked up with a grin. "Having a decent purse again will make me feel like, you know, a decent person. Not a loser with nothing but a bedroll. Thanks, George."

"You're welcome."

"Hey, there's a penny in it." She held it up.

"That's for good luck. I never sell a purse or a wallet without putting a penny in it first."

"Now I need more money to add to it. Lots more money."

She took the purse to the back room and came out with the Windex and a roll of paper towels. She was humming.

"It was nice of you to steer Tish toward the garden club," he said as she headed for the front door.

"I already checked out the paper, so I knew they were meeting on Friday, but I had to act surprised so she'd think she found it all by herself." Smiling smugly, she strolled away in pursuit of fingerprints.

The little schemer. Not that there was anything wrong with making Tish think the garden club was her own discovery, but it was strange.

In the quiet of the slow day, he settled at his computer in the back room and resumed his daily wheeling and dealing online. After checking on a handful of auction items, he dealt with his most pressing paperwork. Then, as a reward, he browsed the Internet for advice on making Greek pizza. He'd been furtively experimenting for weeks, and they were getting better. Better than the Shell station's offerings, anyway.

Mel's scream sliced him like a knife. "No!" she shrieked. "Oh no!"

He ran, papers flying. Halfway through the store he pulled his phone from his pocket. It had to be a tragedy. A homicide on the sidewalk? A vehicle mowing down pedestrians? But he'd heard no gunshot, no sound of impact, no scream but Mel's.

She clung to the door, her face pressed to the glass, the Windex lying at her feet and the paper towels unrolling beside it. "Oh no. No, no, no."

"What's wrong?"

Then he heard a distinctive rumble and caught a glimpse of sunlight glinting on a sky-blue fender. Dunc's 'Vette disappeared around the corner.

"What's going on, Mel?"

Her shoulders slumped. She faced him, her eyes like black holes. "A young guy was driving. He was laughing. And my dad—Dunc—was in the passenger seat. He was laughing too. You know what that means."

"I can't say that I do."

"It was a test drive! That horrible guy will buy it, and I'll never see it again."

"Calm down, Mel. Calm down. I found your dad's ad online, and he's asking too much. He'll never sell it at that price."

Tears crawled down her cheeks. "He'll sell it. He'll lower the price, or he'll find somebody rich enough or dumb enough to pay it." She sobbed and gulped and sobbed again. "I can never afford to buy it. Never, never, never. But it should be mine."

"Now, Mel—"

"No, it's true. Grandpa John told me he was going to give it to me."

"If he honestly meant to give you the car, then it should have been yours, but—"

"Exactly," she said fiercely. "It should be mine."

"But it isn't."

"Then what am I supposed to do?" A tear reached her trembling chin and fell.

He wanted to give her a tissue and pat her shoulder, but more coddling wouldn't help. "You're supposed to go on with your life. You're not entitled to something just because you want it. If you want something, you have to earn it."

"What if it's something I can never earn? Something I can never afford?"

"Then you give up on the idea."

"You're telling me to give up?"

"No, Melanie. I'm telling you to grow up."

"You don't understand! They took the watch back, but they won't take me. Now they're selling the car. It doesn't matter. I don't have a family anymore." She ran for the back room, weeping as if someone had ground her heart underfoot the way she ground out her cigarette butts.

This was what Tish had been talking about, then. Finally feeling the pain. Falling apart. His lectures wouldn't help Mel at all.

He picked up the Windex and paper towels and attacked the fingerprints on the glass. He never should have given her the leather bag. He'd only reinforced her mistaken notion that she only had to wish for something and it was hers.

Thirty-One

A few hours after the 'Vette had cruised by, George was desperate for a breath of fresh air untainted by female emotions. He stepped onto the sidewalk.

Mel was only speaking when spoken to, only smiling when smiled at, and then her smiles were phony. She reminded him of one George Zorbas at fifteen, suffering from his first-ever broken heart, or at least he'd called it that. Mel had been working hard, though. He'd give her that. She must have dusted everything in the store, three times over.

He glanced across the street, where his fellow merchants seemed to be doing a brisk business. Sometimes he wondered if the anti-Mel and anti-McComb forces had arranged a quiet boycott of Antiques on Main. But that was ridiculous.

Come to think of it, though, Dorothea Rose hadn't set foot in the store lately. Trying to remember the last time he'd seen her, he concluded it was the day she'd hidden behind the Luminaire fan and gawked at Tish returning a dog. It was a shame, especially now that he'd read the McComb letters. He would have enjoyed explaining to Mrs. Rose that her grandmother's tongue-lashing had nothing to do with Mrs. Letitia McComb's decision to leave town. The old lady should have been ashamed of herself for treating a recent widow that way.

A flash of movement caught his eye. Tish was running toward him, her hair streaming behind her like a banner. Alarmed, he set off toward her, but when they met on the sidewalk, she was smiling so broadly that he almost thought she'd hug him, right there on Main.

"I have a job offer," she said breathlessly. "Well, it's not an official offer yet, but it's almost certain."

"Congratulations! Where?"

"In Muldro, at a big construction company. I'll be the office manager. It's not much like what I was doing before, but if they're willing to train me, I'm willing to learn." Her eyes shone with laughter. "The people I've talked to so far aren't from Noble. They probably don't know anything about McCombs or Mel Hamilton, so I think I'm in."

"When will it be official?"

"I'll go back on Monday and meet the owner. I met her son today, and he practically promised me the job. Come on, let's go tell Mel. She'll be happy for me."

"I hope she will," he said as they walked toward the shop together. "She's not having an especially happy day herself. After you left this morning, she saw Dunc go by in the 'Vette with a stranger at the wheel. A prospective buyer, maybe. You'd think it was the end of the world."

"Oh, poor Mel. I won't gloat about my good fortune, then."

"No, but there's no reason you can't celebrate it."

"Later," she said. "In private." She downsized her grin to a sedate smile, but her eyes still sparkled.

She preceded him into the shop. They found Mel staring glumly at her reflection in one of the art-nouveau hand mirrors.

"I have some news," Tish told her in a matter-of-fact tone. "I'm almost certain I have a job."

Mel was minding her manners too. Instead of bringing up her own troubles, she set the mirror down and met Tish with a happy expression. "Yay! Now you can buy that black dress before somebody else does."

"I shouldn't. Not until the job is a sure thing. Last time I thought I had a job in the bag, I was wrong."

"This time, maybe they won't find out you hang out with baddies like me."

"Oh, Mel, that wasn't your fault. I'm sorry I made you think it was. And you're not a baddie."

"Whatever." Mel took Tish by the hand and tugged her toward the mannequin in the snug-fitting velveteen ball gown. "Just try it on. If it fits, you can ask George to put it on layaway. Right, George?"

"Right. The dressing room is right over there." He pointed. "I'll leave you two in peace."

He tried to make himself stay on the other side of the store, but within minutes his feet had found their way back to the clothing corner. From his vantage point behind a chifforobe, he sneaked a look.

Tish had already donned the black ball gown and emerged from the dressing room. Facing the narrow mirror beside it, she held still while Mel stood behind her, tightening the laces.

"There," Mel said. "Turn around. Let me see."

With Mel blocking his view, he saw only part of a very pretty picture as Tish spun in a circle. She lifted the heavy skirt a few inches, giving him a glimpse of jeans and bare feet.

"Perfect," Mel said.

Tish laughed. "I think I'm in love."

Still unseen, George allowed himself a small nod of agreement.

Mel stepped away as Tish made another turn, giving him an unobstructed view. The bodice was a snug and solid fit, while the skirt swirled gracefully around her.

"Wow!" The word slipped out unbidden.

Tish stopped moving as if he'd hit her off switch. The skirt settled, hiding her jeans again. "I didn't know I had an audience."

"Sorry. Couldn't resist." He backed up a couple of steps. "You look very nice," he said, as tame a compliment as he dared to offer.

"Thank you. I hope you're not just saying that so I'll want to buy it."

"It's the truth. It's a beautiful dress on a beautiful woman. Don't get skittish, now, just because I've expressed my opinion."

She presented her back to Mel. "Unlace me, please."

George walked away, trying to interpret Tish's mixed signals. He would never understand her until he knew her better. Chance encounters like this didn't help, though, especially with Mel hanging around like a gloomy puppy dog.

Fortunately, Mel was in the back of the store by the time Tish came out of the dressing room with the dress draped over her arm. She'd somehow knotted her hair tightly behind her head. He resisted the temptation to suggest setting it free again.

"Would you like to put it on layaway?" he asked, taking the heavy garment from her.

She sighed, unable to take her eyes off it. "Thank you, but…no. If it's meant for me, it'll still be here when I'm sure I can afford it."

"Okay." He took a breath and blurted it out. "Tomorrow night, if you're free, will you let me cook dinner for you to celebrate the job?"

She met his eyes. In the dead silence, he heard his own breathing.

"It's a little premature," she said. "The job isn't a sure thing."

"Then we'll celebrate a possibility instead of a sure thing."

She smiled faintly. "You cook?"

"Some. Nothing fancy." And wasn't that the truth.

"Thanks," she said evenly. "That would be nice. What time?"

"Say…seven?"

"Okay."

"You know where I live."

"I certainly do."

Thinking he saw something sad or wistful or scared in her eyes, he hesitated. "Don't worry. This time, we won't discuss carpetbaggers and musty old books."

She nodded. "See you then."

He would have preferred more enthusiasm. Maybe she'd accepted the invitation only because he'd accused her of being skittish and she wanted to prove him wrong.

Or somebody, somewhere, had broken her heart. Maybe he needed to let her know she wasn't the only one.

He headed toward the back room with the dress. He wanted to give it to her, just as he'd given the purse to Mel, but Mel was like a kid sister, and a purse was only a purse. In Tish's case, there were proprieties to observe. A gentleman didn't give a lady anything too personal until he knew her very well. He didn't know her well enough.

Not yet.

He hung the garment on the layaway rack. No need to put a tag on it, as it wasn't an official layaway, and he certainly wouldn't forget whom he was saving it for.

Mel wandered into the back room. "It looked great on her. I'm glad she'll have money for clothes soon." She sighed, reaching out to stroke the soft black fabric. "I wish I did."

As his mind tried to formulate a sensible comment about saving her earnings and being patient and responsible, his heart argued that she needed all the blessings she didn't deserve. So he prayed for her instead of lecturing her, and then he started wondering what on earth he could cook for Tish.

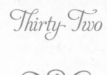

Thirty-Two

The house was quiet and lonesome with Tish gone.

Must be nice, Mel thought. George had invited Tish, and only Tish, for supper. Like they were a couple. Like they belonged together. She'd looked so pretty when she walked out the door, too, in that funky old blue jacket that made her eyes so blue. She'd twisted her hair up in a knot, and she'd made it stick with blue chopsticks that matched the jacket.

Tish had weird taste sometimes. Maybe she was confused about who she wanted to be. She'd said she was like an uptight Sunday school teacher, but when she unknotted her hair and shook it out, it was wilder and prettier than Amanda Proudfit's ever was, even when she was cheerleading.

Yep, Tish was a wild woman on the inside. She just didn't know it yet.

Mel yawned. Her life was so far from wild it was about to kill her. On Friday she'd get another paycheck, but after taxes the whole check wouldn't be much better than the single penny George had left in the purse. She had to earn more money somehow, but nobody would hire her if she didn't have nice clothes for interviews.

She needed her own clothes. Good ones. At least a few outfits. Even Tish would agree. She was the one who never shut up about being responsible, using her money wisely. So, why buy new when she already had plenty of clothes? They just happened to be at the wrong house.

So was the 'Vette, unless it was in some other state by now.

Mel couldn't stop thinking about what George had said about giving up on the car. She would have called him a meanie if he hadn't given her the cool old purse.

She had a wallet now too. Tish had dug it up for her. She'd said it was something she'd had lying around. Out of style but in good shape. Then she'd handed Mel a house key on a ring with a little metal charm in the shape of a sun. Tish had said that was to remind her that she'd have her day in the sun. That she had a future and a hope, if she'd only turn in the right direction.

The house key meant more, though. It meant Tish had finally decided to trust her.

Mel wasn't going to put the 'Vette key on the key ring. It was her last treasure, although it didn't look special. She'd had a hard time picking it out of the slew of keys in the wooden tray on her dad's dresser. Two years had gone by, but he probably hadn't missed it yet.

She'd swiped it once before too, the day after Grandpa John's funeral. She'd driven into the hills, trying to pretend he was in the passenger seat. That didn't work. After about an hour she brought the car back—and got her butt whipped.

She pressed the key to her lips, then zipped it into the smallest inside pocket of the purse. She would keep the key forever. It reminded her of learning how to drive a stick shift in Grandpa John's old truck. Once she could shift gears as smooth as sherbet, he'd let her graduate to the 'Vette.

She smiled, gloating a little. He never let anybody else drive it. Just her. It was his special gift. His way of telling her, *I trust you, Melanie John. I believe in you.* He'd even said it out loud the day he'd told her the car would be hers someday. She'd been so excited. Once she'd realized what "someday" meant though, she didn't want the car. She only wanted Grandpa John to live forever.

She had one cigarette left. If she kept the door closed but opened the windows, Tish would never notice the smell.

Could Grandpa John smell it from heaven, though? He'd always warned her about lung cancer and emphysema, and she knew he was right. It would be awful if she couldn't breathe. She had to stop smoking.

"Do not buy more cigs," she whispered. "Quit. Just quit."

But she would need that last cigarette for her mission. She knew she'd be stressing out about everything.

She shivered. The room was cold at night. Her woolly socks would make a big difference, and nobody would notice if they went missing from the dresser in her old room.

She tried praying again. "Please, God," she said softly, "when it's time, can You keep them out of the house long enough so I can pull it off? It's not stealing. They're my socks, my jeans, my shirts."

She wanted to add *my Corvette,* but she was pretty sure God would side with George on that one.

After a brisk walk down Main, Tish ran up the stairs behind the shop. When George opened the door, she became aware of three things simultaneously: something smelled delicious, George had straightened his cluttered apartment in honor of her visit, and his smile melted her nervousness away.

"Nice jacket," he said as he helped Tish out of it. "Forties or so?"

"That's about right. I found it on eBay. Before I forget…" She reached into her purse and drew out his copy of Miss Eliza Clark's book. "I hardly care anymore what Nathan and Letitia did or didn't do, but thank you for letting me borrow the book."

"You're welcome."

George placed the book on the coffee table. Where it had held stacks of Watergate-era magazines before, now it held a bottle of white wine, two wine glasses, and a glass tray of simple appetizers. A small dining table near the window held a vase filled with white alstroemeria, a pale orange lily, an assortment of vivid mums, and a single pink rose.

She breathed deeply, fighting off a memory of a snowy road and a deer blundering into the path of Stephen's car. She'd never seen the flowers he'd picked up that night except in that terrible front-page photo in full color. Scraps of bright petals in the roadside snow beside a mangled red car.

"Pretty flowers," she managed.

"I picked 'em myself—at the grocery store," George said with a grin. "Shall we drink a toast to your new job?"

"Yes, but it's not a sure thing, remember?"

He poured wine for both of them, not filling the glasses too full, she noted with approval. "Here's to your new job," he said. "May it materialize quickly. May it be a stable and enjoyable place of employment, and may your McComb ancestry and your friendships with assorted baddies never come to light."

"And may I hold my head high even if they do. Cheers."

"Cheers."

As they clinked their glasses together, she reminded herself not to be skittish. George was a friend. A kind and attractive friend.

He picked up the tray. "Let's bring this to the kitchen. You can nibble while I cook."

The kitchen was a narrow, one-person galley. While George cooked, Tish leaned in the doorway sipping her wine and sampling olives, spicy little crackers, and tzatziki sauce with pita chips. Whatever he was making, he took it seriously, whether he was slicing a tomato or stirring a sauce over the blue flames of the stove.

She kept imagining him in a nice suit. He had the build for it. Solid. Muscular but trim. He looked good in jeans too, so what made her think he was built to wear expensive suits? Maybe it was his shrewd look. Like a successful attorney—or a winning poker player. Or it was simply the way he moved. Not arrogant, but calm and confident.

That was it. He walked like a rich man. Unhurried. Setting his own pace.

"You seem to know what you're doing in the kitchen," she said.

"Only when I keep it simple."

"I can ruin even the simplest things, though. Like grilled cheese sandwiches the other night. Mel pretended hers wasn't burnt, but I think that was all part of her—"

He pointed at her with the business end of a wooden spoon coated with a red sauce. "No more about Mel tonight. We've already discussed her and her problems out the wazoo."

She smiled. "Okay, then. Tell me, what's this exotic dish you're making?"

"Pizza. Greek pizza. The crust is ready and the oven's nearly hot enough, but I'm cooking down the sauce." He turned the flame down low and glanced over his shoulder with a smile, his shaggy hair falling over one eye. "Some things need to simmer for a while."

Her nervousness was back.

She turned toward the window that opened to the balcony. The lights of Noble twinkled for blocks. "You have a great view of Main Street and beyond."

"I do. It's better than TV. You wouldn't believe some of the things I've seen."

"You're a native of Noble, right? So you know everybody who walks by."

"Just about. And you're from Michigan, but where exactly? What's your hometown?"

"The place I lived longest was Ames, about here." She held up her hand, showing him the town's location near the base of Michigan's thumb. "But we moved so much, I don't have a hometown."

"That's not all bad. My mom used to say a hometown's just a place you'll want to leave someday."

"Maybe that's true, but we never stayed long enough to get attached to a town. I never felt like I belonged at any school. I didn't even get an invitation to my ten-year high school reunion, but I found it online and sort of invited myself because there were a few people I wanted to see again. None of them remembered me." She made a face. "Is that too much to wish for? Just that somebody would remember me?"

"No, but it's funny that you want to be remembered. Mel would rather be forgotten. She was thrilled when one of her teachers came into the shop and didn't recognize her."

"I thought we weren't talking about Mel tonight."

"You're right. Sorry." He started spreading sauce on his pizza crust, then sprinkled the other ingredients over it. He had it in the oven so quickly that she wondered if he'd been making pizzas all his life.

"There," he said. "Pizza's in the oven and the salad's ready."

Seated across from him at the small table with flowers in the center, she took a bite of the salad and closed her eyes in bliss. Mixed greens, feta cheese, the right kind of beets and olives and onions, and genuine Greek dressing.

She opened her eyes. "I haven't had an authentic Greek salad since the last time I went to Greektown in Detroit."

"I'm glad you approve."

"With a name like Zorbas, I presume your father is or was Greek. Did he teach you how to cook?"

"He was Greek, but I didn't learn much of anything from him. He and my mother split up when I was young, and she was anti-Greek everything for years. I'm just now educating myself about Greek food."

"Do you like gyros?"

"I have never had gyros."

"George! You poor, sheltered man."

He gave her a rueful smile. "What can I say? I've lived a boring life."

They continued chatting over their salads and then over the pizza. Neither of them mentioned Mel. After they'd finished, George poured a little more wine, and they sat on opposite ends of the couch with the sleeping dog between them.

Now Tish felt awkward and didn't know why. "This is a nice place," she said for lack of something better to say. "Convenient too, being above the shop."

"I guess you've wondered why I'm in my late thirties and still living in a bachelor pad."

"I did wonder if you lived with your mom until she passed away."

"No. I never lived at home after college. I dabbled in a couple of career choices, then moved back to Noble, bought Antiques on Main, and moved in above the shop. Close enough to look out for my mother, but not under the same roof."

"I see."

His eyes searched hers. "You might say I came back to Noble to lick my wounds after a few big heartbreaks."

Dread clenched her stomach. He was one of those men who insisted on swapping heartbreak stories on first dates—if this qualified as a date.

"My first serious girlfriend was—well, let's call her the morally challenged one. She was a sweet, generous girl, always bringing gifts for no special occasion…except she wasn't buying them. She was a shoplifter." He shook his head. "I broke up with her. You can't build an honest relationship with a dishonest person."

"No. That must have been difficult."

"But the next one was a little too honest. She always spoke her mind. I cared about her—I cared a lot—but she was a drama queen. I couldn't handle her meltdowns." George studied his wine glass. "Then there was the almost-perfect one. Sweet, funny, generous—and honest but kind. But I wanted to talk about marriage and she didn't, so that was the end of that."

"Must have hurt," Tish said.

"It did, but it was a long time ago." He cleared his throat. "So there you have the gist of my romantic history. Boring, isn't it?"

"No. Those relationships must have been quite complicated when you were in the middle of them. Or leaving them."

George shrugged. "Everybody's heart gets broken a few times, I guess."

A loud motorcycle roared past on Main, and the room seemed quieter than ever.

Daisy stirred, yawned, and went back to sleep. Dogs lived such simple lives.

It was inevitable. She had to tell him about Stephen. The fewer details the better. But even as she formulated the simplest version possible, she found herself clenching the stem of her wine glass as if she wanted to strangle it.

Forcing herself to loosen her grip, she kept her eyes on Daisy's tiny face. "I guess you want my romantic history too. I fell in love just once, about six years ago. He died."

She looked up, and the shock in George's eyes made her wish she'd softened the story and segued into it slowly.

"Tish, I'm sorry," he said. "I don't know what to say. I'm…that's…it makes my little hurts look like kid stuff."

"Don't compare hurts," she said. "You just can't."

There was another long silence, while she tried to understand why she felt incapable of giving him the details. What was the big deal? She'd finished grieving for Stephen—she knew she had—yet she wasn't ready to talk about him. Instead, she kept wanting to blurt something about that stupid deer.

She took a small sip of wine because she didn't know what else to do. She wanted to run.

George returned to the kitchen and brought back dessert plates and a larger plate that held small slices of baklava. "Store-bought," he said. "You can find almost anything in Muldro if you know where to look."

They passed a few more minutes in chitchat, but the frequent gaps in the conversation told her he felt as awkward as she did. She couldn't focus. She couldn't think.

She set her plate on the coffee table. "I'd better head home. Thanks for having me. Everything was delicious, and you're good company. I'm just afraid I'm not."

"No, Tish. You're great. I understand, though. I'll give you a ride. If we sneak out quietly, Daisy won't wake up and I won't have to bring her."

He went to the closet for her jacket and held it out while she slipped her arms into the sleeves. When she faced him, he seemed to be on the verge of saying something, but then he only opened the door. Quietly, leaving the dog undisturbed, they walked down the stairs. The chilly air felt wonderful on her warm cheeks, but she would have given anything for a different ending to the evening.

Finished drying the dishes, George hurled the salad tongs into the drawer, slammed it shut, and walked into the living room. He'd forgotten the wine glasses and dessert plates on the coffee table, a testament to a botched evening.

What a fool. Oh, sure, he'd had her figured out. He'd decided, in his great wisdom, that she only needed a cozy conversation with an understanding man who'd known his share of heartaches. Sure, everybody gets their heart broken a time or two, baby. Loosen up.

Daisy let out a sharp, short yip. Pricking her ears, she stared at the door.

Then George heard it too. Footsteps on the stairs. Someone knocked.

He opened the door. Tish stood there with tiny droplets of rain misting her hair. No blue jacket, no blue chopsticks. Her hair hung in damp and beautiful reddish-brown curls against the shoulders of her stark white shirt.

"I'm sorry, George, sorry to bother you, and I know it's late, but…I wasn't ready to talk about Stephen before. Now I am. I think. I mean, if you want to hear it."

"Come in. You must be freezing."

Instead of taking a seat, she walked to the window and looked out over the sleeping town. "Bear with me," she said. "I'm still figuring things out."

"Take your time."

"I think I've been afraid to connect with people. Living people, I mean. It must have started when Dad and I came down here after Stephen died. For a while, I took comfort in connecting with the past. With family history. My ancestors couldn't abandon me. They couldn't die. They were dead already."

"I see." But he didn't. Not yet.

"But then my dad died too. I put away the family history, and I threw myself into my work and into being available to my mom because it was a tough time for her too. We were like a pair of widows, although I hadn't married Stephen, of course."

"Tell me about him."

She turned toward George but didn't quite look at him. "We met when I moved to Ames for my first job after college. He came from a big farming family. My parents loved his parents and vice versa. My dad even talked about moving there and staying put." She paused. "I remember taking one of Dad's blank genealogy charts and filling it out for me and Stephen, including our wedding date. My life had been so unsettled, but I was becoming part of his family, his roots, his town."

Not knowing what to say, George nodded and let her keep going.

"He was the youngest of six boys. Farm boys. His brothers all loved their pickups, but he drove a fast little car. Bright red. Sometimes I'd see it flying down the road like a red arrow against the snow…" Her voice faltered. "One night he was coming to pick me up for dinner, but a deer ran in front of his car. If the deer had waited just ten seconds, Stephen would have been safely past. We would have gone out to eat, and we would have been married three weeks later."

"Three weeks?"

"We were so close to starting our life together. Our future had become so real in my mind that it seemed like a parallel life, a road we'd already taken, except it was over before it started."

"I can't even imagine."

"Here's what's going on, I think. I've always blamed the deer for the accident, but I think that was only so I couldn't blame Stephen. He was always running late, driving too fast whether the road conditions were good or bad." She took a deep breath. "You can't forgive someone until you realize you hold something against him. I've finally realized I hated the deer so I wouldn't hate Stephen for ruining our lives. Our dreams."

"Aw, Tish." George moved closer, wanting to pull her into a hug.

"Here's the rest," she said. "I loved Stephen and I lost him. Now I know that when you connect with someone, you risk losing that connection later. Your heart goes dark, and there's nothing. It's like…like a power failure."

He spoke softly but candidly. "And you're afraid of going through that again."

She nodded, her eyes filling with tears.

Afraid he'd say too much, George hesitated. But he had to say it.

"I don't know of anybody who doesn't use electricity because they might lose it someday, Tish. I'd say it's worth the risk to have light and warmth while you still can."

"I know," she said with the barest trace of a smile. "That's why I came back."

He took another step closer, and another. She didn't shrink back.

He cupped her face in his hands and brushed away a teardrop with one thumb. She leaned toward him, her breathing audible in the silence, and their lips met. Her skin smelled like flowers. Her hair smelled like rain. Her fingers, when they slid past his ear and into his hair, were both soft and strong.

"I've always wanted to play with your hair," she whispered, laughing and crying at the same time.

"Not as much as I've wanted to play with yours."

Somewhere between kisses, laughter won the battle. When he drew back to study her, her eyes shone with something deeper than tears.

Thirty-Three

$\mathcal{T}$ ish consulted her GPS again and was almost disappointed to be so close to her destination already. The hostess for tonight's gathering of the Noble-Muldro Garden Club lived in a lovely area of tree-covered hills sprinkled with lakes and creeks. It was a pleasure to drive through such beautiful scenery, even in the failing light, and it was a pleasure to have time alone after spending most of the day with Mel.

Mostly, it was a pleasure to think about George. She just wished he wasn't out of town, but he'd closed the shop early and left for his car show.

She had taken Mel to Muldro to deposit her paycheck, but they'd used the drive-through, so they hadn't run into either Marian or Farris. Mel was so sweet too, offering to chip in for groceries when she'd hardly made any take-home pay.

She'd just better remember to take the dog out. If Daisy peed on the floor, it was the last time Mel would be dog-sitting.

Tish spotted the right number on a roadside mailbox and hit the brakes. A long, winding driveway led through a gorgeous yard studded with magnolia trees. A two-story house blazed with lights in the dusk. She parked on a gravel strip behind a string of other vehicles and climbed out into the chilly evening with her pasta salad for the potluck.

"Mingle, mingle, mingle," she said under her breath. She'd mingle for the fun of it, though, not to troll for job leads. If her prospective employer happened to be a member of the garden club, that would be the icing on the cake.

So much had changed in only a couple of days. She'd had a home-cooked dinner date with George. She'd told him about Stephen. The anger was gone. She didn't hate the deer, she didn't hate Stephen, she didn't hate anybody. And George, suddenly, was more than a friend. A kiss was just a kiss, sure, but a kiss could be a turning point too. Like a house that had lost power and had it turned on again, she'd felt life and light and warmth humming inside every corner of her. Electricity.

Now she even dared to join a gathering of longtime local residents and introduce herself as a McComb or even as Mel's friend without worrying about the fallout.

A pair of young women walked a few yards ahead of her, talking a mile a minute. At the front door, one of them smiled at Tish and held it open for her.

"Thanks," Tish said.

"You're welcome," she said, and went on chattering with her friend.

Scouting out the crowd, Tish knew she was underdressed. She'd thought most gardeners would wear something along the lines of jeans with a nice top, as she had, but these were high-class gardeners. Pillars of the community. Everyone around her had somehow achieved some combination of being fashionable yet comfortable. She felt about as fashionable as a hobbit—but she honestly didn't care.

I am Tish McComb. You can't change who I am.

The house was picture perfect. A chandelier hung from the high ceiling of a foyer that opened to an elegantly appointed living room on the right. On the left, the chairs had been removed from around a dining room table that was set up for a buffet. The tasteful assortment of beautiful serving dishes would make Tish's practical plastic container a country bumpkin in a crowd of porcelain-skinned princesses.

She didn't care.

A buxom, blond-gray woman bore down on her. Wearing a grandmotherly apron over a stylish dress, she jingled with jewelry. "Are you Tish? The gal who called for directions yesterday?"

"Yes, I'm Tish."

"Thought so. Welcome, hon. I'm Becky." She put a hand on the arm of a woman walking by. "Samantha, take her dish off her hands, will you?"

Samantha gave her a quick hello and whisked the salad off to the buffet table.

Tish smiled at her hostess. "Thanks for having me."

"I'm glad you came. Gardeners are the best kind of people, always willing to share. Didn't you tell me you're from up north somewhere?"

"Yes, I'm from Michigan." Warmed by Becky's welcome, Tish felt herself relax.

"And where do you live now, hon?"

"In Noble, on Jackson."

"There are some wonderful old homes on Jackson. Which end of the street?"

"I'm on South Jackson, where it starts to curve around the hill. Five houses from Main. The yard needs some serious cleanup, but I haven't done a thing with it yet."

"You'll have a lovely garden in no time, especially if you join tonight. Then you can jump right into the online forum and our classes and meetings. The perennial swaps are the best meetings of the year. Each person brings a box or two of extra plants, and we trade around. Everybody goes home happy. It's only open to members, but my goodness, you'll make back your dues with one swap. It's only ten dollars a year."

"That's a bargain. Where do I sign up?"

"Let's track down our secretary-treasurer. She was in the den a minute ago." Becky checked her watch. "Then I have to run back to the kitchen and pull my cheese grits out of the oven." She set off through the crowd. "How do you like it down here so far?" she called over her shoulder.

"It's like any move. There are pros and cons. The pasture always looks greener on the other side of the fence, but then you learn there are cow pies there too."

"The cow pies are the fertilizer, darlin'. They help make the grass green."

Tish glanced into a cozy den and did a double take. Steel-gray hair. A tall and trim figure. Marian Clark-Whoever was leaning over a low table to rearrange a bouquet of calla lilies in a gigantic crystal vase.

"Sometimes I think I'm a cow pie in another person's pasture," Tish said with a nervous laugh.

Becky laughed too, slowing her mad dash. "Oh, there she is. Marian! Stop playing with the flowers and sign up a new member. Tish, this is Marian. I'll leave y'all to it and check on the food." She hurried away.

Marian finished tweaking the flowers before she straightened and turned around. Recognition flashed in her eyes, but her smile remained in place. "Hello, Letitia. Or do you prefer Tish?"

"You can call me Tish. How are you?"

"Just fine, thanks."

Tish considered asking her if she'd read the copies of the McComb letters. No. It didn't matter. Ancient feuds didn't have any place in a modern garden club.

"I'd like to pay my dues," Tish said, pulling her wallet from her purse. "Ten dollars, right?"

"Correct." Marian reached into a big canvas tote bag sitting on a wing-back chair. She pulled out a receipt book and a pen, flipped the book open, and started writing.

Tish dug out a ten. "I guess I don't have to tell you how to spell my name," she joked.

"You certainly don't," Marian said briskly. "I'll write my e-mail address on the receipt. E-mail me with your phone number and address, and I'll add you to the roster and give you the password for the forums."

"Thanks. I'm looking forward to it."

"I hope you're enjoying the house and the yard. Si and Shirley certainly did. They used to be members here, you know. Poor Si. He loved all those perennials and flowering shrubs. Especially those gorgeous old camellias. Now he'll hardly have room for a geranium on their balcony." Shaking her head, Marian pulled the finished receipt from the pad.

"I hope they'll be able to buy a home again someday," Tish said. "I really do."

Marian handed over the receipt like a ticket to board the train for a guilt trip. "Here you are," she said in a grim tone.

"Thanks." Tish tucked the receipt into her purse. "I'm looking forward to being part of the group." Especially the plant swaps, as long as Marian didn't try to send her home with poison ivy or stinging nettles.

Walking out of the den, Tish began to comprehend her situation. She was among Si and Shirley Nelson's loyal friends, who saw her as the woman who practically stole their house from them, then sullied it by installing that incorrigible Mel Hamilton in the guest room.

Tish entered the dining room where fifteen or twenty women and a handful of men formed two straggly lines on either side of the table. They seemed to have divided themselves by age, with younger people on the left and their elders on the right.

A chill ran down her spine. It was entirely possible that one of those formidable older women was her prospective employer.

Tish took her place at the end of the line on the left. No one joined her there, and the woman ahead of her didn't turn around.

She didn't feel bullied; she felt ignored. Snubbed. It was the more refined version of her uncomfortable experiences at Bag-a-'Cue. The hostess, Becky, was kind, but Tish hadn't seen her since she'd disappeared to tend to those cheese grits.

With her plate filled, Tish scouted out the living room for available seats. Like the new kid in the cafeteria, she hated to butt in where she wasn't wanted. She settled on a padded folding chair in a corner. As she ate, she listened to the conversations swirling around her.

She would tough it out and stay for the whole evening, but she would keep her mouth shut. She'd be less conspicuous that way. Less likely to make enemies.

I have not failed, not once. I've only discovered a whole mess o' folks who don't want to be my friends.

Mel was freezing by the time she turned the corner onto Rock Glen Drive, coming in from the back of the neighborhood. She pulled the hoodie's zipper up so high that it nicked her throat, and she pulled her hood low over her eyes. It was so dark now that it probably didn't matter. Keeping to the back streets had added some time to the walk, but it was better that way. If she'd walked down Main, half the town might have noticed her under the streetlights. Even her parents might have seen her. They would have driven down Main on their way to Muldro and their anniversary dinner.

She bit her lip, wondering if they'd gone to Carlita's, her favorite Mexican place. They went there for her seventeenth birthday, and the whole family had laughed and talked and kept their waitress hopping. Jamie and Nicky had made cute, sloppy "Happy birthday, Aunt Mel!" cards.

Nick, she reminded herself. He was ten now. And he knew too much about her plans. He wouldn't have forgotten, either. He never forgot anything.

She planned to take his advice. She wouldn't take much, so her folks would never notice anything was missing.

She had plenty of time. They were going to a movie, so they wouldn't get home until at least ten. Tish might have an earlier evening than that, though, and Mel needed to get back first.

She'd brought her purse, and it held gloves, a borrowed flashlight, and two shopping bags. She wouldn't take more than she could fit into the bags.

As her feet crunched through dry grass, the code kept repeating itself in the same rhythm: *3808, 3808.* In a few minutes, she could forget it forever. She would never go back.

A dog barked somewhere down the street. She told herself not to worry about it. He wasn't barking at her.

That reminded her of Daisy, all alone in that big old house. She'd better not have an accident. Tish would want to know why. *Where were you? Why were you so busy you couldn't let the dog out?*

There was the house she'd grown up in. They'd left those bright security lights on. A single light shone above the doors of the stand-alone garage, farther back on the lot, and more lights glared down from each corner of the attached garage. She'd have to move fast and pray the neighbors wouldn't look out at the wrong moment.

She didn't belong there anymore. Even her memories seemed like they were from somebody else's life. It must have been somebody else who'd climbed off the school bus at the corner every afternoon. Some other little girl had had a playhouse in the backyard and a Shetland pony in the field behind the yard. He was named Boswick's Big Boy, the dumbest name ever, so she'd called him Buddy. Her mom said that was an awfully redneck name for such an expensive pony, but Mel didn't care. Buddy was a good name for a good pony. They sold him to a family in Muldro when she was thirteen, and she'd made them promise to keep calling him that.

Walking quickly, she crossed the lawn. She slowed down when she reached the shelter of the bushes. Hiding there, she checked out the situation. There weren't any cars in the driveway, and there weren't many lights on in the house. Just the dim ones they always kept burning.

She reached into her purse for those stretchy little knit gloves. Pulling them on, she felt like a burglar. A criminal. But she was only rescuing a few things that belonged to her. She wasn't stealing.

"God, help," Mel whispered, eyeing the little black box that covered the keypad. "Help me pull it off. Please."

She hurried across the driveway. Wishing she had an invisibility cloak, she raised the black box on its hinges. A soft light came on, shining on the keypad. She typed the code and hit Enter with her gloved fingertip, then held her breath.

The garage door rose—quietly, of course, because the Hamiltons always bought the very best—and the overhead light came on, shining on her mom's car. The other spot was empty, so they'd taken her dad's vehicle.

The moment the door rose high enough, she ducked inside. She tiptoed past the car to the door that led to the kitchen and hit the button on the wall. The garage door slid down.

Her legs went weak. She'd made it in. The rest would be easy.

The door to the kitchen was unlocked, as usual. She stepped inside and hurried to her bedroom. Once she was there, the night lights weren't enough to go by. She had to use the flashlight.

Leaving the gloves on, she shone the light into one drawer after another. She chose jeans, a sweatshirt, two T-shirts, and a few pairs of her superwarm socks, the expensive kind. Then she went into the closet and shone the light over her hanging clothes. She grabbed some dressy pants and shirts for interviews plus a little knit dress that wouldn't take up much space, and two pairs of shoes.

This was her last chance. With everything packed into the shopping bags, she flashed the light around the room. Her jewelry tree glittered. She pulled off a pair of plain silver hoops and a silver chain and dropped them to the bottom of her purse. Nobody would miss those. It felt wrong to take anything to pawn, so she didn't.

She played the flashlight beam over the window, remembering how many times she'd climbed in after curfew. Remembering, earlier than that, how Grandpa John had helped her paint the walls that soft blue.

She backed out of the room. She didn't want to look at anything else. She didn't want to remember being a little girl in that house, having a ton of toys and grandparents who came over to help her play with them.

In two minutes, she was outside again, the garage door sliding down behind her. She re-armed the security system and closed the box over it. She was good to go.

The night had turned cold. Nobody was out, and nobody was driving by. The stillness of the neighborhood made her feel as if she were the only person in town who hadn't gone out with friends or family on a Friday night. Maybe she was.

Glancing toward the smaller, newer garage, Mel wondered if the 'Vette was already gone. Maybe the test-drive guy had bought it, or maybe he hadn't. She had to know.

Her dad always used the same code on both garages because he was too lazy to memorize different codes, so she'd probably be able to get in and take a peek.

The blinds and drapes at the neighbors' houses were still closed. She still didn't see anybody around.

She walked down the short driveway that veered off to the left, leading to the second garage. Horribly exposed by the security light, she lifted the keypad's cover with her gloved fingers and entered the code a second time.

The door began to rise. The overhead light came on. Clapping one hand over her mouth to keep herself from crying, she watched the blue Corvette come into view. The chrome glinted like silver, bringing back memories of helping Grandpa John polish it.

She ducked inside, hurried to the driver's door, and bent over to look through the window. It seemed like yesterday that she'd sat there, one hand on the wheel and the other on the gear shift, while Grandpa John told his corny jokes and sang along with the radio. All that moldy-oldy music like the Beatles and the Beach Boys. He'd loved their dumb songs about cars. *"Melly, you can drive my car,"* he'd sung, and something about fun, fun, fun in a T-Bird.

When nobody else trusted her, he'd let her drive his car. Only on the back roads, and only after she'd proved she could drive a stick without grinding the gears—but still, he'd trusted her. He'd loved her.

"I love you, Grandpa John," she whispered. "I miss you so much."

She wanted very badly to start up the engine for old times' sake, but that would be so, so stupid.

Thirty-Four

Tish's Saturday started with Daisy whining outside her bedroom door before sunrise. Mel's enthusiasm for adopting a dog for the weekend must have worn off already, but it wasn't the dog's fault. Half asleep, Tish staggered through the routine of taking her out, bringing her in, and feeding her. By then, she was wide awake so she started the coffee and made toast for breakfast. Through it all, the door to the guest room remained closed.

Eating her toast, she wondered how the car show was going for George. Maybe she would call him later. Hearing his voice might help her recapture a little bit of that lovely, heady happiness she'd felt on Wednesday night. Because, somehow, she'd lost track of it the night before, sitting in an elegant living room surrounded by fashionable gardeners.

By the time the sun came up, Daisy was snoring softly on the couch. Tish put on a warm jacket and work gloves. She headed outside with a trash bag to start the yard cleanup. Si and his wife had left the place in a state that would have horrified the members of the garden club. Broken bird feeders. Old clay pots. Windblown trash.

But it was her yard now, and she'd have it cleaned up in no time. Standing at the bottom of the back steps, Tish smiled. Now she could raise her own vegetables. She had plenty of room. She couldn't grow mangoes and avocados, but she would have camellias at Christmas the rest of her life.

One of the camellia bushes stood apart from the others. Most of its petals had fallen in a circle around its lower branches, like a pink slip that a girl had dropped past her ankles to land on the floor, but some of the other camellias hadn't bloomed yet. Their bloom times were staggered instead of making one brief show of color.

Last year, they'd been Silas Nelson's camellias. Before that, they'd belonged to George's mother, Jerusalem James Williams Zorbas, better known as Rue. And before that…Tish had no idea, but she'd read that a camellia bush could live a hundred years or more, with proper care. It was possible—barely— that Nathan and Letitia had planted at least some of them, but they probably wouldn't have tended them with their own hands. They would have hired someone. She hoped Nathan had paid decent wages, but she suspected he hadn't.

Tish wondered how many times the property had changed hands. Public records would go back only so far. There wouldn't be any records of the Native Americans who'd once lived on the land. They were the true native southerners.

Mrs. Nair's lithe black tomcat stalked around the corner of the house, leaving a green trail through the dew-silvered grass. So big that he could have beat up George's tiny handful of a dog, the cat prowled through Tish's yard without giving her a glance.

"Snob," she said. "You should join the garden club. You would fit right in."

She had to admit, though, that the hostess and several other people had been friendly and welcoming. Either they weren't up on their local history and gossip, or they'd decided to overlook it.

It was nearly ten and Tish had moved on to raking leaves when Mel finally wandered onto the back porch. She waved, then sat on the top step and pulled a cigarette out of a new, uncrushed pack.

"How was the garden club?" she called, lighting the cigarette.

"I learned all about iris borers and Japanese beetles and other pests."

"Yuck."

"Exactly." Glad to give her blistering palms a break, Tish came closer, dragging the rake behind her. "But it inspired me to get busy with the basic yard cleanup."

"Want some help?"

"Yes, I do. It's part of the deal, remember? Housework and yard work."

"Yeah, I remember. Sorry." Mel took another drag from her cigarette. "Can I finish my cigarette first?"

Tish watched the smoke drifting into the clear air and sighed. "Go ahead."

Mel sighed back. "Thank you *so* much."

"Are you feeling all right?"

"Yeah. I'm just tired."

"But you were already in bed when I got home last night."

"That doesn't mean I slept well. So, did anybody freak out last night when they learned your name?"

"Most people didn't pay any attention to me, and nobody mentioned carpetbaggers. I've decided not to worry about those old stories anymore. Every family has at least one skeleton in the closet."

"Yeah." Mel stared at the sky. "Everybody does terrible things sometimes."

Tish took a hard look at her. "How did you spend your time while I was gone?"

"I went for a walk. A long one."

"Did Daisy behave herself for you?"

"Huh? Yeah. Yeah, she was great. Thanks for taking care of her this morning." Mel ran down the steps, dropped her half-smoked cigarette on the grass, then ground it out and kicked it under a bush. She reached for the rake. "I'll do the raking." Her voice cracked.

Tish hung on to the rake. "What's wrong, Mel? What's going on?"

"I'm helping with the yard work. That's what's going on. You want help, don't you?"

"Yes…" Tish's sore hands settled it. She let go of the rake.

Mel took the rake and disappeared behind the camellias.

Tish tilted her head, listening. She'd never heard anyone rake so fast and hard. The rake was a weapon, and Mel was slashing the ground with it.

George walked slowly across the crowded parking lot through blue smoke and delicious aromas. The first full day of the car show was winding down, and the folks who'd come prepared had hauled out tailgate parties and grills. He enjoyed the freedom of being dogless, but he wished Tish could have been there with him. It would have been at least twice as much fun.

He'd already gleaned a wealth of information from his fellow Chevelle enthusiasts, and he'd picked up a few necessary parts from vendors—after calling Calv to make sure they were the right ones—but the sense of camaraderie was beginning to fade.

These people didn't necessarily like him; they liked his car. He was just a man alone. He would spend the night in a small and overpriced motel room, eating carry-out with no company.

The show would end tomorrow afternoon with the drawing for the charity raffle. He'd stay until then, on the off chance that he'd won one of the big prizes, but he'd be home in plenty of time to wish Mel a happy birthday.

On impulse, he pulled out his phone and called Stu. Given the way their last conversation ended, it might be awkward.

"Too bad," George said under his breath.

Stu, when he answered, sounded wary but not hostile. "What's up?"

"Not much. I'm wandering around a car show. Just thought I'd call and remind you that tomorrow is your sister's birthday."

Stu was silent for a moment. "Yeah, I remember."

"Good. I'm sure she'll be happy to hear from you."

Stu sighed. "Not if I tell her the Corvette's sold."

"It is? Oh boy. She fell apart when she spotted somebody taking it for a test drive."

"Yeah, that's him. The one and only guy who took it out for a spin. He's buying it. Go ahead and tell her if you want to."

"That's not a conversation I'd care to initiate."

"Me either," Stu said. "Poor Melly."

"Melly? I haven't heard you call her that since she was about eight."

"I feel sorry for her. First the watch, now the car. Not that there's any comparison, value-wise, but you know what I mean."

"I've been wondering who ended up with the watch. Did your dad give it to you?"

"Yeah. He said that's what he'd planned to do all along." The edge to Stu's voice said he was skeptical, though.

So was George. "Good for him," he said.

"But now that I know how much it meant to Mel, I won't enjoy having it."

"Give it back to her, then. She would love you forever."

"Not a bad idea, except Dad would be furious."

"What you do with it is your business. You don't have to tell him a thing."

"Good point. Yeah. Yeah, I like that idea. I could give it to her for her birthday."

"Excellent plan. Let me know how it goes."

"I will."

"Hey, Stu, did you ever hear that we've pretty much cleared up the mystery of why Mel's cash drawers used to come up short?"

"She said something about that," Stu said slowly.

"She just didn't have a clue about how to count change. I think there's more to it than that, though. Have you ever wondered if she might have a learning disability? Dyslexia or something similar?"

"Come on, George. Dad was on the school board. Mom ran the PTA. You think they didn't pay attention to how she did in school?"

"Think about it. She's smart, obviously, but she never did well in school. Sometimes I catch her staring at price tags like they're written in Farsi, and it's like pulling teeth to get her to write anything. I wonder if something keeps her from processing information the way the rest of us do. I've tried to broach the subject a couple of times, but she'll never talk about it."

"Huh," Stu said. "It's something to look into."

George smiled, dodging an elderly gentleman who blundered into his path. "Let me know what you find out."

"Okay. Hey, George…thanks for giving me a kick in the butt."

"Anytime."

Still smiling, George continued walking between rows of shiny muscle cars and smoking grills. His tuxedo-black baby stood at the end of the last line of vehicles, locked up tight.

Of all the cars he'd ever owned, the Chevelle was his favorite. He'd sell it in a heartbeat, though, if somebody flashed enough cash. As much as he tried, he couldn't understand how Mel could be so attached to a car that had never been hers…unless she'd learned how valuable it was. That could explain it.

He called Tish next, wanting another dose of that fast-talking Yankee voice. He wanted to know what she'd thought of the garden club too.

Her phone rang several times before she answered, and then she sounded peeved with him.

"Uh-oh. What did I do?" he asked.

"Not you. Mel. How much bad behavior can she pack into one day?"

"Is she neglecting her dog-sitting duties?"

"Yes, but that's not the worst of it. Not even close."

"What did she do?" he asked.

"What didn't she do? I'm starting to see why her parents threw her out. She's impossible."

"You want to give me the details?"

"She's gone into a tailspin, George. She's like a different person. A very difficult person. She helped me with yard work for a few minutes this morning, but then she smarted off and went inside. While I was still outside, working, she went into my office and used my computer without asking. When I said she needed to ask permission, she kicked my computer chair, and then she ran downstairs and slammed the door to her room."

"That's not acceptable behavior," he admitted.

"It gets worse. She knows she's not supposed to smoke in the house. I caught her once already and chewed her out. So what does she do? She lights up a cigarette in her room and doesn't even try to hide it. She left the door wide open, like she was taunting me. I was so tempted to kick her out."

"Why didn't you?"

There was a long silence. "I don't want her to be on the street again," Tish said.

"I don't either, but maybe it's time to draw a line in the sand. Tell her if she crosses the line, she's out on her ear."

"But what if she crosses the line?"

"Then she's out on her ear."

After another silence, Tish said, "Gotta go" in a wobbly voice and ended the call.

He'd forgotten to ask how she liked the garden club.

George unlocked the Chevelle and climbed in but didn't start the engine. He couldn't forget what Calv had said about Mel. All her mess-ups were some-how related to abusing other people's property. Taking things or breaking things. More than that, though, Calv had guessed that her parents hurt her somehow, so she tried to hurt them back.

But Tish had never hurt Mel. Tish had only helped her—or tried to, anyway. Returning the watch to Dunc hadn't helped, unless Stu was serious about giving it back to Mel.

About to call Tish back and tell her Stu's plans for the watch, George decided to keep it under his hat. If Mel went off the deep end, Stu might change his mind. He still might keep the watch and ditch his little sister.

Thirty-Five

*T*he cinnamon rolls for Mel's birthday breakfast were staying warm in the oven, their yeasty aroma filling the house, and Tish had finished decorating the dining room. Guessing that the birthday girl wasn't into pastels, she'd festooned the chandelier with balloons and crepe paper streamers in red, turquoise, purple, and lime green. She'd draped a colorful "Happy 21st" banner across the doorway. She'd put yellow napkins on the table, filled a small crystal vase with cherry-red camellias, and tucked the gift into a nest of apricot-colored tissue paper in a small gift bag of vivid orange.

The gift, like the color combination, was over the top, but she wanted Mel to know her birthday was worth celebrating in spite of her bratty behavior. And, if nothing else, giving away treasured possessions was good for the soul. Once Tish had given them away, she wouldn't have to worry that someone would steal them.

"You can't take it with you," Tish told herself in a whisper. With a lump in her throat, she placed the heavy gift bag at Mel's place.

The downstairs shower finally went off with a heavy thudding in the pipes. Tish placed the cinnamon rolls and fruit salad on the table, then poured milk for Mel and coffee for herself.

Waiting at the table, Tish checked the clock. She hoped she'd be free in time to walk down the street to a church she wanted to try. The service started at eleven. If she didn't pick up friendly vibes…well, that was one thing about the South. There was a church on every corner.

The bathroom door creaked open. Mel's bare feet padded down the hall with the scent of shampoo preceding her.

"Something smells yummy," she called. "Where are you?"

"Dining room."

Mel stopped in the doorway, her hair wet and her eyes wide. "Whoa! Wow!"

"Happy birthday," Tish said.

"You shouldn't have bought all this stuff. Balloons and flowers and everything."

"It's nothing. The decorations didn't cost much, and the camellias are from the backyard."

Mel noticed the gift bag. Her eyes filled. "You bought me a present?"

"Actually, it's something I've had for a long time. I hope you don't mind that it's not store-bought and new."

Mel shook her head vigorously. "No, I know what it's like when you can't afford to buy somebody a present." She sniffled. "When am I supposed to open it?"

"Right now, if you'd like."

Mel sat and reached into the bag, her eyes bright with tears and anticipation. Pulling out one of the silver rings, she sucked in her breath. "It's beautiful! What is it?"

"It's a napkin ring. There are four of them. I've had them for years."

"It's so shiny." Mel turned it over, admiring it from all angles. "Is it real silver?"

"It's only silver plate."

"Tish, it's too much. Especially after yesterday—"

"No. Yesterday's forgiven. When you have your own place someday, you can invite me over and use them on your own table. I don't have to own them to enjoy them."

Mel's tears flowed freely as she returned the napkin ring to the bag with the others. "How can you be so nice to me? Nobody else treats me like this. Not even my own parents. My ex-parents, I mean." She used her napkin to dab her eyes, then reached for a cinnamon roll. "Thanks for making these. They look so good."

Quietly amused by the power that food had on Mel's outlook, Tish took a roll too. She passed the fruit salad across the table. "Eat up. If we finish in time, I'd like to walk down the street to church. You want to come?"

"Hmm." She licked her sticky fingers and wiped them on her jeans, as if she were afraid to dirty her napkin. "I'm kinda scared of church and all that. God, you know? God's scary." She frowned, craning her neck to see past Tish to the window. "There's a cop car out front."

Tish turned to see. A squad car parked squarely in front of her house was an unsettling sight even for an upright citizen. "Maybe they're stopping to talk to one of the neighbors." She resumed eating her breakfast while Mel kept an eye on the police car.

"Somebody's getting out," Mel said. "Ooh, it's Darren. Remember him? The cute guy who stopped to talk when I was at the gazebo that night?" She flashed a smile that was bright but not warm.

"I remember him." Tish watched Mel's face carefully, trying to believe she'd have no reason to fear an officer of the law.

We all do terrible things, she'd said, and she'd been mysterious about how she'd spent her evening alone on Friday.

"Ugh," Mel said. "Robot Face is getting out too."

"Robot Face?"

"I don't know him. He's the new cop in town, and he has a weird, square face like a robot. He always looks mean."

Again, Tish turned to see. An older officer stood by the driver's door, using his phone. Mel had described him perfectly.

The younger officer, Darren, headed straight toward the front door. His expression was somber but not angry. Worried, maybe.

Tish glanced at her beautiful table. The basket brimming with perfect cinnamon rolls. The healthy, yummy fruit salad. The birthday decorations, the bright napkins and crockery. She might have congratulated herself for achieving something that could have come straight out of *Southern Living,* except her scenario included the police at her door.

"Do you have any idea what they might want?" she asked.

"I haven't done anything wrong," Mel said in a faint voice. "Honest."

"Then you have no reason to avoid talking to them. Let's go."

"Um, yeah. Right."

Tish led the way, glad to hear footsteps behind her. Reaching the door, she beckoned to Mel. "Come on."

Mel followed Tish onto the porch as Darren reached the top step. Blond, blue-eyed, and handsome, he reminded her of Stephen, except this young man seemed to be the serious type.

"Good morning," Tish said.

"Good morning, ma'am. 'Morning, Mel."

Mel smiled back. "Hey, Darren. This is my friend, Tish McComb."

"Glad to meet you, Miss McComb. I'm Darren Chapman, and I'm afraid I'm here on official business." He studied Mel. "Is there anything you'd like to tell me before the lieutenant gets involved?"

She regarded him with big, innocent eyes. "No, I don't have anything to tell you. Want to come in for a cinnamon roll? They're fantastic."

Darren shook his head. "Thanks, but I can't."

The older cop swaggered up the walk and stopped beside Darren to glare at Mel. "Are you Melanie Hamilton?"

"Yes, I am."

"Good. Talk to me. Tell me about the Corvette that's missing from Duncan Hamilton's garage."

Tish stifled a gasp and searched Mel's face. The girl was pale but calm. Too calm, as if she'd rehearsed this moment.

"Of course it's gone, Officer," Mel said politely. "He sold it, didn't he?"

The lieutenant let out a peevish sigh. "The buyer left a deposit. He planned to pick up the car today, but your dad opened the garage this morning to make sure it was ready to go, and…" He held his hands wide and raised his eyebrows in mock surprise. "Somehow, between Wednesday night and this morning, the car vanished. In spite of a good security system."

Mel's eyes were wet. "I'm sorry to hear that. It's a beautiful car."

The lieutenant sighed, shifted his weight, and addressed Tish. "Ma'am, I understand there's a garage at the back of your property."

"Yes, there is."

"I'd like your permission to take a look inside."

Her mind roiled with questions—Didn't they need a search warrant? Would they find a stolen car? Could her prospective employer find out?—but she could only manage a faint, "Why?"

"Because Miss Melanie Hamilton is the prime suspect in the disappearance of her father's 1956 Corvette."

"He's not my father anymore," Mel snapped. "And it's not his car."

"Sure, he sold it, but the buyer hasn't taken possession yet."

"That's not what I mean," Mel said. "I mean it's my grandfather's car."

Darren stepped forward. "Your granddaddy's dead, Mel," he said gently.

Her eyes swam with tears. "You think I don't know that?"

She turned to go inside, but the lieutenant gripped her shoulder. "Stay put," he said. "I'll want to ask more questions."

"Fine." Mel drew back, trying to escape him. "And go ahead and snoop in the garage. You won't find anything."

Tish gave her a warning look, then turned to the officer. "If you'll let go of her, I'll get the key to the garage."

Reluctantly, he set Mel free. "Don't go anywhere, young lady."

She brushed her fingers across her shoulder as if to rid herself of his touch, but she didn't argue and she didn't run.

Tish went inside and ran upstairs, her heart pounding. She didn't want to think of the consequences of having a stolen car in the garage. A car worth sixty grand.

She hurried down the stairs with her keys but took a moment to compose herself before opening the door. In two minutes, she'd know. And then she'd have to figure out what to do next. Of all times for George to be out of town.

When she walked onto the porch, Darren was trying to make peace between Mel and the lieutenant, who were practically nose to nose.

"I'm staying right here on the porch," Mel said.

"Why don't you come with us, Miss Hamilton," the lieutenant said. It was plainly an order, not a request.

"Come on, Mel," Tish said. "I don't know about you, but I have nothing to hide."

Mel let out a huff. "Oh, all right. Let's go."

Tish led the tense, silent trek to the garage. Very much afraid of what they'd find, she scrutinized the sandy ground for tire tracks. The closer she came to the garage, the more slowly she moved, excruciatingly aware of everything in her path. Weeds, stones, pine cones—and tire tracks, but she didn't see any fresh ones. As far as she could tell, they were all old ones from George's and Calv's comings and goings.

Mel had been falsely accused before. If this was another false accusation, it could explain her hostility.

Stopping in front of the garage, Tish glanced over her shoulder. Mel stood with her arms folded across her chest, her eyes burning with defiance. The lieutenant and Darren stood squarely behind her. If she ran, she wouldn't get far.

Tish opened the padlock, lifted it off the hasp, and said a quick prayer. She shoved the stubborn door to the left—and let out a sigh that seemed to leave her chest as empty as the garage.

"See?" she said. "We have nothing to hide."

The lieutenant left Darren to guard Mel and walked in. He strolled in a large circle, taking in the huge assortment of tools and what George called the clubhouse furnishings: a fan, camp chairs, and a cooler.

"Somebody's been working on a car in here," Robot Face said.

"George Zorbas," Tish said. "He's renting the garage from me, but he took his car out of town this weekend."

"And his car is the only one that's been in here?"

"Yes," Tish said. "I walk out here almost every day, and I've never seen a car here except George's Chevelle."

"Miss Hamilton," the lieutenant said, "your daddy tells me the last time the Corvette disappeared, about six years ago, you were at the wheel. You come back to town, and your daddy's car goes missing again. Strange, isn't it?"

"He's not my daddy and it's not his car," Mel said between clenched teeth. "It never was. It was my Grandpa John's."

"There's another funny thing too," the cop said. "This morning, your dad ransacked his house looking for his spare key, but he didn't find it. Last time he remembers seeing it was a couple of years ago. Just about the time you left town."

Mel kept quiet, her lips pressed tightly together and her eyes narrowed.

He moved closer. "Admit it, Miss Hamilton. You stole the car the first time when you were fifteen—"

"I did not steal it."

"Okay. You took it for a joyride."

"A joyride? A *joy*ride? When my grandpa had just died?"

"Come on, Lieutenant," Darren said. "There's no car here."

"But it's somewhere, and I intend to find it." The lieutenant glowered at Mel. "Stop wasting my time, young lady. If you won't tell me where it is, I'll find it anyway. I'll turn the whole county upside down if I have to, but I'll find that car."

"Go right ahead." Mel shot a pleading glance at Darren. "I'm not a thief. I'm not."

"We'll see about that." The lieutenant began the long walk back to the house.

Darren studied Mel with worried eyes. "Melanie, I'll ask you one more time," he said softly. "Do you have anything you need to tell me?"

"I see what you're doing, Darren. Y'all are playing good cop, bad cop. No, I don't have anything to tell you."

"Are you sure?"

"I'm sure. You think I'm a criminal, don't you?"

"It's not looking good," he said. "The sooner you come clean, the better."

"The sooner people stop calling me a thief, the better." Holding her head high, Mel started after the lieutenant.

Hands on his hips, Darren watched her disappear behind the camellias. "Miss McComb, do you have anything you'd like to share with me?"

She hesitated. Although the Corvette wasn't on her property, that didn't prove Mel's innocence. "How can I reach you if I think of anything?"

Darren handed her a card. "Here's my number. Call anytime. Thanks."

He paused, running his fingers over the neat stubble of hair on his head. "Sometimes I worry about that girl." He walked away.

"I do too," Tish whispered. Her fingers shook as she pulled the door closed and padlocked it. She had to call George.

In the distance, church music floated on the air. It was an organ, flying high and happy over the congregation's singing. As near as she could figure, it was the little white church two blocks away.

Sooner or later, she'd find a church. For now, maybe she needed to find a lawyer.

Thirty-Six

D aisy snuffled around on Mel's bed, hunting for pretzels in the folds of the quilt. She gave up and gave Mel one of those sad looks.

"They're all gone. Sorry." Mel sighed. "George would kill me if he knew."

He would kill her for a lot of reasons.

She flopped over on her back. "He doesn't trust me," she told the dog, softly so Tish wouldn't hear. "He only lets me baby-sit you because he doesn't care about you. He hopes you'll run off and never come home. Like my folks would've been glad if I'd never made it back from Florida. If that pervert had left me dead by the side of the road, I never would've embarrassed them again."

Mel grabbed her pillow around her ears so she couldn't hear cars going by on the street. She was the only twenty-one-year-old in town who didn't have her own vehicle. Anybody else could go anywhere, anytime, but she couldn't even walk down the block. The cops would be watching. She was trapped.

It reminded her of the time she'd helped Stu paint the porch when she was five or six. She'd painted herself into a corner. He'd laughed his head off, and then he'd reached over and picked her up with his long arms.

Now she'd painted herself into a different kind of corner, and it wasn't something her big brother could get her out of even if he wanted to. And he wouldn't want to.

She'd never had such a miserable birthday. Stu never called. Her parents never called, of course, but Tish was being too sweet, like that awful principal at the middle school who'd thought she could get kids to talk by treating them like her little buddies.

"You are a dead duck, Melanie John," Mel said quietly. "Dead. Duck."

She lit a cigarette from the pack she'd bought on Friday night on her way to pick up her clothes. She didn't bother to crack the window. "Sin boldly," Calv had said.

Then she tried to decide what to do.

Pack, she decided. She could unpack later if a miracle happened and she could stay, but if she had to make a run for it, she'd be ready to go.

It didn't take long. Even now, including the "new" clothes she'd stashed under the bed, she didn't have much to take with her. The clothes rolled up nicely in the sleeping bag, but she couldn't think of a good way to pack the shoes.

Whatever. So she was down to one pair again.

My little barefoot beggar, Grandpa John had called her when she ran around barefoot all the time. He'd said a barefoot beggar was ready to step onto holy ground. Another one of his weird little sayings.

She hesitated when she saw the napkin rings on top of the dresser. It didn't seem right to take them now, but it would be rude to leave them. She didn't know what to do.

So she lit another cigarette. She didn't usually do that, one after another, but her nerves were shot. She couldn't even focus on smoking. She picked up her cig, put it down, walked around the room, tried to think. Tried to pray.

Her life was a mess, but she didn't have a better life anywhere else.

She'd just remembered the toiletries in the bathroom when Tish knocked on the door. Mel lowered the bedroll to the floor and tried to sound innocent. "Yes?" she said.

"You've got company," Tish said.

"Great," she grumbled, picturing Robot Face on the porch. "Here we go again."

Shoot, maybe it was Darren. She would smell like smoke, and she hadn't even brushed her teeth.

She padded to the bedroom door and opened it. Tish had walked away already, not even trying to explain who it was.

"Tish," she called softly. "Who is it?"

No answer.

Pretending to be calm, Mel walked into the living room. And there stood Hayley with a big grin on her face.

"Happy twenty-first birthday, doll!"

"Oh my gosh! I thought you forgot."

"No way! We're going out."

"I can't afford—"

"My treat. I'm taking you out for your first legal drunk. I mean drink." Hayley giggled.

Mel put her finger to her lips and widened her eyes in warning.

"Oops," Hayley whispered. "Of course I remembered," she said in her usual voice. "I didn't have a number to call, but I heard you were staying here."

Tish came in from the kitchen, drying her hands on a towel. "Introduce us, Mel."

Mel raced through the introductions in a hurry. Hayley managed to act sweet and dignified, but Tish must have heard that little slip-up because her eyes held more suspicion than friendliness. Or maybe Hayley's tattoos bothered her. Mel loved them and wanted some too, but she'd promised Grandpa John she wouldn't get any skin art, ever.

"Get dressed up a little, Mel," Hayley said. "We're gonna have fun."

Tish's lips thinned to a tight, angry line. She crooked her finger and gave Mel the stink-eye. "Melanie, may I have a word with you?"

Reliving how she'd felt when she was six and she broke the goldfish bowl, Mel slouched after her into the kitchen. "What?"

"I heard what she said about drinking. You're an adult, and I'm not your mom, but your friend looks like trouble."

"No, she's a good person. She's the only real friend I've had ever since, like, kindergarten."

"You don't take care of a friendship by doing something stupid like drinking and driving."

Mel rolled her eyes. "I won't drink."

"On your twenty-first birthday? You expect me to believe that, after what Hayley said?"

"She said it. I didn't. I might have one little drink, but that's all. I promise."

"But what about Hayley? And she's driving! There are some things you can't undo, Mel, like getting a DUI and having it on your record forever, or getting in an accident."

"If she has too much, I'll drive."

"You don't even have a license. Oh, Melanie." Tish folded her arms across her chest. "You're an adult. Please act like one. I won't wait up for you."

"Trust me. I'll stay perfectly sober."

"All right. That's your line in the sand. Don't cross it. Cross that line and you're out on your ear. Got it?"

"Got it. Now I'd better change my clothes."

"Oh, and now I'm supposed to take care of the dog for you again?"

"You know you love her."

"I do not!"

"Yes you do, because she's George's dog and you love George."

Mel escaped Tish and returned to the living room, where Hayley stood gawking at that awful old portrait. "Wait in the car," Mel told her. "I'll be right out."

Hayley nodded and slipped outside.

In the bedroom, Mel knelt on the floor and unrolled the sleeping bag a little so she could pull out one of the nicer thrift-store shirts and the favorite jeans she'd taken from her old room. The jeans were a little baggy, but she wasn't as skinny as before. She hoped Tish wouldn't notice they were different jeans.

She brushed her hair and put on the silver chain and earrings she'd rescued from her old bedroom. That would have to do. And if ol' Robot Face was keeping an eye on her...well, that might help keep Hayley on the straight and narrow too.

She wondered if there were any cute guys around town anymore, or if they'd all gone off to college. Or turned into cops, like Darren.

He wouldn't want her now. If he was out of her league anyway, it didn't matter. Nothing mattered. She'd have one last fling with Hayley, and then she'd hit the road for...somewhere.

She left the bedroll in the corner again, fatter than before. All packed and ready for her when she came home. Except this wasn't home.

Mel tiptoed down the hall and peeked into the living room. No sign of Tish.

She tiptoed across the room to the front door. Still no sign of her.

"Bye, Tish!" Without waiting for an answer, Mel stepped onto the porch. Hayley's beater of a car waited at the curb, and old Mrs. Nair's curtains fluttered.

Mel ran to the street and climbed in. "We're off!"

"We're way, way off!" Hayley pulled away from the curb and cranked up the stereo. It was almost like high school except they didn't have to use fake IDs anymore.

Mel started laughing when she remembered she didn't have any ID, real or phony, so she couldn't drink. At least she could use that as her excuse.

Thirty-Seven

*T*he Chevelle's noisy engine woke Tish from a troubled sleep. Groggy, she glanced at her bedside clock, expecting it to say eight or so.

Five? Made sense. The windows were still dark.

But it *didn't* make sense. George must have left his motel room in the middle of the night.

He'd called late last night after the car broke down in a small town on the way home from the car show. An electrical problem. He'd fixed it, but he was too tired to drive the rest of the way. He'd planned to spend the night there and leave early in the morning so he'd be home in time to open the shop—and to talk to Mel about the missing Corvette. Tish had called him after the police left, and they both knew Mel was involved somehow.

The whole town knew. Even Mrs. Nair had hobbled across the street after Mel and Hayley drove away. Mrs. Nair had heard the rumor from her daughter.

Tish closed her eyes in the dark and opened them again with a groan. She needed to tell her mom what was going on, but where to start?

The engine's grumble grew fainter as the car drew farther from the house. In a minute or two George would start walking back through the yard, past the house, and back toward Main in the dark.

She wanted to run downstairs and intercept him so they could talk things over, but he had to be exhausted. Mel and her problems could wait until daylight.

Had she even come home?

Tish lay awake, listening to the steady thrumming of the furnace. As many times as she'd moved in her life, she'd always liked to get acquainted with the sound of each new furnace. Each one had its idiosyncrasies. If she knew them well, their clunks and shudders in the middle of the night couldn't make her think they were the footfalls of an intruder.

An unreasonable fear crept into her thoughts. Just as she'd already learned the voice of the furnace, she'd learned the voice of the Chevelle.

The Chevelle wasn't what had disturbed her sleep.

George wasn't back from the car show. Neither was his car.

"No," she whispered in the darkness. "No, no, no."

But her suspicion wouldn't go away. She threw off her covers. She had to know.

She turned on the light and put on her robe, then picked up her purse from the chair by the door and reached into it for her keys. Searching for the padlock key, she shook her head. The key had to be there.

She started over, one key at a time, all the way around her key ring. The key to the garage was missing.

Tish dropped her phone into the pocket of her robe and went downstairs. Remnants of the birthday décor remained. The balloons had begun to shrink, the crepe paper streamers drooped, and the banner had come loose on one end and hung straight down from the doorway.

"Happy twenty-first, you little thief," she said softly.

She flipped on the hallway light. Mel's door was open. Daisy was asleep on the bed. Alone.

In the kitchen, the flashlight was missing from the top of the fridge.

She put on her Crocs and left through the back door. The sky was still dark, and a chilly wind bit into her. She maneuvered her way through the yard, nearly running into several bushes but staying on track. She rounded the line of camellias and saw a sliver of light at the bottom of the garage doors.

As quietly as possible, she walked to the garage. Putting her ear to the door, she heard Mel's voice.

"You are so stupid," Mel said clearly. "Stupid, stupid Mel."

Tish placed her hands on the heavy sliding door and prepared to push it to the side. She braced herself, gave it one hard shove, and stared at the shiny rear bumper of a classic, sky-blue Corvette.

Mel gasped, standing precariously on Calv's tall stool with a folded newspaper tucked under her arm. She wore a roll of duct tape like a bracelet on her left wrist, and she wore red gloves—the ones Tish's mom had passed on to her.

Mel gaped down at her. Tish gaped up—and then at the car again. Her mouth went dry at the beauty of the machine and the insanity of what Mel was attempting. Either she didn't know right from wrong, or she had her own definitions.

Tish stepped into the garage and shoved the door closed again. "What are you doing?"

Not that she needed an answer. It was obvious. Mel had covered three windows with newspaper, and she was working on the last one.

"I'm covering the garage windows." Mel's voice sounded breathy. Panicked. "So nobody can see the car."

"I thought so." Tish marveled at her own calm. "And you…borrowed my gloves so you wouldn't leave prints?"

"Uh-huh. Don't worry, I was gonna give 'em back." Finished taping the paper across the top of the window frame, Mel ripped off another length of duct tape for the left side.

"I take you in, I trust you, and you steal a car and hide it in my garage?"

"I didn't." Mel taped the right side.

"Who did, then? Was Hayley involved?"

"No! My dad stole it from *me*!"

"Shhhh! Keep your voice down, Mel, you'll wake the neighbors."

Tish reached out to touch the fender of the Corvette. Sixty grand, George had said. Sixty thousand dollars' worth of stolen property.

She imagined herself in prison. Then she imagined herself pulling her phone out of her pocket, right now, and calling the police. Being a hero.

Mel taped the paper across the bottom of the window frame, lowered herself to a seated position, and slid off the stool. "I've got to get out of here."

"And leave me holding the bag? How dare you! No, you're taking it back. Right now."

"No way!"

"It's only a fifteen-minute trip. We'll be there before daylight." Tish held out her hand. "Give me the key."

Mel reached into her pocket and produced the padlock key.

Tish took it. "Thanks, but now I want the key to the Corvette."

"Why? Are you taking it somewhere? Where are you taking it?"

"*You* are taking it to its rightful owner, and you're going to apologize to your father."

After a heart-wrenching sob, Mel dug deeper in her pocket and pulled out a small, ordinary key. Tears rolled down her cheeks. "It was Grandpa John's key. When I took it, it wasn't so I could take the car. I only wanted something of his to take with me when I moved out."

"When you left home? You've had the key since then?"

Mel nodded. "To remember Grandpa John by. But when I got into their house—"

"Whose house? When?"

"My parents' house. On Friday night when I knew they wouldn't be home. I walked there to get some clothes, but then I peeked in the garage and the car was still there, and I already had the key with me. So I—I started it up, and I kind of kept going. It's an awesome car, you know? I could've driven a thousand miles. But I didn't take it far. I hid it in an old barn outside of town and I walked home."

"Do I understand this right? On Friday night you put the car in a barn somewhere, but now you've moved it here? Why?"

"Robot Face said he would turn the county upside down, but he won't check the garage again because he already did."

"Don't count on it. He's not stupid."

"But God will help me again. I prayed, and He answered. First I asked Him to get you out of the way on Friday, and He did—"

"No, that was *your* doing. You pressured me into going to the garden club."

"But I couldn't make you go. That was God, see? You actually went. And I asked God to keep the cops away when I took the car on Friday, and He did, and He kept the neighbors from noticing. And when I walked to the barn after Hayley dropped me off, I asked God to keep the cops away again, and He did. It took five whole minutes to get it here, but I didn't see a single car. Not a cop car. Not any kind of car." Mel stopped her breathless recitation to wipe her eyes. "It was a miracle."

Tish shook her head. "I can't believe God wanted to help you hide an extremely expensive car that belongs to someone else."

"It's mine," Mel said fiercely. "Grandpa John said it was. George did too. He said if Grandpa John honestly meant to give me the car, it should be mine."

"*Should* be. But legally, it isn't." Tish walked to the door and shoved it open, then returned the padlock key to Mel. "I'll pull the car out and turn it around. You turn out the lights, lock up, and hop in."

She climbed into the driver's seat before she could change her mind. Before Mel could argue.

It was a three-speed. Piece o' cake. Driving a Corvette couldn't be too different from driving any other car. Gas, brakes, clutch. Headlights. That was about all she needed to locate. Oh, and ignition.

She found the ignition, depressed the clutch, and turned the key. The engine started right up, the noise hammering the walls. She could only hope the neighbors would think it was George, inconsiderately firing up his Chevelle at five in the morning.

Biting her lip, she focused on finding reverse. There it was. Checking the rearview mirror for the camellias, she backed the car out of the garage. She swung the car around—with some difficulty, because it didn't have power steering—and waited.

The garage went dark. A minute later, the dome light shone on Mel as she opened the passenger door and climbed in. She was crying softly.

"Do you want to drive, Mel?"

"No! I don't even want to go!" Mel slammed her door and turned up the volume of her weeping.

"Please be quiet and let me think."

Again, Tish eased up on the clutch and fed the engine some gas. The Corvette leaped forward, its headlights shining on the sandy track that had once known the beat of horses' hooves. She could understand why Mel had kind of kept going. It was an awesome car.

Thirty-Eight

We made it down Main Street without any trouble," Tish said, not expecting an answer.

Mel huddled in the passenger seat in the dark, alternating between weeping and whimpering. Once in a while, she issued petulant orders.

Tish hadn't driven a stick shift in several years, but it had come back to her, as easily as riding a bike. It wasn't a smooth ride, though. Nearly sixty years old, the car didn't have modern suspension or power steering or power brakes. Boy, could it move, though. It throbbed with barely restrained energy.

Tish nearly laughed, remembering how she'd tried to be sweet and respectable and inconspicuous at the garden club. How she'd never taken produce boxes from Kroger without asking the manager first. Now she was driving a very loud and very stolen Corvette through town in the predawn stillness.

If they were caught, she could forget that job in Muldro. She could even forget George, who'd ditched one of his girlfriends for shoplifting, as he certainly should have.

"Go faster," Mel pleaded.

"No. The police are on the lookout for this thing, and I don't want to attract any more attention."

"Oh, so you want to be on the road *longer*?"

Tish checked her speed. Forty. Maybe there was some wisdom in shaving a few minutes off their time. She'd already decided against taking the back roads, in the interest of time. On this side of town, at this hour, even the main roads were empty of traffic.

"We're nearly there," she said to reassure herself as much as Mel.

Then they would have a long walk home. At least Mel was dressed for it. Tish sure wasn't.

"I'd better call George," she said, digging in the pocket of her bathrobe.

"Why? So he can turn us in?"

Tish called his number but got his voice mail. "Good morning," she said after the beep. "You like honest people, right? Let me be perfectly honest. I'm doing a stupid, stupid thing." Her voice cracked. "If you want to give a couple of felons a ride, we'll be walking home from Dunc's house in a few minutes if the police don't nab us." She sniffled. "Look on the bright side. I won't need a job if I'm in prison." She put her phone back in her pocket.

"Prison? No!"

"It's about time you thought about the consequences of your actions."

The sky had barely lightened in the east. Mel said Dunc was an early riser, though.

Letting up on the gas, Tish downshifted and made the turn onto Rock Glen Drive. The thunder of the car seemed even louder now, and the speed bumps were murder on the stiff suspension. No wonder Dunc had campaigned against them.

If Farris went for a run and saw her at the wheel of the Corvette…so what? He'd already decided against hiring her. If anyone at the construction company in Muldro heard about it, though, that job was toast. She couldn't in a million years justify her behavior—except it might keep the fresh-air kid out of prison.

She'd thought nothing could feel more dangerous than that short stretch on Main, but Rock Glen was worse. One by one, the darkened houses slipped past. Nothing but thin panes of glass stood between the noisy car and the neighbors' ears.

"Slow down, we're almost there," Mel said.

"I see it."

Tish slowed to a crawl. She pulled into the Hamiltons' driveway and killed the engine. The sudden quiet was eerie. The sun was behind them, its earliest light glinting on the front windows of the house, competing with the white security lights.

"Think your dad is up by now?" she asked.

"Probably."

"Get it over with, then."

"Come with me," Mel begged. "Please."

They climbed out. Tish shut her door first, the sound like a gunshot to her hypersensitive ears. Mel's door was the second gunshot, and then they walked to the front door.

Mel stood motionless, not lifting a finger.

"Ring the doorbell," Tish said.

Like an obedient child, Mel did as she was told.

Tish pressed the car key into the girl's hand. "When he opens the door, tell him you're sorry and give him the key."

Mel nodded woodenly.

There were soft noises somewhere inside, and then the rattle of a deadbolt. The door swung open, and Dunc Hamilton stood there in sweats and a snug white T-shirt.

"Well, well." He looked past them to the car. "I thought I heard something." Ignoring Tish, he studied Mel. "You have something to say to me?"

"Yes sir." Her voice was emotionless. "I'm sorry."

She held out the key. He took it.

"It's about time." He met Tish's eyes. "Thank you, Miss McComb, for returning my property."

"What about your daughter?"

His eyes flickered over Mel and back to Tish. "She made her choices. She can live with 'em." He shut the door and locked it.

Tish's hand shot out to pound on the door and hot words danced on her tongue, but some vestige of common sense saved her. She took a deep breath and backed away.

"Let's go." She tugged Mel into a turn. "Even if he won't let you in, there's a place for you. There will always be a place for you. God isn't like Dunc Hamilton."

"Good thing." As they passed the Corvette, Mel trailed a shaking hand along the rear fender, but she kept moving.

She was still wearing those red gloves, but fingerprints didn't matter now. Dunc knew his culprits.

The sky was lighter now. Birds were chirping. People would be up. Pouring their morning coffee, looking out their windows, walking their dogs.

On their fifteen-minute drive, Tish had hardly been aware of ditches, uneven pavement, barking dogs. Now, on foot, she noticed everything. And she was working up a sweat in her thick robe and flannel pajamas.

Mel sniffled at regular intervals and sometimes gave in to soft sobs. Glancing over at her, Tish wondered what she could do for a girl whose family wouldn't have her. She needed a new family.

Calv, a surrogate grandpa. George, the big brother. She, Tish, the big sister. An unemployed sister, of course, because word of this escapade would spread fast.

She wasn't the kind of employee a business would want. Not now. And she wasn't the kind of woman George would want. Compared to this, George's ex-girlfriend's wrongs were meager, wimpy little sins. Shoplifting? Ha! Boring.

Years from now, he might tell some other woman, *Then there was the one who swiped a car. Morally challenged. Reckless. Irresponsible.*

She should have looked for another option. A sane option. She could have called Stu and begged him to come get the car—and to keep his mouth shut for his sister's sake—but it was too late.

Mel burst out with a groan. "He probably turned us in already."

"Probably."

"We're dead ducks. Dead. Ducks."

"I've got the right pajamas on," Tish said. "With duckies."

"Huh? Oh." Mel laughed, just for a second.

They reached the main road and turned left, walking on the shoulder against traffic. Fortunately, there was very little of it.

Her heart hammered her ribs when she recognized the sound of the Chevelle, far down the road. "Here comes George."

"No way. Oh no. You're right."

The headlights approached slowly. George must have been afraid he wouldn't see them in the dim light. As he came closer, Tish waved.

He pulled over on the shoulder, leaving the engine running. The headlights made Tish think of prison spotlights.

George got out with his phone to his ear. "Right," he said to someone. "Yes. Thank you."

"Oh boy," Mel whispered.

He lowered the phone and walked around the car. Nobody spoke.

George shook his head. His dark eyes were hard to read, especially in the half light of early morning.

He opened his mouth to speak.

"You traitor," Mel said, her voice shaking. "You called the cops!"

"No, I called your brother."

"I don't have no stinkin' brother!"

"Get in," George said. "Both of you."

He opened the passenger door and tipped the front seat forward. "Melanie," he said. "Back seat."

She shot him a murderous look but climbed in.

George returned the front seat to its position and met Tish's eyes. "I was almost home from the car show when I found I had an interesting message from you."

"Honestly, I don't even remember what I said. It has been a rough morning."

"This isn't the way I'd pictured your first ride in my project car."

For a moment, she thought he might smile. He might tell her everything was going to be fine. He might even kiss her by the side of the road, ducky pajamas and all.

No. The lights had flickered out. Power failure.

She climbed in, shaking, then had to act fast to keep George from catching the hem of her bathrobe in the door.

She'd gone from being overheated to freezing. The hems of her pajama pants were wet with dew. She wanted to ask him to turn on the heat, but…no. She wouldn't ask anything more of him. Giving them a ride was enough.

He sat behind the wheel. "Anybody want to explain?"

"No sir," Mel said politely. Two seconds later, she was bawling.

"The Corvette is back where it belongs," Tish said. "Please don't ask questions."

He put the car in gear and pulled onto the road. "One thing I'll say for you, Tish. You hoped people would remember you? I will remember you."

She couldn't tell if he meant it as a farewell or as encouragement.

He shifted gears, and the Chevelle answered with a surge of speed. Tish closed her eyes, afraid she'd see flashing blue lights.

When George shifted into high gear, the car seemed to settle into some kind of mechanical contentment. A plateau of speed. The car sailed along, needing nothing from its driver but a hand on the wheel and a foot on the gas.

"Let's go back to your place, and I'll make breakfast," he said.

"You've got to be kidding," she said. "I can't think about food."

"I'll cook. You just sit back and relax."

"Relax? You're insane."

"Not as insane as you are," he said mildly. "But I guess I'm an accessory to the crime now."

Mel entered into a new spate of tears, but Tish only closed her eyes and released a deep sigh. If George crashed the Chevelle into a tree and killed them all…well, she would wake in heaven—which might be preferable to going to prison—but she wasn't sure about Mel.

George's hand wrapped hers and squeezed. "We're in this together, y'all."

Ever so slightly consoled, she squeezed back.

George shut the oven door on the breakfast casserole, a rough approximation of the one his mother used to make in that very oven. Daisy went into her Sphinx position on the floor mat by the sink, keeping her hungry gaze on the door.

"And now we wait," he said.

Tish, seated at her kitchen table, regarded him with bleary and skeptical eyes. She'd ditched the bathrobe and pajamas in favor of jeans and a U of M sweatshirt, but she'd left her hair wild. Just the way he liked it.

"Today's the day I'm supposed to find out about the job," she said. "I'm supposed to sit down with the owner and do my best to impress her. If I'm not in jail."

"Everything's going to be all right."

"Do you know a good lawyer?" she asked.

"Maybe we won't need one."

"Huh. Optimist." She put her elbows on the table and rested her chin in her hands. "I can't afford an attorney. And I won't get the job now."

"Don't worry. I won't let you starve."

"They don't let you starve in prison either, I guess. How am I going to explain this to my mother?"

"Not knowing your mother, I have no idea." He checked the time on his phone. "Excuse me, I need to make a call."

The sun was shining when he stepped onto the porch, the wet street sending up a mist that reminded him of a malignant vapor in a scene from Tolkien. There were no orcs or dwarves, though. There weren't even any neighbors out and about.

Mel's sobbing caught his ear, just on the other side of the window. She'd holed up in her room with the dog. Poor kid. She'd brought it on herself, though.

About to call Calv and ask him to take charge of the shop for the day, George remembered Calv was on the road, returning from that wedding in Florida. He wouldn't be home until the day was over.

By then, Dunc might have made a decision. Stu might have too. Awakened by George's call, Stu had remained groggy throughout their conversation. Even if he'd fully comprehended the situation, he wouldn't necessarily buck Dunc.

The door's hinges creaked as Tish joined George on the porch. "Anything new?" she asked.

"No." He put his arms around her.

She leaned against him, talking into his chest, her voice muffled. "I'm glad I made her take the car back, but I wish I'd handled it better."

"At least you did something."

"Something that's going to bring the law down on our heads. You'd think we would have had a visit from the police by now, though."

"It could take a little time to file a report."

She raised her head and met his eyes. "What could they write on the report? 'Perpetrators returned stolen car to rightful owner,' maybe?"

Unwilling to contemplate the possibilities, George shook his head. "We'll soon know."

"Will they be any easier on us if we go to the station and turn ourselves in?"

"Possibly, but we're not doing that without an attorney."

"You said we don't need an attorney."

"I said *maybe* we won't need one."

"I shouldn't have done it," she said. "It was a lapse in judgment. A terrible lapse."

"What's done is done."

"Yes, George. I realize that. That's the whole problem." Her voice broke. "I am Tish McComb, and I can't change who I am."

A funny thing to say, but perfectly true. "Good," he said. "God made you to be Tish McComb, and I wouldn't change a thing about you."

She let out a laugh that had tears behind it. "Not even my budding police record?"

"Not even that, if it comes to that." Closing his eyes, he leaned his head against hers.

The ordinary sounds of morning sifted through the air. Birds sang. A dog barked. Inside the house, Daisy barked back. A vehicle passed the house.

He could smell the casserole baking. Sausage, eggs, cheese.

Another vehicle...was slowing in front of the house.

He tensed. He didn't want to open his eyes and see a police cruiser.

A car door slammed.

"George," Tish said, pulling away from him, "it's Stu."

George opened his eyes. Stu came around the front of the SUV, walking slowly. He entered the yard but didn't seem to see them there on the porch until he was halfway up the steps.

"Stu," George said. "What brings you here?"

"Mel. Is she here?"

"There's nobody here but us car thieves," Tish said.

"Car thieves and scoundrels," George added. "Mel's inside."

Stu looked at Tish. "May I go in and talk to her?"

Tish shrugged. "Sure, she's your sister. She's holed up in the bedroom on the left."

Stu nodded and walked inside, his shoulders not as slumped as usual.

They waited, hearing a muffled sound that might have been a knock on the bedroom door. Then Mel's indignant "Go away!" came clearly through the window.

After a long silence, she spoke again, her words indistinguishable but her tone even more indignant.

"Oh, Mel," Tish whispered, "for once in your life, admit you're wrong."

Mel screamed. Tish jumped, covering her ears. Mel screamed again.

Abandoning Tish, George ran inside and charged toward the bedroom. He heard Tish behind him as he made the corner into the hall.

Mel bolted from the room with tears rolling down her cheeks. Stu was right behind her, mumbling something, but George couldn't hear him over Mel's high-pitched voice.

"You know why Stu's here? You know why? Because he loves me." Mel spun around and crashed into Stu, who wrapped his little sister in a bear hug while her shoulders shook. A little gleam of gold in her hand was all that George saw of the watch.

Tish grabbed his hand. "What on earth?"

George leaned over to whisper in her ear. "Stu brought the watch back." Leaving Mel and Stu inside, they returned to the porch and sat on the top step.

Maybe Dunc had decided not to press charges. Maybe sleepy old Stu had stood up to him at last. George only knew that if Tish hadn't come to town, everything would have turned out differently…and probably worse.

She reached for his hand, lacing her fingers together with his. "If I never find a job in this town, I don't care. It would be worth it, just to see Mel and her brother reconnected."

"It would." He shut his eyes, listening to the low murmur of Stu and Mel's conversation inside the house. Stu had a backbone after all, and a heart too. "I think everything's going to work out just fine. I just have one request."

She yawned. "What's that?"

He smiled, remembering the first time he laid eyes on Tish, taking pictures of the house. Tish, weeks later, taking charge of a runaway dog. Taking Mel in. Taking the watch back. Taking the 'Vette back. Taking his world and shaking it to life. She was a take-charge kind of woman.

He lifted their entwined hands to his lips and kissed her knuckles. "Well, I know you understand there are two kinds of Yankees."

"Yes…"

"Please be the kind of Yankee that stays."

Epilogue

ummertime in Alabama was green, hot, and humid, with fewer flowers and more thunderstorms than Tish had expected. She hoped the power wouldn't go out again just when she had a crowd over for a potluck. The western sky was black. George had finished grilling the burgers and hot dogs in the nick of time and stuck them in the oven to keep them warm.

The scent of rain wafted through the house as she hurried into the office to shut the window. She crossed to her bedroom and shut that window too, while tree branches thrashed in the rising wind just beyond the glass. The clouds had massed together like bullies about to gang up on someone, but the storm would pass quickly.

She turned from the window and smiled at the rather startling gift George had given her. The black ball gown hung on her closet door waiting for a special occasion, which this wasn't.

Well, yes it was. Mom and Charles were up from Florida, staying in the guest room for a few days, and Tish had invited some friends over. That was as special as anything. Time with people she loved. That, not the food, was the real feast, and so many people had shown up that she could justify using her big percolator for after-dinner coffee.

Pausing at her dresser, she found her antique honeybee button and pinned it beside the crisp collar of her sleeveless chambray shirt. She took a quick look in the mirror and fluffed her hair.

About to head downstairs, she pulled her phone from her pocket to read an incoming text. *"C U in 5 w pot salad,"* it said.

Tish smiled and sent a quick reply. She'd finally met her next-door neighbors, Jim the hunter and Billie Jo the quilter. Billie Jo made the best potato salad ever.

Running down the stairs, Tish went over the menu in her mind. She'd provided the burgers, the hot dogs, the Detroit-style Coney sauce, and all the fixings. Mrs. Nair, recently widowed, had brought chips. Mom had provided guacamole and fruit salad.

Becky from the garden club would be late, but she would bring the ice cream.

Tish couldn't remember the rest. She only knew they had plenty of food and too many people to fit around her table, so they'd moved the chairs away and set up a buffet.

The rain had started by the time she hurried into the dining room. She stopped in the doorway to savor the sight of sleepy-eyed Stu and long-legged Janice standing by the food table with their boys and Mel. She'd been living with them since April. Janice had taken charge of her kid sister-in-law, making her meet her learning disability head-on, and what a difference a few months of therapy and tutoring had made. Mel had stopped smoking. Her eyes shone. She held her head high, and she was adorable with her new, sassy haircut.

Dunc Hamilton, not Mel, was the loser. Tish shook her head, refusing to waste another moment's thought on him.

Kindhearted Darren was there too, being a good friend to Mel, and Calv leaned against the wall holding his Alabama ball cap in his blackened hands. No matter how long and hard he scrubbed, he could never erase all the automotive grease from his hands and nails. Sometimes she suspected he wore the grime with pride.

She stopped beside him. "Would you mind asking the blessing, once a few more people walk in?"

"I'd be honored, Miss Tish."

"Thanks."

She crossed the room to stand beside George, who was chatting with her mother and Charles. Daisy sat in the crook of George's arm, eyeing the food. Tish took his other arm, content to listen without joining the conversation, and inhaled. The Coney sauce smelled fantastic.

The percolator from 1940 gleamed on the sideboard. Having recently gone through the box of family history, Tish had certain dates clear in her mind. Letitia had died in 1940 at ninety, so it was possible that she was alive when the percolator was manufactured. She'd lived to see the age of electric appliances and airplanes, yet she'd been a young woman when Lincoln was shot.

Awed by the history one woman's life had spanned, Tish decided that was why she loved antiques. They were visible reminders of overlapping lives and events. The continuum of the generations. No generation would ever stand alone.

Jim and Billie Jo walked in with their potato salad, their clothes speckled with rain. Calv raised his eyebrows at Tish. She nodded. There might be more stragglers, but it was time to eat.

"Folks, let's quiet down and ask a blessing," he called out. The room stilled as he began to pray.

Tish prayed along in her heart but kept her eyes open to savor the gathering. She'd imagined everyone joining hands in a tidy circle, but they stood in disorganized little groups, overlapping and connecting.

She glanced up at George. His eyes were closed, his long black lashes lying handsomely against his olive skin.

Calv was still praying. He had a way of turning a prayer into a sermon. "We can't afford no feast or fancy robes and rings, but You can, and You give them freely to Your children. We're Your prodigals, Your hungry prodigals, and You've got good chow. Help us remember that we'll sit at the banqueting table one day with the loved ones who've gone before us. Make us mindful of the folks on the highways and byways. They're somebody's loved ones too. Bring them home like You're bringing us home, a step at a time." He let out a long sigh. "In the name of Jesus, our Savior, amen."

Tish's mother leaned toward her. "I'll go get the burgers and dogs," she said.

"Thanks, Mom. Listen up, everybody. Drinks and cups are on the kitchen counter. We have lots of sweet tea and pop."

Her mom raised her hands and did a little dance step on her way to the kitchen. "And I'm a Michigander so I brought Vernors and Faygo," she announced.

"Once you've grabbed your plates, sit anywhere," Tish said. "The kitchen table, the living room, front porch, back porch. And mix it up a little, you guys. I don't want all the Yankees on one side of the house and all the southerners on the other."

"In other words," George said, "mix it up between the folks who say 'you guys' and the folks who understand that 'y'all' makes more sense."

"Watch it, Zorbas." Tish smiled at him, then at Mrs. Nair. "Why don't you go first, Mrs. Nair? Everybody else, line up after her." She motioned toward the table. "Dig in."

Stu's boys were second and third in line, taking their plates with hands that weren't exactly clean. That was all right. Kids got dirty. So did prodigals. Sometimes, so did the people who loved them.

The crowd sorted itself into a buffet line, and the conversations started up again. All too soon, though, the house would be empty and silent. Tish had to work on Monday, and her mom and Charles would hit the road for Tampa.

Hayley, now sporting a streak of blue in her hair, slipped into the room from the other side, looking ill at ease until Calv greeted her. "Miss Mel's right over there," he said, pointing. "She's gonna be so glad you came. I am too."

Tish retreated to the living room, her heart as full as her house, and took a moment to listen to the rain pounding her solid roof. She had so much to be thankful for.

Stopping before the portrait, she locked eyes with Letitia's regal stare. *I am Letitia McComb. You can't change who I am.* But lately Tish had settled into a different way of seeing things.

"I am Letitia McComb," she said softly. "One of God's children. Nothing and nobody can change that, ever."

The floor creaked behind her, and she knew George by his footfalls even before he placed his hands on her shoulders. "Having a chat with the old girl?"

"You caught me. Yes, I have a lot on my mind."

"I like a woman who has a lot on her mind." He nudged her into a turn and frowned at her shirt, then looked up with sorrowful eyes. "Aw, Tish. You made your nice old button into a pin? You've ruined its value."

Blinding blue radiance filled the room simultaneously with a rollicking roll of thunder. The lights flickered. Braced for another lightning strike and a power failure, she held her breath, but there was nothing but a new downpour of rain, falling so hard she thought it must have scared the lightning out of the sky.

She started breathing again. "The button's monetary value doesn't matter if I don't sell it, and I'll never sell it." She stretched up to give him a quick kiss. "I never get rid of the things I love."

"I don't either." He gave her a slow smile and then a slower kiss.

"Anyway, you can chill out about the button, buddy," she whispered against his lips. "I only used a safety pin."

Lightning and thunder crashed again, making her jump. George laughed and pulled her tight, and they waited together. The lights flickered, but they stayed on.

Readers Guide

1. Southern hospitality is world famous, but a sleepy southern town can be somewhat resistant to newcomers of the Yankee persuasion. How might the descendants of all parties of the Civil War, including the descendants of slaves, be reconciled with one another? As fellow citizens, what are our responsibilities to each other?

2. Tish wants to find her niche in her new community. Given her family's history of frequent moves, what are her chances of putting down permanent roots in Noble? What might improve or hinder her chances?

3. In some ways, Tish resembles the elder brother of the parable of the Prodigal Son, Luke 15:11–32. She's a responsible person who expects her good behavior to be rewarded. Meanwhile, Mel hasn't earned anyone's respect, but she's quick to justify her bad behavior. Is either attitude better than the other? Why? Are you able to empathize with one character over the other?

4. The parable in the book of Luke mentions the prodigal's stint as a farmhand feeding pigs, and also the ring, robe, and sandals given to him upon his return. What is Mel's "pigsty," and what significance do jewelry, clothing, and shoes have in her story?

5. Some of the locals snub Tish because she's descended from carpet-baggers, and Farris the banker refuses to hire her because she has befriended Mel. Do these rejections harden Tish's heart? Or do they soften her heart toward Mel, another reject?

6. Mel's undiagnosed learning disability has kept her from reaching her potential. Why are some of us so reluctant to confess our secret battles and handicaps?

7. George admits that his history in the romance department is "boring," while a tragedy destroyed Tish's plans for marriage. How can two people build a future together when they come from such different experiences?

8. George saw his mother kick his Uncle Calv out of the family because of his drinking. How much might this affect both men in the way they relate to Mel?

9. Mel's Grandpa John showed her unconditional love, but her father requires more of her than she can give. When we have less-than-ideal father figures, how do they affect our perspective of God the Father?

10. Tish is so upright that she has never even had a parking ticket, but eventually she breaks the law for Mel's sake. What might have happened if Tish had reported Mel to the police instead? Do you think either of them is likely to break the law again?

11. During Tish's unsettled childhood, she clung to her identity by repeating "I am Letitia McComb; you can't change who I am." Late in the

story, she says instead: "I am Letitia McComb; I can't change who I am." What has changed in the way she sees herself?

12. Some of the story's characters own—or covet—vehicles, jewelry, antiques, homes, and so on. But "you can't take it with you." In your opinion, who is richest in the unseen possessions of the heart? Who is poorest in that sense?

13. Imagine what Tish could have discovered about her ancestors and their personal perspectives if, somehow, she could have shared the same time with them for a while. If you could time-travel a hundred years into the future, what kind of legacy would you hope to find you had left your future family?

ACKNOWLEDGMENTS

The writing of a novel is a solitary occupation but one that can't come to fruition without the help of many people. I'll start with Chip MacGregor, whose agent-wisdom steers me through the sometimes murky waters of the writing life. Chip, thanks for being there.

Big thanks go to my excellent editors, Shannon Marchese, Jenny Baumgartner, and Pamela Shoup, as well as those who worked behind the scenes. Special thanks to Kelly Howard for cover art that captures the joy at the heart of the story. I salute the unsung heroes in every department: editorial, production, marketing/publicity, and sales. It's a privilege to work with all of you at WaterBrook Multnomah.

I don't know what I would do without my church family and my friends who are so generous with their encouragement, wisdom, and prayers. Special thanks to Suzan Robertson for educating me about the special needs and quirks of Maltese dogs, and to Lindi Peterson for those spur-of-the-moment phone calls that keep us connected even when life gets crazy.

My dear friend Deeanne Gist is a godsend. She braves my rawest, messiest rough drafts and helps me turn them into viable stories. Beyond that, she's a beautiful person who radiates the love of Jesus. Dee, you're a treasure.

I'm also indebted to my precious friend Sherrie Lord, who can brainstorm like nobody's business and fine-tune a sentence until it purrs. Sherrie, you've taught me so much about writing and about life. I'm honored to be your sis.

Michelle Truax, thank you for years of friendship forged through good times and bad. You're family, now and forever.

Most of all, I'm thankful for Jon; Sam, Cindy, Lizzie and Karis; Brent and Stephanie; and Scott. I don't deserve you, but I'm glad I have you. You're my best treasures.

My deepest gratitude goes to our Elder Brother who invites the hungriest, dirtiest, most messed-up prodigals to share His inheritance and rejoice. Jesus, You are my King.